SPENDING THE JACKPOT

TOM ALAN

BLOODHOUND BOOKS

For Jill (and Giuliani).
Plotting is like planning a menu...

PROLOGUE

Win the lottery? The jackpot? He's waited ages for this moment. Since 24 May 2002 to be exact, his eighteenth birthday, so over twenty years. He's won a few times, not the jackpot, but enough once for a long weekend in Crete, five stars. And then another couple of times, that he told nobody about...

He dreams of a big win. Well over a million is what he wants, what he craves. He wants the large house in a better area; private school for the kids; Carrera for himself, maybe a little soft-top thingy for Alice; Rolexes for them all; holidays in the Seychelles; a flat, or even a villa, in Spain; and more important than any of that, the thing that consumes him day after working day (and a lot of the weekends too) he wants to give up the job he loathes. So, maybe five million might be nearer the mark.

What will surprise him most of all, when it happens, won't be the feelings of jubilation, freedom and opportunity he's expecting, that anyone would expect. No, what will shock him will be how quickly, and how bitterly, he'll come to regret it...

PART 1

WINNING

1

THE WIN

'The draw's starting, love!'

Freddie settles back into his favourite armchair and opens his lottery book (volume 3). He's kept a book since day one: a record of all the numbers ever drawn with his numbers highlighted in fluorescent yellow whenever they come up. He riffles through the pages, a nervous tic he indulges twice a week, and watches the little yellow marks flash by like nuggets of gold in a fast-flowing river: all he has to do is pan six – last time he got none.

'Num-ber sev-ennnn...'

His fists clench. And his teeth. Alice's birthday! It had given him an unexpected headache when he'd got engaged to Alice. He'd quietly dumped his sister's number 30 and used Alice's birthday instead. He did it on the quiet because he didn't want to upset Susan although, having emigrated to Australia years previously, it was unlikely she'd ever get wind of it. But then he had a bit of a panic. What if Susan's birthday came up (30) but *not* Alice's (7)? So, what to do? Obvious really: buy two tickets.

It didn't take him long to realise this didn't solve everything: what if both numbers (30 and 7) came up and not one of his others? He'd have to buy seven tickets to cover all the combinations. (Freddie works in a bank, so he's good with this type of calculation.) And, of course, when Ryan was born, and subsequently Poppy, he'd had worse problems. Luckily (not that he'd actually put it like that), his parents had both died by the time the kids had come along, so it had been easy to ditch their numbers without offending them. So out had gone Graham and Brenda (17 and 25), and in came Ryan and Poppy (10 and 22).

'*Num-ber twen-ty-twoooo...*'

Good old Pops! He punches the air, slightly self-consciously; Freddie's no extrovert. There's a little tingle in his spine. Two is good, but the *first* two is better. You don't have to be that much of a mathematician to work that out: the odds of getting three, four, or more, are suddenly much reduced once you've got the first two. He feels another little tingle at the thought, this time in his sphincter.

'Hurry up, love. You're missing it. I've got two...'

Of course, when he replaced his mum and dad's dates with Ryan and Poppy's he'd run into the same problem, but bigger: what if Graham's number 17 came up one week? Or Brenda's 25? Or both of them? The number of tickets he'd have to buy to cover all possible combinations from (what was then) nine numbers in total had increased horrendously. So, he'd reverted to one ticket a week, with his newest numbers (no Susan, no Graham, no Brenda), but sometimes bought two, or three of the possible combinations, and his blood pressure, and bank balance, suffered accordingly.

'*Num-ber tennnn...*'

Blimey. Ryan's birthday. Three in a bloomin' row! This hasn't happened before. He's got three, but never the *first* three. The statistical possibilities start to shimmer like a desert image coming into sharper focus, now looking more oasis than mirage. He stands up. Sits down again. Breathes in and out. There's sweat on his brow; his heart's pattering. He goes to the door to call Alice again, but it's too much to think about now. The next ball is coming out...

'*Num-ber thir-ty-niiiine...*'

39! His favourite Scalextric car from when he was a kid, racing them round the track in his bedroom. It was a silver Porsche Carrera 911 with headlights and taillights that actually worked. It wasn't really number 39. It didn't have a number at all, but ten-year-old Freddie had made one with a disc of paper, a black felt-tip, and a bit of Sellotape. He can't remember why he chose 39. He certainly wanted a bigger number than his green (with white roof) Mini Cooper rallycross car that had come with a number 3 on the side – but why 39? He's no idea.

Four. Four in a flippin' row! He's well into fibrillation territory now; his hands are shaking. He puts his book down, stands up, stares at the screen, not believing what his senses are showing and telling him. He wonders if he might pass out. His heart's beating faster, his breathing is–

'*Num-ber twen-ty-foooour.*'

Freddie sways on the spot. His eyes widen, his mouth droops open. His birthday, May 24. Five? *Five!?* Upstairs he can just about hear Alice reading Poppy her bedtime story; there's a plinking and peeping from Ryan's room. But down here, in the living room, his life, well, all their lives, are on a cliff edge. If he gets the next ball, everything changes. All he needs now is his lucky number from childhood...

'*Num-ber foooouuur!*'

2

THE FAIRY-TALE BEGINNING

'SOMEBODY'S BEEN SLEEPING in *my* bed!' Alice growls in her deepest Daddy Bear voice. Poppy snuggles up closer, clinging to her mum's arm and tugging at her cardi. Alice catches Poppy's eye and mocks a look of shock. Poppy giggles and squeezes harder, her eyes wide with pure, unadulterated seven-year-old excitement.

'And somebody's been sleeping in *my* bed!' Alice breathes in a slightly more comfortable Mummy Bear voice. Poppy gasps, audibly. It's ridiculous, Alice thinks, Poppy's heard this story a million times, but every time it's like the bears are in the room – in her bed. There's no acting going on; Poppy's the same every time. Alice loves reading to Poppy.

There's a bit of a kerfuffle out in the street, Alice can hear. Somebody's shouting. Bit early on a weekday night for anyone to be drunk – the pub's on the corner. She carries on, hoping they'll move on.

'And somebody's been sleeping in my bed, and they're *still there!*' Alice squeaks in her best Baby Bear voice. Poppy's up on her knees now; yet more genuine, so real it's almost worrying, pee-her-pants wriggling. Alice would love to get inside Poppy's head; prays she'll never grow out of this ability to sink into a story and leave the world behind...

The noise in the street is getting on Alice's nerves. It sounds like someone's right outside their front door. They're singing one of those ridiculous football chants: Olé – olé olé olé. Why isn't Freddie out there shooing them off? Actually, she vaguely recognises the voice. In fact, now she thinks about it, and really listens, it sounds like–

If this were a film, Alice muses, she'd rub her eyes and then they'd pop out on cartoon springs. But instead, she stares incredulously through Poppy's bedroom window and wonders if Freddie's running a fever. Getting him to dance at a wedding is almost impossible unless he's a little tipsy. Drunk, and he'd be dangerous, but he's never drunk. So really, it's tipsy or nothing if you want him to attempt a boogie to 'Dancing Queen' or 'Hips Don't Lie'. But he doesn't drink at all on a weekday night. What day is it? Wednesday.

Oh God!

'Freddie, stop it! Come in! What's the matter with you?' Alice hisses. He's behind the lamp post that's outside their front door, *shimmying*. It's the only word she can think of that gets close to the sort of dance he's doing. It's not even really a dance; Freddie doesn't know any dances; he can't even waltz, not properly. If Freddie's waltzing with you, wear your steel toe-capped Dr Martens. He's doing that hips and arms thingy that Hugh Grant does at the top of the Downing Street stairs to that Pointer Sisters' song in *Love Actually*. Except Hugh's able to pull it off – Freddie looks like his phone might have malfunctioned and is giving little electric shocks to his buttocks every half a second.

Alice stomps (quietly) down the garden path in her slippers

and tries to grab him, but he shimmies left and then right, out of her reach, each time she goes for him.

'Come in! The neighbours will see.' She looks across the street but, mercifully, can't spot any curtain twitching. And behind her, the only open mouth and wide-awake eyes are Poppy's, who's gawping out of her window with a look that Alice would only expect to see if Santa and the reindeers landed in the street on Christmas Eve. (Ryan doesn't do Santa anymore, but Poppy is still a card-carrying member, and long may that last.)

'Freddie!'

'We've won!' Freddie says in a conspiratorial whisper, clasping his hands behind his head and gyrating (well, wiggling) his hips in a manner that Alice is sure he'll regret in the morning. 'Two point three mil. We're rich, love. *Millionaires!*'

Alice snatches his wrist and gathers him in, like a rather portly sheep ready for shearing and dipping. Now that she's got him, he won't resist.

'Come inside. I'll put the kettle on.'

He hugs her, lifts her off her feet. She'll be rubbing Deep Heat into his lower back in the morning; that's now guaranteed. She bustles him inside as soon as he puts her down, which isn't long.

Poppy is standing on the bottom step of the stairs looking concerned.

'Is Daddy all right?' she asks Alice in a careful whisper, as if she thinks Daddy doesn't look capable of understanding, let alone answering, a simple question.

Alice marvels at Poppy's calm reaction to Freddie's erratic behaviour. Ryan, it seems, has missed this impromptu edition of *Strictly Come Shimmying*; the plinking and peeping from up the stairs continues uninterrupted.

'He's fine, Poppy. Just a bit excited. He's won a little money on the lottery.'

Poppy's eyes brighten. 'Can I have a new bike? I keep bonking my knees on the handlebars.'

Freddie laughs a manic cackle and clasps Poppy's pink face in his slightly pudgy hands. 'A bike, my beauty? I'll buy you the bike shop!'

Alice guides Freddie towards the kitchen, feeling a bit like Lassie, at the same time ushering Poppy back upstairs with a promise to rescue Goldilocks in a few ticks.

As she skips up the stairs, Poppy says over her shoulder, 'I only want a bike.'

Alice sits Freddie down at the kitchen table and flicks the kettle on. But he's up and behind her before she's got the cups out of the cupboard.

'Dance with me,' he whispers in her ear. 'Dance with a millionaire.'

Alice turns and lets him hold her in a *first dance at a wedding* pose as Freddie hums what she thinks is a sort of techno 'Blue Danube', and they shuffle stiffly around the kitchen until the kettle boils.

'Of course, we should be having champagne,' Freddie announces grandly, as Alice drops the teabags into the cups. 'And caviar. Have you ever had caviar? I haven't. But we should try it. It's something to do with fish. You have it on toast, I think. Like Marmite. Actually, we could employ a cook now. Take all the pressure off you. Though you won't need to work anymore. And neither will I. Blimey, love, I can give that jumped-up schoolgirl my notice in the morning. God, I've dreamt of this for so long.'

Alice fusses with the cups, pours the water, lifts and dunks the bags a couple of times – but her mind is elsewhere. As is Freddie's.

'We can afford to move now. The house we always dreamed of, out of this dump, away from all the oiks. And we can get the kids into a good school, or good *schools*; I've heard the best schools are single sex. Ryan can play rugger, like I did, it's character building. Never did me any harm. Sorts the men out from the goats. And Poppy can mix with a better class of girl, away from all the... you know. Not that I'm prejudiced, but the teachers don't have the time if they're forever having to, you know...

'And I can get the Carrera, after all these years. Can you believe that? Might even get a number 39 painted on the side.' He smiles to himself. Then his face changes. 'Although, maybe not. Might look a bit naff. And you can choose a little runabout for yourself. What about a soft-top? There are some really nice ones out now. Not too expensive either.

'And the Rolexes, of course. I've always wanted a Rolex. In fact, I'll delay my resignation until I've got it, so I can shove it under Little Miss Big Boots's nose when I tell her I'm off. See what she thinks of that. Can't wait to see her face.' Freddie's face is, at this moment, a picture of longing, delight. They say some people have poker faces; they don't say that about Freddie. Freddie has a snap face, every emotion as obvious as a tabloid headline.

'And think of the holidays we can go on now, love. Think of it. The Seychelles, always wanted to go there. Maldives. And you fancy Thailand, don't you? And when we go to Spain, in the summer, we could shoot two hippos with one bullet,' Freddie says, smiling to himself.

He's developed this little tic of adjusting popular sayings

using his own idiosyncratic formula to keep the children on their toenails – as he puts it. Only trouble is, Ryan's reached the eye-rolling stage, and Poppy's still parked in the Clueless in Norwich zone. At least Poppy hasn't started rolling her eyes, in fact she'd still be clueless if he said he was going to kill two birds with one stone, or he wanted to keep them on their toes. Poppy still takes everything literally.

Alice worries Poppy might never exit the literal stage – stage left or right – while Freddie has probably eaten more than he can swallow with this little attempt at Crazy Daddy humour. The really worrying thing is that Freddie has started playing these little linguistic games even when the children are out of earshot. Like now.

'Meaning?' Alice replies, her eyes begging for a clue.

'If we went to Mallorca as planned, but upgraded to one of the new six-star hotels, we could have the holiday and look at some flats and villas at the same time. Depending on the prices, of course. But first let's see if we can upgrade the hotel. Yes, we should definitely start looking for a place out there. See what we could get for our money. We do love Mallorca, don't we?' He pronounces it My York-ah! Just like the locals do, and the teacher when they had their one and only Spanish lesson, free as an evening 'entertainment' at their three-star hotel, more of a pension really, Casa Lola. 'What do you reckon?'

Alice shrugs. She's on board for the holiday, is pleased that Mallorca is still the suggested destination, relieved he isn't planning on scrounging a fortnight on Necker Island, but worried that he might try.

She leads him to the living room, brings the drinks in to land, their usual evening routine with their feet up in front of the telly when the kids are safely tucked up. Plus, four chocolate digestives this time, to celebrate; they usually only have two. She sits opposite him in one of the armchairs rather than next to him on the sofa.

How on earth is she going to tell him?

3

THE OTHER FAIRY TALE

ALICE IN WONDERLAND. It was Alice's favourite book as a child. Partly because of the name, of course. Well, mostly. But she did love the idea of a Wonderland. A land where wonderful things might happen. Is that where she is now? A land where wonderful things might happen? Or is this a different sort of wonder? The I wonder what the fuck's just happened sort?

She should've seen this coming. At least she should've said something. She's had so many opportunities over the years. Maybe as many as fourteen million, she muses, sardonically. It would've been so easy to say what she really felt. But she'd always bottled it. And she knows why.

Why didn't she tell him? Why has she always nodded and smiled and said very little to contradict him as he'd trashed their small life with his gripes and complaints and outlandish dreams of what he'd do when he won? Simple, really: she's never said anything because she always thought it was such a long shot that she didn't need to worry about it. Fourteen million to one, didn't they say? The odds of winning the lottery? So, he's won the fourteen million to one shot. And she's lost it. She's only got herself to blame. She knows it.

She knows it's a small life she lives. They live. She knows the area isn't the greatest, the most impressive part of what is anyway an unremarkable city in an out-of-the-way corner of the country. It might call itself a 'Fine City', but Norwich is a little off the beaten track – and any fast railway tracks. It might be in the south, but it has pockets of poverty that would have benefited from some of the levelling-up promises, had any of them meant anything.

Small life it may be, but it's *her* life. And dare she say it? If only to herself? She loves it. She really does. She loves her small life. She loves taking the children to school, hearing their little tales. She loves Freddie, in her own way. He's a good guy, if a little grumpy at times. Well, often. Especially now that he's worked out why. Now that he knows...

And he's never shouted at her. Imagine? He's such a softie. His worst swearwords are bloomin' and blinkin'. He'll occasionally drop the F-word, but it's his own bespoke version – flippin'. Or flippin' heck if he's really annoyed.

And she knows their house isn't what Freddie dreams of. Actually, it's not really what Freddie's dad had dreamed of, for Freddie, before he died. But Alice likes it. It's close to the shops; she can walk or bike with the kids to school; the garden is manageable; the mortgage is still affordable, just – even after that Truss woman had practically doubled their payments; the sun hits them in the afternoons and evenings; their neighbours are nice. What more could anybody want?

You'd have to ask Freddie that...

The kids, of course, are her pride and joy. That's what she sometimes calls them, secretly, to herself: Ryan is Pride, and Poppy is Joy. She loves being Mummy to them. They'd been easy babies. Well, that's the way Alice likes to remember that time. And now they are good children: kind, polite, friendly, helpful. Nobody would contradict that description. Ryan is clever. Always top marks at school, seemingly without trying much. He's also popular with everybody, easy-going and trustworthy.

Poppy, on the other hand, flies under the radar. So far under, she's more like a mole than any sort of aircraft or (low-flying) bird. She's usually away with the fairies. And if not with the fairies, then she'll be with the unicorns or the dragons. Who knows besides Poppy? She reminds Alice of herself as a child: happier in a book or listening to a story on a CD – or, better still, one read by Mummy. But she's a hard worker who would rob banks and mug old ladies if any of her teachers asked her to. If you looked at her for any length of time, you'd conclude she was a bit of a deep thinker. She watches. But Alice thinks fairies. Her teachers heap nothing but praise on her: she listens, answers questions if asked, is kind to the other children, seems to get along with everyone but – there's always a but – she needs to push herself forward more. She should be a leader, whereas she's actually a bit of a follower. They think it's hard to tell what she's really like: she's so deep.

They've never been much trouble, either of them. They always bring their problems to Alice: a grazed knee, a lost sticker, a torn page in a favourite book. Alice loves 'fixing' their lives for them. Loves being the person who they know will be able to sort that kind of stuff out. Like that time when Barbie's leg had come off. Oh, the tears! Poppy's were tears of deep, deep sorrow. Alice's were of pure mirth: in private, after she'd miraculously reattached Barb's missing limb in a tense operation, Ryan soundlessly passing the Sellotape, Poppy mopping Alice's brow with a hankie. When the operation was finally over, and Poppy was nursing Barb through some rigorous physiotherapy, Alice had hidden herself upstairs to shed her tears, into a pillow to muffle her laughter. Her pride and joy.

So now Freddie's planning to send them to private schools.

Single-sex private schools! Away from their little friends. Wearing poncey uniforms and adopting highfalutin airs. Why hadn't she said something whenever he'd paraded that pipe dream, as he regularly had? Was it simply the fact she was so sure it was never going to happen that she didn't want to bother starting a debate, a row, over it?

And as for Ryan playing rugger, and it being character building, and not doing Freddie any harm? Freddie had *hated* his private school. Hated bloody rugger – which was what he usually called it. *Bloody* rugger. Now, suddenly, it's going to turn Ryan into Boris Johnson – or Jacob Rees-Mogg. He'd voiced his hatred for his old school a thousand times, said the resources were pitiful, especially compared to the local comp where his older sister went. His biggest complaint was about the toilet paper. What was it called? Izal? Something like that. He said it was completely useless, like trying to wipe your bottom with a plastic bag. Funny thing was, he got all nostalgic for his old school whenever Ryan and Poppy's school hadn't done as well in its Ofsted reports as Freddie had wanted.

Or when he suddenly, unexpectedly, won the lottery.

And Ryan won't want to play rugger anyway, Alice muses. Bloody rugger. Ryan is a footballer; he's been a ball boy for Norwich City, has the shirt: Todd Cantwell, number 14, signed, although the shirt doesn't fit him anymore (Ryan that is). Plus, they sold him (Todd) to Rangers.

And as for Poppy going to some Malory Towers type of boarding school? What was it they often wore? Boaters? Poppy in a boater? Over Alice's dead body. So why hadn't she ever said that? Well, maybe not *that*, but why hadn't she simply expressed a view that maybe Poppy enjoyed her school, had some nice little friends, maybe not enough, but that was Poppy, not the school. Whatever happened to Kelly? Alice suddenly wonders. Poppy and Kelly used to be almost inseparable. Sleepovers, that kind of stuff. But Kelly hasn't been around for weeks. She makes a mental note to ask Poppy if they've had an argument.

And him in a Carrera and her in a 'little runabout soft-top'? Well, maybe she'd go for that, although what was wrong with their rusty but trusty Astra, and did they even really need two cars? Freddie got the bus to work, and she walked or biked; they only used Rusty for the shopping and trips out to the Broads or the seaside. And how would they get the four of them into a bloody Carrera anyway? Do they even have back seats, or would the kids be in the boot or a little trailer? Like the ones cyclists sometimes use to carry dogs. She smiles at the thought. But she could give ground on the cars. An estate would be useful as the kids got older.

But Rolexes? Why on earth would he want to waste God knows how many hundreds, or possibly even thousands of pounds, she's no idea, on fancy watches? Ryan would lose his or break it, while Poppy... well, Poppy would probably swap hers for a nice scrunchie or a multicoloured plastic bracelet. And Alice certainly doesn't want a Rolex. She has a nice watch that keeps perfect time and cost her £9.99 at the garage and has a really comfy suedey sort of strap. All those fancy watches have metal straps that would make her skin itch.

She would like a nice holiday, a few more stars on the hotel would be fun. That would be good. Although she'd miss the couple (Lola and Don Antonio) who run Casa Lola, the little hotel they've stayed in for a few years now, just outside Palma. Actually, she wouldn't simply miss the Alcántaras; she'd feel guilty. Their children, Carlos and Rosalita, get on so well with Ryan and Poppy. Alice adores the name Rosalita, the sound of it, the musicality, the stress on the letter i that's pronounced like a double e. She's also captivated by the fact that the *ita* suffix means 'little'. So, little Rosa, Rosalita's grandmother's name.

Alice also loves Ryan and Poppy having Spanish friends,

European friends. She'd always been against Brexit. The children play together; go shopping together to pick things up for the hotel; all the time enjoying practising their school Spanish and learning new words and sucking Chupa Chups on the way back.

So, why did it have to be the Seychelles or the Maldives or any of those other really far-away places that Freddie reeled off whenever he was – or used to be – complaining about their small, lottery-jackpotless life? They enjoyed Mallorca, and it only took them a couple of hours to get there. How different would the sea and sand be if you spent half a day on a plane instead?

And would there be anything to do except lie on the sand or swim in the sea on those far-away islands? She liked to see places. Palma is a lovely town; it has shops, restaurants, a beautiful cathedral, cinema in English, things to do if the weather is a bit iffy or if you get tired of the beach or the pool. And let's be honest, Freddie soon gets tired of the beach. He hates putting on suntan cream, but he burns like kindling when he doesn't bother. So, he usually spends all his time squeezed under a toytown-sized palm-frond brolly grizzling that his back hurts while she and the kids slap on the lotion and frolic in the surf. At least they might have some bigger sun brollies in a six-star hotel to keep him better protected if he continues to resist the sun cream treatment.

Alice loves their week in Mallorca for other reasons: she loves the Spanish way, as she calls it. So relaxed, so unpretentious. Especially with Lola and Don Antonio in their little hotel that no longer feels like a hotel. It feels more like visiting friends.

There's something very... *Spanish* about the beach in Mallorca. It's not like an English beach. Her usual shyness at wearing a bikini *at her age*, not that anybody has ever said anything to her, is always challenged as she watches the local women, all shapes and sizes and colours and ages, marching up and down the shoreline, chatting and laughing with friends or family. There's a constant procession going up and down the *playa*. It reminds Alice of a fashion show catwalk. They walk at about the same pace as the models do: purposefully, like they have somewhere important to get to. But then ten or fifteen minutes later, you see them all marching back towards where they came from.

None of them seem to give two... two... two whatever Spaniards would freely give away, about what anybody might think regarding their shape or size or appearance – and some of them, not only the young slim ones, go topless! Without a care – or a bikini top – in the world. Amazing. She finds it strangely liberating, watching them, their hands flapping and waving in the air as if they're swishing at swarms of wasps or conducting an orchestra, as they tell their tales then cackle like witches around a cauldron, or maybe a paella pan, their breasts swinging like two melons in a plastic bag. And sometimes, not in a plastic bag. Alice, on the other hand, feels sure she'll still bring her bag-for-life swimsuit... Spain might feel liberating, but she's not sure she's ready for that much liberation.

The men are interesting too. They all do the long march along the shore as well, but they're different in a way she finds hard to define. They're slightly more restrained, not quite at the pace of the catwalk señoras, as if their stroll along the beach in swimming trunks still has the residual aura of a business meeting. The older ones nod at each other gravely; the conversation often appears serious; they keep their hands lower than the women do. Pot bellies are ten a penny, or maybe that's ten a centimo over there.

'So, what do you think?'

'Sorry?'

'A yacht?'

'*A what?*'

'A yacht? What do you think?'

Alice realises she's been sitting there for five, maybe ten, minutes, and Freddie's been rattling on all the time, and she hasn't heard a word he's said. Are the kids now heading for Eton? Well, Ryan. Is Poppy off to Roedean? Or Hogwarts? She hasn't started HP with Poppy yet, is waiting till she's a little older. A little more 'mature' – although, much as she can't wait for the boundless pleasure she knows she'll get from reading HP with Poppy, she doesn't want Poppy to grow up any time soon, if at all. Has he traded the Carrera for a Roller? Are they buying Trump Tower now instead of a vil–

'We'd have to have lessons, I suppose,' he continues into his private sunset. 'You couldn't simply sail off into a gale if you didn't know your mainsail from the other one. Maybe hold our ponies on the yacht? What do you think?'

'Yes,' she says, relieved that she might have started some sort of a fightback.

4

THE TRADITIONAL COUPLE

ALICE WOULD DESCRIBE THEM AS A 'TRADITIONAL' couple. Traditional in the 1950s sense of the word: Freddie does the car, the DIY, and the money; Alice does everything else. She's not really sure how they've ended up like this. It reminds her of her own, sadly departed, parents. It shocks her that she's mirrored their relationship so closely, and so effortlessly – or should that be thoughtlessly...?

When she says Freddie does the car, what that means is he'll look at it if it makes a funny noise, or is leaking something, or doesn't go at all. He might even open the bonnet, if he can find the little lever that seems to move to a new location whenever he needs to use it. And then he'll scratch his head, spend twenty minutes on the internet muttering darkly about 'the big end or the bloomin' tappets' before phoning the garage. So, in that sense, yes – Freddie *does* the car.

And DIY? Freddie does that as well. But the doing bit wouldn't feature on any of the makeover shows that seem to litter the TV schedules like... well, like litter. Not unless it was one of the disaster types where everything goes wrong: some bodger tries to fix a leaking tap in the upstairs bathroom and ends up with a sinkhole in the living room big enough to swallow a bus. Norwich has form as far as sinkholes swallowing buses goes but, as far as Alice knows, Freddie wasn't responsible for that little catastrophe. No, Freddie's approach to DIY is always safety first. His modus operandi is clear: why buy a full set of Black+Decker power tools, when you've already got some Sellotape and Blu Tack? But he won't touch electrics – 'you need an expert' – and he's not keen on plumbing – he had a nasty experience with a stopcock once – and he doesn't do paint – sets off his hay fever.

There have been times when Alice has considered searching at the back of the cupboard for a hammer and a nail to rehang a picture of the children that's fallen off the wall – but she always resists the temptation, fearful she will embarrass Freddie who, for some unfathomable reason, seems to think he's a bit of a DIY natural. She can only square this view by thinking about how birds build nests; they're obviously DIY naturals – and they don't have a full set of Black+Decker power tools either. They just bodge it with twigs and bits of string. But she bets their pictures aren't always falling off the walls in the summer, when the Blu Tack warms up and stretches and can't hold the weight anymore. More than once, she's rushed out to the shops to get a bit of glass for the frame and added an extra bit of Tack to the Blu (or Blu to the Tack, who knows?) so Freddie doesn't come home to shards of glass and a new episode of *DIY Bodger Disasters* in his own living room.

And Freddie does the money, which involves setting up the direct debits on his bank account to pay the bills. Yes, he does that. Well, he's done it. *Did* it. Years ago.

So, Alice does everything else. That's the house (minus 'repairs'): cleaning of, tidying of; the garden: planting, sweeping leaves, the odd bit of pruning, although Freddie does the mowing; the food: buying of, cooking of, stuffing of into sandwich boxes; and the children: getting them ready for school, picking them up from school, solving all their little problems – including the occasional orthopaedic operation. Oh, and transferring clothes from the basket to the washing machine and knowing which buttons to press because Freddie can't get the hang of them. Seriously. She's tried and he's tried her patience. But whenever she thinks she's (or he's) cracked it, she finds two pairs of socks and a vest on a two-hour cotton wash and she reverts to doing it herself or teaching the kids, who are desperate to be allowed free rein on the washing machine – and the cooker.

Talking about the cooker, that's another Freddie-free zone. She's never known him to cook anything. Not even beans on toast or a boiled egg. The most he ever does is toss cereal into a bowl and slop milk over it. Oh, he can also slip a slice of bread into the toaster and then add butter and marmalade without the assistance of a Delia Smith hardback. But cook? Use the oven? Even the microwave? No, Freddie never cooks. Although that isn't strictly true...

She smiles in amusement at how she's never noticed this before. If they're ever having a barbecue, then Freddie grabs one of her aprons and takes control, like Alice is in danger of burning herself on the hot coals. No, Freddie always cooks when they plan a barbecue. Well, he usually *under*cooks, and often burns, but he's there with a spatula and a long fork, prodding sausages or spending ages trying to roll a drumstick that's prominently displaying that highly unusual culinary colour combination that is Freddie's barbecue speciality – pink and black.

Another realisation broadens her smile. In Spain, at Casa Lola, whenever Lola and Don Antonio plan *la paella*, it's Don Antonio who dons an apron in order to gather the wood, light the fire, and unleash unimaginably delicious smells into the patio surrounding the swimming pool – with Freddie by his side. Ha! She laughs. Yes, with Freddie suddenly all interested in the mysterious cooking process, and taking one of the *paellera-pan* handles to help Don Antonio display *la paella* to the salivating hordes, smiling proudly as if he has contributed at least half the culinary skill or labour, rather than simply having stood at Don Antonio's side and watched, while attempting to ask questions in English, of Don Antonio, who speaks precious little of it.

Not that Freddie has ever entered the kitchen to ask Lola, who produces everything else they eat at Casa Lola, what she's cooking or how she does it. How does she turn fresh sardines from the dockside into those deliciously toasty fillets, slathered in extra virgin olive oil and a mysterious concoction of spices? No, Freddie only ever shows an interest in cooking when it's done outside and there are matches involved.

The children are keen in the kitchen. Alice decided, very early on, that part of her mothering duties included making sure the children saw the kitchen as a place of creation. From a tender age, she had Ryan, and subsequently Poppy, at her elbow, mixing and kneading and rolling, no matter the price to be paid later cleaning the extra utensils, the countertops, the floor – and often, the children.

They love helping so much – even from the age when they weren't providing any help at all – that Alice long ago decided to extend their homemaking duties to include the cleaning. She discovered, after one or two false starts, that there's nothing more fun than cleaning the house with the kids scooting around the place with two of those little handheld vacuums, seeing who can collect more 'bits' in the transparent 'bits' that collect, er, all the 'bits'. And their rooms are always immaculate: dirty clothes in the basket, duvets plumped up, toys in tidy piles (colour and size coded in Poppy's case).

Shopping with the pair of them is another of Alice's joys, as Poppy and Ryan add up various combinations of items in the trolley to practise maths or translate the foods into Spanish. Even Alice is picking up a bit of the lingo through these shopping games. She knows that bread is *pan* and lettuce is *lechuga*. And, banana is *banana*, but there's no *ahhhh* sound in the middle. Yes, she's getting the hang of the old *español*.

She's not quite sure how she and Freddie slipped into such traditional roles. Alice read Mary Wollstonecraft at university, Germaine Greer too, although she doesn't remember exactly what either of them said. But she got the gist. She burned her bra – metaphorically. Well, she was studying English Lit; a metaphorical burning seemed appropriate enough. And less of a waste of money at a time when she had precious little of it. But then Freddie went down on one knee following steak and chips and a couple of glasses of Mateus Rosé at a Bernie Inn a few weeks after her graduation. What decadence, she remembers now, what sophistication, and only just into their twenties. And then? They both simply 'slipped into role'.

He was working in the bank by then; he won her over with his interest rates, she always joked. He, working full time, became the main provider; she, having recently started her teacher training, and then working part time when the children were young, maybe going to full time later, sort of turned into a housewife, at least a part-time one, without filling out any application forms or signing any sort of documentation. They never actually discussed it. They just did it. 'Slipped' into it.

And to be fair, she enjoyed her role. She was good at it. She loved all the mothering stuff, still does. They were pretty easy babies, mostly; they ate and slept and pooed and smiled, usually in that order, then did it all again. They didn't have that many sleepless nights. Of course, she tried to encourage Freddie to join in the duties and, again, to be fair, he was keen, and he did try. But when he vomited all over Ryan on his first attempt at a nappy change, and a second a couple of weeks later, well, that didn't take off. And him working full time left her with the playgroup run when she went to work part time, and the school run after that. And she loved it all. She loved being with the children. They got on so well: Ryan, such a nice, gentle, caring big brother; Poppy, in awe of him, taking his hand (and Alice's) whenever they walked to school. They shared and played together; he read books to her – when Alice let him...

So, yes, a traditional couple. A traditional family. A normal, run-of-the-mill, bog-standard, average family.

Until now...

Alice stares at the ceiling. She lies and worries. Lies? Both senses of the word. Why haven't they talked? Ever? About this? To be fair, Freddie talks. Rarely stops. But he's either moaning about their small life or planning what he'll – what they'll – do when he wins the lottery. And what has she done in response? Listened. Smiled. Humoured him. Why? Because it was better than his moaning. He was happy when dreaming of his lottery win, so why make him unhappy by telling him? By telling him that... What? That she wasn't sure she really wanted what he wanted? Or said he wanted. But she'd never thought he'd win so she hadn't. So, it was her fault really. Why hasn't she talked? Talked to him? Instead, she lies, by not telling him the truth.

The children haven't taken much notice of Freddie's lottery dreaming. He tried to include them when they were younger, but Ryan, having announced that playing for Norwich City would be what he wanted most if, when, Daddy won, lost a bit of interest when the game went on and on, week after week, with nothing but dashed hopes, tickets in the bin,

Daddy suddenly glum, and no sign of the promised money and Ryan's name on the back of a Norwich shirt. A real one. And Poppy still wasn't old enough to understand what a million pounds was worth. She wasn't very good at maths: couldn't really get her head around a tenner. *What would you want if you won the lottery, Poppy? A new bike.* Right. That's Poppy sorted, now let's all move to Monaco, or San Francisco, in the new yacht, wearing our Rolexes, or whatever his latest dream is.

Freddie's off with the sandman. He's just won the lottery but he's sleeping like a baby hippo, all snuffly and contented. The sex had been nice. A bit quick. As usual. But nice. Nice to see him happy. Relaxed. Instead of his normal...

But what about her? Was there something wrong with her? You've won the lottery, girl. Why doesn't she feel anything?

Except dread?

And why does she feel she can't say?

Is she simply afraid to admit, now the moment of truth has arrived, the fork in the road, all the other clichés she reads in her novels, that they're simply not... not what? Not on the same page? Not in tune? Not marching to the same beat? Like she'd always thought, or hoped, they were. Has this win opened the Pandora's box that she's never wanted to explore? Is she afraid of what it might ignite? What it might reveal? What it might destroy? If he stops talking about what he wants to do, and is suddenly able to start doing it? And she's forced to finally say, to confess, to admit, guilty as charged: 'That's not what I want...'

It's not even as if she knows what she really does want. She simply knows she doesn't want what he wants. But she's not sure she'd be able to say what she does want – except what she has: Freddie (as was, pretty much, maybe a bit happier at work), the children, their home, their life together, the holidays they have, the games they play, the programmes they watch. Isn't that enough? Should she want more? For them? Like Freddie does…? Is she somehow limiting them all by not wanting more?

She's managed to get Freddie to agree not to tell the children how much he's really won – yet. 'A little win' they're calling it, 'a few thou'. Which is true – ish, if you twist the definition of *a few* using Johnson's revised rules of English usage – that's Boris, of course, not Samuel. Enough to buy Poppy a bike, and something for Ryan. She argued that the kids would blab to everyone in the school and they'd be a freak show: their friends pestering them for money; hundreds of begging letters cascading through the letter box for Poppy to sort by colour and size; satellite dishes on vans in the street outside; local reporters following them to Tesco and asking them why they aren't now shopping at Waitrose or getting deliveries sent up from Harrods. She's working on a plan that they never tell the children how much they've won, but first things first.

She's had to think quick. Why hadn't she been ready? Had a plan in place? A contingency? Like they had plans for nuclear war, for floods, explosions, Covid? Although that hadn't turned out so well, so maybe she shouldn't blame herself too much. But she should have had a plan for Freddie winning. She should have had a plan. She should have one.

Instead, she lies.

5

THE SCHOOL RUN

Poppy's devouring her latest library book in the back seat. She's actually finished it, but any book's better than no book on Planet Poppy. It's a series about pets and their exciting adventures: kittens getting stuck up trees; ponies lost in forests or shopping malls; puppies wrestling with miles of unravelling toilet roll. Each book has some adorable kitten or puppy or whatever on the front cover, with huge sad eyes and a soulful look that would melt even Trump's heart. There are twenty-six books in the series and counting. Poppy's on number sixteen: *Puppy Down the Plughole*, or something like that. If number seventeen isn't available in the library, Poppy will choose something else until it's there. Alice has explained that it's not the sort of series where each story continues on from, or even refers back to, the previous book, or any of the previous books but, Poppy being Poppy, she likes to keep things ordered, or sequenced, or whatever it is she does.

Should she be concerned about Poppy's little fixations? Books in strict alphabetical order by author and then title on her bookshelves? Fair enough. Felt-tip pens in rainbow-coloured order on her desk? Okay. Teddies and dolls in an order on her bed that only Poppy knows? Hmm... There are others: Milk into the bowl before the cereal. Fish Fingers eaten before the chips, chips before the beans. In fact, she always eats the parts of any meal separately, in sequence – even with breakfast cereal, where she tries, by carefully draining the milk off each spoonful before eating the cereal, then finishing off by spooning all the milk down with a contented (relieved?) smile. Left sock and shoe on before right. Ryan into the car before herself. Ryan hasn't noticed this little tic, but Alice has spotted it, quite recently: Poppy hanging back at the front door, fannying around with her shoes or bag, 'forgetting something' in her room... Alice wonders if Poppy's been doing this for years and even she hasn't noticed – or is it a new one, to add to the collection? Like how Poppy's recently started gathering the post from the mat every morning and laying the pile on the breakfast table, carefully arranged into colours and size order. She'll be wanting access to Alice's emails soon, to sort them by weight or font or something.

Ryan's sorting his football cards.

They usually walk. But it's starting to drizzle, threatening rain, so she's taking Rusty. She prefers to walk. Poppy always holds her hand, and although she doesn't offer a lot, she will answer questions quite willingly: about school, her friends, which book she's going to get from the library. Poppy also skips sometimes, which lifts Alice's heart as high as (nearly) anything else she can think of. She's often tempted to skip herself, to see the look on Poppy's (or Ryan's) face, but she daren't; she doesn't want to draw attention to Poppy's skipping – in case she stops. Alice knows she'll stop one day. You never see an adult skipping, do you? Everybody stops, not that Ryan ever really started. But Poppy will stop, and Alice doesn't want to do anything that will hasten that moment. Is it a hormones thing? Stopping skipping? Something to do with your legs getting too long? She doesn't know, but she dreads the day.

'Can I still have a new bike?' Poppy suddenly asks from the back seat, looking up from the plughole as if she's just remembered there are other people, other things, on the planet. Planet Poppy.

'Of course,' Alice says, catching her eye in the rear-view mirror, giving her a conspiratorial wink. 'You sure you don't want the whole shop?'

Poppy smiles, and the delicious little shared secret understanding brings Alice such a warm sensation that she feels slightly dizzy.

'What's that?' Ryan says, suddenly intrigued, sounding annoyed, Erling Haaland slipping from his fingers and fluttering into the footwell. 'Why's Poppy getting a new bike? Mine's older.'

Alice nods. She's pleased with this chance to 'break the news'. They'd agreed last night to tell the kids this evening: a *small* win; a *little* holiday; maybe a new car; bikes even...

'Dad's had a little win on the lottery. A small one. And Poppy wants a new bike. You can have one if you want. Or something else?'

'The new Norwich kit?' His face lights up like a firework. He's been angling for the new kit for a while, but they've promised it for his birthday.

'That might be possible,' Alice says, calculating cautiously what two point three million take away a hundred quid would leave. 'We'll talk to Dad.'

'Brilliant!'

Alice sighs silently, hugely relieved that she's been able to manage the expectations so well, no chance of Freddie blurting out that they're millionaires and he's planning on sending them to posh schools, miles away from all their friends. She'll square Freddie later, tell him exactly what happened: Ryan asked when Poppy had mentioned the new bike. Job done.

Alice pulls up outside the school and offers her cheek for kisses: Ryan brushes the lightest of Italians; Poppy gives her the full Dyson. Then they're off: Ryan sloping in like a rather small teenager, Poppy at a gallop, her bag swinging on her shoulder, threatening to cut the legs off from under her. Her teacher is chatting to another member of staff in the playground. That conversation's end is nigh, Alice thinks with a smile...

Poppy's teacher this year is Ms Gibson, but you have to say *Mzzz*. It means you don't know if she's married or not, but she isn't, because Poppy asked her when she told them all what Ms meant. She's got a boyfriend, Arturo, who's Spanish and works in the deli on the Unthank Road. Ms Gibson's first name is Anne, short for Annette, but she doesn't like Annette. She has a kitten called Bonkers and likes Taylor Swift, reading, and chatting with her friends in coffee shops. Alice is confident that Poppy will have her bra size and National Insurance number by the end of the year.

Ms Gibson will soon be chatting to Poppy – well, she'll soon be listening to Poppy. Alice waits for a few seconds – you're not allowed to hang around too long in the drop-off zone – and sure enough, Poppy hovers while hopping from foot to foot, waiting for Mzzz to notice her presence, then, when permission is granted with a smile, Poppy latches on to Mzzz Gibson's arm like a lonely limpet that's finally spotted a space on a rock.

Alice can guess what she's rattling on about: books, what book Mzzz is reading, what Mzzz did last night: all the things Alice has to wring out of Poppy under bright-light interrogation over the weekends, but which appear like greyhounds out of the traps whenever Poppy has her teacher within range. Every year, Alice thinks it impossible for Poppy to love a teacher more. Then the new term starts, and the next one is 'even nicer', a phrase Poppy can fill with more power, passion and meaning than any of the offerings from the last dozen Booker champs.

Alice wonders if she minds, decides that Poppy 'loving' her teacher (again) is well-worth the price of sometimes feeling taken for granted, until it's bedtime story time, when the world rights itself again. Cos, although Mzzz is good, nobody reads a story like Mummy – Poppy says so.

Alice turns the car and heads for her own school.

6

____

THE BUS

FREDDIE'S ON THE CORNER, waiting for the bus. He dodges the drips from the drizzle that are bouncing off the leaves of the conker tree. There's no shelter, and he's forgotten to bring his brolly. This isn't what he was expecting. This isn't what he's been imagining. The morning after his big lottery win? He's dreamed of this moment a thousand times, more, but it's never been like this: waiting for the sodding bus to arrive in the blinking rain. To be honest, his dreams have always started at work, never at the bus stop. He's dreamed of arriving late; flashing his lottery ticket under his colleagues' noses, especially Tasha, his jumped-up manager who's at least ten years his junior and is only his boss, he's recently discovered, because she has a degree and he doesn't.

Sociology. That's her degree. Nothing to do with banking, or money, or maths, or economics. It's just *a* degree. Only a 2:2, it's rumoured. He's not sure; he started the rumour so how would he know? Not his usual style, rumour-mongering, but she gets right up his nose – and into his ears and his eyes. Every orifice he's got, actually. He's hated her since the moment they met. He remembers the day, the interview. *The* interview. The interview when he realised, when it all finally made sense...

It must've been his fifth or sixth for a manager's post, and it was the one, when it was over, where everything suddenly slotted into place and he realised why he was being left to malinger in the deputy's poky little office that was furnished from an IKEA window display, while someone else – anyone who was ten years younger and in possession of a degree, any degree, any class, any subject – was ushered into the manager's office with its huge desk, exec chair, coffee table, Nespresso machine, and easy chairs.

There'd been three other candidates: Tasha, and two guys whose names he can't remember, maybe had never known. The other three all younger by ten years, minimum. All four of them in suits, and showing off: 'I like your Armani, looks good'. Freddie, in his M&S new-year-sale special offer, from five or six years ago, still his 'best' but now with shiny elbows and knees, prayed they wouldn't ask him where his suit was from.

The conversation had moved on to schools. None of them had heard of Freddie's, which quietened the room for a while. Until Armani asked what degrees they all had. Tasha's was sociology; Armani was history; Ralph Lauren was some marketing nonsense. And they'd looked at him. And to his shame, he'd lied. Maths, he'd said. He had the A level, grade A, so it seemed a safe bet.

Freddie is a modest man. Unkind friends might say he has a lot to be modest about. He comes from a modest background; attended a modest little village school; scored a handful of modest GCSEs and three slightly more than modest A levels at an extremely modest private school hidden behind a forest of tall dark trees somewhere in North Norfolk. Enough to get him into a modest university – had his father not leaned on him with talk of student loans becoming workers' debt and Freddie probably never being able to afford a mortgage if he 'wasted' three years getting a degree that he didn't need.

His parents had sacrificed a lot to get him into the small private school in the middle of Norfolk's nowhereland that his dad had gone to – 'keep up the family tradition' – and there was nothing left, according to his dad, when all his friends were applying for university. What his dad never confessed to Freddie, was that there was another reason why the family finances were in difficulty – Graham had treated himself to an impressively large house backed by an endowment mortgage. It later became evident that the endowment was never going to pay enough to cover the mortgage debt, let alone leave any sort of inheritance for Freddie and his sister. Graham, unable – well, unwilling – to confess his mismanagement of the family finances, hadn't even told Brenda that they were, in effect, bankrupt.

The news he wouldn't be going to university came as a shock to young Freddie. He'd assumed he'd go, his elder sister, Susan, had gone, so he was devastated to learn that the new fees were too high. Sod Tony Blair: he'd never vote Labour, he vowed, in revenge.

His dad had been persuasive: his argument that Freddie 'couldn't start his adult life with that much debt' seemed unanswerable, when it landed, like a hand grenade in his bedroom, while all his mates were making their plans. His dad had sugared it as best he could: 'Get in early, like I did, and you'll steal a march on all the rest who'll waste three or four years getting drunk. By then, you'll be well on your way to being a manager. That's what I did – I never needed a degree.'

How could Freddie argue? But then it turned out that the three or four years weren't wasted after all, and Freddie was quickly overtaken by all the graduates with their totally irrelevant degrees in archaeology or anthropology, any olyology, it didn't seem to matter, and their Armani suits. Tasha's was Armani. Or so she'd said. Freddie wouldn't have known an Armani suit from a suit of armour.

There was a sting in the tail when Susan emigrated to Australia with her 2:2 in media studies to marry a sheep farmer she'd met on a Greek island. So, having initially lauded Susan's 'achievement' of being the first in the Cash family to 'make it' to university, Freddie's dad used her to argue how unnecessary degrees were, at least for her – and her sheep.

Worst thing about it was that the manager's job was for his branch. Freddie was the internal candidate, had assumed he was a shoo-in, until he realised he had the wrong suit; went to the wrong school; and crucially, it was now clear, had no degree. Within a week, Tasha, as his new manager, had asked him, by-the-by style, but with a knowing look, 'I thought you said you'd studied maths at university...?' He'd had to bluff it, but she knew, and he knew she knew. She must have found his degree-free CV in the files...

The bus arrives and he clambers aboard. Why is he in his usual workday grumpy mood when he's a millionaire?

'Morning, Ready.' Natalie, one of the cashiers, giggles as Freddie lets himself in behind the counter.

'Morning,' he grumbles back. Why does she always giggle when she talks to him? And she must know he hates the nickname. All the fault of the previous manager, Trevor, who thought he was a wit: Freddie Cash, Ready Cash. Ho ho. Very funny. What were his parents thinking? His dad should have spotted it, what with all the 'Cash by name, Cash by nature' nonsense he was always spouting.

Ah well, at least it's not the first Monday of the month,

Freddie's least favourite day of every month – dress-down Monday. Freddie loathes dress-down Monday. One of Tasha's innovations, designed, she'd said, to 'bond them as a team'. He knows they all snigger behind their hands at his supermarket jeans and trainers, his pastel-coloured polos or jumpers. But how do you look cool when you're fumbling your way around forty? He fears he'd look more ridiculous if he wore the expensive brands – unless he was emerging onto a Greek dockside from a superyacht with a supermodel draped on his arm. Difficult look to pull off on the Unthank Road – the nearest water being the Norfolk Broads. You don't see many superyachts on Hickling Broad.

But, he considers with a shudder, at least it's not Halloween! Freddie's least favourite day of all time now that Tasha has decreed, another team-bonding innovation, that they must dress as ghosts or ghouls or zombies, whatever they are. Even Poppy and Ryan didn't have to dress up for Halloween at school. What is Tasha on? Freddie scuttles through to his micro-office with its doll's-house furniture and closes the door.

He pings on his computer and sits back in his exec chair (grade 2), listening to it squeak and groan like a cheap pushchair going up a steep hill. How much longer will he have to tolerate this? He'll definitely wait until he's got his Rolex. Shame the bank doesn't have its own car park. How he'd love to come in early one day in the Porsche. That would set the tongues wobbling. He smiles bitterly and logs on to the system with a weary sigh.

He spends a pointless and dispiriting hour annoying some of the bank's commercial customers by ringing and trying to sell them more 'services': wireless credit card machines and all the other tosh that hadn't existed when Freddie joined the bank. It's the part of the job he hates the most, apart from everybody calling him Ready, and having to dress down every fourth

Monday, and dress up every Halloween. In their monthly performance management meeting, Tasha hints that everyone else is enjoying the promised bonuses for hitting their targets while Freddie's arrows or bullets or missiles soar away into the trees. To add insult to a virus, as Freddie has described it to Alice, she'd even sent him on a training course, to help him 'achieve his potential in sales'. That had been a disaster. He shudders as the memory sneaks up behind him wearing a *Scream* mask.

They'd gathered at a small run-down hotel somewhere near Gatwick. It was a nightmare journey for Freddie, so, to make the nine o'clock start, he travelled down the night before. The noise from the planes and the smell of urine in his room meant he didn't sleep well and woke up late, leaving him no time for his buffet breakfast – included in the price of the room. At five to nine, the *youf* on the desk informed him that, despite the email claiming the course was being held at the hotel, it was actually hosted by a partner hotel a twenty-minute walk away. 'You want me to call you a taxi?' Freddie arrived twenty-five minutes late to find that coffee and biscuits were still being served. The course eventually started nearer to half ten, as most of the attendees phoned in to say their trains were delayed, meaning he could have made it with time to spare had he got the early train that morning. But getting to the course was nothing when compared to the actual course.

It was run by an irritating American who called himself Billy Wild, although Freddie didn't believe that was his real name. Billy, or whoever, had clearly run away to the circus somewhere in Nebraska as a child and spent the subsequent years training to be a clown. His face had the elastic properties that all clowns' faces, and Jim Carey, seem to possess. His eyebrows brushed his hairline whenever he asked a question, which he did while bending at the waist and almost touching the noses of the seated participants with his own. His mouth would expand to a size that could comfortably accept a whole Ogen melon whenever he wanted to express surprise. And his hands made obscure shapes and karate-style chopping movements, not always obviously linked to whatever he was saying. Of course, they started by wasting another hour doing ludicrous 'icebreaking' activities involving balloons of different colours, sizes and shapes. And, when they eventually started the course, the whole thing was run through – Freddie's least favourite activity in the world, even more hated than dressing up as a ghost – role play.

'I want somebody to phone me and sell me an upgraded property insurance policy...' Billy gurned, thumb and pinky extended and held to his ear and chin, as Freddie attempted to shrink into the stuffing of his chair. 'Freddie! Be a sport!' The memory sends a shiver through his already sombre mood.

At ten o'clock he does a quick tour of the branch, sorting a couple of minor issues, but mainly listening to the gripes and groans of Natalie and the other cashiers, wincing as they all titter when they call him Ready as if none of them have ever heard the nickname before. Tasha's door is firmly closed. As usual. On the phone lining her Armani pockets with commission, no doubt. He makes himself a cup of instant in the cupboard-sized staffroom with its industrial-sized tins of economy coffee and whitener. Only the manager gets the Nespresso machine in their office, little fridge for fresh milk, tins of quality biscuits (whatever that means). He can't bloomin' wait to tell her where to stick her sodding biscuits.

Back in his room, he surfs onto the lottery website and finds he has to call them for such a big win. He pudges the number with an almost steady finger on his desktop phone.

Twenty minutes later, Freddie ends the call and rubs his hands together, delighted with himself. It's finally happening. He can hardly believe it. Here he is, in his office, a millionaire. A *double* millionaire. Two point three million pounds. Two – point – three – bloomin' million. How much is that? It's twenty-three hundred thousand pounds. Two hundred and thirty lots of ten thousand pounds. Two thousand three hundred thousands. Twenty-three thousand hundreds. Two hundred and thirty thousand tenners. Four hundred and sixty thousand fivers. Two point three million pounds. Two hundred and thirty million pence. Freddie has always been good at maths.

It's a delicious feeling, being here at work and they don't know. Yet. He relishes the moment, and dreams of the day when he comes in, flashes his Rolex, maybe with the Carrera parked on the kerb outside, hazards blinking, and resigns. He can hardly wait. He's tempted to do it now. Stand up, walk into the lobby, announce that he's won two point three million pounds and is off. Goodbye. No resignation letter, no period of notice. But it will be better with the Rolex. And the Carrera.

He feels he deserves a little treat. He rattles open the bottom drawer of his battered desk, scrabbles around amongst the old staplers, dried-up highlighter pens and boxes of paper clips, pulls out an old phone and a charger, plugs them in. He pings the phone on and waits for its tiny screen to liven up, his heart pattering a little faster than usual. Then he pudges in her number.

It's not saved on the phone. Nothing's saved on the phone: no numbers, no messages, and it's too antiquated to run apps. He only ever uses it for this call. They call them burner phones in the spy and detective stories he devours on the TV or on his Kindle. He likes the thought, a small smidgen of excitement to liven up another dull day. It's his guilty little secret. He can go and see her more often, now that he has more money. An hour this Friday should be perfect, maybe he'll ask her to suggest some new positions he could try, something a bit more 'exotic' than his usual tastes. His heart quickens further...

The call connects but, as is usual, the line is silent.

'Hello? Mandy? It's Freddie.'

'Freddie, nice to hear from you. Are you coming tomorrow? Usual time?'

'Yes, usual time. But, um, something... a little different this time? Something, ah, a bit special, maybe...?'

'Oh, Freddie. You naughty boy. Something a bit special?'

'That's right.' He always trusts Mandy to lead, to suggest things; she's the expert.

'No problem, Freddie, I'll be waiting for you. I'll have something ready. Usual time. See you tomorrow...'

There's a giggle on the line as the call disconnects.

Freddie wipes the call history, unplugs the charger, and drops it into the drawer. The phone blinks to zero power, its usual state, and Freddie puts it back amongst the old staplers, dried-up highlighter pens and boxes of paper clips. If anybody ever discovers it, and asks, he'll say he found it on the counter ages ago, threw it in the drawer and forgot about it. He sits back and smiles with a delicious shiver of anticipation.

Something a little special, for Friday evening.

With Mandy...

7

THE BIG SCHOOL

ALICE PARKS the Astra and sets off across the playground, laptop bag slicing into her shoulder. A group of year-seven girls emerge from under the trees and run at her like cheetahs who've spotted a lame gazelle limping across the plain. They're the youngest in the school, just out of primary, and they've yet to develop the *Who gives a shit?* attitude of many in the upper years. They want to carry her bag, open doors for her, talk about the homework they had, and get in out of the drizzle.

Can they help to give out the textbooks? Can they sharpen the pencils? Can they clean the board? Alice thinks she likes this part of the day even better than the teaching. There's often a little confidence shared: a problem at home; boyfriend issues (usually the lack of a boyfriend); and occasionally, more recently, *girl*friend issues. She's touched by how much they trust her; worried at how widely, easily, and maybe carelessly they might share their problems.

Does she want to give this up? This contact with young minds who look up to her like some kind of mythical big-sister figure – font of all knowledge on the important issues in life: Jane Austen? Taylor Swift? Who might like whom on *Strictly*?

She dreads the day when she feels they might start to see her as some kind of a mother figure. She plays that role with Ryan and Poppy; here, she's big sis. She's heard one or two of the year sevens whispering that they've seen her name on the register – *Alice* – shared reverentially, with a shiver of admiration, approval, membership of a secret club.

She's good at this bit. She knows it. The bit most people who talk about teaching and teachers know very little about. The bit they mention in training but don't really cover in much detail. You're left to sort it out for yourself; make it up as you go along. Yes, she loves all the books, the authors, the words, the stories. She loves all of that. But this... This contact, between her experience and their young, developing minds. To Alice, these are priceless moments. Good training, perhaps, for the years to come with Ryan and Poppy?

She can remember herself at their age. It was Miss Potter for Alice. English again, form tutor, and she was colossal. Not physically, she was quite a small woman. But in the personality sense, in the place she occupied in Alice's life, she was gargantuan. Someone Alice would have trusted with any secret, asked any question, confessed any transgression. She knows she's modelled herself, a little, on Miss Potter. But she's Mrs Cash.

Wouldn't she miss the banter in the staffroom as well? It's quite a young staff; where isn't nowadays? She occupies a kind of middle position in the school: she's young enough to get invited to all the meals out (although she always cuts and runs before the ones wearing the fewest clothes head for the clubs); yet experienced enough to be sought out to give advice on a range of issues both in and out of school. Should a young member of staff move in with her boyfriend? Should another seek promotion? She sees it as a community. She feels part of it. A valued member. Near enough to the leadership grades to be trusted to know stuff, but far enough away from them to be trusted with stuff – stuff you might not want your boss to know anything about...

She also loves her position as 'English guru'. Any confusion or uncertainty the younger members of staff have over a spelling or a grammatical construction, especially when it's report-writing time, they all trust Alice more than the Word spell or grammar checker. She also enjoys trying to use a few words that they might not know, not in a show-offy kind of way, just her establishing a certain personality for herself: mature, educated, *different*. Plus, it's a little attempt to keep alive some of the words that were common in her youth but now seem to have slipped out of usage. 'Swanky' was the latest of these. She said she'd bought Poppy a swanky new coat and half the staffroom didn't know what she meant.

She knows teaching has its downsides: the pay's not great; there's the marking and the prep and the meetings. But she's experienced enough to be able to rely a lot on last year's planning, and she knows which corners can be cut so some of the square pegs slide easily into round holes. She always finishes and leaves at four, so she's able to collect the kids, usually walking out with it all done. Ready for her 'other' job. Her other role. Which she also loves.

Does she really want to give up this part of her life, as Freddie seems to be expecting?

The bell rings. Her tutor group, year seven, comes in with cheery hellos and chatter. Reda, a recent arrival from Palestine, has brought little home-made iced cakes as it's her twelfth birthday.

'Will you sing to me the "Happy Birthday"?' she asks shyly.

Alice shrugs. 'Course we can,' she replies with a wink. 'We can dance as well, if you like.'

This turns Reda's timid smile into a huge grin, as the other girls start to twirl and swirl around her, and the boys raise their eyes boyishly, but quickly turn them towards the cakes in the box. Reda's from quite a conservative family, but not conservative enough to want to deprive her of an education. Alice considers the singing of 'Happy Birthday' to be an important part of Reda's education.

'Everybody ready to sing?' Alice calls, clocking the boys with meaning over her glasses, then throwing a glance at the cake box on her desk. They smile, a little bashfully, but they know which side their cakes are buttered on.

Yes, Alice is good at this bit.

Very good...

Later in the morning, when she's on a free, Daniella, the head, calls Alice into her office.

'How are things?' Daniella asks as they sit in the easy chairs, a sure sign that she wants something. If you're in her naughty book, you get directed to the upright chair in front of her table. Alice rarely sits there.

Alice wonders how 'things' are. Should she say they're great; she's a double millionaire? Knows she can't, so mumbles something bland about getting by okay. Daniella pulls her chair close and leans in.

'Look, don't breathe a word, but Norman's told me he's going to take early retirement at the end of next year. We'll have to advertise it externally, of course, but I want you to apply. I want you to be head of English. I can square the governors, no probs. What do you think?'

Alice tries to stay calm. Norman's been head of English since teachers went home with chalk dust on their fingers. He's old-school, lets you get on with it, trusts you to do your job, doesn't go in for learning walks and all the other modern paraphernalia that has become essential: checking that your shoelaces are tied, and you've put the lids back on all the felt-tips. Ordinarily, she wouldn't want this. It'll be extra work for a pittance of extra pay, and she'll lose some of her contact time with the children. Extra paperwork and extra meetings have never seemed a good swap for time in the class with the children, for Alice. But if she doesn't take it, who will? There's no other likely internal candidate, so it would be somebody new, somebody from outside, maybe bringing with them all those new brooms that are sweeping so many teachers out of the profession?

Then, of course, there's the elephant in the room. Or, rather, the two point three million elephants. While Freddie's clearly expecting Alice to quit work too, Daniella will almost certainly suggest that she ups her hours. She wouldn't mind that, as long as it gave her a bit more classroom time as opposed to paperwork time. She and Freddie are going to have to talk about this. And a whole lot else.

'Let me think about it,' she says, trying to look as pleased as she would have, had she not recently learned that she was a double millionaire. 'I'll get back to you.'

'No rush,' Daniella replies with a smile that says she's happy with her first move in what she clearly thinks shouldn't be too long a game of chess. 'End of next academic year, so we won't be appointing until next Easter. You'd be so good at it, Alice. You know you would. The children love you; parents are forever whispering in my ear about getting their child into your exam groups. And, between you, me and one of Jane Austen's four-poster bedposts, I don't really want a whiz kid in the English department. It's running well. And if you accepted, I'd get you in on the appointment of your replacement. An ECT that you could mould to your ways? Plus, I could offer you a few more hours. Maybe go to eighty per cent? A bit of extra money on top of the promotion? Win, win, win, Alice...?'

Yes, Alice thinks, *win, win, win.*

The only thing troubling her, is who exactly is doing all this winning...?

8

THE BIT OF NEWS

'BIT OF NEWS. I called the lottery people today; they're coming Saturday,' Freddie says, like he's booked the car in for its MOT instead of invited someone to drop off two point three million pounds into their lives.

'Coming? What, here?'

'Yes, it's standard practice for a big win. They need to see your ID, check that the ticket's not a fake. They have people to give you financial advice, but I said we wouldn't need that, what with me being a banker. She also said they could put us in touch with life-coaching experts, whatever that is, and what she called a luxury concierge service, ditto with that; we don't need either. It shouldn't take long. We can drop the kids off at swimming and get it all done.'

The kids are having their tea in front of the telly, a rare treat conceded, Alice can now see, so that Freddie can share this bit of news out of earshot. She nods and saws into a fish finger, wonders if this is really happening. The world doesn't seem to have changed: the kids piled into the car at home time: Ryan rabbiting non-stop about being picked for the school football team; Poppy as excited as a lottery winner at having bagged number seventeen in the *Pets in Trouble* series from the library: *Kitten Down a Coalmine*, apparently.

Alice has a rather idiosyncratic take on encouraging her children to read. If she wants Poppy to enjoy Austen or the Brontës later on, then sending her down a coalmine with a kitten first seems the obvious thing to do. And as for Ryan, who's already been hooked by the algorithm? They should never have bought him a PlayStation, but at least he doesn't complain about the time limits they set him. So, to encourage him to read? Buy him all the football magazines he asks for. There might be lots of pictures in them, but he likes to read the player biographies and do the *You are the Ref* bit. Before you know it, she hopes, he'll be buying Dickens with his pocket money – you can but dream...

Why are they sitting here having fish fingers and chips when they're millionaires? Shouldn't they be out, painting the town every colour in the paintbox? Mostly gold? It is utterly bizarre. Even Freddie seems his usual self, a bit less grumpy she'll concede. He hasn't yet started huffing and puffing about small boats or the price of petrol or the latest suspected romance on *EastEnders*. And he hasn't mentioned work at all: their (usually one way) conversation has been Tashaless all evening, quite the rarity. This meeting on Saturday is the only mention he's made of 'the win'. Has she somehow killed all the excitement with her call for utmost secrecy? Should they have told the world? Like other, 'normal' people do?

She tries to imagine the scenario. How would they do it? Who would they tell? Their parents are all dead; she has no siblings; Freddie's sister lives in Oz and they barely speak. Freddie, she's sure, is still envious of her 'wasted' degree, now that he's fully realised how much one could have meant to him? So, who? School? No, she'd hate her pupils to see her in any other way. Like a celebrity? That would be awful. Their friends? Neighbours? She's on chatting terms with most of the street but, again, it would change their relationships completely. Old Mrs Bailey, down at number seven, she's always worried about the price of bread. How could she tell her that they were millionaires without giving her some money? She can suddenly see, maybe even understand, why Freddie would want to move away. It's going to be bad enough when Freddie rolls his sports car into the street. Tongues will wag then.

And then she realises another complication: Freddie's determined to resign in a flurry of Rolexes and Carreras. That will let the cat out of the bag, probably the title of one of Poppy's upcoming books. It will be a secret no more when Freddie makes his grand exit, his Frexit.

They need to talk about... it. Whatever *it* is, or whatever *it* might turn out to be...

She lowers her voice, partly to make sure the kids don't hear, but mostly to remind Freddie to keep his own voice down.

'Are you excited? You know... about *it*?'

'Of course,' he whispers, reaching across the table and grabbing both her hands. 'I've dreamt about this for years...' And he's off. Like the start of the Grand National, he's away at a canter, well, more of a gambol: giving up work, the Rolexes, the Carrera, the villa in Spain, the holidays on the moon or Saturn... His eyes suddenly shining like they used to when they had their first couple of 'dates', when he was a newly minted cashier on the Unthank Road, and chicken in a basket and a glass (or even two!) of Mateus Rosé were the pinnacle of fine dining and sophistication.

He was never the coolest or the most fashionable amongst the group of children from the boys' and girls' schools, who met at the bus stop every day, but she always liked him because he wasn't the coolest or the most fashionable, the quickest with the jokes and the smart remarks. He was steady, trustworthy. You could rely on him. He wouldn't let you down. He wasn't always mauling you, trying to shove his hand up your skirt or down your top like a lot of the other lads. He treated you with a bit of respect. He liked to talk. Mostly about his plans, in those days to be a bank manager – like his dad and granddad. He was full of ambition for the future. He was a safe bet. And she did like him – *love* him. But where had he gone?

When had that Freddie turned into grumpy Freddie, who hated his job and his colleagues and suddenly, during Brexit, discovered that he also hated asylum seekers and European bureaucrats? Where had that new Freddie come from? The one who suddenly, out of nowhere, started banging on about sovereignty, and how much he needed it? She'd never been entirely sure that he knew what it meant.

When had he turned sour and bitter about his job and the state of the country and all the other things he moaned and griped about? She'd barely noticed it happening, until one day she noticed it had happened. They didn't talk about it, but she was sure the situation at the bank was at the root of it all. She'd once got collared by Trevor at one of those bank dos Freddie always felt he had to go to with her in tow, and Trevor had sucked air in through his yellowish teeth and intimated to Alice that Freddie's lack of a degree had put a ceiling on his promotion hopes. She's sure Jekyll started turning into Hyde sometime after that.

He'd always done the lottery. But it was a game at the start: sitting on the sofa as he filled in his lottery book, oohing and ahhing together as his numbers came up – or didn't. It was only more recently that he'd started to look at the lottery as some sort of a salvation, an exit route. It had slowly replaced his ambition to become a manager, with a desire, and then a sort of desperation, to get out. Like his own small boat, or big yacht, but going in the opposite direction. Not north towards Dover – but heading south, and then God knew where... She sometimes wondered if the rich people heading for sunnier climes in their private jets were also counted as economic migrants. Or was that term reserved for the poor buggers in the dinghies heading the other way?

And now, suddenly (again), grumpy Freddie has gone, to be replaced by a third Freddie. Not the old Freddie with simple ambitions for his career, the children. But Freddie with grand plans, plans that he now has the means to put into action. Plans that would change all their lives in ways that she was pretty sure she didn't want.

He's looking at her expectantly. He's asked her something and she's no idea what. She hasn't been listening, although she knows she can list what he's been saying, more or less: good schools for the kids, cars, boats, and a never-ending shopping list of other dreams that feel like nightmares to her.

'Sorry?'

'You? Are you excited?'

She takes a breath. Does she dare tell him? Maybe in a slightly muted way? Not: *There's no way the kids are going to single-sex private schools; I don't want to live in a place where all the neighbours will be snobs; I don't want to give up work...* But a gentler, *Yes, of course I'm excited, but it's a big thing, isn't it? We need to talk about it properly, together. Work out what we want, what we all want...* Yes, that's the tack she should–

'Ahem!' Ryan and Poppy in their judo kits, standing by the door, looking extremely pleased with themselves.

She double takes. Triple takes.

'Right. Umm, yes. Sorry. Let me get the car keys...'

Ryan is letting Poppy practise a new throw they're learning. It sounded like *Harry Goshy* when the instructor was demonstrating, but Alice sometimes zones out whenever the kids prattle on about judo. They're paired tonight, which is unusual, Poppy being a head shorter than Ryan. But Alice loves the way Ryan lets Poppy throw him over her shoulder, then pretends he's winded, tells her what a brilliant throw she's executed. When it's his turn, he lands her gently, like he's putting down a newborn lamb. She could cry at his consideration for her. Good old Ryan.

But she doesn't cry. Her main emotion tonight is relief. And that's confused her. So, relief and confusion. But the relief is the main one. Why is she feeling relieved? She's feeling relieved because the kids interrupted her incipient questioning of Freddie's plans about what to do about *it*. Or with *it*. Why is she relieved that they stopped her?

Is it because she thinks Freddie will be angry? She hardly thinks so. Freddie doesn't do angry. Sure, he gets cross about his work, and the gas bill, and small boats, and the rivers being full of poo while the bosses pay themselves obscene bonuses for dumping it there – but he never gets angry. Not properly angry. She can't remember the last time she heard him shout. Never at the kids, but then neither has she, and she honestly can't ever remember him shouting at her either. She's shouted at him. Not often, but she has. Like when he didn't lift the seat and left drips when he went for a waz on one occasion. But then, she was upstairs, so she had to shout down for him to hear her. She'd also wanted Ryan to hear, which was probably the main reason she'd shouted. Apart from that, only to call him. No, she wasn't afraid Freddie would get angry.

Then it hits her. Of course. It's clear now. She's afraid Freddie will be disappointed. He's always so happy with his lottery dreams – what used to be dreams – that she's afraid she'll make him unhappy if she starts to pop his bubbles, one by one.

She'll have to talk to him. Gently. She'll go on the holidays, although she likes their usual little three-star hotel on Mallorca. Lola and Don Antonio will be disappointed when Freddie cancels and transfers to the six-star all-inclusive he's already set his eyes on. And a new car would be good. An electric, preferably. Poppy's already starting to talk about climate change. But the schools? No. That's a red line. Blood red. She's not pulling the kids out of their school, separating them from each other, and their friends, just so Freddie can make an offering to the ghost of his dad. She'll draw the line there. She will. And the bigger house? In the 'better' area? She's really not sure about this. She likes where they live. She has friends here; the children have friends here. If it was a bigger house not too far away? Well, maybe. It would depend...

The children have now been paired up by belt colour and are doing *randori*, a sort of sparring session. Ryan is working with a boy who's a little taller than him while Poppy is fighting a girl who's a lot sturdier than she is. Calling it fighting is a bit grand; it's more like struggling. The children tug at each other's jackets and try to trip or throw each other, but none of them have the strength or the skill or the timing to do anything more than tugging and pushing until they run out of puff and collapse onto the mat where they try to strangle each other or hold each other down on their backs. It sounds good, with all the fancy Japanese names, and the judo suits, and the coloured belts, but in reality, it's wrestling. Ryan is entwined with his partner in the middle of the big mat. They look like a strange white four-armed and four-legged creature that's been trapped, and is now too exhausted to move much, the air slowly being crushed out of its lungs as its resistance levels hit the red zone.

Alice thinks she knows how it feels.

9

THE DANGEROUS LIAISON

Friday. Four o'clock sharp. Freddie collects his coat and heads for the exit with a spring in his step. Two springs. When he was appointed deputy manager, he was awarded an hour 'study time' each week, to be taken whenever and wherever he wanted. He takes it every Friday at four o'clock. So, as he leaves the bank, instead of heading for the bus stop, he turns the other way, heading for Mandy's small flat. He's strict about the hour, always makes sure he arrives home at his usual time. His 'study hour' is his secret.

Well, his and Mandy's.

And Mandy is *very* discreet.

10

—————————

THE NEW TELLY

EVERY WEEKDAY EVENING, Alice and Freddie organise 'the homework table'. It's usually after tea, when they've done the washing-up and tidied away. Freddie sits at one end, calculator by his side; Alice sits at the other end, tablet powered up. The children do their homework in the middle, while Alice and Freddie do crosswords, or sudokus, or Duolingo, or read – the classics or some women's fiction or crime (Alice), detective or espionage (Freddie). At any time, the children can slide to one end or the other if they need help. Freddie is there for maths, Alice for pretty much everything else (hence the tablet), although Freddie isn't bad at geography. He can name the fifty states of the USA in alphabetical order, one of the indispensable life skills that his modest private school education has bequeathed him – not that either of the children have ever needed him to demonstrate it, yet...

Ryan always does his maths first and then moves down to Freddie's end because he likes Freddie to check it. In reality, Alice is sure, Ryan wants to preen, wants Freddie to see how well he's doing, how quickly he's learning. Freddie does a lot of chin scratching and frowning before usually nodding with a pleased look on his face, which makes Ryan glow. Freddie's reputation as a 'maths genius' is unassailable – Poppy, more than once, having whispered reverentially to Alice that he *never* uses the calculator! Ryan will then get on with the rest of his homework, often asking Alice to check his SPaG, as one of the three Rs has morphed into: Spelling, Punctuation and Grammar. Alice wonders how anybody (herself included) ever learned to write in the days before SPaG had been invented. If Ryan needs other help – science, history, that sort of thing – then Alice has the wonders of the World Wide Web at hand.

Poppy's homework often takes longer than Ryan's. She always wants to practise her reading: *Pony in a Panic* being her current bestseller, or is it *Dog in the Doghouse*? Alice can't remember, Poppy gets through them so quickly. There's also usually a project for geography or history that will involve a lot of Sellotape and glue, maybe even a stapler. Last of all, Poppy will slowly take her maths book down to Freddie's end of the table where he will gently coax her through the mysteries of the four times table or adding hundreds, tens and units with carrying. Alice can't help but sneak glances at Poppy's face as she first marvels at Freddie's pencil hopping and skipping, with all the numbers obeying him like a team of huskies effortlessly pulling a sleigh; and then, Poppy will often glance up, in awe, at Freddie, like he's a magician on a stage. It's one of Alice's favourite times.

Homework completed: Freddie is frowning at Mick Herron; Ryan is bleeping and peeping on the sofa; Poppy is panicking with her pony; Alice is reading *Pride and Prejudice* for at least the umpteenth time. Except, she isn't. The words are there on the page, her eyes are following them as they usually do when you're reading, but the meaning of them can't find room in her brain because it's chock-full of money – and Freddie's plans.

'I've had a thought about...' has become his go-to catchphrase that sends shivers down Alice's spine and a few other unprepared body parts. She can't think of anything that could turn her mood dark so quickly, except maybe a gang of masked robbers coming in through the bay window. The latest thing he's had a thought about is – the telly.

They have a nice telly. It's big, very thin, and it's colour. She thinks they bought it less than five years ago. It does exactly what it said on the box: it shows programmes that you can see and hear perfectly well; it has a little doofer that lets you change the channels and the volume and a few other things that she doesn't know about from the comfort of your armchair. They even have Sky for the football (Ryan, and recently Poppy as well) and cartoons (mainly Poppy, now). What more could you ask your telly to do? Well, Freddie has had a thought about it and discovered a feature their telly is lacking...

It needs to be bigger. You see (she didn't, but she does now), somewhere in the underpants of the interweb, there is a conversion chart explaining what size of telly you should buy depending on how far you are going to be seated away from it. The further away you are, the bigger the telly you should have.

To get a 75-incher, you need to sit 150 inches away from it. That's twelve and a half feet. Alice is tempted to argue that any internet page that uses feet and inches to cover a technological issue is probably not to be trusted. But she knows he'll say it's American, so to be trusted – not that Freddie'd trust the Americans with much else. Freddie has calculated (without the use of a calculator, no doubt) that if they drag the sofa back up towards the kitchen door, and site the (new, 75-inch) telly down in the opposite corner on a swivelly bracket thingy by the bay window, then that's as near to twelve feet as they can get. So, they'd be watching the telly across the room on the diagonal. They'd have to twist the sofa around to an appropriate angle, and the telly would swivel out at an opposite angle, so they could look straight at it. It's something to do with the hypotenuse, Freddie has attempted to explain to Alice, but Alice suddenly understood Poppy's ingrained fear of anything mathematical as soon as Freddie mentioned Pythagoras and his hypotenuse.

If she wasn't so worked up about Freddie and his thoughts, she'd be tempted to suggest they knock down the back wall, build a conservatory, and sit out there. That would give them at least another six or eight feet, so they'd probably be able to get an IMAX screen fitted and sell popcorn to the neighbours. She daren't think how big an IMAX is; she's never been to one. But she also daren't (even jokingly) suggest such a plan for fear that Freddie might scratch his chin, frown, and then pronounce it a wonderful idea. They'd also clearly be able to afford four pairs of high-powered binoculars so they could see the damned thing.

Alice's trepidation about the new telly doesn't stop with the size and watching it at an angle from across the living room. In theory, she can see there's not really a problem watching it at an angle. But it simply doesn't feel right. She can imagine guests coming to visit and wondering why their telly is on the wall down near the bay window while their sofa is up the other end of the room by the kitchen door. She fears Freddie explaining to everybody about the swivelly bracket thingy and the hypotenuse: 'Look, we'll show you...' She shudders.

But apart from the funny looks they might get as guests silently wonder if Freddie has dropped the plot down the back of the sofa, she's worried about the children. You see, the children often like to lie on the floor, between the sofa and the telly. Would a 75-incher affect their eyesight if they were regularly watching it from within the twelve-foot exclusion zone? And would she and Freddie have to turn the volume up to max to be able to hear it themselves from a sofa sited in another continent, thereby damaging the children's hearing as well? Would the neighbours complain about the noise? Freddie has calculated that the party wall is the best habitat the telly could occupy in their semi-d.

Alice attempts to return to Liz and Will by reminding herself that whenever Freddie usually has a thought about something, he'll disappear into the internet for a few days in order to discover things that most (sane) people don't know and couldn't care less about, then he'll explain his new thought to Alice, engendering yet more fears that the life she likes is being ripped from her grasp (not by a gang of masked robbers, but by her husband). Then, after she's gently attempted to puncture a couple of small holes in his latest wheeze, he'll announce it'll probably be best to wait until they're in the 'new house', a fear which Alice had forgotten about because she was too busy worrying about the new telly/car/watches, delete as appropriate.

Freddie closes his Mick Herron and switches the telly on. There's snooker tonight...

11

———————

THE HANDOVER

ALICE FEELS SORRY FOR HER. On the face of it, you'd be hard pushed to guess why.

She arrives in a newish-looking silver car. Alice can't see the brand so has no idea what make it is, but it's a nice little four-door hatch. Very trendy. Possibly Japanese. Or maybe French. She dresses well too: a smart, grey two-piece suit, flowery blouse, grey kitten heels to match the suit, a sprinkling of jewellery, a dab of make-up, and a whiff of fruity perfume. Very fresh.

And she speaks nicely, like she might have gone to one of those single-sex private schools that Freddie wants to ship Poppy off to – over Alice's buried body, not that he knows this yet. She's got a smart little name badge, with the crossed-finger logo on it. Her name's Cherry, Cherry Norton. Sounds like a railway station to Alice, but never mind. She's also got a load of kit: clipboard, leather-bound books of rules and regulations, tablet, laptop, smartphone, in an exec-looking briefcase that really makes her look the girl-about-town. She's probably late twenties, maybe thirty, at a push, very pretty, petite, engagement ring, relaxed smile.

But Alice feels sorry for her. It's pity, really. She pities her. Well, imagine. She probably earns, what? Thirty grand? If that. The car might be company, but it hasn't got the logo, so maybe not. But thirty grand, and what does she have to do for it? She has to tour the country with millions in her gift, doling it out to people like Freddie. What must she think, what must she feel, as she enters their living room, knowing that she's going to leave behind two point three million pounds? Some people might imagine it to be a lovely job: making so many strangers happy, like a doctor curing the sick. Alice thinks she'd rather muck out stables than face people like Freddie, who has a smug little grin of anticipation and financial superiority on his face.

Alice has got the kettle on ready and brings in tea and chocolate digestives. It's clear Cherry has a patter and she's keen to patter through it. 'You must be so excited? Making plans already? Nice holiday somewhere? New car? Oh, I do envy you...'

That must stick in her throat, every time, Alice muses as she smiles. Imagine saying that day after day, dropping millions in Norwich and Cromer and Six-Mile Bottom, then going home to thirty grand, a microwaved ready meal, and a holiday in a caravan in Hunstanton? Alice wonders if she ever totals it all up: two point three mil this morning to the smug guy with the quiet wife in Norwich; six and a half this afternoon to the old bloke with the limp in Colchester. That brings the week's total to thirty-three million, a hundred and fifty for the month, maybe as much as a billion for the year? Given away to people she doesn't know, changing their lives. Alice thinks she'd sooner hang herself than do that job.

She feels strangely detached. Like she's watching it all happen on telly: some fly-on-the-wall reality TV nonsense on a 75-incher. It probably does actually exist somewhere in the satellite programme guide, down amongst the fortune tellers and reruns of *The Waltons*; it would be fascinating to watch all the different reactions: people screaming, dancing, crying – and the smug ones.

Cherry moves from chirpy intro to 'the business', as she calls it, while snapping a neat bite-sized soldier off her biscuit, making sure all the crumbs land on her plate. Alice silently bets Cherry won't dunk it – and wins yet again. Freddie bats away all offers of financial advice, telling Cherry he's a banker, like he works on the top floor of a Docklands skyscraper, or on Wall Street, and he jetted in last night, rather than in a six-person rabbit hutch on the Unthank Road. He also smiles away the offers of lifestyle coaches and luxury concierge services like he already has a book full of contacts who will see him right. Alice never got round to looking up what they were, Freddie isn't interested anyway. 'And publicity?' Freddie looks at Alice, who shakes her head stiffly. No publicity. Cherry nods gravely.

'Very wise.'

She checks his ticket, which Freddie makes a grand show of leaving the room to collect from its secret hiding place, like they've got a wall safe behind the fridge with one of those twisty combination dials that cowboys blow off with sticks of dynamite in the old movies. Cherry tippy taps on her tablet, sends messages on her phone; Freddie clasps and unclasps his hands. Alice watches her life changing, she doesn't yet know how.

She feels slightly sick. Like she's losing control, somebody's mugging her, snatching the life she enjoys out of her hands in a dusky, dank alleyway; kicking her out of the house they were so excited to buy and then do up; yanking the children out of the school they love...

Then Freddie has to sign. Freddie has to sign papers in triplicate. 'Sign here; just there, another scribble at the bottom, there.' He scrawls on the tablet and suddenly Cherry's packing her kit away, thanking Alice for the tea and biscuits, 'so kind', then standing up, shaking his hand, Alice's too, although Alice isn't sure why. She's a spectator as her life is signed away and she feels powerless to do anything about it except feel weak and sick and confused and betrayed. She bats away an embryonic tear as Freddie ushers Cherry towards the door.

The kids will come home to a completely different family, Alice thinks. As different as if two new substitute adults will be waiting here for them. She's read in the papers about Russian husband and wife spy teams, who lived undercover in the USA for dozens of years, whose children didn't know their parents were Russian until suddenly they were unmasked and deported back to Russia, the children unable to speak Russian, having no connection at all with the country or the language or the people.

Is that who Alice and Freddie have suddenly become? A rich couple, stinking rich, with posh cars and expensive holidays, and God knows what else rolling down the gold-plated pipeline? Are Ryan and Poppy suddenly going to be deported into a new house in a new town, or gated community (another of Freddie's thoughts), and new schools where they won't be like the other children at all, because they'll have been *born* rich, just like those unfortunate American children won't be like their new classmates because they'll all have been born Russian.

They watch from the porch as the silver car drives away. Alice feels like her old life is tied up in the boot with a hood over its head alongside the children's and Freddie's. Like sacks and boxes full of stuff from the upstairs cupboards and the attic that they used to use, and play with, and love. Now on their way to the tip. In the boot of Cherry Norton's silver hatchback. Alice is beginning to wish she'd answered the door herself and strangled Cherry Norton before Freddie had set eyes on her.

Freddie smiles and waves as their old lives disappear around the corner at the bottom of the road. A cloud covers the sun: a portent. Alice usually loves this word, so full of threat and menace, and bare branches scratching at grimy windowpanes. Fine when applied to the heroes and heroines in the books she reads. But, she suddenly realises with a shiver, it works in real life too.

A portent...

PART 2

SPENDING

12

THE FAMILY MEETING

FREDDIE CALLS A FAMILY MEETING. They've never had one before, so Alice isn't sure what he's got in mind. They gather around the dining table, Freddie proudly taking his place at the head, the rest of them swapping bemused looks, Poppy giggling with excitement like he's told her he's going to do magic tricks.

'Now, as you know, we've had a *little* win on the lottery,' Freddie begins, stressing the 'little' and rubbing his hands together. Alice can't banish the thought that he looks like a year seven or eight pupil auditioning for the role of The Godfather in a school play. 'So, I thought it would be nice if we all chose something that we maybe couldn't afford before, but we *might* be able to afford now. I'm not talking about things that would cost a hand and a foot, just a little *treat* each...'

He gazes around expectantly, but is met by silence, and Poppy now looking confused. Alice wonders if she's included in the choosing, or is this only for the children? Freddie's given her no warning that he was going to do this.

'Norwich City season ticket,' Ryan suddenly blurts; you don't need a master's in psychology to see that this is heartfelt. This really is the first thing Ryan would buy if he won two point three million pounds. Freddie's face loses a smidgen of its pleased-with-his-prospects Godfather impersonation. Football isn't really his thing. You'd sooner find him twelve feet up a climbing wall at the local leisure centre or practising synchronised swimming with a team of lithe teenagers in sparkly swimsuits. Freddie has taken his son to the occasional match, but Ryan has always wanted a season ticket. Freddie makes another Mafia-boss face, like he's wondering if this might be too big an ask out of his 'little' pot of winnings, and how much a bag of cement might cost.

Alice's heart twinges. Surely Freddie can let Ryan have a season ticket. It's Norwich City, not some rough, hooligan-infested stadium that Alice can't name, because football isn't really her thing either. But she knows they're called the Canaries; how could you be a hooligan at a team called the Canaries? Wearing a yellow shirt? Freddie's looking like the decision is going to be a no.

But Poppy, somewhat amazingly, comes to the rescue. 'I'd like one as well,' she chirps, if canaries chirp, sending Freddie's face into the type of shocked category you'd expect to see had Poppy asked for driving lessons, or had Don Vito's wannabe been told he had to dance the Charleston – it was a musical version of *The Godfather*.

'You don't like football, Pops,' Freddie responds, a little sharply, like he thinks she's trying to trick him.

'I do,' she says, stiffening, bottom lip threatening a wobble.

'She's got a Hannah Hampton poster on her wall,' Ryan cuts in, giving Poppy a proud little nod of encouragement and welcome to whichever is the noisier end of Carrow Road.

'Who?' Freddie is clueless.

'Number one Lioness,' Poppy whimpers, which only increases Freddie's confusion. She looks over at Ryan, like she might need a bit more backup. Ryan gives her a thumbs up and an excited smile, like he thinks Poppy's desire for a season ticket might bolster his own chances, which seemed to have been fading – a bit like Norwich City's chances of winning the league.

And suddenly, Alice sees a gap in the defence; one player's out of position, another's lost concentration. Dare she...?

'Why don't we go as a family?' she hears herself saying, before she's actually thought about it. Five minutes earlier, the idea of her suggesting season tickets for the whole family at Carrow Road would have been ludicrous. Let's plant some marijuana in the garden, for personal use, would have been about as likely a suggestion. But now, it's the most sensible thing she can think of. In fact, it's a brilliant plan. Freddie's constant chatter about moving somewhere better has spooked her. He even mentioned Cornwall in one late-night ramble. But if they all had season tickets at Norwich City, then it might put a break on Freddie's geographical horizons as far as that little venture was concerned.

Freddie looks stunned. Alice forges forward, sprinting out of defence and steaming through the midfield, Ryan and Poppy breaking left and right in support, each with an arm raised, screaming (metaphorically) for a pass to put them through on goal.

'We don't do much together, this would be a lovely thing for us to do as a family. We could go into the city in the morning, have a spook around the shops, lunch together in Jarrolds, or, no, better idea, each of us could take turns choosing where we had our pre-match lunch. But it would be Jarrolds for the first match as it's my idea.'

'Brilliant!' says Ryan, clearly seeing his own ticket firmly within his grasp, what with Poppy on board and (somewhat bizarrely now) Mum rounding the keeper with the ball at her feet.

'Yeah!' cheeps Poppy, equally excited. 'Bags second choice: Pizza Express!'

'Burger King!' Ryan leaps in, probably not annoyed that Poppy's beaten him to second choice, Alice thinks, he'd probably have chosen Pizza Express as his first choice anyway. Alice rolls the ball into the empty net and has a sudden madcap vision of the children hoisting her onto their shoulders and carrying her on a lap of honour around the garden.

They all look at Freddie, who's smiling, but Alice can see past it. She knows this is Smokey Robinson's clown; he might be fooling the children, but he isn't fooling Alice.

She feels guilty at having played Freddie, boxed him into a corner. But he's sprung this family meeting on her with no warning. What was he thinking? Why hadn't he told her what he was planning? So, she only feels a little guilty at having turned the tables on him. And she's sure she could get to like football. And the kids are clearly thrilled. Every second Saturday afternoon, all the family together at Carrow Road? Why not? Better than moving to Cornwall.

———

'I never knew Poppy liked football,' Freddie grumbles after the kids have gone to bed, and he and Alice are having their coffee and biscuits in front of the news.

'She often joins in the playground games,' Alice replies with a hint of pride. 'And they had a half-term of football in PE lessons with Ms Gibson. She really enjoyed it.'

Freddie crunches down on his biscuit, clearly dissatisfied. 'I bet she doesn't understand the offside law,' he grumps.

Alice bridles; Poppy's only seven. 'I don't see how that matters,' she says after a moment's thought. 'I mean, you like to go to the opera, but you don't speak Italian.' Alice had been quite happy to indulge Freddie's occasional forays to the Theatre Royal for opera. She'd googled beforehand, so had been able to follow the story reasonably well. She's sure Freddie had had no idea what was going on, and that he only went in the hope of bumping into Trevor, his old manager before Tasha, during the interval, which they had done on two separate occasions. Freddie's opera-going had stopped once Trevor had retired, and Tasha started asking if anyone wanted to try to get tickets for Taylor Swift at Wembley.

She hopes he's not going to attempt some grubby little scheme to deprive Ryan and Poppy of their season tickets – and her of her home. But he grizzles quietly to himself for a while before letting the topic drop: small boats on the news grabbing his attention instead...

'I never knew you even liked football,' he mutters as the small boats disgorge their passengers onto a beach.

Alice shrugs. 'It's more the idea of doing something all together that I quite fancy.' She suddenly worries that Freddie might attempt to puncture the Norwich City plan by suggesting something else they might be able to do all together: like season tickets at Penzance Bromwich Albion or Queenstown Park Rangers; Alice isn't that clued-up about football teams. 'But I've heard Norwich is a very nice family club. Pete, from school, is a member. He goes with his boys. Says it's great, really brings them together, lots to talk about. It would be a good move for us, especially as Ryan heads for the teenage years, don't you think?'

Freddie huffs, and Alice feels guilty, again. She knows she shouldn't be doing this: fighting a guerrilla war against him, trying to trip him up and undermine his plans. She does like the idea of doing something regularly together. She wouldn't have initially thought of football, though. She wouldn't have ever thought of football if Ryan and Poppy hadn't been so keen. That was mostly to put the brakes on Freddie decamping them to

Cornwall, or the Highlands of Scotland, or wherever his latest 'thought' takes him. But now, she quite likes the idea. She should talk to him, seriously. Like an adult. Tell him her fears. Not try to trip him up with half-baked schemes. He'd understand.

Freddie takes a breath. 'I've had a thought about skiing. Apparently, they do very good lessons for beginners in the Canadian Rockies...'

13

THE UNIVERSITY WALK

'It looks like Hogwarts!' Poppy grabs Alice's hand and swings it joyfully; Alice's heart clangs with all the joy of a cracked bell tolling a death knell in a thunderstorm. Although Alice is yet to start HP with Poppy, she's read books one and two to Ryan, and Poppy has seen the first film on TV. Freddie, not an HP fan, adjusts his tie.

Poppy beams a gap-toothed smile which, Alice knows, is worrying Freddie. He was furious (well, as furious as Freddie ever gets, read mildly peeved for anybody else) the other night when Poppy came home from judo with spots of blood on her *judogi*, and her first milk tooth to fall carefully stowed in Alice's purse. 'Fall' is Alice's euphemism, an attempt to keep Freddie's blood pressure out of the heart-attack zone. In the real world, Poppy had ended her latest judo scuffle by leaving an upper incisor on the mat after it accidentally collided with a small stray elbow. What had pleased Alice was how Poppy had walked off the mat (after bowing to her opponent), blood dribbling down her chin, but smiling. Alice had to send her back to retrieve the tooth. And then, her growing understanding of judo etiquette caused her to hunt a scrap of tissue from her cardi sleeve and usher Poppy back out again, to mop up the spots of blood from the bloody (quite literally) *tatami*. Poppy, domestic duties fulfilled, was as thrilled with the prospect of a fiver for her tooth as she was for passing her grading and earning a new coloured belt – she couldn't remember what colour it was going to be, but she was hoping for Barbie pink.

'Best behaviour now, Pops,' Freddie warns, with an admonishing wag of his index finger. 'They'll be looking at you as much as we'll be looking at them. It's not easy to get in here, it's one of the best. And remember, try to smile with your lips, not your teeth, eh?'

Alice squeezes Poppy's hand and winks, sure that the headteacher of The River Wensum Preparatory School won't suspect Poppy lost her tooth in a fight with a boy. She also takes Freddie's 'One of the best' comment with a mine of Siberian salt. She's had a little google and the school doesn't feature in any of the *Top 50 Prep Schools in Britain* articles that flood the internet. Nor in the *Top 100* category. Not even in the *Top 250*. But it's got a gravel drive, a (small) conical slate roof on one of the buildings, and Poppy's got a lively imagination. So, Hogwarts it is – maybe with warts and all.

Bits of Alice's heart are in her boots and her stomach and her throat. Freddie's pitched this as an enquiry, not a decision. They're 'testing the waters', to see what it's like, and what Poppy thinks. Alice hates the gravel drive and the conical roof with a ridiculous amount of venom. She swallows bile as she lifts Poppy up to rap excitedly with the lion's head knocker. A stern-looking woman wearing a twinset and pearls and a badge saying *Secretary* opens the door for them. Alice also loathes the lion's head fucking knocker.

'Mr and Mrs Cash?' the secretary enquires, with a look and a tone that suggest she fears a newspaper sting operation.

'And I'm Poppy,' Poppy announces, smiling a gap-toothed smile. Freddie winces.

'Yes, of course. Do come in.' The secretary stops them on an absolutely enormous doormat, almost as big as the judo mat, *tatami*, at Poppy's club. Beside it is a large rack full of slippers. 'Now, as you'll see, our main building has wonderful parquet flooring, so *all* the girls, and *all* the visitors, change into what we call day shoes when they enter.' Although she's clearly talking to Alice and Freddie, her intonation is one you'd use with a worried-looking toddler.

Freddie nods his appreciation of the parquet flooring. Alice wonders if this woman is serious, but Freddie is already unlacing his brogues.

The secretary leads the tour up a creaky central staircase. Freddie, like a naughty child, has to retreat after losing one of his slippers on the way up. She chits and chats about the history of the school, founded in 1987. Freddie nods an impressed little nod; Alice bites her tongue against a flippant quip concerning who might have losted it.

The top floor has six classrooms leading off a long corridor. They peer in through the dusty glass panels in the doors at years three and four; Poppy would join year four in September. Inside each class, a teacher sits or stands at the front, the girls arranged in rows of single wooden desks, some with hands up, like a scene from a documentary about schooling in the 1950s. It even seems to be in black and white. The quiet unnerves Alice.

She's spent a lot of time in Poppy's primary school; it's always noisy. Children chattering, playing, investigating, building, scampering along the corridors. Not running, *scampering*. There is a difference, at least in Alice's mind.

There's a buzz about the place. Here, there's no buzz. Not even a bluebottle. If there's any noise at all it's the muted drone of bored-sounding teachers behind the firmly closed doors. Alice's mind wanders into an enormous wooden hive, not that bluebottles live in hives, but her mind isn't behaving well. She'll probably get a detention.

One of the doors at the far end of the corridor suddenly opens. A female teacher in her forties, Alice would guess, and dressed for the forties, she further thinks, emerges. The teacher's hands are behind her back and her head is high, like she's searching for cobwebs hanging from the lights, as she marches towards them. Behind her, a line of small girls follows like a waddling (one of Alice's favourite collective nouns) of ducklings. With their hands also behind their backs they look a little like ducklings, in Alice's mind. But they don't sound like ducklings, not unless somebody has Sellotaped all their bills shut. The line passes in an eerie near silence and heads down the stairs, the only sound being the light squeaking of their day shoes on the pristine parquet.

'Off to playtime,' the secretary whispers reverentially, as if an ageing member of the royal family has passed by, waving. 'The classes leave at one-minute intervals to keep the noise down. Might be best if we head outside ourselves.'

Alice has read about this trend for some schools to make children walk in silence with their hands behind their backs, chest out and nose in the air – the university walk, she's heard it called – although she can't remember ever having seen anybody walk like that in the four years she spent at university. Plenty of stumbling into lamp posts and tripping into the gutter, but not much 'university walking'. Some proponents have claimed that the puffed-out chest teaches children to feel pride. She can see how you might want a bit of order in secondary corridors – but these girls are seven or eight years old. Why can't they have a quick little natter with their friends, or their teacher? She glances at Poppy's face and sees a look of utter bemusement, like Poppy's seen a line – a waddling – of children waddling off to some prison camp. Alice's heart dips further into the sludge.

Outside, they view the playground complete with netball posts, the extensive fields with their hockey goals. The playground gradually fills as lines of girls follow their teachers outside before dispersing. It's surprisingly quiet for a playground, Alice muses. And also, surprisingly static. There's no running, no chasing, no skipping ropes, no balls. Most disconcertingly, there's no screaming. There's always screaming in a playground at playtime. Plus, squealing. A lot of squealing. You can usually hear it from two streets away. There's something deeply wrong, according to Alice, if there's no screaming and squealing in a playground. Alice suspects they're all banned. Especially the squealing. The girls sit and talk, or walk and talk, or sit or walk on their own. It reminds Alice of a scene from a fifties American prison movie, without the basketballs – or the knives. A teacher approaches them straight from an audition for a remake of Miss Jean Brodie. It's like Tom Brook is doing a special retro edition of *Talking Movies*. Alice takes half a step back, nudges Freddie to do the same.

'Hello,' Miss Jean says, her hands behind her back, nose still in the air, but bent at the waist so she's almost at a level with Poppy. 'On a visit, are you?'

Poppy finds herself alone on stage.

'Yesh,' she says, clearly attempting to talk without opening her lips too much. Give her a ventriloquist's dummy in her arms and she'd do okay on BGT.

'And, what's your name?' Jean enquires.

'Hohhy,' says Poppy through clenched teeth with hardly a tremble from her lips.

'Well, what do you think of the school so far? Do you like it?'

Poppy shrugs. 'Is wery wiet,' she mumbles.

Jean laughs. 'I thought you'd notice that. Quiet, inside and out, yes? All the better to study and learn, we say.'

And with that, Jean wanders off, hands behind her back, chalk dusting her fingers, nose in the air, a self-satisfied smile on her lips. *All the better to study and learn...* Alice thinks Jean reminds her of someone. Who is it? Oh yes, the Big Bad Wolf – *All the better to...*

The secretary blithers and blathers about their exam results being the best in East Anglia, where you can buy the uniform, and who the most famous old girls are. Freddie nods and widens his eyes at all the names, Alice knows, he doesn't recognise. Alice doesn't recognise any of the proffered hall of fame either. But, a mercy, at least Hannah Hampton didn't feature, she thinks, with a huge sigh of relief. Poppy thinking it's Hogwarts is bad enough, having her imagine she was following in the Number One Lioness's pawsteps would be a bitter own goal to add to Alice's misery.

As playtime ends, the secretary leads them into a sports hall, now full of more ducklings who also seem unable to quack. A teacher stands in the middle of the girls who encircle her. Alice enviously counts sixteen, knowing there are twenty-six in Poppy's current class. The teacher, also dressed for a post-war dinner party (as opposed to Mzzz Gibson's figure-hugging running kit and snazzy trainers), throws a netball to each child in turn. Each time she throws, she shouts a question: 'twelve times six', 'spell miscellaneous', 'name Henry's fourth wife...'

The responses travel with the ball's return journey: 'seventy-two', 'M-I-S-C-E-L-L-A-N-E-O-U-S', 'ummm Anne Boleyn?'

'Sit down, Charlotte,' the teacher commands with a dismissive shake of the head you'd expect to accompany a red card. She then throws the ball to the next girl. 'Name Henry's fourth wife.'

'Anne of Cleves, Miss.' Not *Mzzz*, Alice notices, somewhat sadly.

And on they go. And out goes the secretary, followed by an impressed-looking Freddie, a stunned-looking Poppy, and an angry-looking Alice, thinking bleakly of Poppy's excitement when *Mzzz* Gibson started football lessons in PE and Poppy begged for a Hannah Hampton poster for her bedroom wall. As they approach the headmistress's door, Alice notices that apart from a few whispered utterances from the secretary, and Poppy's brief Q&A with Jean, none of them have spoken since they entered the school. To do so, Alice fears, might risk a hundred lines.

14

THE HEADMISTRESS'S OFFICE

Mrs Flogstaff rises from her leather chair like a ghoul in a horror movie as the secretary ushers Freddie, Alice and Poppy into the musty wood-panelled office, possibly used as part of the set for *The Munsters* in the 1960s. Alice wonders if the nameplate on the door had been a misprint. Or a joke. Surely? But Mrs Flogstaff offers her hand to them in turn (not including Poppy) and mutters 'Mrs Flogstaff' from below a rather healthy-looking moustache. Alice wonders if Mrs Flogstaff's family tree had once included a Flagstaff who wasn't the town's best speller...

'Now, I see you've brought Poppy today,' Mrs Flogstaff begins, as if they have a dog on a lead sitting meekly in the corner and want it house-trained. 'Is that her real name? We don't allow nicknames here, you see. Cuts out any chance of *bullying*.' She emphasises the word with a hushed sneer, as if its very mention might risk an outbreak among the year three ducklings.

Freddie nods his understanding, and agreement, gravely; Alice is on the verge of lying.

'It's Penelope,' Freddie announces, nodding again to confirm it. He appears a little guilty in the face of Mrs Flogstaff's stern look of disapproval.

'Is it?' Poppy mouths, turning suddenly to Alice, bemused; confusion and disbelief creasing her nose into the shape of a hungry squirrel's. She looks as she might do had Freddie announced that she is, in fact, called Rupert.

Alice pats Poppy's hand and grimaces an apology. They haven't called her Penelope since she was born. They haven't called her Penelope ever, Alice is sure. Alice had chosen Ryan – Harrison Ford, Jack Ryan (she almost went for Jack) – Freddie had chosen Penelope, some great aunt on his mother's side. But Freddie had always called her Pops, Alice lengthening it to Poppy because Pops reminded her too much of one of the imps on the breakfast cereal box. And so, Pops and Poppy had stuck. Alice wasn't even sure that Ryan knew her real name was Penelope.

Mrs Flogstaff is busy scribbling something on Poppy's – probably now Penelope's – application form.

'Does Penelope know her times tables?' Mrs Flogstaff continues, a high-speed train thwacking through a small station, sucking a swirl of litter and small dogs into the vortex of its wake.

'Well,' Alice begins, trying to sound proud, worried by the PE lesson they non-university walked through. 'She knows her twos, fives and tens. We're working on her threes and fours at the moment...'

'Oh dear.' Mrs Flogstaff's moustache droops, like a mouse caught too long in a trap; she shakes her head. 'She's in year three now? Will be joining year four in September? She'll need to know her tables up to fourteen by then.'

'Fourteen?' Alice is seriously beginning to wonder if they've walked onto the set of a yet-to-be-released Ealing comedy.

'We aim for *excellence*,' Mrs Flogstaff erupts, as if merely saying the word is a sign of– of– of something... Excellence, probably. 'The girls know their tables forwards, backwards and in German. Has Penelope started a modern foreign language yet?'

'*Hablo español,*' Poppy, or Penelope, offers proudly in response.

'Oh dear,' Mrs Flogstaff mutters, staring at Poppy as if she's piddled on the carpet. 'She'll need the rudiments of German by September. I can lend you a book. Do either of you speak a modern foreign language? Or Latin? The girls started Latin in year three.'

'I have A level French,' Alice says; she's not at all sure why she does – say it. Freddie looks at his slippers. While he can name the Kings and Queens of England in order from Æthelstan through to Charles III and his immediate successors, including William of Villa Park and Harry of Santa Barbara, his private school hadn't seen fit to equip him with much in the way of foreign language skills. He had studied French, or so he says, but his appalling accent renders any words he might produce in an emergency completely incomprehensible to any French-speaking people.

'Oh dear,' says Mrs Flogstaff again, beginning to sound like a doctor who's returned from a coffee break to find their patient's monitor flatlining. 'Come and sit over here, Penelope,' she continues without a pause. She picks up a couple of sheets of A4 from her table and moves across the room to a small chair and desk in the corner, beside a very dead-looking plant.

Poppy stares at Alice, points at her own chest and mouths, *Me?* Alice smiles weakly and nods apologetically.

'Just a couple of little tests for you, Penelope. Maths and English. I won't give you the German or the Latin, not until you arrive in September.' Mrs Flogstaff returns to her seat and smiles; her teeth have seen better decades. 'Don't worry, Mr and Mrs Cash. We'll soon have Penelope brushed into shape, just you wait and see. Now, does Penelope have a propensity for nits...?'

15

THE FLAMENCO DANCE CLASS

'No,' says Alice, her insides trembling, as soon as Poppy has scampered off to the Assembly House toilet. 'We're not sending Poppy there!'

Freddie looks shocked. Whether he's shocked that Alice didn't like the school, or that she's just said no to him, isn't clear to her. She doesn't care either way. He stirs his tea, allows the waitress to deposit three well-toasted teacakes onto the table, then sighs.

'They get such good results,' he says.

'*Penelope?*' Alice almost squeals. 'They'd insist on calling Poppy, *Penelope?* You're up for that? No hint of asking Poppy what she'd like? To stop bullying? That's the bloody definition of bullying, Freddie.'

Freddie shrinks into his jacket, shushes Alice's *bloody* with his eyebrows and a horror stare. Norwich's genteel Assembly House tearooms will rarely have heard such incivility, certainly not in the mid-afternoon. The chaperones will be swooning giddily to the floor.

'I can't go to parents' evenings and listen to them talk to me about a girl called Penelope.'

Freddie shrugs, which irritates Alice immensely. 'She'd get used to it,' he replies, not sounding at all convinced. 'You know how things like that are what make your schooldays. She'd laugh about it when she was older.'

'You don't laugh much about your schooldays. You told me they used to hit you with plimsoles. The teachers, that is. Some of the boys were worse. What was it they used to call you? You said you hated it.' She knows damn well he was called Tubs at school. Doesn't really want to use that bullet unless she really has to. She knows she won't be able to once Penel– Fuck! Poppy returns from the loo... But then her mind does something weird. It zeroes in on the fact Freddie's said 'she'd', not 'she'll'. Alice wonders if this is the chink she needs.

Freddie shrugs again, doesn't jog her memory with Tubs. Alice's fists clench at another shrug; it's like dealing with a year-seven lad who's been accused of swearing. 'It can be character building,' he says quietly, still without any conviction.

'And Latin? What on earth good would that be to her? She's just started Spanish. She loves it. We're going to Mallorca again; she's so excited about learning it she's asked me to buy her a phrasebook so she can practise with Rosalita and Carlos. Freddie, you can't take that away from her.'

Freddie looks distinctly uncomfortable, like his best-laid plans are suddenly showing signs of subsidence.

'We could send her to an after-school club for Spanish. You see them advertised everywhere.'

'What? She'd have time for an after-school club with the amount of homework old Mrs Bushy-Whiskers said she'd be getting in year four? Three hours a night, the same on the weekends? She'd be behind all the other girls in every subject. I'm meant to start teaching her two-years' worth of German and a year's worth of Latin over the summer holidays. Times tables up to fourteen? Plus, she said her spelling wasn't up to scratch, two sheets of spellings to teach her over the summer. Miscellaneous? Architecture? Bourgeoisie? Have you looked at that list? I bet you can't spell half of them.'

'It simply shows the school she's at doesn't push her. They spend all their time dealing with the kids who don't speak English.'

Alice stares angrily at the scones in the display cabinet, as if she's considering grabbing one and hurling it at him. She doesn't share Freddie's views on this matter; he knows that. It's one of the subjects they usually dance around, circling each other before moving away, like an awkward little Austenesque *Boulangere*, to keep the peace at home. Alice sees the mention of this subject as a very low blow. Freddie appears to suddenly realise he's got mud, or something worse, on his court shoes and changes the record rapidly.

'Besides, Latin helps with lots of languages. Even English. Take a word like submarine. If you spoke Latin, you'd be able to work out what it means.'

'I know what it means. I'm quite sure Poppy knows what it means.'

'Yes, but if she knew the roots, she'd... you know, it would help her.'

'And speaking Spanish would help her a damn sight more than Latin or German. Plus, she's so keen, she's practically teaching herself. God, Freddie, she's blossoming. I know we've had some worries about her, but she really is happy where she is. What if she doesn't get on with the girls at this school? What if she doesn't make friends? She's only recently got into football, but there isn't a football pitch in sight there, it's all netball and hockey, and playtime seems to be a ball-free and fun-free zone. There were no little gangs of girls making up dances together.'

They sit in silence for a few moments, Alice's heart thumping heavily. They rarely argue; she doesn't like it. But, and it's a big but, the more she makes her case against sending Poppy to the school, the more important, and convincing, it seems to be. This is Poppy's childhood. She's happy where she is: dashing about the place; playing football with the boys; screaming at playtime or dancing to Taylor Swift songs with her little chums; worshipping *Mzzz* Gibson who's got a cat called Bonkers and a Spanish boyfriend working in the deli on the Unthank Road – just the boyfriend, not the cat. Poppy doesn't spend her playtimes sitting on a bench practising how to spell *bourgeoisie*. She might not have anything in common with the girls at this private school. She has a few little friends where she is. What if the other girls at the private school take against her? All in their settled groups, no room for somebody new to upset the balance? Especially someone who isn't really like them. Alice has seen how children often suffer at a new school, especially girls, how delicate their friendship groups can be, how fragile. She hates how it works, but she sees it. New boys? As long as they play football, they're pretty much sorted. But girls? Poppy's age?

'Freddie, she's seven, she's a happy little girl, she plays judo, football, loves Spanish. It would be a horrible summer for her, working all the time to catch up on her tables, German, Latin. She'd start to think she wasn't good enough. And to be honest, I don't want to be the one driving her through all that German and Latin over the summer. She'd hate it. She'd end up hating me. Would you like the job?'

He sighs. Looks away. His sighing irritates her, but she swallows her anger, thinks reason might have a better chance against him.

'Look,' she says, taking his hands in hers, 'it's not the right time to move Poppy. She's too young. There's too much that could go wrong. At least let's ask her what she wants to do.'

'But we move Ryan?'

Alice feels guilty, like she's been given a sort of Sophie's choice of school, and she's choosing Poppy to survive, but leaving Ryan cast to the fates. She knows it's not the same. Justifies herself with the thought that Ryan was moving up to secondary anyway. Ryan has even said that one or two of his friends are also considering going to the boys' school. But it still hurts her. She still feels she should be standing up for them both. Standing up for herself.

Freddie shrugs. Is that a yes? Has he agreed? With year-seven kids, a shrug often translates into, *Okay, whatever...* Poppy returns from the toilet.

'Poppy,' Alice says, in her best schoolteacher voice. 'What did you think of the school?' Alice keeps her face straight, stern, hoping Poppy might read her mind and tell them she thought it was shit. Well, maybe not 'shit', exactly. That might only convince Freddie that he needed to enrol her immediately.

Poppy bites into her teacake.

'Didn't you like it?'

Poppy looks from Alice to Freddie. Back again. Chews slowly.

'The truth, Poppy. What did you think? It's an important decision. We want you to go to a school where you'll be happy.' Alice suddenly wonders: is this the choice Freddie never got? *Do you want to go straight into the bank or go to university first?* Is this Poppy's chance to choose, where Freddie got no choice?

'Nobody spoke,' Poppy whispers, looking bemused. She stares at her shoes, a very un-Poppyish move. And then it gushes out, lifting and breaking Alice's heart at the same time. 'Except the secretary, and the horrible teacher with the moustache who doesn't want to call me Poppy. And they don't do Spanish. And nobody plays football at playtime. They don't even have football goals on the fields. And none of the girls came over to say hello.

Mzzz Gibson says, if we ever see a new boy or girl looking around the school, we should say hello, ask them their name, make them feel welcome...' Alice knows the power of 'Mzzz Gibson says...' It pours out of Poppy's mouth like projectile vomit at the dinner table, in the car, on the way to the shops. 'Mzzz Gibson says this', 'Mzzz Gibson says that', 'Mzzz Gibson's cat says the other...' And Alice feels she could hug Mzzz Gibson for engendering such loyalty and enthusiasm in Poppy. And Poppy stops suddenly, like she's only just realised what she's said, and is wondering if she should have. There's a single tear on her cheek, with the threat of a further bucket-load in her eyes.

'It's a very good school, Pops. You'd learn a lot there.' Freddie's eyebrows flutter skywards, willing her to agree.

Poppy looks at Alice. Alice returns her stare, attempts telepathy.

'What do you think, Mummy?' Poppy finally says.

Alice takes a breath; Freddie has made his preference clear.

'We want you to go to the school where you think you'll be the happiest. We think you'll learn better if you're happy.'

Poppy nods gravely. 'It looks a bit like Hogwarts.'

Alice's heart sinks...

'Will all my friends be going there?'

...and rises again.

'No, Poppy. Your friends will go into year four at the school you're at now. You'd be moving to this new school on your own. If you really want to.'

Poppy nods slowly; then she nods more quickly.

'Well then, in that case... I'd like to stay where I am, with my friends, where I can learn Spanish. And because Mzzz Gibson told us, she's moving up to year four with us in September.'

Olé! Alice almost screams, wondering if there is a chance

she could find a flamenco-dancing class in Norwich. Something she and Poppy could do together, perhaps? She also seriously wonders if she'll be able to stop herself from kissing Mzzz Gibson the next time she sees her.

16

THE CHEEKY LITTLE NUMBER

'THERE'S A DELIVERY FOR YOU, LOVE,' Alice shouts as she hears Freddie come in from work. It looks and feels like a bottle of something. Wine, possibly, she's guessed, as the package is stamped *VintageVino*.

'Oh good; that was quick,' Freddie replies, coming through into the kitchen and giving her a peck on the cheek. He picks up the box and takes it upstairs. Alice looks at the children. The children, who have been gawping at the package like it's got muffled meows seeping out of it, and have been waiting impatiently for Freddie to arrive, stare back. They look surprised, disappointed, intrigued – although Poppy might not know that particular word yet. Since the win, Alice muses, Freddie seems to be enjoying his ability to evoke a bit of intrigue.

At dinner (shepherd's pie) the contents of the package reappear at the table. Everybody stares at Freddie, who has his *I've got a little surprise* smile Jackson Pollocked across his face. Alice wonders if there's another family meeting in the offing.

Alice is now certain it's wine. Freddie's unwrapped the parcel to reveal a dark-wood box with a clasp like they used to have on old-fashioned suitcases, the type of case you saw on films where you could push down the window on the train door and hang out for a kiss goodbye. She's shaken the package and has heard liquid. The children have practically juggled it between them. She hopes now it isn't champagne or the ceiling's about to be washed in the stuff.

'You remember, at the last family meeting' (*only* family meeting, Alice thinks to herself) 'we all got so involved with the football tickets that I forgot to mention my own choice of special treat. Well, here it is. Better late than... Um, better late, than... Well, better late than a stitch in time.'

Poppy's excitement overwhelms her confusion; she's squirming in her chair like Santa has just walked in, taken off his coat, and tipped a sackload of presents onto the table. Freddie picks up his box and unclips the clasp. He opens it like a book, displaying the contents à la Trump showing off a new law, proud as a three-year-old who's filled his nappy. Inside – the box, that is – Alice can see it's lined with deep-red silk, and sitting in the middle is a fancy-looking bottle of red wine.

'It's all dirty,' Poppy frowns. She's right, Alice notices. The bottle is decidedly dusty; the label looks like it was designed in the eighteenth century and has been stored in a damp cave ever since. Even the metallic cork cover is torn and rumpled.

Freddie smiles the kind of *I know something you don't* smile you'd usually see on the face of a magician with a saw in their hand. 'That's because it was bottled in 1954. It's a vintage.'

'Nineteen fifty-four?' Ryan gasps incredulously. Like Freddie's said 1066. 'Won't it have gone off?' He leans across the table and sniffs the bottle suspiciously.

Freddie chuckles to himself. 'Wine matures as it ages. And this is a particularly fine bottle. And that's my new hobby, wine.'

'But you've always had wine?' Poppy protests, like he's suggesting Poppy take up a new hobby – reading.

'Ah, but the wine you buy in the supermarket is a very poor imitation of what vintage wine tastes like,' Freddie preens as he removes the cork cover, which is barely attached to the bottle. He lifts a waiter's corkscrew out of the box and plunges it in.

'Oh look, there's free stuff,' Ryan gasps, hauling a silver pourer and drip-stopper out of the silk. Poppy delves into the depths and lifts out a thermometer.

'Is this in case you drink too much?' she asks.

The cork comes out with a very satisfying *plop!*

'What is it?' Alice asks, winking at Poppy.

'Umm, it's a...' Freddie twists the bottle. 'It's a Marqués de Riscal,' he says, squinting to read the faded writing on the distinctly grubby seventy-year-old label.

'Lovely,' Alice says, not that she'd have a clue about the difference between a Marqués de Riscal and a Grand Old Duke of York. 'What sort of wine is that?'

'Umm...' Freddie squints again, rubbing some of the dust off the label. 'I think it's a Rioja. They're very nice. Especially the Gran Reservas.' He fetches two wine glasses from the cupboard and moves to pour into Alice's glass.

'Shouldn't you let it breathe?' she asks, covering her glass with her hand. 'I mean, it's been bottled up since 1954.'

Freddie looks mildly embarrassed. 'I think it'll be all right.'

Alice smiles, pleased to see him happy; she takes her hand away. Freddie pours for her and then himself.

'Can I try some?' Ryan asks, eyes wide and eager.

'Me too,' demands Poppy, looking delighted, if a little less sure.

Freddie looks at Alice. She nods at him.

'You can have a sip of ours,' she says.

Freddie passes his glass to Ryan. 'You should sniff it first; the aroma is part of the tasting experience.'

Ryan nods gravely, pokes his nose into the glass and takes a huge, snot-assisted sniff, his eyes scanning the table suspiciously, like he's checking that this bit isn't one of Freddie's jokes. Then he takes a sip. 'Mmm. Not bad.'

Alice passes her glass to Poppy, who sniffs, hesitantly at first, then with great enthusiasm. 'It smells like flowers,' she announces. Then she takes a sip, considers the taste – and screws her face up like she's got a mouthful of vinegar, seventy-year-old vinegar.

'Gross!' Poppy announces, stand-in wine of the year judge's verdict on one of the finalists.

Alice, smiling, offers her glass for Freddie to toast. They clink; she drinks. Not bad, she thinks: a cheeky little number. A nice 1954 red – thank goodness she's made shepherd's pie...

While Freddie's brushing his teeth, Alice sneaks downstairs and logs on to their laptop, and scrolls through his email account, intrigued by how much Freddie has spent on his new hobby. One bottle of wine? She thinks, maybe, he could have spent up to thirty pounds. A silly indulgence when there are people reliant on food banks. But it is nice to see him happy – ish.

Three hundred and sixty pounds. She gasps. Looks again. Has she misread it? Checks it's not for a case, a dozen bottles. No. Three hundred and sixty pounds. She considers this news. It's a shock. She'd never have thought Freddie capable of spending three hundred and sixty pounds on a bottle of wine. The wine had been nice. She's no expert, but she'd even call it very nice. But three hundred and sixty pounds? She can't stop saying the amount, under her breath, as if she's trying to take it in, really understand how much he's spent. Three hundred and sixty pounds. On one bottle of very nice wine? Was it really that much nicer than a £9.99 bottle from Sainsbury's?

Alice doesn't do conspicuous consumption. In fact, she's quite scathing about it. She doesn't buy brands, encourages the children not to be sucked in by them. She scoffs at people who spend over the odds for things and then bore you with details of how much better they are than the cheap stuff you buy: baby clothes, lawnmowers, whisky. Not always the same people, of course. And as for those jeans that are ripped and frayed before they're even in the bag? Well, Alice considers them the fashion farce of all time.

She loves watching car adverts. All those beautiful shiny cars cruising down mountain passes, next to white-sand beaches, through rolling hills. Where does she see these cars next? Hooting their horns in a dismal traffic jam on a drizzly Grapes Hill. No, Alice sees through a lot of it.

And Freddie has never been one of those people. His shirts are M&S. So are his pants and socks. Suits, too, although some of the older ones are C&A. They could never have afforded him to have been a conspicuous consumer. Has he now been revealed as a closet brand magnet? A logo limpet? Is he now planning on frittering away a huge chunk of this money on overpriced booze? Simply so he can show off? Three bottles would be over a thousand pounds. On wine? Twenty glasses, at a push? A thousand pounds...?

She shuts the computer down. Three hundred– She feels numb, slightly sick at the thought. Wishes she'd never looked.

17

THE DINNER INVITATION

ALICE MAKES friends with the woman across the street. By coincidence, they leave their houses at the same moment, clearly heading for the corner shop, unless either (or both) are planning a visit to the park using their bags for life as sort of DIY wind-resistance training aids. As Alice crosses the road and joins this woman on the other side, they're marching almost like an army patrol. So, they smile, and they talk. It's not a long walk to the corner shop, but by the time they get back (Alice waits for Emma after she's paid), they've agreed to have a cuppa and a chat.

Alice likes Emma immediately: she's open and friendly, a bit scatty. There are piles of toys wherever Alice tries to sit, which Emma sweeps into bigger piles. Emma's a nurse, lots of shifts. She and her 'other half' (she doesn't say husband – or even wife, Alice thinks, with a smile) have only recently moved in. Alice remembers a *To Let* sign that has disappeared.

Alice has a few spare mornings and afternoons to fill in her part-time teaching week, and a cuppa plus a chat is always better than a cuppa without, in her eyes.

Emma's oldest has joined the local primary school: Mags is

in the parallel class to Poppy. Alice promises to ask Poppy to look out for Mags. There's a toddler at playgroup.

By the end of their chat, Emma has invited Alice and Freddie to an 'early dinner' one evening, the children being provided with a picnic snack that they can have outside in the Barbie-sized garden, weather permitting, 'to save on babysitting'. Alice accepts gratefully...

...and isn't surprised when Freddie sighs, almost silently, when she tells him. It's not that he doesn't like them, they've only recently moved in, so he doesn't even know them by sight, but he always prefers to 'sound people out' before getting hitched into any neighbourly dinner-go-rounds.

First 'con' in Freddie's mental *Debrett's*, Alice knows, is that they're across the road, in the terraces, whereas Freddie and Alice have a semi-d. So, there's that. And they have a Fiesta, he's noticed while peering through the lace curtains without twitching them. Old one. Lots of dents and faded paint. It's not that Freddie's a snob, Alice attempts to convince herself; even she couldn't help but notice that Emma's pushchair for their little one did look less sturdy than the toy Poppy uses for her dolls and teddies.

Freddie says little to Alice, but she suspects, well, she knows, because he's said it all before, that there's a long list of things they should check out before accepting a dinner invitation. But Alice is damned if she's going to play the enclosed nun simply because Freddie would prefer to act even posher than he pretends to be. She's sure, given a chance, he'd devise a questionnaire, a sort of application form, for prospective dinner friends to fill in before any invitations are made or accepted.

What paper do they read? If any? Anything other than the *Telegraph*, *Mail* or *Express* would automatically lose them twenty points, a vote for the *Guardian* being an instant disqualification. Who did they vote for last time? Conservative (Freddie never uses the word Tory), twenty points; LibDems, minus twenty points; Labour, instant disqualification. How did they vote on Brexit? Leave, gold star; Remain, instant disqualification. And on and on he'll go, views on private schooling, private health, small boats, picking up dog shit from the pavement...

Alice is a smidge disappointed to notice Emma kissing a handsome chap goodbye on her doorstep the following morning: introducing Freddie to a pair of lesbians might have broadened his horizons somewhat. It would have been good for him to see the world as it is, as opposed to how he would like it to be (his default position), and it might have been quite entertaining for her – and possibly even the lesbians.

The following Saturday, bottle of Rioja (2019 vintage, £9.99 from Sainsbury's – Freddie wishes she'd let him choose the wine) and a box of After Eights in Alice's grasp, they cross the Rubicon from the semi-ds to the terraces.

It's poky, Freddie judges, silently, happily, hoovering up wedding and baby pictures from the windowsill, the smell from the kitchen pervading the living room. The three-piece is too big for the room, and Freddie and Alice find themselves sardined together on the one-and-a-half-seater sofa. The whole place is furnished like a doll's house, he muses with a sigh of satisfaction.

Mags hugs Poppy as soon as they arrive. It obvious she has some sort of a problem with her eyesight. She's wearing thick glasses, and comes right up to Poppy, as if she's checking who it is. She then grabs Ryan's hand and hauls the pair of them out back where a tent that Barbie and Ken would have trouble sharing chastely awaits them with paper plates full of sarnies and sausage rolls, and paper cups and cartons of economy (Freddie notices with a raise of his eyebrows) juice.

'The sausage rolls are veggie,' Emma blurts. 'I forgot to ask; we're all veggie–'

'It's fine. They'll eat anything,' Alice replies with a dismissive wave. 'Keep your eyes on your drinks coasters, mind, in case they mistake them for biscuits.'

They watch for a moment as Mags offers plates and paper cups and the children all squeeze into the tent like they're preparing for a big finale finish at a stage magician's show.

The handsome chap is Keith, 'store manager', all nervous tics: pill-rolling fingers, bouncing knee, raucous laughter at the slightest excuse. Freddie's eyes widen and his brow furrows when, at the first squeal from the toddler upstairs, it's Keith who heads up to settle her. Alice smiles weakly when Emma notices Freddie's confusion.

They finish the Rioja at the dinner table. Start another bottle. Might be another Rioja, Freddie has no clue. His glasses are a little steamy from the food and the single glazing in the rotting wooden frames (he's noticed; his own are uPVC doubles, installed with the help of a small inheritance they received when his mother died). Even if he could read the label, it probably wouldn't make any difference. Freddie hasn't done the wine snob course yet, but he's on the waiting list.

The food is vegetarian, as announced, but Freddie would have guessed: falafel to start, almost certainly home-made as they fall apart in transit from bowl to plate; some kind of vegetable lasagne thingy to follow, lots of crunchy carrots and courgettes; and a cheeseboard of odd-flavoured cheeses, so obviously not containing whatever it is that makes cheese unvegetarian and, at the same time, edible. The coffee is instant, the milk probably powdered.

Alice is enjoying herself, Freddie notices. She's certainly sloshing back the wine as the conversation makes stops at the usual stations: where they're from, their jobs, their children, the school, but steers clear of politics and religion. Alice had insisted on these off-limits limits in the days before the meal, memories of a disastrous dinner up the street a couple of years previously when Freddie had launched some small boats and was greeted at the shore by silence. Still, Freddie thinks to himself, renting a terrace, veggie food, they're obviously tree-huggers so probably best to keep the train on the tracks and the boats back in Calais. He does bridle, however, at not being able to be himself in his own castle, should a return date be deemed appropriate, which Freddie doubts, having spotted a *Guardian* slumbering next to the (extremely small) telly.

His mind wanders: he scans the bookshelves behind Keith, where he spies a le Carré lurking amongst a lot of women's stuff in green jackets. So, Emma's the reader. He wonders if Keith ever finished the le Carré; decides not to ask in case he's a bit of an aficionado with the rest of them on a Kindle with notes and cross-references. Freddie gave up on *Tinker, Tailor*. Couldn't make sense of the film either.

'Oh, I had to put my foot down, didn't I, Freddie?'

'Wha–'

'Your *investments*,' Alice giggles, half whispering, eyebrows dancing, another glug of wine, stressing the word like she's saying 'porn'.

'Which investments?' he asks, shaken back to a conversation where he is, apparently, the object under the microscope. Keith and Emma are smiling. Freddie doesn't know why.

'You remember. You bought those ice thingies. Lost half their value within the month. I made you promise you'd stop.'

She doesn't reveal that it was a condition of her agreeing to marry him.

'ISAs,' he corrects with a sigh. 'I had others that made money, *if* you remember.'

But the train is already moving out of the ISA station before Freddie can clarify that, in the main, he'd been quids in on his investments. A tidy profit. But they're talking about some TV drama Emma thinks is wonderful, and Alice is promising to watch. Which means he'll have to watch it as well. Something about blinking social workers...

'Aren't they nice?' Alice asks as they're getting ready for bed. She knows he hasn't been impressed, but she's enjoyed their company, and the wine is making her feel like putting down a mini marker.

'They're okay,' he mumbles, as he might were she asking about a new brand of biscuit they'd tried. He climbs under the covers and opens *Tinker, Tailor, Soldier, Spy*. 'Aren't those terraces small, though?'

She smiles to herself, notices how they circle each other. She's happy they don't argue, of course she is, but it does mean they don't discuss much, neither wanting to dig up the patio, fearing what they might find underneath. They're too far into their relationship to change much, she fears. But this lottery money is worrying her, and she still doesn't know how to raise it.

'By the way,' he says, without looking up from his book. 'The money came through, and I've transferred the extra point three into your account. Bit of spending money. You can treat yourself, whenever you want. Thought you'd like that.' He looks up at her quickly, smiles.

'That's lovely. Thank you,' she says, but her mind is

juddering, like a car attempting a hill in too high a gear, losing power suddenly, kicking and bucking until it stalls, and starts rolling backwards. This doesn't feel right and she's not entirely sure why.

The extra point three? So, what? Is the rest of it his? Is that what he's just said? It's awkward. He's just, in effect, given her three hundred thousand pounds. Shouldn't she be genuinely grateful? But it kind of implies that the rest of it, two million pounds, is his. Is that what he's suggesting? Shouldn't she ask for half? She can't. What he's done is a sign that he recognises something. A little something. She can't start an argument when he's just given her three hundred thou. Can she? No, she can't.

She slides into bed, kisses him on the cheek. He smiles again, nods a little nod in appreciation of her thanks, for his beneficence. What the fuck?

'Thought you'd read that?' she says, knowing she's changing the subject because she doesn't know how to pursue it. Where would the discussion go?

'No, I was busy and left it for too long. So, I'm starting again.'

'We enjoyed the film, didn't we? Although I can't remember much about it.'

'Yes, it was very good. Whatshisname was good as Smiley.'

'Yes, very good. Night, night, love. I think that wine's gone to my head. I'll be asleep in seconds. Lovely evening.'

'Yes, lovely,' he says.

She lies down, turns her light off, but is awake for hours after he puts his book away, kills his own light, and starts snoring contentedly.

18

THE POSH WATCH

Where to buy a Rolex?

If you want to buy a new Rolex, you'll almost certainly have to wait. Some jewellery stores sell second-hand Rolexes for which there won't be a waiting list. But for new watches, get yourself on the waiting list – pronto!

Freddie's face drops. A waiting list? That's a shock. He consoles himself that it probably improves the exclusivity value, but he's a bit disappointed. And as for a second-hand one? Well, you must be joking. He tries Amazon. Surely he can buy a Rolex on Amazon? You can buy anything on Amazon.

He's at work. Technically it's his coffee break, so he's having a little google – looking for a posh watch. To his relief and delight, up they pop. They look wonderful: thick and chunky, with luminous displays and rotating bezels, and that little crown he's seen on the tennis. Why are all the hands set to ten past ten? Who knows? He dives in. Some of them have three smaller dials on the watch face, he's not sure what they're for, but they look impressive. One of them has a little blue sky with a moon. Phases of the moon, maybe? Could be useful. And then, he spots something...

Thirty-nine quid. *Thirty-nine quid?* For a *Rolex?* Freddie squints closer to the screen. Between the hands set at ten past ten, and under the little crown, where he thought he read ROLEX, on closer inspection he can now see it says OLEVS. He clicks back to the main search result: more OLEVS, most of them at thirty-nine quid. There's a Breitling at a smidgen over seven thousand pounds. That's a bit more like it, he thinks, although he's not really sure how much a Rolex, a new one, actually costs. Ten thousand? Twenty? He's never checked. His dream has always been that: a dream. He simply knew they'd be out of his price range. Like the Porsche. He's never checked the price of one of those either. What would have been the point? Except to rub his own nose in the impossibility of ever being able to afford one.

So, he reverses out of Amazon and googles again: *buy a Rolex* and finds himself on the official site where men in white coats and wearing white gloves assure him that his watch will have *balanced weight* (that sounds sensible) and will *nest* in a *presentation box that is both protector and keeper.* He'll need to locate an *Official Rolex Retailer* where they'll prepare his watch: adjusting the bracelet to the perfect size, placing any excess links in the presentation box, winding the watch, setting the time, date and day, giving him an instruction manual and then filling out the guarantee card that will certify his watch's authenticity. His heart flutters when he discovers that there is, in fact, an *Official Rolex Retailer* in Norwich.

Freddie claps his hands together and plans a little retail therapy. Then he spots another link.

How long is the waiting list for a new Rolex?

He clicks apprehensively.

Two to four years or longer...

'Blooming heck!' Freddie gasps. 'Two to four *years?*' But it gets worse. Having ordered your watch, while you are waiting, if the price of it goes up, then you'll pay the higher price.

Freddie sighs. He never thought it would be this complicated. Then he spots yet another link. The internet is beginning to feel like a chapter of *Alice in Wonderland* – except he never seems to reach the wonders. *Want to beat the Rolex waiting list? Top tips.* He clicks again, to what he's sure will be another rabbit warren.

Tip number one is *Dress like a Rolex wearer*. Freddie sits up. Well, that's obvious, he thinks. He's got his suit and tie; he wouldn't think of wearing anything else. He remembers the white coat and white gloves from the website; it's a serious business. He imagines a lower order of people are probably attempting to buy Rolexes nowadays. A younger, get-rich-quick brigade with more money than sense and precious little class. He knows the type. What do they call them? Gen Zeds? Break dancers? Something like that. He's seen them on the TV. Stockbrokers, computer programmers, DJs. Riff-raff, he calls them. All dressed in tracksuits and chunky gold chains, playing loud washing-machine music through the open windows of top-of-the-range (but classless) cars: VWs, BMWs, the new Mini Coopers, which aren't at all mini anymore. Completely classless bunch of idiots.

Tip two is *Build a relationship with the Rolex dealer*. Well, duh! He'd hardly go in and ignore the guy. Or woman! Course it could be a woman. No reason why not. Freddie is a liberated kinda guy – and good at building relationships. Not a problem. Freddie builds relationships all the time at work, except when busy shopkeepers put the phone down on him as he tries to rent them card readers or hawk them a loan. But this would be the other way around. Freddie with money in his pocket wanting to buy. No problem.

Three: *Wear a Rolex when visiting a Rolex dealer*. What?

How the hell is he meant to wear a ruddy Rolex when he's attempting to buy one? He doesn't know anybody who owns a Rolex who could lend it to him for a morning. Keith, across the road? His watch (Freddie checked) looked like a nine ninety-nine jobbie out of the garage, the kind of cheap thing that Alice wears. The nearest Freddie's ever been to a real Rolex is probably seeing the tennis players at Wimbledon putting them on after they've won, ready for the on-court interview. Well, he's never actually been to Wimbledon; he's seen it on the telly. So, not actually that near after all. He'll ignore that bit.

Four: *Know your stuff and show that you're serious!* Freddie's heart sinks. He's seen enough on the internet already to know there are dozens of different types of Rolexes, and he really isn't that interested to learn about the differences between them all. He wants the gold one they show on the adverts in the papers when Wimbledon's on. That's obviously the best one.

He sits back and pulls the face Poppy displays whenever he tries to help her with the intricacies of bus-stop division. It's one of utter bemusement. How the hell is he meant to show the dealer that he's serious? Is he meant to slap a wad of fifty-pound notes on the counter as soon as he walks in? He reads further. Apparently, he should show his credit card and tell the dealer if he has any holidays booked, so they don't call him to say his watch is in while he's out – on holiday that is. Mercifully, you don't have to tell them whenever you go to work, or to do the shopping. This still irritates Freddie. Christ, if only the oiks who came into the bank showed a tenth of this much respect for him... He'll have a think about that one.

Five: *Don't faff about by changing your mind.* Right. He can do that. Or, rather, not do it: change his mind, that is. The gold one. The one on the Wimbledon adverts. He can use the internet to choose the watch he wants and then march straight into the shop – sorry, 'authorised dealer' – slap his credit card on the counter, open his Filofax to show his holiday dates, and then announce the exact watch he wants. The gold one.

Six: *Make sure the dealer doesn't think you're going to sell the watch on for a profit.* So, what? He's going to have to sign a declaration saying he won't sell it? But why shouldn't he? Not that he's planning to, but why shouldn't he, once he's bought it? It'll be his. They can't tell him what he can and can't do once it's his. He has read, however, that Rolexes do appreciate in value quite quickly. So, maybe he will want to sell it, upgrade it, to a newer one. He has another little google to settle his nerves.

How much is a Rolex?

He finds a website that, luckily, has pictures next to the watches. There's a black one with a huge chunky bezel for a little over ten thousand pounds. He doesn't really know if that's cheap or expensive. He doesn't want to buy one that marks him out among aficionados as some kind of cheapskate Rolex wearer. He wants the real deal, the dog's whatsits. The next one has the three little circular faces inside the main watch face, but it doesn't have the little moon. That one's sixteen thousand. So, the black one is toast. There's one at eight grand. Swipe left. Then he spots a gold one for eighteen thousand. He likes the gold. He's sure he's seen Roger Federer wearing the gold one. He quickly flicks through the selection, moving past anything that isn't gold and is less than eighteen grand. He finds a gold one for thirty-seven grand, but it has a blue face that he doesn't think looks nice. He's never seen one like that on the Wimbledon adverts. It's also got the day displayed in a little window at the top, in capitals. He doesn't like that: makes it look like a child's watch, in his mind. He knew there were a lot of models, but he'd no idea there were this many...

He goes back to the eighteen-thousand-pound gold one, without the day in a window, clicks on it. It says it's unworn and fully stickered. He wonders what that means. Ryan and Poppy collect stickers. Why would his Rolex have stickers? Would they be to put on your Filofax? Or the back of your phone? Surely not. Why is this so bloomin' complicated? Then he notices that the condition is described as *like new and unworn*. So, is this one of the second-hand ones? It says it comes with the original box and original papers. A new one would obviously come with all that, so this must be second-hand. It's a 2022 model, so not that old. And then the kicker – *in stock...*

He decides to pop into the Norwich authorised dealer for a chat, and if he's not happy with anything, or they don't show him enough respect, he'll come back and get this one. Sorted.

He checks the time. Half past eight. Half past *eight*? It can't be half past eight; he's at work; he's never at work at– Oh! He notices, with a mildly embarrassed smirk...

His watch has stopped.

19

———————

THE TREAT

Alice is in John Lewis on one of her half days. The poshest shop in Norwich. Well, the poshest shop in Norwich that she knows. There are probably posher shops, but she's never been in them. Doesn't know anybody who has. Doesn't know where they are. Doesn't really know what they're called or what they sell. Probably posh clothes, or posh jewellery. So, she's in John Lewis. Attempting to treat herself...

That's what Freddie had said. 'Treat yourself'. He's bought himself some posh wine, is looking for his posh watch, so she's going to treat herself to something. She's not sure what; she's not sure she knows how. How to treat herself. It's simply not her style.

They've never had much extra cash for treats, whatever they might be. They have coffee out, occasionally, in the Assembly House. They used to do those lovely coffees that came with the little plastic bucket with the lid balanced on top of the cup, that the hot water dribbled through. What were they called? Rombouts! She used to love the wait, and the smell, as the coffee trickled through into the cup. Luxury. They've all gone now, replaced by capsules. Still, that's what Alice thinks about when

113

she considers treating herself. Maybe push the medium-sized boat out and have lunch? That'd be a treat! Even a pudding? Glass of wine? Lordy!

But a light lunch followed by a well-buttered toasted teacake isn't the kind of treat she thinks Freddie is envisioning. He's got his mind on millionaire treats. What would a millionaire – or a millionaire's wife, she thinks, a little grumpily – deem to be a treat? She's considered googling 'millionaire treats'. There are probably dozens of websites, blogs and podcasts that would enlighten her, but there's something that stops her looking. A fear that she won't like what she sees, perhaps? She doesn't like the idea that she might have prejudices – but she feels, well, she knows that she does. She'd despise them all. Posh people in expensive clothes, smugly ignoring the camera and draped in bling: how she hates that word.

She and Freddie have never really been short. Not that they inherited a fortune from any of their parents, but they have a house, a car, an annual holiday. They're warm in the winter and not too hot in the summer. They have enough to eat. Maybe she can treat them all in the food department; she doesn't usually shop there. Some special ready meal? Then she feels pathetic. She knows that's not what Freddie means when he says 'treat yourself...' He means something for her. Not a family-size chicken korma in a posh-looking box with biscuit-sized naan breads included.

She heads for the women's department. Not ladies, *women*. There's probably a deeply significant, sexually political difference between the two that many women, or ladies, maybe even some men, know about, have read about, in books by Germaine Greer, and possibly some even more up-to-date people who she hasn't read. She should read more, she thinks.

She steps onto the floor and is confronted by handbags. An

army of them. She's not sure where handbags end and suitcases begin. There's every colour, every style, although how would she know whether there was or there wasn't *every* style? She's never been a handbag person. Handbags, for Alice, have always been a utilitarian purchase. She's got her phone, her purse, a pen, a notebook in her handbag. It's a dozen years old, doesn't have any holes in it, the strap isn't in danger of breaking: why would she want to change it? Upgrade it? Like a car? She has a posh one, the one she uses when she goes to bank dos with Freddie: a clutch bag. Called clutch because...? She's not entirely sure. Because it's got no handles or straps, so you have to hold it, *clutch* it? Bizarre, really. Why would anyone invent, why would anyone buy, something that was so user unfriendly? A bag you can't sling over your shoulder by a handy strap? Even hook over your elbow by the handles? She never really understood fashion. Always loved reading the children in her classes that book: *Bill's New Frock.* No pockets...? That always made the girls sit up and think! Sometimes, some of the boys as well.

But she's not in the mood for handbags. She's never in the mood for handbags. And she's damned if a lottery win is going to change her into the sort of woman, or lady, who really gives a fig about handbags. So, she moves on – and finds herself in shoes.

Now, being a teacher in a busy secondary school, Alice is a bit set in her ways in the shoe department as well. There are some younger teachers who wear heels – when did that become a euphemism for high heels – but Alice doesn't. She has a pair of kittens, for parents' evenings: that's as high as she ever goes. She usually wears flats. She's sure Germaine Greer advised her to, when she was at university. Not that Greer was strictly part of the Eng Lit course reading. And it could have been someone else. It was a while ago. Weren't high heels some male imposition? Like the Taliban with their rules for women's clothing? She's lost touch with all these issues. Yes, she really should read some more. Some up-to-date stuff. Germaine Greer. Maybe she's got a daughter...?

She browses, quickly, past the heels, *Christ, some of them are enormous, they look like they'd weigh a ton*, shooing away the young sales assistants who attempt to approach with advice or help. But she soon loses interest in shoes, she has more than enough anyway, and heads for fashion...

Big mistake. She thought there were a lot of handbags, and shoes, but half the floor seems to be fashion. Should she buy something for school? A smart two-piece? Maybe a trouser suit? For the HoD job? Although didn't Germaine Greer have something to say about trouser suits for women that she's forgotten as well? What about something for herself, as opposed to for school? Something that Poppy would comment on? *What a lovely top, Mummy*. Yes, that's it: She'll look for a top.

Of course, John Lewis doesn't group all its tops together like it does its handbags or shoes. No, there's no sign hanging high with *TOPS* written on it in John Lewis's own font and colouring. Tops are scattered around the place grouped with their own brand-named clothing.

She likes the look of something that a sign says is a *Spot Print Cotton Blend Batwing Top*. But it's a John Lewis own brand, and she wanted something a bit 'special', and it's in the sale for twenty quid, and she really doesn't know, and doesn't want to ask, what batwings are. She scuttles away before one of the young assistants attempts to explain or, God forbid, unfold them...

She turns a corner and finds herself in the Sweaty Betty section. She's tempted to do a swift one-eighty but there are a couple of young assistants chatting by the till and she doesn't want to draw attention to herself like she's just walked into a sex shop by mistake. So, she surveys the Sweaty Betty tops like she really might buy one. She sees a sign for a *Sand Wash Cloud Weight Crop Hoodie, Trek Green* and picks one up, merely to see if *Cloud Weight* actually means anything. She's also not sure if the *Trek* is part of the article. The comma suggests it's part of the colour. It feels nice. She wonders if she dares try it on. She looks at the label. Ninety quid. *Ninety quid!* For a top! One of the assistants suddenly breaks away from her conversation and heads menacingly towards her. Alice puts the *Sand Wash Cloud Weight Crop Hoodie, Trek Green* back as quickly as she can. Then she spots a couple of no-more-than-fourteen-year-olds holding up other Sweaty Betty tops and realises she's in completely the wrong section and why aren't they in school...? She curses the demise of Top Shop and wishes Poppy was old enough to come with her and explain what batwings are and cloud weight...

She finds herself in the Baukjen bit, but keeps moving, not being sure how to pronounce it: would it be a hard J or a softer, Spanish, throaty-clearance one? She flicks a label on a *Hattie Organic Cotton Denim Shirt* and speeds up as she sees a hundred and sixty-nine pounds flashing into the distance.

There's a lovely *Lace Detail Blouse, White* in *Mint Velvet* but it's ninety-nine quid! It doesn't even have any batwings and isn't cloud weight, so she keeps moving before she's ambushed by any of the lurking assistants.

She buys a top. She feels she has to, or the whole excursion will be a complete failure. It's not much of a success as it is. It's a John Lewis own top. Green. No batwings; not cloud weight. Simply a top. It didn't even have a label with eight or ten words of unfathomable description. It simply said *Sale*. Twenty quid – reduced from thirty-nine so it's sort of a win in the treat yourself stakes.

She exits, almost running, through Whistles, where a *Long-*

Sleeve Ultimate Silk Shirt is a hundred and fifty-nine pounds. *A hundred and...* The problem is that she likes it. It's a lovely deep blue colour. She doesn't stop long enough to discover if it's royal blue, or ocean blue or whatever other kind of funky blue the Whistles marketing wonks might have dreamed up. It's just blue. She remembers some advertising tosh on the telly once, 'a new blue whiteness'. Maybe this shirt is a new blue *blueness*, possibly? And a hundred and fifty-nine pounds. *A shirt?*

She'd imagined herself as Julia Roberts in *Pretty Woman*, wearing a massive hat, three or four of those big paper bags swinging from each hand, full of Sweaty Betty clobber or Mint Velvet gear, 'treating herself', as she exited on to Fifth Avenue and hailed a taxi. But she's got one John Lewis plastic bag at her feet as she cowers in the store's coffee shop with a cappuccino and a slice of lemon drizzle cake, wondering what's wrong with her.

Why does she think Freddie has taken leave of his senses for spending over three hundred quid on a bottle of wine? Why can't she spend a hundred and fifty on a nice shirt? *Ultimate* shirt? Ultimate *silk* shirt...? It would last a damn sight longer than his bloody wine. She'd have it for years. Imagine if she wore it once a month for a year? Special occasions? Not that they have twelve special occasions a year – but never mind. What would that be? Just over ten quid a wear? That's not excessive. Compared to over three hundred quid for a bottle of wine. Sixty quid a bloody glass. Poppy probably drank a tenner's worth and almost spat it out.

She scans the coffee shop: Norwich's great and good enjoying a morning out. Who are these people who don't work? A fair number are obviously retired, and able to afford John

Lewis coffees and lunches. Some of them have glasses of wine. At lunchtime? Probably that expensive Marqués de Wherever stuff that Freddie bought. If they make a white. The majority are women, in little clutches of twos and threes, well dressed, carefree laughter, more bags piled onto the adjacent chairs than Alice has managed (dared?) to collect. And she bets none of them are even millionaires. Where would the millionaires be? They wouldn't be in John Lewis, would they? In Norwich? No. They'd be in Monaco, possibly on a yacht. Or on Fifth Avenue, New York, in Macy's. Or is it Bloomingdale's? Which is the posh shop? The Harrods of NYC? Is it both of them? And do any of them have an apostrophe?

You see, that's part of the problem right there. Not the apostrophe. The posh shops in New York. A millionaire would know which of them was posh. A millionaire, a real one, would know how to buy a yacht; they'd know how many staff you'd need to hire in order to crew it. Alice and Freddie don't know any of that stuff. And, she muses further, there must be different types of millionaires, mustn't there?

She sips her John Lewis cappuccino and attempts to construct a hierarchy of millionaires. There's royalty. Prince Harry and all that mob. They're millionaires, probably billionaires. But they'd never rub shoulders with the likes of her and Freddie. Same with the Beckhams. They're never going to be coming over for tea. So, what sort of millionaires are she and Freddie? Second division millionaires? Non-celeb millionaires? Is that the difference? Celebs and non-celebs? Or are there other categories of millionaire before you get to the Freddie and Alice type? There are inherited millionaires who aren't necessarily royalty, dukes and barons and the like; there are people who've earned their money by building multi-million-pound businesses in their garage. Are the lottery winners yet another category? She has a feeling the lottery winners might be the lowest division in the millionaire league. She imagines the royals, the celebrities, the inherited, and the earners probably all look down on the lottery winners. She's no idea why she thinks this, and whether or not it's really true. And that's partly what scares her about Freddie's plan to 'move away from the oiks', which she fears is code for moving to a gated community where millionaires live. Real ones. Although maybe not the royals. Would they be ostracised by the other divisions of millionaires when they discover that Freddie and Alice are lottery winners? Freddie never considers this type of thing, but it can keep Alice awake at night. It's pretty confusing, however it's organised. And imposter syndrome is crushing her like a welcome hug from an ogre.

She tries to clear her mind, wipe it of any background and habits that she has. What does she want to do with all this money? Even thinking about the three hundred thousand Freddie has gifted her, what would she do with that? What is she going to do with it? Private schools for the kids? Even a mixed one? No. She's quite sure about that. She feels even more guilty now about having let Freddie get his way over Ryan. Wonders if she can still find a way to short-circuit that decision. So, how about the six-star holiday Freddie is researching? She knows she's happy at the three-star Casa Lola, with their friends. But maybe once? She could compromise over that, couldn't she? Although, if she was making the decision, then no, she'd go back to where she knows they're happy. And the house move? That's really tricky. A new house not too far away from where they live now, so that she and the children wouldn't lose touch with their friends? Maybe. But a new town, far away, where they know nobody? Maybe in some kind of a gated community? With all the other categories of millionaires looking down on the lottery winners...? That seems too much like an exercise in inviting the Beckhams or Prince Harry and Megan over for tea.

She hoovers up the last crumbs of her cake, drains her cappuccino, picks up her twenty quid top in the John Lewis plastic bag and wonders if she's ever going to be able to adapt to Freddie's new life of luxury. Wonders what he'll think of the new top that she's treated herself to? Will he even notice?

As she steps out onto All Saints Green – no hat, one plastic bag – she has a thought: should she, could she, hail a taxi? It's a thought a real millionaire, or millionaire's bloody wife, would have without thinking – if it's possible to have a thought without thinking. She tries to remember if she's ever hailed a taxi before. Not phoned for a minicab. A real taxi. Like they have in London or New York. Hailed one? On the street? She's sure she's seen black taxis in Norwich. She's simply never considered hailing one. She likes this word, *hail*, she's realising.

And then, like a vision, one appears tootling around the corner and she panics. What does she do? Does she have to shout 'Taxi'? Like they do in the films? Leaning out into the street, one arm up, fingers stretched out.

'Taxi!'

It's as she's shouting, leaning out into the street, with her arm up, and her fingers stretched out, that she notices two passengers in the back. And that little yellow light above the windscreen? It isn't on. So, the taxi keeps tootling on past her. And she wishes the ground would open up, not as unlikely an event in Norwich as it might be in many other cities. But it doesn't, and she scans the street to see who might have witnessed her humiliation. Hopefully, no one she knows. But nobody is paying the millionaire's wife any attention. And, lo and behold, here comes another, with its yellow light on above the windscreen. And she... she can't. She nearly does, but she can't. What would be the point? What would it prove? She likes walking; it's a beautiful day; she can detour along the River Wensum. If being a millionaire means choosing what you want, then that's what she wants. She wants to walk home, through the park, along the river, swinging her John Lewis bag.

She strolls along Riverside Walk, crosses Pull's Ferry and sashays past Cow Tower, feeling good. Feeling for all the world like a millionaire. She spots a table on the terrace at The Ribs of Beef and orders herself a sandwich and a half of shandy, spur of the moment, almost giggling as she watches herself, as if on a stage. *This is what millionaires do*, she thinks as she watches a fit-looking young guy row one of those racing canoes or kayaks or whatever they are along the river. She lifts her glass to him in salute, and he nods back. They do exactly what they want. They have time and they have money. She's made her walk home slightly longer than it needed to be, but she doesn't care.

For, bonus upon bonus, she's wearing a pair of her oldest, most comfortable and, mercifully, flattest shoes.

20

THE OLD BOYS' NETWORK

FREDDIE'S TAKEN the day off work. He and Ryan are on a visit to Freddie's old school, Grewsomes, out in the wilds of North Norfolk. Alice has cried off, unable to bear the prospect of a morning of Bunteresque backslapping in the school Freddie used to describe as a hellhole but is now convinced is exactly what Ryan needs.

They've had a hushed discussion. It wasn't a row, but nearly. She'd made her pitch: all of Ryan's friends were going to the local secondary; it would be a two-hour round-trip, morning and evening, for someone; it would add two hours to Ryan's day; their results weren't actually that much better than the secondary his friends were going to; she thought he was being pompous and Ryan would pay the price.

She didn't actually voice this last objection, although she got close. She was worried for a while that Freddie was going to hit her with 'Well, you got your own way with Poppy, so I'm going to get my own way with Ryan', and she would have hated it if they'd come to that. But he didn't, to her relief. But he probably thought it. His heels were dug in, stronger than hers, even though his were even flatter than hers. He'd offered her the Porsche for the school run; he'd have got it long before Michaelmas term started, he said.

Alice wondered if she'd heard right. Michaelmas? It was as if Freddie was having a full relapse back into the good old days, which not very long ago had usually been called the bad old days. Was this really happening? Did she still recognise her husband? When was this madness going to end?

So, she couldn't go. Couldn't set her face into a rictus smile for the hour or so it would take to wander along the musty corridors, passing men (all of Freddie's teachers had been men) dressed in dusty mortarboards and capes (gowns, he'd corrected her). So, she'd stayed at home. And cursed Freddie. And cursed herself.

The only chink of something that wasn't dark and musty and old-fashioned and pompous was that Ryan seemed almost keen. Well, he hadn't objected. He simply looked a bit small and defenceless and in danger of having a big decision go against him, just like Freddie had, when his dad decided Freddie couldn't go to university. So, Freddie could take him on his own. This was his decision; she wanted no part of it. And if it all went wrong, as she feared it might, she'd murder him – in one of the unspeakably painful ways she's read about in her novels.

'Cash,' Freddie says, proudly, as the heavy oak door opens with an eerie creak, and he extends his hand. He's already explained to Ryan how the boys all call each other by their surnames, well, usually. One of the many little quirks Ryan will come to love, Freddie has promised. He's also dying to introduce Ryan to Mr Wiseman. *Can't believe he's still alive, let alone still working.* Mr Wiseman was Freddie's favourite teacher. Well, he was the only teacher, pretty much, that Freddie actually liked. Taught maths, which had been half the appeal. It had given Freddie such a thrill when the secretary had told him that his appointment would be with Mr Wiseman.

'Sorry?' says the spotty-faced youth in the sports jacket – without gown or mortarboard – as he grips Freddie's hand tentatively.

'Freddie Cash,' Freddie says, unsure now.

'Oh! I *see*,' says the youth, relief flooding his spots. 'I thought you were looking to get a bill paid. No matter. Charlie Wiseman.'

'Oh,' Freddie gasps, his face dropping. 'I thought–'

The youth stares at him.

'I was a boy here; Mr Wiseman used to teach me maths. I thought–'

'Oh, right,' replies the youth. 'My uncle. Died a few years ago.' He smiles, like it wasn't news that caused him any sorrow. Might even have celebrated by the look on his face. 'Come in. And this is Ryan?'

'Yes, Cash,' Freddie says again, louder, staring expectantly at young Mr Wiseman, who simply looks confused.

'Hi, Ryan,' says the youth. 'Come on in.'

Freddie's eyes widen and his jaw slackens as they enter the lobby area. He's prepared himself for a little time warp experience: dark-wood panelling; twisty staircase; shiny parquet flooring, probably with old Dodgem, the caretaker, giving it a polish with that noisy machine he never seemed to be without. But no, Freddie's TARDIS has malfunctioned; the place has been gutted. The dark-wood panelling has been replaced by brightly painted walls, those that still exist. It seems bigger, there used to be a wall here, another over there. The wooden staircase has gone too. In its place, a lift, all glass and shiny steel. The stairs are now over in a corner, more shiny steel. And the flooring is now some sort of lino. It looks like the head office of a bank – a better bank than the one Freddie works in.

'Changed a bit since your day, eh?' young Mr Wiseman says as he leads them down a corridor and out into what used to be a quadrangle – they called it the quad, he's prepared Ryan – but is now an extension of the original building, but done in poured concrete, pretty brutally. They finally reach a playground. Freddie has warned Ryan that the boys aren't allowed to play football at playtimes. They're encouraged to talk or read. So, the multiple games of shirt-sleeved football in progress raise a smile of relief and pleasure on Ryan's face, and a frown on Freddie's.

'We didn't play football at recess in my day,' Freddie grumbles.

'Really?' says young Mr Wiseman, looking like he's expecting Freddie to bore him with news that they held conker championships instead, or had hopping races.

'No. We walked. And talked.'

Young Mr Wiseman nods and turns towards the games fields. The school's pride and joy in Freddie's day. Less than half of them are still there. The rest have been covered by an enormous single-storey building. It looks like a sixties temporary prefabricated building, possibly housing scientists testing anthrax. Freddie's frown gathers a layer of shock.

'My God,' he gasps.

'Progress,' young Mr Wiseman says, proudly. 'This is the new STEM block.'

'Stem?'

'Science, technology, engineering and maths,' Ryan says. 'They've just opened one of these at our local school...'

Freddie's eyes search beyond the building; his frown deepens further.

'I can only see one rugger pitch,' he says, almost as an accusation.

Mr Wiseman nods. 'Yes. Football has become very popular.'

They walk further on, and half a dozen more soccer pitches appear from behind the STEM block.

'We didn't have any football pitches in my day,' Freddie moans.

———

Freddie is quiet in the car on the way home; Ryan chatters excitedly about the school having three football teams. In his briefcase, Freddie has placed the school brochure, also available online, plus a number of curriculum documents that the school prepares for new boys, advising them on the catch-up work they should do over the summer. Freddie also has a list of private tutors he might wish to employ in order to bring Ryan 'up to speed', especially as the school has accelerated programmes for all the STEM subjects, so Ryan is almost certainly 'a little way behind' the other boys.

It doesn't really matter, Freddie reasons to himself as he considers the invasion of football, the disappearance of the quad, the plethora of female teachers they spotted on their tour, the absence of gowns and mortarboards, the boys shouting Christian names at each other. And, possibly the biggest change of all, since his day, not that this mattered at all, they were all obviously very bright. Had to be, didn't they? They wouldn't let them in if they weren't. Would they? But he had noticed. No prejudice, of course. He's not in the least bit prejudiced. But he had noticed, just an observation, nothing more – there were an awful lot of colonial-coloured faces in evidence...

Alice hugs Ryan when she sees his smiling face and hears his news about football in the playground and football fixtures on the weekends, *and tennis*. Freddie puts the kettle on.

'So, you like it?' she says, tentatively, hoping Ryan's face won't drop as he remembers some of the non-football features of his new school.

'Yeah, it seems okay. I saw one boy who went to our school last year, can't remember his name.'

Freddie brings the teas in as Ryan escapes into the garden.

'Go well?' Alice asks, a sliver of hope in her voice and on her face. Maybe a new start for Ryan will be good for him? At least he's happy, or seems to be. It's a concession she can make; a card she can play later on – when Freddie attempts to move them all to Cornwall, maybe? Or onto a yacht in Monaco. *We can't move Ryan twice, so disruptive.* Yes. She keeps a poker face as Freddie stirs his tea.

'It's changed a bit,' he says.

'For the better?'

He takes a sip. 'Not sure. It wasn't Mr Wiseman we saw. His nephew. Mr Wiseman's dead.'

'Oh. That's a shame. You wanted to see him, didn't you?'

'I suppose so. But I should have known. He had to be close to retirement when he taught me.'

'Has he got a lot of catching up to do? Ryan? Over the summer?'

Freddie shrugs. 'Some. I can help him with it. But it will do him good. Push him on.'

Alice suppresses a shudder at the thought of Ryan having to study during the summer. Ah well, one summer; maybe it will help him, in the end. She accepts the risk with a heavy heart. She still hates the language of it: all the pushing that children seem to need, according to certain pushy adults. She prefers the thought of children pushing, or pulling, themselves, like Poppy with her Spanish. Out of interest, asking for books so she can talk to Rosalita and Carlos. But Alice is already regretting having signed her up for Duolingo Spanish. Poppy's asking to be on it more and more. Why is everything so complicated? Alice is toying with the idea of suggesting Spain over New Year, as well as in the summer. Poppy would die with anticipation, and Alice is happier for Poppy to talk with real Spanish children instead of a pixelated owl. And it would be interesting to see Mallorca out of season. Don't the Spaniards do those Christmas market thingies? Alice wants to show willing for the jet-set lifestyle. As long as Freddie doesn't go the whole hog and suggest Christmas in the Maldives, or Vietnam.

'They still swishing around with their hats and capes on?' she asks, hoping to lighten the mood a little.

He sighs. 'Gowns! No. They seem to have dropped all that. Plus, there are some female teachers on the staff. Young ones, too.'

Alice smiles at the idea of a staff meeting, sometime in the last twenty years, when they'd decided to 'modernise' the school, ditch the mortarboards and *gowns*, replace them with women. She can imagine angry teacups flying across the common room (as Alice has been taught it's called); furious mortarboards frisbeeing in the opposite direction; huffing and puffing on the front page of the *Grewsome Mercury*.

'A lot more colonial pupils than in my day,' he says, quietly. 'I'm not being prejudiced. They say Indians are brilliant mathematicians. Even the girls. Might drive the standards up.'

'What? Have they started admitting *girls*?' She's teasing him now. Always her bypass around an argument.

'No! Gracious no. I mean, no real reason why they shouldn't, of course. But, you know, tradition and all that...'

Alice can see he hasn't got an argument. Just a bunch of

tentatively held prejudices that he doesn't think too hard about, and she's never brave enough to challenge him on.

'Are they still doing French and Latin?'

'Yes, but Spanish is also an option, instead of French. Ryan was pleased with that.'

Alice takes his hand. *This might work,* she thinks. *This might work...*

PART 3

THE ALL-INCLUSIVE HOLIDAY

21

THE SPANISH SWANS

It's Freddie's holiday. His treat, he's taken to calling it. He's cancelled their week in the three-star Casa Lola (that they've used for years, and Alice and the children really like) and booked them into a six-star, all-inclusive hotel up the hill for a fortnight.

According to Freddie, six-star luxury hotels are springing up all over the island, but this one has been there for years, so is probably the best. You'll love it, he insists, having browsed Booking.com for all of twenty minutes. He's even cancelled their Ryanair tickets and instead reserved business class (there was no first class, to his annoyance) on British Airways from Heathrow into Palma. It's a bit of a hassle, because Ryanair fly from Stanstead (just down the M11) and BA fly from Heathrow (all the way round the M25). But it'll be worth it, he says, as LHR, as he's taken to calling it, is a much nicer airport – not that he's ever flown from there.

So, Freddie is as excited as he was as a six-year-old on his first trip to Butlins, and the rest of them are a little bit flat – although a two-week holiday instead of their usual one has softened the blow somewhat.

Alice accepts it, is at least willing to try it. She'd have preferred two weeks at Casa Lola as the best of all possible options. It's being threatened by the growing plethora of six-star megahotels that are loss-leading with BOGOF offers, two weeks for the price of one, undercutting the smaller, family-run places. Like Casa Lola. But six stars should be fun, and she likes seeing Freddie so happy. So proud. His achievement. His treat. And Freddie is set on six stars, whatever it means.

But underneath the cover of all the excitement, Alice can see Ryan's a bit put out; she knows he likes Ryanair: *Ryan* – air... And he and Poppy are clearly a little glum cos they're not staying with Rosalita and Carlos. The four of them have become good friends, despite communicating mostly in Spanglish and off-the-cuff sign language. Moreover, since Ryan and Poppy have started studying Spanish at school, their holiday friendship with Rosalita and Carlos has acted as a motivator. Poppy, in particular, has become almost obsessed with looking up any and every Spanish word she hears.

Alice herself is also slightly disappointed, mainly because she knows the children are, and that they're trying hard to hide it – but also because she won't be having her own little chats, her Spanglish *charlas* (Poppy's informed her it's a sort of Spanish for chinwag) with Lola. Casa Lola, Poppy has also reliably informed her, means Lola's house. It's a funny relationship that's developed between Alice and Lola.

Alice speaks very little Spanish; *pan* and *lechuga* are her party pieces. But Lola has a front-of-house command of English which, while so heavily accented it sometimes makes it sound like she's speaking Greek, is actually quite serviceable. The best thing about Lola is she's so very patient, and dogged, and she really seems keen to make time for their little *charlas*. She's always determined to make sure she understands what Alice is attempting to say, especially when she isn't ordering a lettuce sandwich. And Alice is linguistically aware enough to speak slowly, stick to the present tense, listen as Lola offers her interpretation of what Alice might have said: 'So, you say Don Freddie, he no like hees work, he want new work, what he can do?'

Alice also admires Lola – running her own business with Don Antonio, a smile always decorating her face, doing all the cooking (except for the weekly *paella*) because she wants to, enjoying seeing people eating the food she's prepared. And then, when the day is done, she's always keen to join Alice and Freddie around the pool for a glass of wine and an attempt at international relations which, being Spanish, mostly means talking about the children.

But Freddie says they won't actually be that far away from Casa Lola, and they can maybe visit for a day, or an afternoon, or a meal. To say *hola*, he says, with a laugh. Pretty much all he is able to say *en español*, Alice thinks, with a laugh. Ah well, she concludes, at least they'll probably have bigger parasols at a six-star hotel, so Freddie might not end up with a cricked neck, or sunburn, or both. And thank God he hasn't decided to book the Seychelles or Thailand. He's stuck with Mallorca, he says, because he thinks they should explore the idea of a villa, depending on the prices, or maybe a luxury flat. Not a bog-standard flat on the Costa del whatever it is on Mallorca – but a luxury one.

'We should take evening wear,' Freddie suddenly says as they're packing.

Alice looks at him like he's suggested squeezing the stereo system into his case. *Evening wear?* she asks with her eyes and eyebrows. A bit of a bemused nose and lip curl combo, too.

'You know! They'll probably dress for dinner. Like they do on *Downton*. Dress to the tens!'

Alice wants to laugh. She does know what evening wear is.

She simply hasn't got any. Well, not the stuff she knows Freddie is imagining: the ballgowns and tiaras that Lady Grantham dons when the king comes to visit. She's got a couple of nice floral frocks; her mother always called them that. That one out of C&A, before it went belly up – C&A that is, not the frock – is pretty. Quite nice... still. And she has a string of fake pearls. But Freddie, she knows, isn't thinking C&A; he's thinking Dolce & Gabbana, Stella McCartney. Although, he isn't, she quickly concludes; the only Stella Freddie's in any way familiar with is Artois.

'I'll pack a suit,' he says, nodding gravely. Like he's got a choice of at least a dozen and is going to be hours choosing. 'Might pick up a dicky bow in the hotel shop. You know...'

Does she? She actually wonders which channel she's tuned to. One of the comedy ones, for sure. A dicky bow? He'll have to get a clip-on, cos he certainly won't know how to tie it, and neither does she. She wishes now, sort of, that she'd bought a pair of heels when she was, or wasn't, treating herself in John Lewis. And she should have checked out their evening wear. She'll have to go back, she thinks, with a shudder. Or maybe, she suddenly remembers, she could go on a little spree in the Corte Inglés.

El Corte Inglés is a sort of Spanish John Lewis; there are two branches in Palma. She could take Poppy; they could ask what batwings are. Or, rather, Poppy could ask, having first translated it into Spanish. She might even understand the answer. If it ever rains on their holidays, or it's too hot for the beach, or if they simply fancy a change, El Corte Inglés is Alice's go-to alternative. The kids are always game: El Corte Inglés has multiple coffee shops and *restaurantes* (that means restaurants – Poppy) in every store. Freddie is always keen, too – anything to get away from the heat and the sun and the too-small loungers and the too-little shade. Plus, all the staff in El Corte Inglés are super helpful and deferential, and many of them speak *inglés* (that's English – says Poppy). But Alice thinks she knows another, almost secret reason why Freddie is keen to spend a morning or an afternoon in El Corte Inglés – the staff always call him *Caballero*.

The way Freddie preens whenever he's addressed as *Caballero* makes Alice suspect that, in his mind at least, it means something very prestigious – like Your Honour, or Lord. He preens in a similar way whenever Lola and Don Antonio call him *Don* Freddie, which is almost always. *Caballero* sounds a bit ridiculous to Alice's English ear, like they're taking the piss. But she knows they aren't; all the men are addressed as *Caballero*. And Freddie clearly thinks it's his due, whatever it means. She'll ask Poppy.

'I'll tell the children to pack something nice...'

Alice watches him skip out of their room. It's lovely to see, so much enthusiasm and anticipation. He's possibly more excited than the kids, although Ryan has packed his Spanish textbook, trying hard to keep up with Poppy who's graduated on to a kids' phrasebook. At least that's one bit of his summer prep they won't have to 'push'.

Poppy is positively volcanic with *ganas*. It means enthusiasm, she's lectured Alice gravely. They also have a word *entusiasmo* (*entusiasma* for the girls), but *ganas* is somehow better, according to Señorita Poppy, cos it has more of an 'up for it' vibe. Poppy's certainly up for it. She also wants to be called Amapola while they're in Spain. La Señorita Amapola. It's Spanish for poppy, the flower. Alice guessed that straight away, but feigned ignorance so that Poppy– sorry, la Señorita Amapola – could preen, just a little.

So, Alice is very much looking forward to going on holiday – with her three children.

They're off early the next morning. Ridiculously early. And only because their business-class tickets entitle them to visit the British Airways private lounge, and Freddie doesn't want to miss that. Well, he doesn't want them, the children that is, and maybe Alice, to miss that.

Alice thinks he's like a squirrel, alone under a fully laden oak tree on a windy day: *Look at that, smoked salmon*, like they've never eaten smoked salmon before; *Look, there's Brie...*

'Is there any caviar?' he asks the uniformed server, as Alice attempts to do a David Blaine style disappearing trick.

'In the evenings,' comes the cut-glass reply.

'Of course,' says Freddie with a knowing nod and a blush.

So, why has he booked lunchtime flights? And in both directions?

They're enjoying the freebie grub: Poppy and Ryan indulging in plates piled high with crisps; Alice has a cheese baguette; Freddie's plate is stocked with things Alice doubts he knows the names of. Some of them are seafood, not his usual choice if he's paying. But today, it's free, so he can take a risk. Alice thinks he's more excited than the children. He's certainly more edgy.

'Where's my passport?' he splutters all of a sudden, flakes of a puff-pastry thingy snowing into his lap.

'You put it in your trouser pocket.'

'No, I took it out of there because you said I'd bend it when I sat down.'

'So, where did you put it?'

'I thought I put it in my bag. But it's not there. And I remember thinking I'd need it to hand when we went thr– Ah! Here it is, shirt pocket.'

'That's a good place for it.'

'I think I'll put it in my jacket...'

On board, he plays with his seat, which reclines into a fully flat bed. *Look at this!* The children play with theirs for less time than Freddie.

'The drinks are free, aren't they?' he asks as the steward arrives.

They're picked up at the airport by a limo – Freddie's surprise – which cruises out towards their, well, his, very own Camelot. There are more drinks in the limo. If he says limo one more time (*limusina*, Poppy informs them all after a quick check of her phrasebook) Alice swears she'll scream. But, hey, they're on holiday, he's happy. Well, he's a bit sloshed actually, since the steward on the flight unwisely told him that even the champagne was free. And there's more champers in the *limusina*. Alice takes a water (*agua* – Poppy) to Freddie's quizzical look; Ryan has another Coke; and Poppy's now crossing and uncrossing her legs.

The hotel is impressive; Alice will grant him that. Lots of concrete and glass, lots of places to lounge, lots of flunkies piling their luggage onto one of those bellhop trolley thingies she thought only existed in American movies, and Freddie hasn't got any euros to tip them, so he has to do it in pound coins and apologies. Ryan has opened their French doors onto the terrace and Poppy's found the toilet just in time.

The children have an adjoining room with their own balcony, twin beds and en suite. The towels are on the beds, expertly folded into the shape of swans – *cisnes*, says Poppy, *nariz* in the dictionary part of her guidebook again. Poppy wants a photo; swears she won't wash for the whole fortnight. Then she discovers that Freddie and Alice's swans are bigger, made from bath towels, *cisnes grandes*, positively *enormes*. So now Poppy needs a photo of the whole swan family, and Alice is worried that none of them will be allowed to shower. The baby swans – *cisnes* – are reverentially carried through to join Mummy and Daddy *cisne* for the photo shoot.

'They might do giraffes tomorrow,' Alice whispers, in jest. But it sends Poppy into the *in need of resuscitation* category, and Alice starts to wonder if maybe it's going to work out fine...

'Well! This is nice,' Freddie announces, as they gather on the balcony after photographing the swans in every conceivable 'wedding day' combination – Cash family and *cisne familia* all together; la Señorita Amapola and *cisne familia* together; Amapola and Ryan with baby *cisnes*, etc., etc., ad nauseum. They stare down towards the enormous blue pool, which is surrounded by enormous blue parasols, Alice is relieved to see. 'A swim?'

There are sunbeds aplenty, fluffy towels available from a small *quiosco*, drinks orders taken within moments of them settling. Alice and the kids are in the water in seconds. Not long afterwards, Freddie is snoring. No more than a quarter of the sunbeds are occupied, so either the place is near empty or most of the guests are on the beach, a short walk down some steps. But Freddie's snoring would disturb hippos were there a nearby waterhole; it wouldn't even have to be that nearby.

Alice hurries out of the pool and tries to shush him. Not happening. So, she gives him the sort of hefty shove that usually quietens him. What was that TV programme they used to enjoy? *Waking the Dead?* Not this one. So, last resort, she shakes her dripping hair over his chest, showering him with cold water. He shudders, his eyes open, but there's nobody at home.

'Freddie! You're snoring,' she snaps at him. 'People are staring.'

She can see he's working hard to keep his eyes open, but the effort is too much, and they close like two bleary suns executing a synchronised setting manoeuvre over the Mediterranean. She shakes him again and sprays him with more water, this time in his face.

'Freddie! Wake up.'

'Wha–?'

'Wake up! You're disturbing people. You're snoring.'

He takes a huge breath, sighs it out, then looks around like he's no idea what continent he's on.

'I'll take you to the room,' Alice says, lifting his hand. 'You can sleep it off there...'

22

THE OYSTERS

FREDDIE LOOKS splendid in his black satin dicky bow, albeit a clip-on, despite the splitting headache, he's confessed to Alice, which has appeared post his *siesta*. Alice has on her C&A summer frock, her fake pearls, a splash of perfume, and the highest heels she owns. Ryan is smart in his best dark shorts and a crisp shirt and mini dicky that Freddie also bought in the hotel shop. Alice has almost successfully put a crease in Ryan's shirt and shorts by hiding them under the mattress since their arrival. Poppy is in her favourite swishy skirt and spaghetti-string top combo. (Spaghetti is *espaguetis*, she tells anyone who'll listen.) Freddie leads them proudly down to dinner.

Half the dining room is in darkness: chairs at the far end upside down on tabletops, curtains drawn, mothballed. They're shown to a table set for six, near a window, by a waiter in uniform; the cloth napkins in more origami shapes, delighting Poppy. Alice now has more photos of fabric animals than she does of their poolside frolics. She vows to reverse that ratio by the time they get home.

Mercifully, the menu is in English, and the children point excitedly at the fish fingers, nuggets and burger options at the bottom, underneath all the *emulsions*, *essences* and *smears*, *nestling* (or, maybe, *nesting*) amid the *harvested* or *foraged* food aimed at the adults. Freddie orders a (hand-selected) Rioja, Alice wondering how it might otherwise have been selected. Might a dog have picked it out with its teeth? 'Probably not up to the standard of the one we had back home, but no matter, it'll be a good one,' Freddie informs them all.

They order their food and settle: Freddie happy to find the word steak amid the *mousses*, *jus* and *foams*, while Alice chooses fish in something unfathomable, cooked in a way she suspects even Jamie Oliver wouldn't recognise. Ryan and Poppy are thrilled with fish fingers and chicken nuggets respectively and assume the chef will know how to cook them without *emulsion*. Alice, Ryan and Poppy then compare the first blush of sun on their arms – Freddie keeps his jacket on. But not for long. The windows are open, and the air is warm, so he sheds it onto the back of his chair and rolls up his sleeves as their food arrives – ready to tuck in.

The dining room is filling up – a bit. There is a fair mixture of types although, there are two in predominance. The first are the twenty-somethings: males in loud-coloured Hawaiian shirts and tailored shorts; females in skimpy, tight, and occasionally extremely short cocktail dresses in uproarious colours usually seen in Poppy's paintbox. Freddie's eyebrows bounce in surprise. The second grouping are elderly, certainly more elderly than Freddie and Alice and, credit to him, Freddie was right, they have 'dressed for dinner'. Just a different type of dress – from a different era, and possibly a different social class. Or maybe they're filming an episode of *Downton Abbey* on Mallorca, and these are the extras for a Grand Ball.

There's a pair of this second set halfway across the room. He's wearing a striped blazer, sky blue with a red pinstripe. He's also got on one of those coloured shirts, it's pink with a white collar, and the tie suggest 'a school'. She's in an evening gown, red satin, blood red, but slit down the front to her belly button; she looks like she's heading for the Oscars red carpet, but she isn't. And suddenly, it becomes clear why the waiter has put them on a table with six chairs around it...

'Oh! They've started,' striped blazer barks with a loud jolt, as the waiter peels away and the red dress stands beside him, staring like they're waiting to join the Cash family in a jacuzzi, but have spotted a bobbing turd.

'Oh, I'm sorry, we didn't–'

But Freddie's embryonic apology is stillborn as the blazer is occupied with pulling out the dress's chair and settling her on it before sitting down himself. There is a silence, during which Alice catches Ryan's eye and communicates with a hard look that he shouldn't stare so brazenly at so much brazenly displayed cleavage. Hopefully, Freddie won't need a similar pep-stare. The silence is eventually broken by the blazer.

'Terrance,' he announces with an odd little shake of the head, 'and Kathleen. So pleased.'

'Oh, right,' Freddie stumbles. 'I'm Frederick, and this is Alice, Penelope and Ryan.' He stretches across the table in an effort to shake Terrance's hand, but Terrance rears backwards like *Frederick's* pulled a gun.

'First day?' Terrance asks, as Freddie eases himself back into his seat, hand unshaken, gun back in its holster. 'Delightful couple sharing the last fortnight, Winston and Melanie, *very* nice people. Excellent conversation. Eton and Roedean.'

'You've been here a fortnight already?' Poppy gasps, like Terrance has informed them that he owns the hotel.

Terrance turns and stares at Poppy as if a parrot from the garden has landed on the table. 'Been here a *month*, young lady. Be here *another* before home.'

Poppy's eyes and mouth show a degree of shock usually

displayed by the audience at late-night showings of Stephen King films. Freddie suddenly notices that Terrance is wearing a Rolex. Why hasn't he got his yet? He's tempted to compliment Terrance on his choice, tell him about the model he's considering for himself, the gold one, but even Freddie can feel that this might come across as somewhat needy, trying too hard to impress.

'So, you like it here?' Freddie offers instead, a little stiffly, like he's desperate not to put his foot in something he can't quite imagine. 'Would come again?'

'Been coming for twenty-eight years,' Terrance roars, his voice getting louder with each syllable as if he can't understand why Freddie hasn't known this. 'But this might be the last.'

'Oh.' Freddie looks crestfallen.

'Going downhill, you see? Losing custom hand over fist, so they've upgraded the old place to try to keep up with the newer six-star hotels being built in the area. I can tell you, nothing's changed here except the zoo-animal origami towels and a new chef. However, they've somehow managed to attract the riff-raff, as you've no doubt noticed.' Terrance opens his palm in the direction of a table of twenty-somethings who have noisily discovered that cocktails are available with dinner. There's a bit of whooping and giggling, and everyone seems to be ordering Sex on the Beach.

'We've got swans,' Poppy announces, proudly. 'Baby ones, too.'

Terrance glances at her like she's farted, loudly.

The waiter intervenes momentarily, long enough for Terrance to mumble, 'The usual,' with a weary nod.

'Do carry on,' Terrance suddenly says, pointing towards the four plates that nobody has dared touch since he uttered his shocked, 'They've started!'

Freddie picks up his knife and fork. 'Oh, right. Sorry. We didn't know we'd be sharing a table…'

There's a prolonged silence as they start to eat again, and Terrance eyes the Sex on the Beachers. 'So, your first time here?' he finally asks.

'Mmm.' Freddie nods, chewing on his steak, which is a bit – chewy. 'We've been to the island before, but this is our first time at El Paraíso.' He pronounces it Par-hay-so, which elicits a frown from Terrance, like he thinks they may be staying somewhere else.

'We liked Casa Lola,' Poppy suddenly says, breaking the monopoly of male voices with a spirited squeak, causing Freddie to wince.

'Don't know it,' Terrance growls.

There's another silence as Poppy shovels nuggets and Ryan picks a fish finger up and bites the end off it. Freddie starts to sweat.

'School?' Terrance coughs.

'Sorry?'

'School? Which *school* did you go to?'

'Oh,' Freddie mutters. 'Grewsomes.'

Terrance looks puzzled. Shocked, even. His eyes widen, the corners of his mouth droop like an unhappy bloodhound.

'Norfolk,' Freddie mumbles, as if it might explain everything. 'You?' he continues, as he forks an emulsion-slathered chip into his mouth.

Terrance stares at Freddie with a look of bafflement, then he points, both index fingers, at his tie: black with thin light-blue diagonal stripes.

'Oh, right, sorry,' says Freddie, nodding a *silly me* nod.

Terrance sighs an almost imperceptible sigh, his head shaking minutely, like he's discovered it's time to put down an old dog.

'I go to Unthank Primary School,' Poppy announces, proudly. 'It's also in Norfolk. In Norwich,' she clarifies when nobody responds.

Terrance and Kathleen's food arrives: oysters on a shell-shaped silver platter with crushed ice and lemon wedges.

'What are those?' Poppy blurts, eyes fixed warily on the slithery *mariscos*.

Terrance sits bolt upright and inspects her carefully, like he suspects she's pulling his leg. 'You've never tasted oysters?' he gasps. *You've never brushed your teeth?* He looks at Freddie like he's the worst parent he's ever met. Poppy shrugs.

Ryan intercedes, to Freddie's evident horror. 'My friend, Calum, at school, said he had them once. But I didn't believe him.'

Terrance smiles at Kathleen. Kathleen raises her eyes to the ceiling: *I blame the parents.*

'You must try them,' Terrance announces, Father Christmas doling out parcels. 'Who's first?'

Poppy flinches, like there's a live snake on the table.

'I'll go,' Ryan says, looking half as brave as he sounds. Terrance hands him an oyster and a small round-ended knife. Ryan puts the oyster shell onto his plate, picks up his fork, and tries to slice off a piece of the meat, like he's eating a fish finger the way Freddie would like him to.

'No, no, *no!*' Terrance gasps: *The youth of today!* 'Like *this*.' He holds the shell in his palm and slices under the oyster with the knife. Then he picks up a wedge of lemon and squeezes it over the oyster before tipping his head back and letting it slip off the shell into his mouth. 'Delicious,' he announces after he's chewed and swallowed, before Kathleen repeats the demonstration with the flourish of a magician's assistant. Poppy and Ryan stare like Terrance and Kathleen have removed most of their clothing, which Kathleen could obviously achieve in less time than it took her to down her first oyster of the night. Terrance hands the knife, and another oyster shell, back to Ryan.

Ryan picks up the shell and shoves the knife under the oyster's flesh. He saws backwards and forwards with the concentration of a brain surgeon, but maybe less finesse, then checks the oyster has parted from the shell. Then he squeezes on the lemon. Freddie, Alice and Poppy study him like he's about to undertake a spacewalk. Terrance and Kathleen, meanwhile, stare at Freddie, with no less interest. Ryan tips the oyster into his mouth and chews for a moment or two. There is silence around the table – and more Sex on the Beach next door.

'Well?' Terrance asks, as Ryan swallows.

Ryan nods. 'Mmmm, not bad. I could develop a taste for them.'

Terrance looks thrilled, nudging Kathleen with his elbow.

'Your turn, Poppy,' Ryan says, suddenly sounding like an international connoisseur, or gastronome, not that he could spell either, but they'll probably both be on his homework spellings for the summer. He hands her the knife.

Poppy picks the smallest oyster on the platter and prods at the flesh with the knife, shying away from it like it's a live cockroach wriggling in her hand, threatening to run up her arm and down the front of her *espaguetis* top. She then squeezes lemon juice all over the front of Freddie's shirt, and everybody laughs – except Freddie, who starts a flurry of huffing and puffing and flapping with his napkin. Undeterred, Poppy lets the oyster slip into her mouth, her eyes screwed tight.

'You have to chew it,' Ryan commands after a few seconds, expert in all things *mariscos*.

'Well?' Alice says, sounding worried.

'Poppy?' Freddie whispers, still dabbing at his shirt.

Poppy's face slowly changes from tight-eyed fear to tongue-expelling disgust and the (unchewed) oyster flies from her mouth, bounces once on the table, before exiting to the floor through the gap between Terrance and Kathleen. It ends up halfway to the Sex on the Beachers' table.

'Dis-*GUST*-ing!' Poppy bellows, coughing and spluttering onto her plate, as the others smile or laugh – all except Freddie, again, who looks distraught, and Alice, who's breathing a sigh of relief that the expelled oyster managed to avoid slipping down the front of Kathleen's dress. *That* would have been a disaster.

Poppy's expulsion of the oyster even silences the Sex on the Beachers for a moment...

Alice dabs at her make-up with a cotton ball. With Terrance insisting that they always drink a Chablis Grand Cru with oysters, Freddie ended up polishing off most of the Rioja on his own. So, she can now hear him snoring in the bed, and the children laughing through the partition door.

So, this is luxury? she thinks, wondering if she recognises the woman in the mirror. *The highlife?* She's surprised Freddie didn't make a great show of downing, or whatever you do, a few of Terrance's oysters. 'Don't agree with me,' he'd claimed when invited. 'Had them at bank dos,' he'd said, when she'd questioned him later about oysters not agreeing with him. He's never been to a bank do without her, always insists she comes, 'good form'. So, she knows that bank-do food never includes oysters. Sausage rolls from LIDL; cheddar cheese on cocktail sticks; floppy ham sandwiches with the crusts chopped off and cut into triangles was the nearest the food at a bank do ever got to the high life... She's no idea whether she'd like oysters or not. She's not really interested, and she certainly wasn't going to 'perform', like a seal, in front of Terrance and Kathleen. She smiles at the thought of her children – well, Ryan – eating oysters. Then she laughs at Poppy's reaction to the high life. Similar to her own, she thinks.

Freddie has disappointed her tonight. Fawning over Terrance and Kathleen like they were royalty. He reminded her a little of Basil Fawlty – a shorter one – bowing and scraping and trying to impress. She'd asked Freddie which school Terrance had gone to. The black and blue tie? He admitted he didn't know, even though he'd clearly pretended he did. Saving face. She remembers a bank ad she'd seen a few years back, on the TV, about saving face. It was a big thing in the Far East, the ad had claimed. Perhaps they'd meant the Far East of England.

This isn't the Freddie she married. Freddie's always been a little bit pompous. Only a little bit, though. It's hard to be that pompous when you haven't really got much to be pompous about. Except now he's staying at a six-star hotel, and will be getting his Porsche, and the children will be going to single-sex schools – well, Ryan. Poppy's saved. For now.

She's a little sad. It's not a state of mind she experiences often. Could she be losing him? Could they break up over this? This change that's happening to him? Like a male menopause. What do they call it? Manopause? Except, Freddie's having a moneypause. She banishes the thought of them breaking up and smiles, weakly, at her wit. She should write. She's always having good ideas. This would be a perfect situation for a novel, she muses. But would it be a comedy?

Or a tragedy?

23

THE CHANCE ENCOUNTER

FREDDIE IS NURSING his cognac-induced hangover under one of the enormous blue parasols surrounding the enormous blue pool. His throbbing head is the result of a second night trying to keep up with Terrance and Kathleen's alcohol-fuelled version of dinner. On the first night, with Terrance incredulously informing Freddie that one couldn't drink a red with oysters, and then he and Kathleen downing their Chablis Grand Cru like it was lemonade, Freddie seemed to think that he had to match them glass for glass with their Rioja. He didn't take account of the fact that Alice kept covering her glass with her hand after her customary one drink. So, the level of Rioja in Freddie's glass rose and fell like an excitable child on a new trampoline.

On the second night, Freddie, when Terrance and Kathleen suggested a cognac, nodded like he had a brandy before bed every night – with his chocolate digestive, perhaps? – having already joined Terrance and Kathleen through two bottles of Chablis Grand Cru, to go with his steak. Alice demurred, guessing correctly that 'a cognac' might in fact be a plural in T&K's bespoke dictionary of alcoholic vocab.

Alice takes the children to the nearby beach. It's straight out of what used to be called a travel brochure – but would now be called Booking.com. The waves are big enough to make Poppy and Ryan squeal with delight, and cause Alice a few wobbly moments. She joins in the squealing, so happy to see them behaving like children. Unlike Freddie, who she's still a little annoyed with for behaving like a child.

The beach seems a better choice than the pool, which has been occupied by the Sex-on-the-Beach brigade who play loud splashing games that Poppy doesn't like. Alice is also not keen on Ryan sharing the pool with such small bikinis, especially as they seem unlikely to restrain such large breasts amid the cocktail-fuelled excitement. They buy ice creams from a *chiringuito*, one of the temporary beach bars that pop up every year for the summer season. Poppy delights in translating all the flavours into English, raising Alice's eyebrows when she turns *ron y pasas* into rum'n'raisin without a blink. What *are* they teaching her at that school...? They stroll along the shore to dry off and are overtaken periodically by groups of loudly chatting Spanish women, wearing 1950s style swimwear and waving their hands like they're practising kung fu.

'So, how do you like the new hotel?' Alice asks breezily, all her trepidation well hidden behind a lick of *limón* – helpfully translated into 'lemon' by la Señorita Amapola.

There is much slurping of *ron y pasas* and *chocolate* – that's choc-oh-*lah*-tay in Poppy's expert opinion – but not much in terms of a reply. Poppy eventually shrugs.

'S'okay,' she concedes with all the enthusiasm of a death-row inmate passing judgement on the last meal menu. 'Are we going to have to eat *ostras* again?'

'Eat what?' Alice replies, staring at Poppy who's chasing a dribble of *ron y pasas* down the cone towards her small pink fist.

'Oysters. They're *ostras, en español*. I looked it up.'

Alice marvels at Poppy's dedication; she's dropping more and more Spanish words into her conversation. Alice wonders if she should worry about a new obsession – or is it simply the sort of genuine childlike enthusiasm she should be celebrating? She decides on the latter, and further vows to do all she can to encourage it, even if it means she might understand less and less of what Poppy says over the coming months – unless she signs herself up for a degree in Spanish at the OU.

'Right. *Ostras*. You'll have to tell Terrance you've learned a new word. He'll be impressed.' Alice isn't sure Terrance will be impressed, but she's damned if she's going to let him squash Poppy's desire to join in the conversation in her own little way. She never quite worked out whether Terrance's invitation for Ryan and Poppy to try the oysters – *ostras* – was a genuine wish to include them, or a nasty trick designed to humiliate them, and possibly Freddie and her as well. She's given Terrance the benefit of the doubt, for the moment, and wonders what 'benefit of the doubt' might be in Spanish.

More worrying is the fact they've discovered, over the first couple of days, that children are a rarity at El Paraíso. In fact, there seem to be only two: Ryan and Poppy. Alice has checked back over their booking details to see if Freddie had missed a bit that said the hotel was adults only, but no, there's no such stipulation. There are, however, a number of subtle hints that might have alerted an eagle-eyed sleuth more savvy in the lingo used in hotel website descriptions.

In its *Activities* section, the hotel boasts nightly *dancing*: ballroom on a Monday, Wednesday and Thursday; disco (with free bar) on Friday, Saturday and Sunday; and Flamenco on a Tuesday. There's no children's disco (without a free bar) listed. In fact, there's no mention of anything that might appeal to children or help adults attempting to holiday with children. There are no slides or water fountains in the pool, no childminding or babysitting services. Alice was confused by the fact there was a children's section of the menu, until she checked on the second night and discovered it wasn't a children's menu at all, it was simply labelled *International Dishes*. Chicken nuggets? Well, fair enough.

'No,' Alice says at last, snapping out of her reverie. 'You won't have to eat oys– *ostras* again. Just say *no gracias* if Terrance offers them to you again, like you did last night. They're not compulsory.'

Poppy smiles, and Alice isn't sure if she's smiling because the threat of more *ostras* has been lifted, or if it's because Alice is joining in the game of learning new Spanish words with her. Almost certainly both.

'Will we have to sit with Terrance and Kathleen every night?' Ryan asks, somewhat sheepishly. Alice winces, her very thought halfway through their first meal as she'd pieced together the jigsaw of the waiter showing them quite deliberately to a six-seater table and Terrance and Kathleen joining them a few minutes later like they were heading for their own dining room. Their second night had confirmed her (and obviously Ryan's) worst fears. At least breakfast had no set places, and lunch was wherever you chose to take it among the hotel's numerous bars and cafés.

'Well, it's sort of traditional, I think, in this type of hotel, that you mix and make friends. Don't you like Terrance and Kathleen? They've introduced you to oys– *ostras*, and you liked them.'

Ryan shrugs, Terrance and Kathleen seem to elicit a lot of shrugs. 'I didn't really. Like the *ostras*, that is. I was only trying to be polite. I didn't like them much; they were like chewy fried eggs with lemon juice.'

Alice hugs him: not sure whether he's gamely joining in with Poppy's everything *en español* game, or if he's doing a bit of catch-up work for his new school. 'Thank you for being so polite. That was a very nice thing to do.'

'I didn't mean to spit it out,' Poppy protests immediately, a look of horror taking over her face. 'It was so yucky, I got a shock.'

Alice laughs and hugs her as well. 'Poppy, your reaction was the funniest thing I've seen in ages.'

'It was epic,' Ryan agrees. 'Best bit of the holiday so far.' They're suddenly smiling, all of them, and Alice realises that the children haven't smiled, or laughed, as much as they usually did – at Casa Lola.

'Really?' Alice says, reading the room, smelling the coffee, licking her ice cream. 'Aren't you enjoying this hotel much?'

The silence and shrugging sadden her heart.

'I like the Spanish lessons,' Poppy squeals, suddenly animated. She and Ryan have signed up for the daily 10am Spanish lesson offered by the hotel, and attended every morning, returning to report to Alice that the other (all elderly) students 'aren't very good, don't listen properly', and 'keep forgetting the new words'. Their teacher, Iñigo, one of the waiters at the poolside bar, has collared Alice to tell her how wonderful Poppy and Ryan are in class, hands up for every question, no fear when invited to speak, and no, Poppy isn't bothering him when she swims over and clambers up onto one of the high stools for a bit of a *charla* – a chat.

There is a shout from behind them, 'Poppeee! Ryyyyan!' They turn. Rushing towards them are Carlos and Rosalita, the children from Casa Lola. They greet Ryan and Poppy like lifelong friends, and Alice marvels at how easily Ryan returns the bearhugs from Carlos, and Rosalita, no sign of any traditional British schoolboy reticence at being hugged by another boy (who hasn't just scored a goal), or, possibly worse, a girl (whether or not she had just scored a goal).

Alice is glad they're on a beach; the squealing and shrieking is ear-splitting as the children swap their news in a mixture of Spanish, English and hand gestures. It's clear Poppy and Ryan are beginning to emerge as sort of (very) amateur interpreters as neither Carlos nor Rosalita have much English, but Poppy and Ryan's Spanish is serviceable enough to mark them out in some rudimentary way as being functionally bilingual. It's only now that Alice notices how quiet her two have been over the past couple of days in the hotel. A machine gun of Spanglish from Carlos ends up with all four children looking at Alice.

'I didn't catch it,' Alice confesses, looking pleadingly, and hopefully, at Poppy and Ryan.

'Carlos said their hotel is right over there. He says you have to come and see Lola and Don Antonio. They'll be very happy to see you again...' says Ryan enthusiastically.

Alice takes a breath. She and Freddie have mentioned they might 'drop in' to say *hola* to Lola and Don Antonio, but neither have mentioned it since and, if she's honest, she feels awkward, like she's let them down somehow, deserting their beautiful little pension in favour of the six-star beast up the hill.

But the children are already fifty metres away, hopping and skipping around each other like an unruly gang of excited pups, still swapping hugs, chattering away like they all know what the others are saying. Alice kicks off to catch them up, failing to invent any suitable excuses on the spur of the moment. She fumbles with her phone to tell Freddie where they're headed and, secretly, feels excited to be seeing Lola again...

24

THE MOVEMENT OF THE EARTH

THE POOL at El Paraíso is almost deserted. The Sex on the Beachers are on the beach, having – fun. Terrance and Kathleen are playing the fruit machines, *tragaperras* (swallow-coins), not that Poppy knows this word – yet. The water in the pool is as smooth as a block of (blue) marble, and the surrounding sun loungers are almost unoccupied. There is one body lying poolside under a Paraíso sun brolly. It's Freddie. Next to him, his phone is warbling disconsolately, juddering and rocking like an upside-down baby tortoise attempting to right itself.

The Paraíso brollies are enormous. Easily big enough to cover you with shade, even if you were to stretch out like a starfish. Freddie isn't stretched out like a starfish. He's sort of slumped, like a drunk in the gutter outside a run-down bar. Although his brolly is big enough to cover him – easily – it's nearly three hours since he lay down, and although his phone is bleeping and pinging with calls and messages from Alice, Freddie is deeply asleep. And while Freddie has slept...

The Earth has turned on its axis, as it does every day. The shadows have moved as the Earth has turned. So, the backs of

Freddie's legs, which had started out in the shadow of the enormous Paraíso brolly, have now been exposed to the sun's rays for almost as long as he's been asleep. It's a hot day. A very hot day. A very hot day in summer, in Mallorca.

And getting hotter...

25

LA CASA LOLA

ALICE IMAGINES the squeeze of an anaconda would feel a bit like this. Or possibly an adult grizzly bear. The air being forced from her lungs creates a whistling sound as it exits. Lola is giving her a very Spanish hug of welcome. An *abrazo*, Poppy will tell her later, after she's looked it up. It's not the hug of a hotel owner greeting a guest. Even a guest who has visited the hotel for a number of years. There is passion to this hug. Real passion. The passion of an extremely hungry anaconda for a stray deer, perhaps. It's a long-lost friend's hug. A sister's hug. Then Lola hugs the children. Then she hugs the three of them. There are tears in her eyes. The little patio that surrounds the modest pool, not even half the size of the pool at El Paraíso, is filled with teary smiles and shrieks of delight.

Lola releases Alice and the children then starts to flap. It's the only word Alice can think of to describe what she's seeing. Lola, dressed in what Alice's mother would have called a housecoat, plus slippers with pom-poms, is turning on the spot with her arms flapping up and down. She looks like a very excited goose who can't decide in which direction to take off. Then she hugs Alice again.

And Alice feels wretched.

She's going to be rumbled. She knows it. A humiliating betrayal. It will start when Lola asks, in her almost passable, front-of-house English...

'But where is the Señor Cash? Where is Don Freddie...?'

And with all four children, and Lola, looking at her, Alice can only tell the truth. He's lying by the pool, at the upgraded six-star Hotel El Paraíso, less than five-hundred metres up the road. A glass and concrete megahotel, probably owned by a German or American company, stealing the custom from Lola and Don Antonio's beautiful, friendly, authentically Spanish hospitality with zoo-animal towels, a new chef, and a marketing budget probably larger than Casa Lola's annual turnover.

Alice feels like she's betraying friends. They've stayed at Casa Lola six times, she thinks, maybe seven. Yes, it's seven. Although there was that year they went to Crete. Poppy had been a babe in arms for their first visit. And although Lola and Don Antonio didn't have great English, they had become more like friends. Especially after the Cash family had arrived for the fourth year, and then a fifth. Actually, they'd come once for a week one Easter. Freddie had got some bonus from work. Probably their best week ever as the weather was cooler and they began to sit together in the evenings like real friends, as opposed to hosts and guests, chatting about their lives and their hopes, in Spanglish and hand gestures, the children splashing in the small pool or playing board games that didn't need much language – just laughter.

When the Brexit debate let rip in the UK, Alice and Freddie danced their most complicated entry for *Strictly*, a sort of high-speed paso doble, constantly threatening to face up to each other before quickly looking or twisting away from the argument. Alice couldn't think about Brexit without seeing

Poppy and Ryan playing with Carlos and Rosalita and wondering how anybody could suggest anything that might threaten such friendships or prevent them from starting at all.

So, there is a little silence as Alice mutters that Freddie's back at the hotel; she points up the road, there's only one hotel up there. A million tonnes of poured concrete; a billion miles (or kilometres, here) of reinforced steel; a trillion acres (or whatever Spaniards use to measure area) of plate glass, looming over Casa Lola like a mega cruise ship bearing down on a paddle-boarder. Lola moves on seamlessly.

'We have dreenks. Poppy, Ryan, what you want?'

'*Yo quiero un zumo de naranja, por favor,*' Poppy says, a little robotically, but with huge pride and confidence in her voice. The patio falls silent as Lola's eyes lock on Poppy: there is surprise in them, maybe a little awe. Alice feels pride spraying from her pores, Poppy shocking all around her with a moment of – of what? Poppyness? But she's also washed in relief, as Alice banishes all thoughts of Freddie lying on a lounger by the pool of the monstrosity that's threatening Lola's livelihood. Then the Spanish screaming explodes around them. Lola is hugging Poppy, Rosalita and Carlos too, Ryan looks slightly stunned and a little proud. Alice smiles, but still feels the burn of shame at having betrayed and deserted such friends...

'You must to stay for the lunch,' Lola informs them. It's not an invitation. The menu isn't offered. This is the agenda for the afternoon: Spanish hospitality enveloping them in its embrace; as unrefusable as a sentence passed by a judge. Lola has already disappeared inside, and the pans are clattering like a tornado is passing through the kitchen. Alice calls Freddie (again), but his phone goes to messages (yet again). She leaves him another WhatsApp.

> We bumped into Rosalita and Carlos. We're at Casa Lola. It's just down the road. Lola insists we stay for lunch. Come down…

Don Antonio appears with bursting supermarket bags, and the hugging begins again: hugs for them all, including his own children who he last saw less than an hour previously. *But where is Don Freddie?* And Alice mumbles away the bare bones of her shameful betrayal as grilled sardines save her, appearing just in time, swimming in extra virgin olive oil, surrounded by the sweetest, reddest, juiciest tomatoes in all of Europe, and the bread is crusty and fresh, and there's no emulsion, nothing is nestled anywhere, and Carlos is teaching Poppy and Ryan how to say *sardinas*, even though Poppy and Ryan refuse to eat them – *yuk!* And, *Sí, claro que sí*, of course they have the *ron y pasas* ice cream. And how do Poppy and Ryan know so much Spanish? And they all look so happy, even Alice, although she feels like she could cry.

They hug their goodbyes. 'Please, come again, and bring Don Freddie, we must to see Don Freddie.' Alice's cheeks are damp from kisses, and the muscles in her face are sore from forcing so many smiles, and Poppy and Ryan skip back towards the beach, batting *sardinas* and *helados* and *zumos de naranja* between themselves. Alice's heart sinks into her sandals as they approach the concrete and glass monolith of El Paraíso, which now feels like some corporate, mega-national monster, throttling the livelihoods of the local Casa Lolas, and Don Pepes because,

Alice had noticed... With a sinking heart she'd noticed something awful. Something terrible. The realisation had crept up on her with Hitchcockian terror until she couldn't deny it. It screamed in her face in all its black-and-white horror – there didn't seem to be any other guests staying at Casa Lola...

26

THE ACE IN THE HOLE

THE CHILDREN ARE desperate to tell Freddie where they've been, and that they must go again, because Lola, Don Antonio, Rosalita and Carlos really want to see Don Freddie. But he's not in the room, and he's not in the bar, and he's not answered his phone or Alice's numerous WhatsApps.

They finally find him, exactly where they'd left him, face down on his sun lounger by the pool, a puddle of drool soaking his towel, and the backs of his legs the colour of a flamingo. Just a little fatter. And without the webbed feet.

Alice has an after-sun cream that she applies once he's hobbled back to their room. She can tell he's annoyed. 'Why didn't you come back and get me?' And Alice gently reminds him that she'd called him, sent him a dozen WhatsApps, but she doesn't retort that he was too out of it to hear his phone after last night's attempts to keep up with Terrance and Kathleen's prodigious alcohol intake. So, they dance around the subject, him slightly grumpy, clearly wanting to somehow blame her for his sunburn, while Alice is resentful about them being in El Paraíso at all, instead of down the road, with their friends, their good friends, their children's friends, enjoying simple but delicious home cooking, and a three-euro bottle of wine, instead of mixing it with half-naked teenyboppers and half-soaked old soaks, and slurping down a diet of emulsions and nests and oysters and sixty-euro-a-bottle cognac.

———

Even Don Freddie can't fail to be cheered on arrival at Casa Lola that evening: he's greeted like visiting royalty. Don Antonio pumps his hand as if he thinks it might somehow solve the Spanish water shortage; Lola hugs him and cries; the children hug him and don't cry, but squeal like there's a mouse on the loose. And there's an awkward little negotiation to be conducted, as Alice and Freddie insist that they buy their meal from the menu, and that Lola, Don Antonio, Rosalita and Carlos join them, as their guests... But the Brexit negotiations are restarted as Lola and Don Antonio won't hear of it. Don Freddie and his *familia* are their guests, in their home, and they haven't got the English, and even Poppy doesn't understand the Spanish, but it seems possible that there is a European directive, or a law passed by Franco, that forbids British guests from treating their Spanish hosts to a meal. Until finally, Alice suggests they go Dutch, which only starts another unintelligible conversation in Spanglish as Alice and Freddie attempt to explain what 'going Dutch' means, and no, they're not planning a holiday in Holland next year.

The sun sets behind the courtyard wall, leaving the eight of them to enjoy the delicious food, a glass or two of tasty local wine from the *supermercado*, and a Spanglish conversation that holds no etiquette bear-traps for Freddie to fall into, or old-school tie expectations to live up to. Everybody tiptoes around the subject of the cancellation of their room, but it burns in Alice's conscience throughout the evening. The children giggle and laugh and teach each other new words. Of course Poppy remembers it's *sardinas* – her eyes to heaven.

It's the laughter that Alice notices the most. Apart from Poppy firing an oyster across the dining room, there'd been very little laughter at their table at El Paraíso. It had all been on-your-guard manners so as not to embarrass Freddie in front of Terrance and Kathleen. The more she thinks about it, the more Alice resents the situation, and the fact that they all, especially Freddie, feel duty bound not to 'show themselves up'. Why should they care? Why can't they simply be themselves instead of pretending to be more refined, or whatever it is Freddie's chasing?

As midnight approaches, they learn another Spanish word, *sobremesa*, the after-dinner table talk they've all been enjoying. And Alice is so proud that her children are still fully engaged in the conversation which, although it's often interrupted as they attempt to find the right words, feels more relaxed than their stilted, guarded, mind your Ps and Qs (and every other letter of the bloody alphabet) evenings they've spent with Terrance and Kathleen. Alice feels a dread at the thought that they're soon going to have to say *adiós* and *buenas noches* and trudge back up the hill, wreathed in shame.

As they're saying their elongated Spanish goodbyes, with hugs, kisses on the cheeks, firm squeezes from Don Antonio of Freddie's shoulders, the children explode with a request that Alice has seen coming from the far side of the moon. It's Poppy's voice that's the loudest, with the other three cheering her on.

'Can we come down to play here tomorrow? With Rosalita and Carlos? Please? *Pleeeeez?*'

Alice looks quickly at Lola and sees exactly what she

expects: the same pleading eyes that the children have. Alice doesn't look at Freddie until she's said the phrase she's had prepared for hours, 'Yes, of course. As long as Lola and Don Antonio don't mind. That okay, Freddie?'

And Freddie shrugs. 'Yes. Of course.'

The days take on a regular pattern. Freddie lounges on his lounger, nose in another le Carré; eyes firmly closed. A gang of Sex on the Beachers are frolicking in the pool, all splashes, shrieks and extremely loosely tied bikini straps. Poppy and Ryan are engrossed in Duolingo Spanish as El Paraíso offers so little for them to enjoy, once Freddie and Alice have banned them from the room full of fruit machines. They're limited to an hour a day of owlish screen time, and they have to share Freddie's mobile, taking turns. They're happy with the rules, wanting to practise together anyway. 'What good is a new language if you've got nobody to talk to?' says Poppy, sounding like a second-year university student. Alice can hear how well they're doing: learning useful phrases such as *the owl and the duck are friends*, and *the owl likes bananas*. Alice wonders how she could encourage her A level groups to revise so assiduously...

Alice, meanwhile, is on her own mobile, but not learning Spanish with an owl. She's hatching a plan. Tentatively. Unsure, as yet, if she dares put it into practice.

The first thing she needs to ascertain, before she decides whether to go ahead or not, is: has the room they had reserved at Casa Lola for next week been booked by somebody else since Freddie cancelled? Alice is hopeful. Apart from their table, the small restaurant was empty last night. And Alice has been unable to rid her mind of the fact she hasn't spotted any other guests, at any time, and there were no towels hanging on any of the four balconies overlooking the pool. So, there's a chance. A good one. And the internet confirms it. In fact, the internet tells her that she can book any one of the four rooms at Casa Lola for next week, sending her heart into the sludge nestling at the bottom of her stomach. She takes a deep breath. Now, all she has to do is get Freddie to agree. She knows there's only one way...

Alice feels mean. It's a low trick, unfair, but – but he bloody deserves it, and he probably wouldn't agree unless she does it this way. So, sod him. She waits for what is becoming a daily request from the children. It's Poppy today who makes the plea, her spoonful of muesli, already drained of milk, halted in mid-air as she petitions once again.

'Can we go down to play with Rosalita and Carlos today?'

Alice takes a breath, does she dare? Yes, she bloody well does. She utters more words she's prepared, like an actress with a big first night tonight, sure of the response they'll provoke.

'Yes, of course you can. You'll be wanting us to swap our booking, spend the second week living at Casa Lola...'

The pause is pregnant. Twins. Maybe even triplets. Poppy's eyes widen; flakes of oat drop back into her bowl. Ryan gapes up at Alice, a look of wonderment crossing his face. Freddie is sawing at a sausage, not paying attention at all.

'Oh, *could* we?' Ryan.

'Oh, yes! Oh, please, please, *pleeeezeee...*' Poppy.

'What was that?' Freddie.

Alice sends the children a look that says, *Well, I wasn't really being serious, but...*

And the pleading intensifies.

'Oh, it would be *so* nice, Poppy and I are there nearly every day now anyway, aren't we? And it's helping so much with my prep for school. *Pleeezzze?'*

'What's that?' Freddie suddenly taking a hit from the mention of Ryan's summer studies.

'Can we change our booking? Spend next week at Casa Lola? With our friends. Our *amigos*. Please, Daddy?' Poppy.

'Please, Dad. We're there nearly all the time, and we prefer it, and we're learning so much Spanish. It's helping me with my catch up.' Ryan.

Freddie looks confused, he hasn't been paying attention to the conversation. He looks at Alice.

'I don't mind,' she says. 'We'd have to check to see if there is a room available at Casa Lola. There might not be at such short notice...'

Freddie puts his knife and fork down, looks from one expectant face to another.

'We'd lose the money we've paid for the rooms here next week. They wouldn't give us a refund.'

Alice has another answer scripted for this objection: Act 1 Scene 3, crafty wife lays a cunning trap for ill-prepared husband. Enter crafty wife from stage left...

'That's probably true but we did get a BOGOF, and it would be nice to have our usual week there, wouldn't it? It's been *so* nice here, but wouldn't it be lovely to have a change for the second week? It's not as if there's a lot for the children to do here, and we're not seeing much of them as they prefer to be at Casa Lola, of course they do.'

Alice looks at the pool where the Sex on the Beachers are now playing a rumbustious game of noisy water polo. A nipple appears around the side of a Barbie-pink bikini and winks at Alice.

'They don't seem to have many guests staying at Casa Lola, and they've been so kind, letting Poppy and Ryan use their pool, giving them drinks, they even gave them lunch yesterday. It would be a nice way to pay them back. And, well, we do have the money...' Alice then plays the ace she's had hidden up her sleeve since the idea of decamping to Casa Lola for the second week first appeared in her mind. Act 1 Scene 4, leading up to the interval: crafty wife plays her ace...

'Look, tell you what, let me check on my phone, see if they've got a room...'

Ryan and Poppy send the furniture skittering; slops of milk splatter the table. Freddie takes a breath; Alice talks over it.

'Let me see. I doubt there'll be anything at such short notice, kids. But we'll have a look just to make sure, let me see...' She has the page surreptitiously bookmarked on her phone for speed of access. Something she didn't know how to do before she googled it last night. She doesn't want Freddie to have much opportunity to voice objections, not until she's wound the children up into a Latin frenzy.

'Yes! Look. Available!' Ryan, jumping up and down, spots it before Alice. Poppy starts what looks like a pretty passable attempt at a flamenco dance, twirling around their table like a spinning top, her dress swirling around her knees. A passing waiter starts to clap and stamp his feet causing Poppy to hide her face in her hands.

'Well, fancy that!' Alice says, the surprise in her voice warranting a Golden Globe, she thinks proudly. 'And look at the price. It's a quarter of the amount we're paying here. And look, all four rooms are available next week. God, they've got nobody staying there at all. Isn't that sad, Freddie? Poor old Lola and Don Antonio.'

'*And* Carlos and Rosalita,' Poppy chimes in, adding a subsidiary in economics to her studies, her voice as sorrowful as if a favourite kitten (*gatito*) had died in her hands, having just been rescued from a nearby coalmine.

'What do you think, Freddie?' Alice asks. 'Only four hundred pounds, and we could have the adjoining rooms, like here, with the big balcony...?'

Poppy dashes around the table, hands in prayer position, eyes pleading.

'Oh, pleeeeez, Daddy. *Pleeeeeeeez! Por FAVOR!*'

27

THE FIESTA

It's like a fiesta, the arrival of the Cash family at Casa Lola. Rosalita and Carlos have hung streamers out over the arched entrance to the small courtyard at the back of the house. Don Antonio has put music on the loudspeakers. It sounds, to Alice, like some kind of entrance of the matador bullfighting music, while Carlos has dusted off a battered trumpet and is tunelessly serenading half the town. Poppy and Ryan are enchanted; they stare at the streamers and listen to the music as if they are extras in a film on the big screen. Lola is wiping tears from her eyes, and Freddie looks genuinely stunned.

And Alice can tell, call it intuition, call it whatever you like, but Alice can tell from the way Lola is wiping her dusty hands on her apron (she's been baking) that it's nothing to do with business or money. This is to do with friendship. And Alice is wiping tears from her eyes too.

Lunch is emulsion-free again, and there are even a few fresh *ostras* on a plate, what Terrance and Kathleen might call a *tapa*, and Freddie is cheered to the terracotta tiles as he downs one. Ryan follows him loyally, as does Alice, but Poppy graciously decides 'not to waste one'.

To Alice's surprise, her children choose not to opt for their usual fish fingers or chicken nuggets that Casa Lola provides for their international (read British) guests. She doesn't know whether it was Ryan or Poppy, but somehow, they've both decided they'd like to eat what Rosalita and Carlos eat, which has always been what the adults are eating. So, they try the *sardinas* and pronounce them 'nothing like the rubbish sardines we get out of the tins at home'. And, whereas before, the huge size had certainly put them off, even though Alice and Freddie had assured them countless times that they tasted nothing like the rubbish sardines we get out of tins back home, now that they've discovered they're *deliciosas*, the Cash children are thrilled at how big they are.

They also discover they've been eating crab, twenty minutes after they started eating it.

'Crab?' Poppy squeals, a look of horror widening her eyes and mouth to *Texas Chainsaw Massacre* proportions.

'*Claro.*' Rosalita shrugs, like she's telling Poppy it's chicken. Poppy looks at Ryan for support, that eating crab is way beyond the pale of English gastronomy. But Ryan raises his eyebrows.

'It's quite nice,' he says, looking a little mystified.

'I know,' Poppy replies, confusion flooding her eyes. There's a moment's silence as the adults watch Poppy getting to grips with the idea that crab might be something she could enjoy eating – might be something she already *has* enjoyed eating. She looks up from her plate at Rosalita, lifts a piece of crab on the end of her fork. 'How do you say this, *en español...*?'

Alice nearly sends her mouthful of wine across the table...

The *sobremesa* drifts on and on while the children jump in and out of the pool, and then, nobody remembers later who suggested this, Rosalita and Carlos fetch their English books from their schoolbags. Their school has started teaching English this year, and Poppy and Ryan begin their teacher training this evening. Alice catches Lola's eye during the first lesson, and she knows immediately that the pride of a Spanish mother is exactly the same as the pride of a British one. As the four adults slowly turn to watch the four children working through a lesson about buying a meal in a hotel restaurant, Alice wonders if a completely silent adult *sobremesa* has ever happened before, in any part of the Spanish-speaking world.

Alice stares at the ceiling, listening to the cicadas, if that's what they are; they could be grasshoppers for all she really knows, or a landslide from the nearby mountains about to engulf the town. The sex had been nice. Nice that Freddie hadn't immediately collapsed into a drunken slumber as he had during their nights at El Paraíso. Here, he obviously doesn't feel compelled to keep up with Terrance and Kathleen's pub crawl of a dinner. Don Antonio, she noticed, makes a glass of wine last until his dessert. Then he has another half a glass before coffee. And that's it. No second bottle, no chasers. So civilised, so continental. Although they did accept a little *chupito*, some sort of lemony antifreeze-like liqueur, to round it all off.

Why can't this be enough? she thinks, wide awake and in a philosophical mood. This! Everything they have. Each other. The children. Their home. Their work. Their holiday with people who have clearly become good friends, even though they barely speak each other's languages. Happiness cascades around Casa Lola: Lola and Don Antonio are so relaxed, and yet they clearly work hard, and Carlos and Rosalita are such nice children.

She wants to understand Freddie, she really does. But it's like he and she don't share the same language. She feels she understands Lola better than she does Freddie. Now. Since the win... She can understand his views on the schools. That's the easy one, and the one she most disagrees with. But she can understand how and why he might support private education, even single-sex private education. She disagrees with it, especially for her own children, but she can understand why he might think it could be a good idea.

But why can she really not understand all the rest of it? The wine? The watch? The car? The six-star holiday hotels populated by a bunch of young Hooray Henrys and Henriettas, and a load of old snobs? The big house corralled behind a fence with other big houses owned by people she fears she won't get on with. People like Terrance and Kathleen. She shudders at the memory of their dinners, walking on eggshells in case she or Freddie said something embarrassing, in case the children said something childish...?

But, besides all of this, which is bad enough, she knows there's something bigger that is bothering her, has bothered her ever since *it* happened. Why is she still unable to talk to him? It embarrasses her that she can't. Or won't. She sees herself as a liberated woman, whatever that means. She sees herself and Freddie as equals. She works. She has as high hopes and expectations for Poppy as she has for Ryan. She won't mind who they love, as long as they choose somebody kind who treats them well. They can marry (or not marry) any race, any religion, any sex. As long as she can see they're as happy with their chosen partner as she was with Freddie when he went down on one knee and looked so frightened in case she said no...

She's not sure the roles they've slipped into over the years really matter that much. She's happy with who she is. She loves being Mummy to the children, organising their lives, all their birthday parties and the sleepovers, so inappropriately named as nobody ever seems to get any sleep. She's so happy with the way they're turning out – she couldn't be prouder of them. She dreads the moment when Freddie might suggest they employ an au pair, or a nanny, or some sort of governess to 'take the strain off her'. Some Mary Poppins figure, parachuting in under her umbrella with her carpet bag and pointy boots, ready to take away all the tasks that Alice loves doing.

She remembers lockdown somewhat fondly – and, therefore, a little guiltily. She'd never claim that Covid was a good thing, so many people died, but she got to spend some extra time being Mummy. Having the children at home was a treat. Freddie locked himself away in the box bedroom from nine to five, with his laptop and his phone, doing whatever he had to do, while she and the kids mucked in together, she helping them when they needed it, and them letting her do her online teaching by working so quietly, Ryan often helping Poppy to save them from disturbing Mummy.

And, apart from the fear of what he might suggest next, Alice is happy with Freddie. That's not to say he couldn't do a bit more around the house. But she simply can't understand why he doesn't want what she wants. Which is what they have. What they already have – each other, the children, nice friends, a holiday they all enjoy together...? Why can't all that be enough?

There could even be more. She wouldn't begrudge him a second holiday each year. Somewhere not too far away. Maybe a sightseeing tour instead of their usual beach. Something the children would find interesting, educational: the ancient bits of Italy? The pyramids? Somewhere they'd all enjoy together, while the children are still young enough to go on holiday with them. She should talk to him about that. She should. She will.

The cicadas mock her from the garden. Sounds for all the world like they're laughing at her.

28

THE WINNER TAKES IT ALL

SOMETHING RIDICULOUS IS CRYSTALLISING in Alice's mind. It's so ridiculous she'd never mention it to Freddie, or anybody else. It really is quite stupid. Mad. But she can't stop her mind from giving the idea the odd swirl...

There's something about their relationship with the Alcántara family that is growing on her rapidly. Her own relationship with Lola has deepened as they've taken the time to watch their children playing, and learning, together. Alice has noticed how her children had been so quiet during their week at El Paraíso but have exploded into life since meeting up with Carlos and Rosalita again, especially now they've moved hotel. It's silly, she knows, but watching the four children together, at times childish, splashing each other and chasing, or playing blind man's bluff (Rosalita's favourite): then at other times more serious, as they explore new words and pronunciations, it's planted a seed in her mind that is growing without any tending from her.

The other morning, this is the really silly bit, she knows: that ABBA song, 'The Winner Takes It All', was tinkling out of Lola's tranny as Alice was lying on her sun lounger with a healthy G&T by her side. And, she doesn't know the film well, she's only seen it six or seven times, but that song conjured memories of Meryl Streep and Whatshisname running up to some hilltop church. It all made her think, this is really, *really* silly – she thought of a marriage, sometime in the future, on some hilltop *Ermita* on Mallorca: Ryan and Rosalita.

Ridiculous, she knows, totally ludicrous, romantic twaddle but – and here's where the silly bit gets totally insane: they're always thinking of their children's futures, planning the schools they'll go to, university, careers, all that normal stuff that normal parents, at some time or other, think about, and make plans about. So, why not this?

And she's not trying to matchmake. She really isn't. She'd never do an Emma Woodhouse on one of her own children, but why not simply open certain doors, or in this case, keep them open, and let opportunity walk through them if it wanted to? They seem to get on so well, especially as the amount of language they actually share is still pitifully small. Moreover, Carlos and Rosalita are both beginning to show more interest in developing their pidgin English, now they've started having English lessons at school. This hasn't entirely pleased Poppy, desperate to improve her Spanish rather than help improve Carlos and Rosalita's English, but she's coped with that admirably.

And here's the thing. Here's what's popped into Alice's mind and won't exit it. Alice has noticed, on more than one occasion, something in Rosalita's eyes as she's been looking at Ryan. And Alice knows they're only twelve, well, Rosalita is nearly thirteen, and Ryan won't be long behind, but Alice knows that girls mature earlier than boys. And there's certainly been no twinkly looks in Ryan's eyes, not yet, but she remembers when she first got to know Freddie: they were twelve or thirteen. And she doesn't remember ever having a fully blown crush on him, but she always liked him, always trusted him enough to walk home with him from the bus stop, knowing he'd never tell smutty jokes or put his hand on her bottom. But look where they are now...

Alice has calculated that, from the look she's noticed in Rosalita's eyes, she would only need to keep up their visits to Mallorca for what? One more summer might light the blue touch paper for that little señorita. She is such a nice girl: sensible, but vivacious, with a glorious laugh that rings around the courtyard, and those deep brown eyes. And they're such a nice family, traditional, like her and Freddie, yes, but in that Spanish way that seems to come with guitar music, a sunset behind palm trees and a lot of garlic, rather than the English way, where he phones the garage while she loads the washing machine.

And so, Casa Lola has become something more than simply a lovely holiday and a Spanish family that Alice is pleased and proud to get along with in more than the traditional hotelier–guest kind of relationship. It's become a sort of stage, for Ryan and Rosalita to maybe... who knows? Not that she's matchmaking. Oh no. She'd never do that. But why not give it a chance? Why not deliberately give it a chance? Something that might be worth more than Freddie's millions could ever buy for Ryan?

But no, it's silly, silly, silly – *stop it!*

29

THE SPANISH PIED-À-TERRE

FREDDIE KNOWS one Spanish word that Poppy and Ryan don't. The word is *inmobiliaria*. As Freddie has discovered through Google Translate, *inmobiliaria* means estate agent. And while the children are frolicking in the pool or, amazingly, quizzing Rosalita and Carlos about the Spanish words for anything and everything they see, Freddie is taking Alice to *la inmobiliaria* – for a browse.

Alice is torn. A villa, or more likely a flat, on Mallorca is something Freddie has been bending her ear about since they won the lottery. And, still feeling guilty at having bounced him out of his embryonic bonding or networking or whatever he was attempting with Terrance (and the lovely, but often sloshed, Kathleen), she feels she might have to give ground here.

If she's honest, Freddie has constructed quite a sound case for a buy-to-let wheeze that might future-proof their (read *his*) plans that they give up work for good. He's already confided that two point three big ones, as he's taken to calling their stash, might not be sufficient for a life of leisure and an enormous house plus the villa (or flat) on Mallorca and etc., etc....

The agent is a very pleasant lad who ushers them into the sparkling *inmobiliaria,* a long (and sweltering) walk from Casa Lola. Freddie had put on his paranoid hat and decided they'd have to choose an *inmobiliaria* a long way from Casa Lola. Spanish businesspeople are thick as robbers, he'd warned Alice. 'They talk to each other at some Chamber of Commerce thingy; they know everybody else's business. We'd no sooner set foot in an *inmobiliaria* in this part of town, and Don Antonio will hear about it.'

How Freddie might know such nuggets of small-town Spanish business machinations, Alice isn't at all sure. But she'll do anything to make sure Lola and Don Antonio don't hear of their plan, so she's quite willing to yomp over to the far side of Palma in the midday sun in order to minimise the risk of them getting wind. She'd suggested they take a taxi – we are millionaires – but Freddie had scoffed at the idea, taxi drivers apparently being the worst for having loose tongues and knowing everybody in town. So, they've walked down into the valley that they'd never noticed was there in Palma. And up the other side. In the scorching sun.

'I'm Stephen, but call me Steve,' the estate agent announces, magnanimously.

'Frederick,' Freddie replies, in his best (but quite damp) suit, but *sin* dicky bow. 'And Alice.'

Steve offers them cool drinks, comfortable chairs and recently activated air conditioning, all the while, Alice supposes, assessing them. Time wasters, bored of the beach, looking for a free day out nosing around some fancy houses they'd never be able to afford? Or genuine potential customers, with money, or at least a ready mortgage, in the bank?

'So, buy or rent?' Steve begins when they've all had a sip of their orange squash.

'Oh, buy!' says Freddie. *How could you ever have thought otherwise?*

Alice has noticed this change in Freddie. He's always been a little pompous, but guardedly so. Like he knows he can't go too far. Not anymore! He's developed this... this *something*, where he adopts a sort of superior air, as if the conversation is a battle and he wants to get the first punches in quick, dominate his opponent, show them who's boss. She thinks he's copied it from Terrance, in the Paraíso, where Freddie always seemed to reel backwards whenever they started a conversation. Is this Freddie attempting to step into Terrance's brown brogues?

'Smashing,' Steve says, ignoring Freddie's attitude, and almost licking his lips at the increased chance of a healthy commission. 'On the island?'

'Yes.'

'Any particular part?'

Freddie looks at Alice. 'We thought Palma, didn't we?'

Alice nods, and is suddenly aware that their 'homework' or 'background research' has been relatively scant, which will probably put Freddie at a disadvantage from here on in.

'Right, smashing,' Steve says again, and Alice has to stifle a smile. 'So, house or flat?'

'Haven't decided. Considering both,' says Freddie with a curt little nod.

'And...' Steve swallows, like he's suddenly a bit nervous, even making quite a comical gulping sound, the sort you'd get in a *Tom and Jerry* cartoon. 'Your price range?'

'Well, the best things in life aren't free, are they? So, let's say, up to... a million,' Freddie says, leaving a little gap before leaning forward and announcing the number, half in a whisper, like he's expecting Steve to gasp, which he does, much to

Freddie's evident delight. He obviously feels he's floored Steve in the first round, will be in the shower before the end of the second.

And suddenly, Alice thinks she's sussed it: she imagines Steve might be in his first job; they could even be his first ever customers. She considers his pasty-white skin: *Not been out here longer than twenty minutes*, she concludes instantly. He's got an eager-to-please puppy-dog demeanour, but behind it, Alice now suspects, there could be a maelstrom of first night nerves, twenty-minutes of training, and flashing dollar, or maybe euro, signs. She wonders if his excitement at maybe making a sale (and thereby impressing his boss) weighs more heavily on his mind than simply remembering everything he's meant to know and ask. She can imagine Ryan coming across in a similar way in this role, in a few years, holiday job, perhaps, while visiting You-Know-Who... She warms to Steve, a little. Poor lad.

'Right, smashing, shall we start with the houses, or...?'

'Flats,' Freddie says, a left uppercut that almost lifts Steve out of his chair.

'Smashing.'

Alice's eyes eventually glaze over, and her mind wanders as Steve twists his wide-screen monitor and clicks his mouse endlessly, walking them through dozens of lounges, bathrooms, bedrooms, communal pools and the mysterious *trasteros*, which Steve doesn't translate, and Freddie doesn't ask, leaving Alice wondering if it's some kind of dungeon, or panic room. She'll consult Poppy – if *she* doesn't know, she'll soon find out.

Freddie makes an appointment to see a flat at half a mil (Steve's words) and a house at one point two five the next day. 'You won't get a house for less than a mil' is Steve's 'expert' (but pasty-white) judgement. Hands are shaken, Steve seeming particularly impressed that Freddie wasn't bothered that they couldn't 'just nip out today', as Steve was alone in the office, and by the fact that Freddie and Alice were on the island for the week.

———

'Shall we bring the kids? Tomorrow?' Freddie asks, as they sit in a small bar with two low-alcohol beers going down like student skydivers who are late for the next training lecture.

Alice takes another slug as cover for a calculation. She could go for a flat, but only as a buy-to-let. Freddie can see the sense in letting out a small flat long-term, rather than restricting themselves to holiday lets, where they'll probably earn less money, just so they can block book a couple of stretches for themselves and the kids.

Secretly, what Alice really wants are more trips to Casa Lola. She likes the idea of strengthening their ties to the Alcántara family: they could stay at Casa Lola for a night or two, any time of year, bring the kids for a long weekend, if they ever needed to check on the flat. Freddie has nodded sagely at this line of argument: the flat let out, probably to a Spanish family, with him, Alice and the kids 'jetting out' now and again to check up on the air conditioning. And maybe Ryan, checking up on the delightful Rosalita or, possibly more likely, the gorgeous Rosalita sneaking up on an unsuspecting Ryan – not that Alice is matchmaking. Heaven forfend...

What Alice doesn't want is Freddie showing the kids a half a mil flat or, worse, a one point two-five mil house, and them thinking they're going to live there, or at least come there for holidays. She wants that clear in their minds if any of this ever happens. She doesn't want the children starting to plan invitations for all their friends to their villa in Spain, and one of Ryan's slightly more confident mates sweeping the lovely Rosalita off her feet and out from under Ryan's nose before he's even smelled the coffee, or her perfume. So, she really wants something to rent out. Preferably for a damn sight less than half a mil. She makes a *not sure* face.

'Let's wait until we know what we want. You know what they're like; they'll love the first place we view and tell all their friends at school what we've bought. Plus,' she goes on as Freddie takes a breath, 'they're having such a nice time with Rosalita and Carlos; they've only got a couple of days left; let's leave them to play, or work, or whatever they're doing...'

Freddie nods, sips beer. 'You're probably right. But we'll have to tell them when we make a decision, won't we?'

'Yes, but we should make sure they understand it's a buy to let, that we might be coming to Casa Lola a bit more often if we need to get any decorating done, or buy some furniture, or whatever.'

'*Muebles*,' Freddie says, although Alice wonders if he's sneezed.

'Sorry?'

'Furniture is *muebles*, I looked it up.'

She smiles at him as he tries to look modestly proud of himself. 'You should tell Poppy and Ryan; they'll be thrilled to know. And even more thrilled that you know.'

As they pay and leave, Freddie has *La cuenta, por favor* off pat, she wonders if this high-wire act she's playing is going to work. She knows she's not being honest with him, that she's manipulating him, but it seems to be keeping him, and the children, and, most importantly, her happy. At least for now.

Steve had offered to collect Freddie and Alice from their hotel, but Freddie, of course, had refused. 'He probably knows the Alcántaras personally,' Freddie explained later to Alice. Alice had doubted this; Steve's lack of a tan suggesting he's not been on the island long enough to withdraw any cash, let alone cultivate a network of business associates. But she hadn't argued, in case Steve arrived at Casa Lola tooting his horn, in a car with *Casas R Us* plastered down the side.

So, sweaty yomp across town number two now completed, Steve drives them all the way back to within three streets of Casa Lola, to view the flat he has assured them would be *perfecto*. Alice isn't sure if the walk, or the end of the drive, especially as they seemed to be approaching the front door of Casa Lola, had caused Freddie to sweat more.

There's a geriatric 'doorman' behind a wooden desk in the poky little vestibule, who 'springs' to life as they enter, dropping his copy of *Marca* as he does. Steve attempts some very stilted *español* but only extracts a shrug in response. Freddie has more luck by offering his hand and dredging a very passable *Hola, buenos días* from somewhere. He exchanges a couple of very Spanish backslaps with his new best *amigo* before Steve herds Alice and Freddie into the lift that grinds upwards with a lot of quite worrying clanking. It's one of those old-fashioned cage-type lifts, with the metal concertina doors that take a bit of tugging and often host a James Bond or Jason Bourne fist fight. Today, luckily, it's empty.

Steve wrestles with a bunch of keys so large it makes Alice think they've been sentenced to life. Once he's broken in, he then excels at the estate agent's traditional job of explaining that the room with the cooker is the kitchen and those with beds are bedrooms. Freddie walks with his hands behind his back, nodding approvingly at the sofa and the sideboard, looking like a particularly sweaty royal on a walkabout in a furniture store.

Alice finds it hard to take any of it seriously. With a rather Machiavellian eye, she knows there's no way they're going to be buying this particular flat. Freddie is still a little undecided on the buy-to-let option, and he's aware that Alice won't countenance rubbing the Alcántaras' noses in it by becoming their next-door neighbours. So, the viewing, in Alice's eyes, is unlikely to lead anywhere. But, she's rapidly realising, that might be no bad thing in her plan to spend – or allow Ryan to spend – more time at Casa Lola, in the company of the delightful Rosalita. The longer Alice can string out the flat-buying process, the more trips to Casa Lola they – and, more importantly, Ryan – can make to Palma. Emma Woodhouse, eat your heart out.

Not that she's matchmaking...

Alice wonders if their life really is about to take a turn into international-property-magnate territory. They don't seem to have discussed it much. Two days ago, it was simply another of Freddie's hare-brained schemes that might, but probably wouldn't, come to something. But suddenly, here they are, in some unidentified Spanish family's sitting room, staring at the photos on the tops of the bookcases, peeking out of the windows at the view from the fifth floor. Freddie is asking questions about how much rent they might charge, and how much the local taxes are, and who would have to pay them.

Even Freddie, proud banker, clearly has little to no idea of the financial implications, especially now that Brexit (which he voted for) seems to have erected more impenetrable barriers between the UK and Europe than ever existed between East and West Berlin when the cold war was at its frostiest. But give him his due, he's trying manfully at least to appear the international property magnate – and isn't *magnate* an odd word? Alice feels like she's playing a game, and hopes she can take it into extra time, and possibly a replay, over the coming months – and maybe years...

The flat for half a mil was a no-no as soon as they realised how close it was to Casa Lola. Nevertheless, Alice enjoyed the opportunity to attempt to spot a few objections: a lot of noise from the street if you opened the windows; with a flat on the fifth floor would you really trust that lift to keep working?

The house for one point two-five mil, however, is another planet. Alice thinks it could be Mercury. That's the really hot one, right?

It's one of those one-storey white concrete boxes with lots of windows. In fact, it seems to be more windows than walls. And lots of curtains. Because if you didn't have the curtains the whole house would be a greenhouse, and you'd grow to nine-foot tall within a month if you drank enough water. But they're not inside the house – it's too hot – they're outside, on the decking, in front of the pool, where it turns out to be even hotter.

The sun is facing them and reflecting off the water like one of those new-fangled solar power generating thingies that can fry an egg in ten seconds or destroy your car if you park it in the wrong place. Alice has her sunglasses on, and a hat, yet still has to squint as the water ripples and the radiation does something that only radiation can do. Freddie's jacket – damp rag would be a more accurate description – is draped over his arm, his shirtsleeves are rolled up like sodden dishcloths, and the rest of his shirt is stuck to him like he's a sure-bet to win the wet T-shirt competition at El Paraíso (second Wednesday of every month, apparently).

'You'd get a nice tan out here,' Steve offers, shading his eyes from the glare; he's left his sunglasses in the car. *Amateur*, thinks Alice, with a knowing raise of her eyes.

They retire inside where the temperature is only at Venusian levels; Steve has been unable to ignite the air conditioning, he thinks the owners have removed the fuse. So, they move through the rooms at pace. It's like viewing an enormous oven. They come to a bedroom at the far end of the property that has three floor-to-ceiling glass walls. Alice imagines some nuclear power stations might occasionally reach such temperatures – Chernobyl, for example...

The only cool(ish) place they can find is on the front porch, which is in the shade of the house. There, they make promises to think about it, and get back to him, and Alice's suggestion: maybe make another visit to the island. This time wearing spacesuits, like the Apollo astronauts did when they went to the moon.

Steve looks like he fears he might have been had by a couple of professional time wasters, bored of the beach, angling for a free day out looking around some fancy houses that they'd never be able to afford. But he still manages a final, perfectly acceptable, 'Smashing' for Alice. He offers to drive them to their hotel but, despite Alice's attempts to contact him by ESP, Freddie demurs, saying they quite enjoy walking – on Venus.

30

THE LONG ADIÓS

They say parting is such sweet sorrow. *Bollocks*, thinks Alice. Freddie and Don Antonio are holding it together well in a very macho style, slapping each other on the back like they're about to set off up the tallest mountain on Mallorca, carrying rucksacks and ropes. However, the amount of brine pouring down Alice, Lola, Poppy and Rosalita's faces would overflow the pool if they weren't mopping so efficiently with paper napkins from the table dispenser. Even Ryan's lip is threatening to tremble.

The goodbyes, the *adioses*, seem never ending: Poppy hugging and kissing Carlos and Rosalita, then hugging and kissing Lola and Don Antonio; Alice hugging and kissing everybody more than once. Don Antonio is driving them to the airport; he instigates one last hug and kiss from everybody for everybody else.

As they're finally getting into the car, Freddie is in the front seat, attempting to discuss the route with Don Antonio; Poppy is waving the hand of a new teddy that Carlos has given her. Alice glances back for a last wave and spots Rosalita looking like her world is collapsing at her feet.

Alice and Rosalita have grown closer over their week at Casa Lola, especially once Rosalita, knowing Alice was a proper English teacher, started to engineer little conversations *en inglés* whenever Ryan and Poppy were busy *en la piscina*. Alice's admiration for Rosalita, and her desire for Rosalita and Ryan to start a little something, has only been strengthened by Rosalita's inquisitive personality, her mature nature, and her cackle of a laugh. But, at the moment, Rosalita looks bereft. Alice has a feeling: this dam is going to burst. Imminently.

As Alice looks on, it's like watching a Spanglish Jane Austen remake; Rosalita chews her lower lip, clenches and unclenches her fists, and fires quick little glances across at Ryan who is clearly oblivious of the effect he is having on her emotions. Suddenly, Rosalita seems to make her mind up, bats the tears off her cheeks, strides over to Ryan and wraps her arms around him like she's going to try to stop him from getting into the car. She then leans back, and instead of the usual Spanish one-two airbrushes on the cheeks, she plants one lingering, very Latina, kiss quite near to his lips. Ryan staggers back as she releases him: his eyes wide; cheeks colouring like the veins in his face have opened close to metro-tunnel size. He stares at Rosalita, who looks partly confused, but also hugely proud of herself. Yes, definitely a Spanglish remake; the Austen-era censors would never have tolerated such a brazen display in public without Rosalita's honour being shredded forever.

Kiss her back, Alice roars silently in her head, as Ryan looks like gravity has ceased to function, at least in Mallorca. Rosalita smiles, her olive cheeks turning a deeper russet brown, relief and pride flooding her face. Alice catches her eye, and smiles. She guesses that Rosalita has been building up to this for days. *Kiss her back*, she yells again in her mind, remembering the scene in that film, the Christmassy one, at the airport. That boy should have kissed the girl back too, Alice has always thought.

Ryan takes a step; Lola has also spotted the standoff. It looks like Ryan might be about to return the kiss, but he doesn't. He simply reaches across and lightly takes Rosalita's fingers in his hand. They stare; they smile. *Good move*, Alice thinks, *leave her wanting more.*

'*Hasta el año que viene!* See you next year!' Alice shouts at Lola, a phrase Poppy has spent half an hour teaching her over breakfast. Then she gathers a blushing Ryan into the back seat and ruffles his hair proudly. If there's a battle over whether to return to Casa Lola for extra long-weekend flat-hunting trips, Alice knows she's recruited a firm supporter and willing bagboy.

'Good holiday?' Alice, squeezed between the children in the back seat, asks as they head out towards the airport.

'*Mar-a-vill-o-so,*' Poppy eventually manages to stutter, almost dislocating at least one tonsil in her attempt to get all the syllables out in the correct order. Alice can't help but smile at her enthusiasm. Poppy Cash, BA Spanish, first-class honours. If William Hill wants to bet, Alice is feeling very confident.

She turns to her other side. 'Ryan?'

Ryan is staring out of the window where the flats above the shops are slipping by. Alice wonders, with another smile, if he's imagining where he and Rosalita might buy one together.

'Ryan?' Alice gives him a soft nudge.

'What?' he starts. 'Sorry?'

'Did you enjoy the holiday? Not bored with two weeks on Mallorca?'

'No! No, it was *brilliant,*' he replies, with a kind of desperation that pulls at Alice's heartstrings.

'I was going to suggest to Dad, maybe we come out for a

week at Christmas? It wouldn't be as warm, but it would probably be sunny. What do you think?'

His face lights up, as it might had she informed him that Norwich City were offering him a trial.

'Could we?' he begs, her boy growing up before her eyes.

'We'll see,' she replies. 'As long as you're doing well at your new school. Not too much catching up to do.'

'I'll be fine,' he shoots back. 'I'll get it all done. Promise.'

She nods. There's another bet she thinks is a banker.

PART 4

THE SPENDING SPREE

31

THE POSH WATCH (2)

ALMOST AS SOON AS the wheels have hit the ground at LHR, Freddie is impatient to get on with the job of buying his 'posh watch'. He's annoyed that he delayed before they set off on holiday, depriving him of the opportunity to show it off to Terrance, maybe share a conversation about other luxury items that he should be purchasing. He's determined not to make that mistake again. He also wants to flash it around at work, especially as he can't think of a way of driving his (soon to be acquired) 'posh car' into the branch, before announcing his resignation.

His planned departure from work is, however, causing him some minor headaches. Like a good mathematician would, he's been doing his sums. And it's rapidly becoming clear to him that posh watches (times four), a posh car (or two), private schools for the children, a new house (somewhere 'nice'), a flat (or a villa) abroad, plus he and Alice never working again – might cost a sliver more than two point three million pounds over the next thirty odd years. If only they'd invent an app that could tell you when you were going to die, he thinks, ruefully.

He's mentioned these worries to Alice, preparing her for the fact they might have to trade in their chance of giving up work for good if they really want that posh car (or two) and that flat (or villa) abroad plus all the other assorted paraphernalia on Freddie's ever lengthening to-do (now-I'm-rich) list. Being a double millionaire is a lot more complicated than he'd ever imagined. Who knew?

But the watch isn't a deal-breaker, it's small change, so he's moving apace on that front. He's already spent a fruitless couple of hours in the Norwich posh watch shop, unsuccessfully attempting to talk his way around the waiting list. Plus, he's discovered that they don't make posh children's watches – or should that be children's posh watches? Alice will know. This is a bizarre mistake in Freddie's view, although the white-coated and white-gloved salesperson didn't seem at all keen to communicate his opinions to the 'top brass', as Freddie called them, only slightly pompously.

So, he's back on the internet searching for a second-hand 34mm watch, last made in 2014, that the salesman has suggested might be suitable for Ryan's eleven-year-old wrist. Poppy, he's decided, will be delighted with a little diamond necklace until her wrist grows big enough to sport a lady's model.

He spends thirty-five thousand pounds on three watches and is then stunned to find that he can get a diamond necklace for Pops on Amazon for six pound ninety-nine. Six ninety-nine? For a diamond necklace? He can barely believe it. But he also feels he can't spend only six ninety-nine on Pops; so, he pushes the luxury yacht out and finds one for fifteen quid.

Ryan, in Alice's eyes, is clearly underwhelmed when he sees his watch. Sadly, the original box and papers weren't available, but

Freddie doesn't make Ryan aware of this little cloud. Instead, he explains all the reasons why this watch is so special: a waffle dial – whatever that is – and a nine carat yellow gold case. He's loath to mention the price, although he's not sure why. A ten thousand pound watch is obviously a good watch, a *great* watch, but somehow mentioning the price seems to cheapen it – surely its greatness should be obvious for all to see? Oh, it's also got a taupe strap.

Poppy is as delighted with her diamond necklace as she usually is when her weekly comic dishes out free sparkly stuff in a plastic bag Sellotaped to the cover. She allows Freddie to close the clasp behind her neck while hopping excitedly from foot to foot – Poppy, that is. The pendant looks wonderful, hanging, as it does, in front of the (slightly grubby) *My Little Pony* design on her T-shirt. Poppy gives a little twirl before running out into the garden to climb the tree.

Alice kisses Freddie on the cheek and wonders how much her watch cost. She'll have to coat the inside of the metallic strap with nail varnish to stop it provoking a rash on her wrist. But then, she'll probably only wear it 'for best'. Apart from that, she has to confect an appearance of delight that she simply doesn't feel. What she does feel is that Freddie is simply throwing money away on things that none of them, well, apart from him, really want.

Ryan already has a watch with a stopwatch and chunky buttons that he adores (last birthday present). At least he was savvy enough not to tell Freddie that his new high-kicking watch looked like something his grandfather might have worn, had he been pompous (or rich) enough.

And as for Poppy with a diamond necklace? Alice can't see the sterling silver chain lasting long as Poppy climbs the tree at the bottom of the garden or crawls in and out of the dens she and Ryan have constructed between the oleanders.

How does she stop him without looking, and maybe feeling, like the biggest killjoy in his life? She miserably considers how she's rarely seen him happier. There's a twinkle in his eye, and a growing hole in his (their?) bank balance. But, to her, the whole escapade has an odd feel to it. The holiday was nice, the holiday was wonderful, but only once they'd moved back to Casa Lola. El Paraíso had been a bit of a letdown, especially for the children. And although he probably wouldn't admit it, even Freddie seemed to relax more when not attempting to keep up with Terrance and Kathleen. He also stayed more sober.

She simply feels confused, and conflicted. Ryan and Poppy receive expensive watches and jewellery and run out to play like they've each been given a bag of crisps. Genuine thanks, but they're gone now. Ryan's watch probably left in a drawer because she knows he'll prefer the one with the buttons and the stopwatch; Poppy's necklace will end up in her 'jewellery box' along with a dozen bracelets and necklaces she's made out of bits of plastic and rubber bands. Either that, or it'll end up in Mags's jewellery box, swapped for some other trinket that Mags had probably traded with somebody else.

And as for her? She sits looking at her sparkly new watch, wondering if it's going to start making her skin come out in a rash, or has it got some 'special' metal that doesn't itch? Are those real diamonds encrusted – she's sure she's never used that word before – in the face? She guesses they must be, but what difference does it honestly make? She'd have to tell someone for it to make a difference. Maybe she could lean over to the table next to her next time she's in the John Lewis coffee shop: *Look, I've got diamonds encrusted in my watch.* What would she expect anyone to say in reply?

She's not even sure she wants to check Freddie's bank statement to see how much he's splurged. She's afraid of another, but bigger, shock than the price of the decades-old bottle of wine. And what difference would it make how much he's spent, except it's another x-thousand pounds off the balance? She guesses she won't feel too bad if it's cost him a couple of thousand. But she'll feel dreadful if it cost, say, ten grand? Go figure that. The more he spends on her, the worse she feels. Because she doesn't want it. It's him; he wants her to want it. But she doesn't. And she's no longer really sure what she *does* want.

'I've been thinking,' Freddie says suddenly, causing her heart to drop.

'What?'

'An earring. A diamond, maybe? What do you think...?'

32

THE COFFEE MORNING

THERE's a letter on the breakfast table, put there by Poppy: Spanish stamp and postmarked Mallorca. Beautiful copperplate handwriting, so probably from Lola. Alice is about to open it when she notices it's addressed to Ryan.

She studies it. The handwriting, now she looks more closely, is not an adult's hand. It's too precise, too careful. Alice's heart flutters. She turns it over. There, on the reverse, in the same beautiful, precise copperplate handwriting is the name and address of the sender.

Rosalita Alcántara Gil, Casa Lola, Palma de Mallorca, Mallorca, España.

Ryan bustles into the kitchen, sits down and starts filling a bowl with bran flakes. Alice drops the letter in front of him.

'Letter for you,' she says, carefree, calm as you like: *Here's your football kit; put it upstairs when you've finished.*

Ryan double takes, stares at the envelope like he's never seen one before.

'Spanish stamp,' Alice says with a nod and a smile, unable to resist.

Ryan picks it up and studies the stamp, the handwriting. Then he turns it over.

Alice picks up her plate. *Give him some space*, she reasons. *It's only fair.* She bustles at the sink, listens to him slicing it open with the breadknife – he'd usually rip it, she's sure.

'Who's it from?' she asks, unable to contain herself.

'It's Rosalita. From Casa Lola.' Like there are a dozen Rosalitas in his orbit.

'Oh, that's nice. I bet she wants you to help her with some English...'

Alice washes her plate for the fourth time, desperate for him to say something, but he's deeply engrossed in the letter now. Funny for her to write a letter, she thinks. So old-fashioned. Why not email? Or is it that they only have one computer, the hotel one; she's seen the children on it occasionally. Maybe Rosalita wanted a bit of privacy... She sneaks a glance. It's A5, folded once, looks like two pages, pale-blue paper, dense writing. Can she smell a whiff of perfume...?

'You should help her if she's asking,' Alice says, as she exits the kitchen towards the stairs. 'Lovely girl...'

***

Alice invites Emma out for coffee – 'my little treat'. She likes Emma, wants to nurture her friendship. In the back of Alice's mind, way back, there's a dark cupboard: inside it is a question, a question that's been nagging at her – she wonders if she could confide in Emma.

The other people she knows in the street are acquaintances. She chats with them, helps old Mrs Wilson with a bit of shopping sometimes, has babysat for the Khans once or twice.

But she couldn't confide in any of them: about the money, about Freddie, about what's happening... She almost wishes her mother was still alive, but she could never have talked to her about Freddie, not about this. Not about anything, in fact.

Alice's mother, Petula, hadn't liked Freddie. Years later, after they were married, Alice had confided this to him. She admitted to herself, and herself alone, that Petula had actually hated Freddie. She'd warned Alice against going out (*consorting*) with him. Petula thought Freddie had too high an opinion of himself with all his 'highfalutin airs' about becoming a bank manager like his dad. Petula said Freddie looked down on her (she worked in the toy department in Woolworths) and Alice's dad, Michael (postman). She went as far as to accuse Alice of trying to marry above her station. This had made Alice laugh.

They'd shared a love of Jane Austen, and Alice, by now, was studying her at A level. She, rather unwisely, likened Petula to a reverse Mrs Bennet, attempting to prevent Alice from making good with Freddie. This, of course, only served to confirm Petula's view, and add the sin that Alice was doing it deliberately. Their shared discussions of *Pride and Prejudice*, and all things Austen, ceased at that point, to both their dismay. Freddie, unwittingly cast as Darcy, was blissfully unaware of the unfolding plot in the Bennett household, the real-life one, for Alice's maiden name was indeed Bennett, but with a double T.

Petula didn't speak to Alice for three days when Alice announced her engagement to Freddie. Then, when she did speak to her, Petula threatened to cut Alice out of her will – not that Petula had much to leave.

Alice feels Emma might be different. Different from her other neighbours, she means. Not different from Petula.

Everybody in the world is different from Petula. Emma is... well, Alice thinks she's like her: ordinary, normal, she'd listen, offer sensible advice. Care!

It's only after she's suggested going out for coffee, and overcome Emma's resistance by insisting, and paid four pounds fifty for each cup of coffee, and the same for each slice of cake – *I insist* – that Alice realises. The penny drops. The eighteen pounds drop. Her 'little treat' is clearly a 'big issue' for Emma. A big financial issue. How could she not have seen it?

It's not that Alice makes a habit of going out for a coffee, but it isn't that big a deal. Certainly not now. The knowledge of two point three million in the bank, even though most of it's technically in Freddie's account, has made the (not a) habit, well, a bit more habitual. But she should have thought. Should have worked out that the resistance wasn't about the time, or the distance, or whether they'd be late to pick the kids up from school. No. It was all about the money.

Alice only suggested 'going out' for a change. She really didn't realise how much a change costs nowadays. She makes a mental note: when Emma insists she returns the favour – she knows she will, and Alice won't be able to talk her way out of that self-laid bear trap – she'll pretend she's had a huge breakfast or lunch so really can't manage a bit of four-pound-fifty cake. She also decides to nurse her coffee, nibble her cake, so that Emma can't suggest another. Not today. Alice even wonders if it's her who has the hang-up about how much the coffee and the cake costs, not Emma. But she knows.

They chit and chat, Alice desperate that it's a good conversation, so Emma doesn't feel the eighteen pounds has been an extravagance. They talk about their pasts, how Emma ended up in Norwich, their families, their hopes. It's at this point that Alice feels her pulse racing: is this the moment when she can bring up the issue? Is it too soon? Does she know Emma well enough yet? But, while she's deliberating, the conversation swirls back to family, to Poppy and Mags.

'You know, Poppy's quite a special little girl,' Emma suddenly says, apropos of nothing in particular. 'Quite a few of the other girls in school steer clear of Mags. It happened in her old school as well. It wasn't deliberate unkindness; they simply didn't have the patience to wait for her. Poppy almost seems to relish the challenge. She'd make a great nurse, you know. Or a primary school teacher.'

Alice laughs. Yes, Emma's right. Poppy is a bit of a waif and stray collector. Injured birds and hedgehogs, even snails that seem to have lost their zip. Plus, of course, the 'special needs' kids at school. Who was it that insisted Tony, the lad in the wheelchair, could enter the fifty metres at sports day, because Poppy would push him? Poppy. They came third.

'Can't the doctors do anything for her?' Alice enquires, aware that they've never discussed Mags's eye issue, Alice always avoiding the subject, in case Emma didn't want to talk about it, waiting for Emma to bring it up.

'Oh, she's on the waiting list. She needs an operation on each eye. But the list seems to get longer and longer the longer she's on it. I did ask the docs if we could go private, not that I agree with it, but they said we'd be talking up to fifteen thousand quid. They could do her in a week. But that kinda money's not an option. Trouble is, she's missing so much at her age. As much as we, and Poppy, read to her, she's not *learning* to read. They say she'll catch up. But what will she miss while she's catching up? And then there's the social stuff, like hanging around and sharing little secrets with a gang of friends. Maybe playing football, like Poppy. She's been a lifeline, you know. At her last school Mags became a bit of a loner. I hope Poppy's not losing other friends, because of Mags.'

Alice covers Emma's hand as she notices tears welling. 'Absolutely not. Poppy steers her own path. Will of iron, that girl. Don't worry about Poppy. She's friends with Mags because she likes Mags. I've watched them. They chatter away non-stop while they play. It's nice to see. I watch other girls, in the playground, they chatter, but you can see it's not always a conversation. More like two monologues, with gaps, but nobody's really listening, if that makes sense? Poppy and Mags? They *listen* as well.'

Emma nods. 'Mags is a good listener. Has to be.'

Alice cringes. How could she have been so careless? So clumsy? Of course Mags is a good listener. *Dummy!* She changes the subject.

Alice refuses Emma's offer of another coffee and can feel Emma's relief. It's nearly time to collect the children anyway.

'Let's do this again,' Emma suggests, one of Alice's top three possible outcomes for her initial approach. Top of the list had been to unload on Emma, about Freddie, and the win, without mentioning specific numbers, just the gist: Freddie wanting X, Alice wanting any fucking letter of the alphabet except X.

'Love to,' Alice agrees with a smile. 'Maybe find somewhere a little cheaper next time. I didn't realise it was so expensive here.'

'Well, look, can I give you my share–'

'No, no! I didn't mean that. Really. I meant next time.' Alice touches Emma's arm. It's not a touch that would prevent Emma from opening her bag if she went for it. Alice simply wants it to be a friend's touch. She feels she's mucked up the whole afternoon: going to a coffee shop; choosing an expensive one; commenting that Mags is a good listener; then, while attempting to protect Emma from a repeat eighteen pounds meal deal, somehow suggesting that she wanted her to pay for her coffee and cake. Alice wants to bang her head against the wall. Why can't she say what she means? Why does it always come out wrong? Or not come out at all?

Emma smiles. Alice smiles. Next time, she'll tell her.

33

THE BIG MATCH

Poppy screams. It's a full-throated scream, straight from a horror film showcasing a varied selection of DIY tools. She starts jumping up and down. Then, while she continues to jump up and down, she starts screaming again.

Alice watches her. She's never seen her so animated, wonders if she's often like this in school. Does Ms Gibson see a very different child? She's almost out of control. She's now shaking her head as she screams and jumps up and down, like a mini thrash-metal guitarist, dressed in a canary-yellow football top. The teams have only just come out onto the pitch, first game of the new season; God knows what she'll do if Norwich City score a goal...

Alice claps along with the crowd. She's quite enchanted by the colours and the sunshine. Somehow, the lush green of the grass – don't they call it turf in football? – and the yellow shirts of Norwich, the bright blue of Wigan, all make it seem like an enormous theatre set. And the noise is numbing. She's never been to a football match before; she never thought it would be like this. For some reason, when she's thought of football, it's been in black and white, an overcast day, the crowd all wearing overcoats and flat caps. There are no women. But there is a white horse. This is actually quite exciting. It's more like a show in the West End. She could really enjoy this.

'Come on, you yellows!' she finds herself shouting, after an old man sitting in front of her shouts it. She catches Ryan's eye. He looks like he's got the cream, a whole tub full of it, sitting there in his scarf and bobble hat, next to Freddie (minus scarf and bobble hat) on a sunny afternoon, his mum shouting *Come on, you yellows*. It's like all his dreams have come true, except the one where he's on the pitch instead of in the stand. But he's still happy enough with this. Not quite in the Poppy completely out of her mind mood, but very happy. A whole season ahead of him. Alice congratulates herself on her snap decision to suggest family season tickets in an attempt to cement them in Norwich, at least for a while, until Freddie comes up with his next suggestion of somewhere worth investigating for the new house. He was touting Northumberland the other day. More good value up there, apparently.

She'd been thrilled when Ryan had reminded them all that it was Mum's choice for lunch, so thrilled she said she'd changed her mind, she wanted Pizza Express, which brought a cheer nearly as loud as the Barclay Stand from Ryan and Poppy.

Now Freddie's shouting something, although she can't hear what it is. But he seems happy – ish. She leans forward and waves to attract his attention, indicates the kids, them all together, all the green and the yellow, a bit of blue, gives him the thumbs up. He smiles, like he's accepted a sort of defeat that he's slowly realising maybe isn't a defeat after all. Now, all they need to round off a happy day together, is a Norwich win.

Simple pleasures, she thinks. And then she realises: if Freddie hadn't won the lottery, they'd never be sitting here, all together, in the sun, with smiles on their faces and nice feelings in their stomachs: Freddie, content – ish; Ryan, happy with his lot; herself, relieved and surprised; and Poppy, off the scale.

Alice watches the match in a sort of trance. Is this what two point three million pounds buys you? An afternoon out, all the family together, at Norwich City? It seems absurd. But here they are. And, bizarrely, she's enjoying it, her very first football match. Why hasn't she ever thought to go before, take Ryan and Poppy?

Ryan, of course, is pleased as a volley of punches. Knock-out blows, all of them. And Poppy, incredibly, is absolutely immersed in the whole experience, soaking up the noise, and thrilled to be allowed to make as much of her own as she likes. Alice soon picks up the *ooohs* when Norwich come close to scoring; and the *ahhhhhs* when an attack breaks down. It's like another new language. She wonders if Spanish football crowds make the same noises. Then she ponders the likelihood of there being a club on Mallorca. Now, wouldn't that be fun?

Even Alice, who knows nothing about football, is beginning to anticipate the noise building when Norwich attack, and how quiet it goes when they have to defend. She notices her heart start to race when Norwich approach the goal, and doom flooding her stomach when they're forced back. How can she care so much, so quickly? It's like a drug, she realises. And suddenly she can understand Ryan, with his hat, and his scarf, his Todd Cantwell shirt, his collection of programmes, his wall of yellow posters. She sneaks a sly glance at him, on the edge of his seat, fists clenched, eyes locked on the ball.

And there's Freddie. She watches him slowly sinking into the atmosphere, getting immersed in the fact that this, this *game*, somehow matters. If not to him at the beginning, then he certainly seems to realise it once Wigan score.

It happens in a flash. Norwich have spent the first half an hour having shots aplenty at the Wigan goal. Then, suddenly, as if by magic, a Wigan player is running with the ball straight at the Norwich goal in front of them. Alice stands, as if she might help the goalkeeper in some way. But the ball rolls into the goal, to an almost unearthly silence, given the size of the crowd. The only noises are a curious scraping sound as the ball spins into the back of the net; and a small group of Wigan supporters, clad mostly in blue, who are going berserk off to their left.

Alice looks to Ryan for... she's not sure what. An explanation, possibly? How can that happen? Norwich have almost scored on three or four occasions, and now they've let a goal in. Ryan shrugs stoically, like it's not a big surprise. Alice wants to hug him, protect him from the pain and disappointment. Poppy is suddenly silent, staring at the celebrating Wigan players in front of her like one of them has stolen her bike. Alice realises that the games to come, over the months to come, might be more of a rollercoaster of emotions than she'd initially anticipated, when the air was full of expectation and the smell of recently mown grass.

'That's not fair,' Alice announces to the glum-looking Norwich fans sitting around them.

Freddie is suddenly more animated, shouting 'Play up!' every now and again as his contribution to the communal yearning for Norwich to equalise. He's up out of his seat every time Norwich attack, and on the edge of it when they have to defend. She's rarely seen this side of him. Where's it come from? He's never shown the slightest interest in football before. Ryan has usually gone with the school, when he's gone at all, free tickets dished out to the local schools in an attempt to fill the ground with some, albeit high-pitched, noise. But here he is,

Freddie, shouting at the referee for not giving Norwich a penalty. Bizarre. But somehow, wonderful.

But most of the time, as the game swirls around her, she's thinking about herself, and Freddie, and what they're going to do. Or, more accurately, what Freddie might do. She knows she should talk to him, but she's chained by the simple fact – they don't talk. Not really. Never have.

And then, Norwich score, unleashing a tsunami of noise and people jumping up and down. Ryan hugs Freddie, Poppy hugs Alice, and they're all jumping up and down deliriously. A few minutes later, Norwich shoot, and the ball hits the crossbar. Everybody seems to be holding their head in their hands, Alice included. And for some odd reason, she finds herself laughing at the theatricality of it all as the crowd all scream 'Oooohhhh!' together. Ryan stares at the pitch; Poppy is red-faced with the effort of her uncontrolled screaming; Freddie is open-mouthed, shocked, like he's just crashed the car into the back of a bus.

The game ends in a draw, but everybody seems delighted, as if Norwich don't usually manage even that. The sun is still shining; there's a lovely atmosphere as they file out of the stadium and on to the streets. Poppy and Ryan are chattering excitedly, their hands moving to show the path of the ball that dipped onto the crossbar: *We nearly won!*

Alice slips her arm inside Freddie's.

'Enjoy it?' she asks, keen for him to acknowledge how easy it's been to spend so little of the money and yet enjoy so rich a day out, together, as a family. Adding the lunch on to the front of the game has been a masterstroke, she thinks, turning an afternoon out into a family day out. She can't wait for a night match, when the floodlights will almost certainly enhance the whole thing, the colours so much brighter, the noise so much louder. Poppy will barely believe it. She even wonders, how they might, one time, go to an away game. Somewhere not too far, not Wigan, obviously, but she's heard Ryan mentioning Luton and Coventry, and Millwall in London. They could be nice places to visit. She might suggest that: a weekend in London and a nice family day out at Millwall...?

They walk back towards the centre of the city alongside the River Wensum, among a sea of yellow shirts. Alice doesn't want the day to end. She hunts for an idea to extend the occasion and suddenly announces, 'Back to Pizza Express for dessert, my treat!' At which, Poppy starts screaming again.

34

THE OFFER SHE CAN'T REFUSE

'I COULDN'T, honestly. I had an enormous lunch,' Alice lies. 'Just a coffee, really. Actually, I fancy an espresso.'

Alice can see the relief in Emma's eyes; it's obvious that she tries to hide it. The fact she returns with two coffees, no cake at all, confirms everything Alice already knew. She takes charge of the conversation. Her hand shaking, she lays an envelope on the table between them.

'Hear me out before you say anything, Emma. But I want you to have this, for Mags. For you. For Keith. For our friendship. And for Poppy. Please...'

Alice has spent sleepless nights wondering if she should, if she could, ask Freddie, should she tell Freddie, and every time, she's come to a different conclusion. The final conclusions she came to last night were yes, yes, and no. So, here she is. What did that sports clothing advert use to say? *Just do it!*

But this isn't a sports clothing ad. She should have told him. Told him first. Before. But did he tell her before he splashed out on his wine? The watches? No. So why should she have to tell him? He'd said she could treat herself. He never said he wanted to vet what she bought. What she did with the money. But she knows the real reason why she hasn't told him. She's afraid he won't be pleased. Won't agree. A bit like moving to Casa Lola for the second week of their holiday. If she'd consulted him beforehand, given him a chance to think about it, he'd probably have said no. So, she'd ambushed him. And it had worked out because they'd had such a good time; even he couldn't deny that the second week was much better than the first, corralled in with all the snobs and the Sex on the Beachers. So, she didn't tell him. Didn't give him a chance to object. And besides, didn't he spend eighteen thousand on his watch without telling her? She's had a peek at his emails.

Emma looks at the envelope like it might be a tax demand. It's a couple of weeks since their first coffee out, where this idea, this treat, Alice's first real treat, had been born.

'What is it?'

'Open it. It would make me so happy. It would make Poppy so happy. Not that I've told her. Not that I ever would.' Ever *would*? She should have said *will*. Assume it's a done deal. No discussion.

'You're scaring me, Alice.'

'Just open it. Please...'

Emma lifts the envelope, turns it over in her fingers like she's feeling the quality of the paper. Then she slits it open, pulls out what's inside, and stares at it.

'Alice, I couldn't.' Her voice is trembling. She places the cheque on the table, sits back from it like it's something dangerous, maybe infectious, possibly lethal. A Novicheque, perhaps?

'Nothing would make me happier, Emma. Nothing would make Poppy happier, I'm sure. Please take it.'

'I can't. Really. It's so kind of you. But I can't take it. I really can't.' She shakes her head but doesn't take her eyes off the cheque. It's face up on the table, fifteen thousand pounds clearly visible in Alice's neat copperplate. Blue ink. She'd deliberately chosen blue. Less formal. A friend's colour.

Alice pushes the cheque a little closer to Emma, pulls out her phone and tippy taps on the screen. Alice has thought long and hard and again and again about this next move. Last resort, she's dubbed it. A Hail Mary pass. Only to be used if the fan is in danger of being painted brown. She takes a deep breath, taps a couple more times on her phone, then turns it to face Emma.

'Listen, Emma. Listen to me carefully. That's my bank balance: over three hundred thousand pounds. We had an inheritance a few months ago. Freddie's going to buy himself a new car. A fancy one. It will cost a lot more than that cheque's made out for. It embarrasses me, but what can I do? He's moved Ryan to a private school and the fees for the year are also more than that cheque. He's bought himself a bottle of wine that cost over three hundred pounds. One bottle. That embarrasses me, too. I think he's gone a bit crazy, but I don't know how to talk to him about it.

'Anyway, he's quite happy for me to treat myself to a few things. I walked around John Lewis for over an hour a few weeks back, trying to treat myself. I bought a nice top in the end, cost me twenty quid. Then I treated myself to a coffee. I really don't know what I want to do with this money. I have everything I need, Emma. I have Freddie, even though he's gone a bit loopy. I have my kids. We have a nice home. I like my job. I have good friends. We have a lovely little three-star holiday in Spain every year. We bought season tickets for Norwich so we could do something as a family that the kids are really excited about. Apart from that, I don't know what to spend any of this money on. It sits there until Freddie buys another bottle of wine and I don't really know what to do with any of it. Except this.' She puts her finger on the cheque, deliberately moves it another few centimetres closer to Emma in the process. 'I know I want to do this. More than anything else I can think of.' She sits back and points at the cheque. Briefly, because she notices her hand is shaking.

Emma goes to speak, but Alice talks over her. 'I simply see it as so unfair, Emma. Pure chance has given us more money than we know what to do with. More money than we need. More money, frankly, than I want. And the only thing I can get excited about, the *only* thing, is the operation for Mags. How happy that would make Mags. How happy it would make Poppy. How happy it would make you and Keith. How happy it would make *me*. Please, Emma, take it. Otherwise, it'll sit in the bank for years because we have no idea what else we would do with it. It's such a small proportion of what we've got. I hate saying this, because it's not me, but we won't miss it. It's numbers in a bank account to us.'

There's a silence. Emma is staring at the cheque. Alice thinks she's close to taking it, so she presses on. All the arguments she rehearsed last night, and the nights before, as Freddie snored contentedly next to her, because she knew she might need them. She's beyond Hail Mary now; this is the full rosary.

'You know, I hate all the etiquette about money that we British have. We won't talk about it. It's somehow bad manners or gauche. I wish we could cut through all the crap. We've got a ridiculous amount of money that we don't really need. A small proportion of it would make a lot of people happy, especially some very small children who are dear to our hearts. Can we not simply cut through all of that and do a little deal together? Two no-nonsense women, rewriting the rules of etiquette?'

Emma pushes her chair back, stands. A tear hits the table between them.

'Thank you, Alice. Thank you, really. But I can't. I'm sorry.'

She turns, bolts for the door. Alice is up, tries to follow, tries to call after her, but people are looking, her bag falls off her lap, empties onto the floor, her phone is on the table, next to nearly ten pounds' worth of unfinished coffee.

35

THE NICE SET OF WHEELS

'GOT SOMETHING TO SHOW YOU ALL...' Freddie shouts from the front door. The kids pelt towards him; Alice's stomach drops.

He's been out all morning. 'A little something to do,' he said, slipping out before she could ask. Norwich are playing away this weekend, so he's got a free day. So, she knows it's *something*. House? Car? Yacht? Cigars? Earring...?! Once again, he's grabbed the reins, given them a bit of a flick, and she's bouncing about on the rump, in danger of falling off.

She wishes he wouldn't do this: spring surprises on them. But the children love it, and Freddie loves it, and she feels a killjoy.

'Wow!' Ryan. But it's a car 'wow', she's sure. He wouldn't be taking them out front for a house, or a yacht, unless it's on a huge trailer. No, even Freddie wouldn't do that, she prays. And, although he might haul them outside to show them a cigar he thought he should have now he's rich, she doubts Ryan would 'wow' over a cigar. And if it were an earring... well, she doubts Ryan would be wowing over that. He'd probably be dumbstruck. So, it's a car. He's gone out and bought his car, she's sure. *His* car. The car he's always dreamed of. And now she can hear it: growling out front like a lion loose in the road. Poppy is squealing. Ryan is wowing again. Freddie will be looking so proud, wishing his dad was still alive, to show him how well he's done. Not that he's actually done anything – simply kept buying lottery tickets. Alice heads for the front door while attempting to morph her mouth into a smile.

It's sleek, and low, and the roof is down, and it's a sort of mustardy-yellow colour, and Freddie's in the front seat, with Ryan beside him, and Poppy squeezed in the back, where there doesn't seem to be enough room for another seat.

'My goodness,' she manages to say, and the three of them beam at her, but none of the beams are as bright as Freddie's. His is a full beam, sparkly fog lamps too.

'Get in,' he shouts, like Ryan Gosling might, or Brad Pitt, from the front seat of a sleek sports car, with the roof down, parked outside their semi-detached house in Norwich. 'Let's go for a spin. Jump in the back, Ryan.'

So, she grabs her door keys and lowers herself into the front seat. It's plush and comfy and seems to fold itself around her like a soft embrace. She feels like she's only inches off the ground. And despite the roof being down, it's got that new-car smell. She's not sure how she recognises a new-car smell, they've never owned a new car. She's not sure she's ever even been in one; Rusty was eight or ten years old when they bought it.

Freddie guns the engine. How does she know that expression? Neither of them has ever gunned Rusty, afraid they might kill it, probably. This car sounds like an animal. Not a lion, now she's close up, but certainly cat-like. A cheetah, maybe, not that she's ever heard a cheetah growl. Perhaps on a David Attenborough, but she's not even sure cheetahs growl. And they're away...

'Go faster!' Poppy squeaks, as Freddie crawls, very un-cheetah-like, around the corner into the traffic, then kangaroo-hops as he tries to belatedly gain speed in front of the honking horns. The cheetah screams and yowls; Ryan and Poppy yelp with unrestrained joy; Alice finds her fingers gripping the seat; and sees sweat breaking out on Freddie's face.

'I'll head for the dual carriageway,' he says, as he crawls down Newmarket Road at a stately 28mph. He takes her up to 48mph when they hit the A11. *Why are cars always female?* Alice wonders.

'You two okay in the back there?' Freddie shouts as the wind starts to make conversation difficult.

'What?' they yell in excited unison.

They seem to reach Thetford on the A11 in less time than it usually takes Alice to boil an egg. But that's probably the excitement because the cheetah's been grumbling all the way like she wants to go faster, but Freddie's very aware of the speed limit so obviously sticks to one mph under it. He turns at a roundabout and they're on their way back, more grumbling from the frustrated cheetah.

As they pootle back along the A11, hanging a sliver below the limit, they seem to be overtaken by more cars than they usually were in Rusty, which never went near the maximum allowed.

'It's well known,' Freddie leans across and shouts at Alice, 'people get jealous when they see a fancy car and feel compelled to overtake it. You're meant to ignore them. Certainly never try to race them. Idiots.'

Alice wonders if he's telling her this simply so that she knows what it's going to be like in a posh car, or because he's fully expecting she might decide to drive this car next time she takes the kids to school? They haven't actually spoken about 'her' new car in a while. Is he thinking she's simply going to go out, like he's done, and buy herself a car from her three hundred thou? She doesn't fancy buying a car on her own. She's never done it. Although, to be honest, Freddie's car-buying experience isn't much better than hers. They bought Rusty together. That's the beginning, middle and end of both their car-buying CVs.

Well, until today.

The kids are in the garden. Poppy's still wearing her 'diamond' necklace, today over an old Care Bears T-shirt. Ryan's trying to beat his keepie-uppie record – twenty-seven – wearing a ten-thousand-pound watch.

Alice is reading her latest book. She likes books about relationships, although, to be honest, most of the relationships in the books she reads don't last long. By the third chapter, they've usually imploded or exploded or simply collapsed, and the woman, usually wife, is left to pick up the pieces. She's not sure why she reads these books. She's read (and reread) all the classics. Most of them are about relationships. So, she sees these as sort of substitute classics. Or maybe they could be classics-in-waiting. Although she doubts that, can't see any modern authors joining Austen or Dickens on the exam syllabus before she's hung up her dry-wipe markers. Freddie's standing at the bay window staring out through the net curtains.

He's been there for nearly an hour. Every now and again, he'll mutter something. 'Those kids from number four are looking at it. That woman from down the road, the one with the stiff leg, she's stopped and is peering in the window.' Alice doesn't know if it's simply pride: wanting to know who's looking at it and for how long. Or is this a private neighbourhood watch scheme? Their own? Just for Freddie's car? Cos he's afraid somebody might steal it...? Or key it?

That's a thing, he told her as soon as they got back: keying cars. It means scratching it with a key because you're jealous. Alice wondered for a moment if he'd come back dizzy from the 'spin', but he said he'd read it in the *Telegraph*. He's not bothered, cos it's insured to the eyeballs. Even against hailstones, he said, because of the soft-top, although she wasn't sure he was being serious.

It's got a bit like that: her not really knowing or understanding what's going on in his mind. He gets a package with three-hundred quid's worth of wine in it. Then another with thirty-five thousand quid's worth of watches. Now he arrives back from a little 'shopping spree' with a sports car. She's no idea how much he's spent. She can't be sure what he'll do next. She wonders if she could turn her predicament into eighty-thousand words and write one of her novels – except this time the man runs off with the car instead of another (younger, prettier, sexier) woman.

They'd not been back from the 'spin' half an hour when he went out again and moved Rusty down a bit so he could shunt the mustard pot directly out front, where he could 'see it properly'. She hopes the neighbours don't complain that Freddie's encroaching on 'their' bit of the road now Rusty has been nudged out of the way to make room for Freddie's new toy.

So, there's another little foible that's entered their life: Freddie affixed to the net curtains to make sure nobody's stealing or keying his car. She'd never heard of keying a car before, and now it's Freddie's new fixation.

She watches him over the top of her novel as he sways slightly left or slightly right, searching for the next neighbour to pass his car and glance at it.

'Old Mr Thomas has slowed down. He's looking inside...'

One Christmas, not long after they'd bought Rusty, Freddie had asked her to get him a leather steering-wheel cover, one of those ones you had to lace up. And a pair of driving gloves.

She'd got the gloves in Jarrolds, had to ask for them. She wasn't sure anybody outside the aristocracy wore such things. But the Jarrolds shop assistant hadn't blinked. 'Driving gloves? Small, medium or large...?' They hadn't been on display, but down under the counter in a dusty box, she remembers with a smile. Will he now be searching them out from the bottom of his sock drawer (he rarely wore them), and unlacing the steering-wheel cover from Rusty, or asking her to get him some of those driving goggles that racing drivers wore way back when racing cars went about as fast as Rusty could go now?

'Here comes Mrs Gibbs with her Dalmatians...'

'I hope she doesn't let them piddle on it,' Alice mutters with a smile.

Freddie stiffens, takes a half step closer to the curtains...

36

THE LONG-TERM LOAN

ALICE OPENS THE FRONT DOOR. It's Emma; she's clearly been crying.

'I've come to apologise.'

'For what?'

'For the other day. For running–'

Alice shakes her head, smiles. 'It's not a prob–'

'It was such a shock–'

'I understand. Really, there's no need–'

Emma sighs. She looks dejected, like she hasn't slept for days. Not at all her usual perky self, steamrollering life's daily problems with a smile and a shrug.

'Come in. Sit down. I'll make us some tea.'

While Alice fusses with the teapot and a packet of chocolate Hobnobs, Emma slumps at the kitchen table, head in her hands.

'I don't think I even thanked you,' she mumbles at the tablecloth.

'You thanked me, Emma. I shouldn't have sprung it on you like that.'

'No, it wasn't that. It's just all so confusing. I worry about

Mags. About her falling behind, not making friends, and then you offer to help, and I turn you away–'

'You didn't turn me away. I sprung it on you, and you didn't know what to do. I'd probably have done the same in your situation. I'm sorry.'

'Oh, please don't apologise. Christ, Alice, you've done nothing wrong.'

'The offer's still there. The cheque's in my bag if you change your mind. Which I would love you to do…'

Alice's heart lifts as the silence stretches. She quickly reaches for her bag and puts it on the table, but says nothing, continues to fuss with her best teapot, desperately trying to control her shaking hands so she doesn't rattle the lid or spill the milk as she's pouring it into her best matching jug.

She watched a programme once, National Geographic channel it might have been, on the Japanese tea ceremony. She'd been enchanted by it. All the tatami mats, the fancy kimonos, the posh hairdos, the dainty little cups. Apparently, the ceremony is meant to create a bond between the people involved: the tea maker and the guest. Part of the ritual, the tea making, is done in silence. While Alice might usually have chatted while making tea, this time, she doesn't. The silence at this point, in Japan, is meant to be meditative, she thinks, so she lets it linger now, hoping Emma is meditating on her bag, on the cheque for *Fifteen thousand pounds only*, made out to *Emma Ings*, in blue ink, which is inside. Alice places her best cups and saucers on the tray. She knows neither of them take sugar, but she puts spoons out as well, eating more time, so Emma can meditate a bit longer…

She brings the tray to the table, still without speaking, trying to remember and imitate, a little, the poise and grace of the geishas in their kimonos. She seems to remember they managed to kneel while holding the fully laden tray and wearing a tight, knee-hugging kimono. She hopes the same meditative atmosphere can be achieved without the kimono – and the kneeling, otherwise Emma is going to experience another Japanese tradition that Alice remembers from the programme – the hot spa bath.

Silently, Alice unloads the teapot, milk jug, cups, saucers, spoons, and chocolate Hobnobs on a plate. She wonders if Hobnobs sell well in Japan. She sits down. Half her mind is quiet, meditative. She feels this is the way to handle it. She's made the offer again, but this time, she won't browbeat Emma. She'll simply let the offer stand, there, on the table, in her bag: *Pay Emma Ings, Fifteen thousand pounds only.*

The other half of her mind is in Norwich City taking a penalty mode. (They had one last week.) She couldn't believe how excited she'd been: standing up, sitting down, not knowing what to do with herself as the referee got all the players out of the way so the Norwich player could clear his mind. A lot of her excitement had been for Ryan; he'd looked so desperate for them to score. But quite a bit of it was for herself. They've been to three matches now, and she's come to see some of the players as friends, people working so hard to achieve what all the fans want. She even knows some of their names. She's waved at them when they've scored and one of them waved back at her. Well, that's what it looked like. She's even shouted at them!

She wants this to happen as much as she wanted Norwich to score their penalty. She wants Emma to say thank you, and take the cheque, and take Mags to the hospital so they can fix her eyes, and she can enjoy a normal childhood friendship with Poppy. If she can't spend such a small proportion of their money on this, then what is the point? What is the fucking point of having two point three million pounds if she can't spend so little of it on the one thing she'd really like to spend it on? Really. Serious question. What is the point? Freddie wants to buy wine, watches, six-star holidays, a flash car. No problem, sir. And she wants to buy an operation for Poppy's little friend.

'Could we call it a loan?' Emma says softly, so softly Alice can barely hear her. But she can hear her, and the words unleash the same feeling of joy and relief she'd felt when Norwich had scored their penalty. Only without the noise that went with it. And Alice manages, this time, not to leave her seat.

'Call it what you like, Emma,' Alice says, covering her hand. 'You can pay me back whatever you can, whenever you can. But remember, from my point of view, I'm giving this to you, for Mags, for Poppy's little friend. I don't want it back. I don't expect it back. They're my conditions. What you do is up to you. I won't fight you over it. If you give me money, I'll take it. You can give me a penny a month for the rest of our lives if you want, but I'll never ask for it. Never. You owe me nothing.'

Emma nods, covers her mouth with her free hand. Alice knows she's trying not to cry. Well, not to cry any more than she already is. Now's the time to leave her seat – silently.

37

THE HOUSE FOR SALE

There's a For Sale sign in the front garden. Alice slows to a halt, almost drops her bags of shopping. There's a For Sale sign in *their* front garden.

'Alice?' It's Emma, coming across the road: apron tied on, flour dusting her hands, concern dusting her face. 'I don't want to pry, but–'

Alice shakes her head. 'Will you take the children for an hour when I collect them from school...?'

He's not in. He must have come home at lunchtime to let the estate agent in, and now, presumably, he's back at work. How *dare* he? She feels like going outside and ripping it down. Breaking the post over her knee. But it looks quite sturdy. So, she paces instead, muttering. 'No, no, no! This isn't happening. This is not happening. We discuss this. You don't put the house up for sale and say nothing to me. Like my views don't count. Jesus, Freddie! What's wrong with you?'

She suddenly realises she's given him too much slack. The

wine. The watch. The car. He's got the impression he can do whatever he likes with the money, and she'll accept it. She had a minor stand over Poppy and her new school, but the price of that had been Ryan. She needs to be stronger. And the house is different, the mortgage is joint: it's theirs, not his. He can't simply decide, on his own, to move them all to Chipping Norton, or Chuffing-somewhere-else. He can't do that.

They'd pushed the boat out a long way when they'd bought their house, with a little financial help from Freddie's parents. She remembers the 'preferential' rate of interest Freddie's dad had charged them: 'much better than you'd get off a bank'. The *much*, Alice learned later, was as good an example of hyperbole as you were ever likely to get. But the house was worth the early sacrifice. It was bigger than a usual first-time buyers' house, and not that much smaller than what an estate agent would call a 'next-rung-up-the-ladder'.

Alice loved it at first sight. Within a week of them taking possession, she'd bought a cherry tree sapling from Notcutts and planted it in the front garden. It was a statement: she planned on them being there a while. They both wanted two children, and the house would easily accommodate a family of four. Freddie had always mumbled in the background that they could trade up, at some time, when he got his big promotion... But Alice could date his real yearning for somewhere bigger; she could even name the occasion.

Tasha had invited them to a housewarming, soon after she'd arrived at the bank. Freddie had been unable to close his gaping eyes and gobsmacked mouth from the moment they pulled into Tasha's drive. The drive had been the eye-popper. There was nothing that special about the drive – it was a bog-standard drive. But it was a drive, and that was what popped Freddie's eyes. And then he'd looked at the house.

Again, in Alice's eyes, there was nothing special about it. It was a nice house. No argument. It was simply a bit bigger than Freddie and Alice's: the windows were bigger; the hall was bigger; the lounge was bigger; the kitchen was bigger; the stairs were bigger, and they didn't go upstairs but, from the footprint of the ground floor (which also had a toilet), it was obvious that it had (more) bigger bedrooms. It also had a conservatory and a nicer garden – also bigger.

Alice spent weeks afterwards pestering Freddie to ask Tasha and Dick back to reciprocate, but Freddie always had an excuse: they were too busy; Tasha was too busy; there was an atmosphere at work; Tasha was away on a course; Dick was away at a conference; there was an R in the month. But Alice knew.

She knew because Freddie was grumpy for weeks after the party, and because when she woke up their computer one day, she found the browser full of the prices of houses in Tasha's area, and he'd idly started pointing out houses in estate agents' windows that had drives and bigger chimneys and dah-dee-dah. But it never went anywhere; they could never have afforded the jump in price. And then he won the lottery...

She looks at her watch, encrusted with diamonds but not (yet) making her wrist itch. She has to collect the kids. And then she needs to talk to Freddie – alone.

Emma takes the children. She might have guessed some of what's going on from Alice's brisk manner at the appearance of the For Sale sign: 'I need to have a chat with Freddie...' But Emma doesn't pry, doesn't ask, doesn't comment. 'As long as you need, Alice. We've got nothing on.' She's a good friend, Alice is realising.

'What's this?' Alice asks, pointing through the net curtains as soon as Freddie closes the front door. She folds her arms across her bust as she says it; but it reminds her of someone from her childhood TV memories: some stocky northern comedian who used to dress up as a woman and complain a lot in a working-class accent. So, she unfolds her arms, but then doesn't know what to do with them, so she folds them again.

'Oh that?' he says, looking out, maybe surprised it's still there. But she's finding it hard to read his thoughts anymore.

'Don't you think we should have discussed this?'

'We have discussed it. And anyway, it doesn't mean anything. It's just testing the waters. See what we might get for it. In fact, I've been wondering. It might be better if we kept it. Judith, the estate agent, said we could earn a nice little stream of income if we rented it out when we've got the new place.'

Alice takes a breath as yet another of Freddie's latest ideas storms her sitting room like a rhino on the rampage. So, what? He's planning on being a property developer in the UK now? As well as on Mallorca? A string of houses let out with 'a nice little income stream'? Bloody hell. How is his mind working?

'Freddie. Stop. You can't put our home on the market like it doesn't matter.' He takes a step forward and tries to put his arms around her, but she takes a step backwards. She doesn't want to be comforted, or whatever it is he's trying to do. This is a new dance, one they haven't practised before. There's a nervousness to it, like someone you're not sure you like has asked for the last dance at the school disco. 'I had Emma across earlier, almost in tears.'

Freddie huffs a little sigh. He hasn't taken to Emma, or Keith, has shrugged off her suggestions that they have them over for a return date. All his usual excuses from his self-published edition of *Twenty-First Century Debrett's*.

'Look,' he says, sitting down and motioning for her to do the same. But she doesn't feel like sitting down. She remains standing, like she might suddenly get her coat and walk out the door. She thinks he can sense her mood, that he's overstepped the mark: she suddenly realises that she likes the feeling. 'I had bank business with Judith this morning and I asked her, just a by the by, how much our house might be worth. She had a free morning and said she'd pop round. She said maybe over a quarter of a mil, although the market is a bit depressed at the moment, so no guarantees. She said they have a fifty per cent discount on their fees if we put a board up this week, but it doesn't mean we have to sell; it will simply give us an idea of what it's worth and how quickly it might move. And it gives them some free publicity in a slow market. Everybody wins. But we're in control, we can keep saying no until we find somewhere we like. We can take down the sign if we don't find anywhere. We'd lose nothing, and it costs us nothing.'

Alice goes to sit, changes her mind, walks to the window, looks at the sign.

'What about the children? It'll upset them, all these changes, what with Ryan already in a new school? I'm not sure it's the best time to be putting the house on the market.' As she says this, she feels herself getting annoyed – with herself. This isn't the *No, no, no!* reaction she'd had at first. This is another shimmy to the left, a shimmy to the right, *not the right time* isn't exactly *No, no, no!*

'We can tell them the truth. We're simply looking to see what it might be worth. Tell them we're not set on moving.'

'Because we're not. Are we? We haven't decided anything, have we?'

'Of course not. We're simply exploring options. It would be silly not to explore our options.'

'Right,' says Alice, but wondering if they're actually

speaking the same language. Do his words mean exactly the same thing in her mind as they do in his? Do her words mean exactly the same thing in his mind as they do in hers?

'Cuppa?' he says. Olive branch? Peace offering? Subject changer? Discussion avoider? Argument evader? Invitation to dance? All of the above?

'What do you think?'

Alice takes the flyer, along with her cuppa. It's a house. One point four million pounds. In Devon. Her stomach lurches. She thought Devon had come and gone. Or was that Cornwall? It's hard to keep up with Freddie's latest financial brainstorms.

'Where did you get this?'

'Judith gave it to me. She's thinking of moving down there, not that she could afford this. But we could. Would you fancy Devon?'

It's the first time he's seriously asked for her opinion. She wants to say, *No, I don't fancy Devon.* But would that lead him to ask her where she does fancy? And she'd be forced to say that she quite likes Norwich. Couldn't they look at houses not too far away? In the Golden Triangle, maybe? Or Cringleford? So she wouldn't lose touch with her friends? So the children wouldn't lose touch with their friends?

'It's got lovely views, look. Although it's quite small. Anyway, testing the swimming pool. No rush. You have to do these things carefully. I've read that moving house is one of the most stressful things you can ever do. Along with dying. I think that's what it said. I'm going to check out other locations too. You should also have a look. See if there's anything, anywhere, you like.'

She nods. Has he forgotten asking her if she'd fancy Devon? He leaves the flyer on the table, switches on the telly.

'I've been thinking,' he says, sipping his drink, flipping the channels, DCI Banks is getting a rerun somewhere in the pants of their TV. 'How old do you think is too old for a tattoo...?'

38

THE KNOCK ON THE DOOR

DCI Banks is playing his jazz. The lights are low. Annie is sitting on his sofa looking alluring. Banks is pouring two glasses of red wine from an almost-empty bottle. There's romance in the air. Again. But Alice and Freddie have watched this episode before, and Alice knows that there'll be a knock on the door, or Banks's phone will ring, or Annie's phone will ring, just when you think they're going to kiss...

There's a knock on the door. Funny, Banks is still moving closer to Annie, handing her a glass of red wine, a sparkle in his eye, two in hers. Hasn't he heard it? Is he ignoring it? Go on, Banksy – *kiss her!* Banks's phone starts to ring. There's another knock on the door. Freddie's up.

'That's our door...'

'But we have a bell...?'

There's another knock on the door. Banks is answering his phone. Annie's phone is ringing. Alice hits pause and tries to hear who's at their door. It's a man's voice, a bit of a monologue; she hears the word 'charity', said angrily, more than once. She can't hear Freddie saying anything. She hears the door closing.

Freddie comes in looking confused. DCI Banks is frozen,

while talking on his phone, looking angry, disappointed. Freddie sits back down next to Alice.

'That was Keith, from over the road.'

Alice braces; there's a sliver of trepidation hugging her.

'And?'

Freddie opens his fist. Inside are twenty or so small pieces of ripped paper.

'I didn't quite understand what he was saying. He was in a state, angry about something. Kept saying he didn't want charity. Rammed these into my hand.'

He leans forward and wipes the pieces of paper onto the coffee table, making more room by pushing aside the coffee cups and the plate full of crumbs. He starts to turn all the pieces the right way up, like he's about to do a jigsaw. Well, not *like*; he is about to do a jigsaw.

'I know what that is,' Alice says, recognising the colours of her bank, of her fountain pen: blue, a friend's colour. Her heart is thumping, but Freddie's already got the four corners in position. They don't do jigsaws together; he'd be good at them, clearly.

'Uh-huh...' He's obviously not listening, too involved in solving the little puzzle, the little jigsaw that Keith has slapped into his palm.

'It's a cheque,' Alice says, deadpan, almost to herself.

'Look. It's a cheque.'

'I wrote it.'

'Wha–?'

'I wrote it for Emma. For Mags.' Alice thinks she's going to cry.

Freddie stares at her. Then he stares at the jigsaw. He moves another little piece into place: it's the bit with most of Alice's signature on it. She can see a shred that says *thousand,* could easily move it into position for him. It's like his mind is captured by the jigsaw. She wonders if he's connected the jigsaw on the coffee table to the cheque she's telling him about. Is he too distracted by the puzzle? He moves another piece. Then he looks at her, a little guiltily, like he knows he's not paying attention.

'You–'

'She needs an operation on her eyes. Mags. She's on a waiting list but there's no sign of a date. They could get it done privately in a week or so. She's missing so much at school, and socially. I wrote the cheque for Emma. I meant to tell you. It must've slipped my mind...'

It's a piss-poor excuse, she knows. She feels grubby. Lying to him. Hiding what she was doing. Hiding it because she didn't trust him to agree. She feels shitty that she didn't trust him. Feels like she's let him down. Let herself down. Why, at least, hasn't she told him before now? Before Keith came round banging on the door and slapping it, torn to shreds, into Freddie's palm. She was going to. Wasn't she? *Wasn't* she? She's not sure.

She waits for him to say something. Wills him. Anything. *Why didn't you tell me?* She's answered that. She was going to. *How much did you give her?* But he's moving the *fifteen* piece into position and it fits perfectly. There go the two bits that make the word *pounds. Fifteen thousand pounds.* Are they going to get to the point where she says – maybe shouts – you spent more money on your car...? Will she be angry enough to say – to shout – your fucking car...?

She hopes not. She's not religious, but she prays not. She doesn't want to argue with him. She can't remember the last time they argued. What they might have argued about. Not sending Poppy to the girls' school was probably it. Although it wasn't really much of an argument; he gave in quite easily. Especially when she sacrificed Ryan. Jesus. It's like their life has become some *Thick of It* episode, each trying to outmanoeuvre the other with some clever, underhand wheeze.

He finishes the jigsaw. *Pay Emma Ings Fifteen thousand pounds only.* Then he sweeps the pieces into his hand and heads for the kitchen.

'Another cuppa?'

'Yes,' she says. Instinct. Wanting to move on. Move away. But also, not wanting to. There's a part of her that wants to have it out with him. This is the perfect opportunity. Confront it all. When he complains about her giving fifteen thousand pounds only to Emma Ings, she can come back at him with his plans to move them away from here; uproot the kids from their friends; the six-star holiday with half-naked teenagers and drunk, ageing snobs who looked down on them; God knows how much money wasted on a car that he spends more time looking at through the net curtains than he does driving. Is this the moment to do it? To take him on?

'Another biscuit?'

'Go on then.'

And yet, she feels relieved. At what he's doing. He's doing exactly the same as she does. He's avoiding it. Sweeping it away. Making a cuppa. Another biscuit. But shouldn't they... talk? But she fears talking because too many people talk nowadays. Modern couples discuss everything. And then they argue about everything. And then they split up. And then they divorce. Leaving the children with a broken home...

So many of their friends have married, then talked, then argued, then divorced, children now alternating homes on a weekly basis, old friends bitching about older friends. That's Alice's nightmare. Her marriage failing, like so many others, because everybody else *does* talk? Share? Unload? Unburden? And then they divorce. Is that why Alice has never told Freddie what she thought about his dreams? His dreams for her, and for the children?

Or have Alice and Freddie found the holy grail? She should write a book. Not a novel, but one of those *How to* books that solve the mysteries of the universe in two-hundred pages: *How to Avoid Divorce, for Dummies.* Or better still: *Happily Married Couples are from Jupiter; Divorcees are from Uranus.* Avoid those subjects that send marriages into tailspins? Could she drag that out into two-hundred pages? Is that really how they've survived? Is that how they will survive? Does she simply have to accept his car and his bottles of wine but quietly try to manoeuvre him away from a house in Great Snoring or wherever his latest brainstorm is, like she rescued Poppy from Hogwarts? Is that how they'll get through this? By *not* talking about it?

'Home to Coventry on Saturday,' he shouts through from the kitchen. 'Big game.'

Big game, she thinks. *But who's winning...?*

Freddie re-enters, refill coffee and extra biscuits on a tray.

'Rea-dy to crum-ble...' he announces, boxing MC-style, as he always does whenever he brings the biscuits in. Alice smiles, as she always does, whenever he does his rea-dy to crum-ble gag; their usual life re-established, as if Keith and the cheque has never happened. 'You know, I've been thinking,' he continues, DCI Banks still on pause, still looking angry, disappointed.

Alice steels herself. What on earth is he going to spring on her now?

'I'm not sure we're going to be able to afford everything we'd like, with the money we've got. We might have to make some choices. It's been looking at the houses that's made me realise. They're all a bit more expensive than I'd thought, and this place isn't going to fetch what I'd imagined. The market's a bit more depressed here than I'd realised.'

Alice's heart lifts. Her stomach, for once, stays in neutral.

'Really?'

'Yes. It's giving up work that's the issue. Together with a new house. If we gave up work, and didn't spend any of our money on a new house, then we could probably survive on what we have, and the interest, quite happily. It's so difficult to calculate, you see, if inflation's going to rocket again. What will happen with interest rates? Will they pick another economic illiterate to be PM? Are Ryan and Pops going to university? Those sorts of things could hit our calculations. Anyway, I've been thinking, if we looked for the new house somewhere cheaper. Or, maybe waited until the market improves. A year or so...?'

Alice nods encouragingly.

'The less we spend on the house, the more we have left to live on. Do you see?'

She nods again, wishes he wouldn't speak to her like he's explaining how to play Ludo to a three-year-old.

'So, I've been looking at some of the places where we'd get more bang for our doubloons, as they say, as an option, testing the water. Maybe get somewhere bigger and nicer than in Devon, but for much less money. How would you fancy Newcastle...?'

39

THE SANDWICH BAR

If she wasn't a teacher, Alice would like to own a sandwich bar. Just a small one, maybe near the university where she could have all the clever young things, in their torn jeans and colourful T-shirts, arguing about Marx or discussing physics or child psychology, all serious with raised voices and high ideals for the future, dropping in for a latte and a sarnie. In her dreams she would meet some of the students she'd taught at secondary and reminisce a little – or, maybe, a lot – and share in their hopes for the future.

She'd have all the different breads ready on one side: white, wholemeal, granary, rolls, baps, bagels, baguettes. Next to them would be the spreads: butter, marge, healthy non-marge stuff, olive oil, houmous or hummus, however you chose to say or spell it; she wouldn't care. Then all the fillings in a display cabinet: the meats; all the different cheeses, tomatoes, fruits and veggies.

She has these thoughts most weekday mornings when she's making the packed lunches for the day. Ryan's is the easiest. Anything is fine. Any bread, any spread, any filling. He probably wouldn't complain if she sourced some horsemeat from Spain or frogs' legs from France, especially if she picked out all the horseshoes and made sure there were no obvious webbed feet sticking out between the crusts. She always gives him a banana and usually slides a little 'something' she knows he really likes into his canary-yellow NCFC lunchbox: a two-fingered KitKat or a Club biscuit.

Poppy's pretty uncomplicated too, although she's recently gone off bacon. And ham. Alice thought she might be going vegetarian, but sliced chicken is still okay, and she still eats bacon as part of the regular Saturday morning fry-up. Poppy always likes a satsuma (recently two; she's a growing girl), and an orange Club (recently two, keep an eye on that), all slipped into Barbie's pink safekeeping.

Freddie has a spreadsheet. Well, not really, but he has a list: Monday, Wednesday and Friday it's wholemeal bread and meat, he's not bothered what type, but don't forget the HP sauce. Tuesday and Thursday it's white bread and cheese, always mature cheddar, with a swipe of Coleman's mustard. An apple a day keeps the dentist away, according to Freddie. All this in a two-seasons out-of-date, hand-me-up NCFC box that fills his otherwise empty briefcase.

Alice hoovers up the leftovers, often an eclectic mishmash of whatever probably won't survive the weekend in the fridge. She tries not to look too closely at what's going into her granary roll so that when she opens her cast-off, hand-me-up My Little Pony horsebox in the staffroom, she often has a nice surprise. And sometimes, just a surprise.

Yes, she'd enjoy running a sandwich bar. Piece of cake. Now, there's an idea for next week: Ryan does like a Mr Kipling...

40

THE REGENCY TALIBAN

ALICE IS UP TO SPEED: all her marking and prep is done, housework acceptable, shopping away, dinner organised, Freddie not yet home, Ryan playing football, Poppy *Rescuing a Racoon* – or possibly a rabbit. She has an hour or so to herself. Luxury time, she calls it. And in her luxury time? TV mini-series? Hairdo? Long soak in the bath? Nail bar? None of the above. In her luxury time, Alice reads. Sometimes, a rerun of a classic. Often, Jane Austen. Sometimes only a favourite scene, read for the hundredth time.

She flips open her Kindle. There was a time when she swore she'd never get one. She loved books, real books, too much. But in the end the weight in her suitcase on the way to Spain convinced her otherwise. And now she's a convert. She always stares at the pixels mishing and mashing on the screen before informing her that her latest book is 'downloading'. This is a kind of magic for Alice, having grown up in the previous world where 'buying a book' meant leaving the house, walking into the city, hunting along the shelves of WHSmith before purchasing it, with notes and coins, then carrying it home again in a paper bag, and using the receipt as her bookmark. Every paperback on her shelves has the original receipt tucked between the yellowing pages.

She still misses this ritual, even as she marvels at her new book downloading through thin air, and the rooms and roof above it, and the thinner air above all of that. The moment never fails to arrest her, cause her to wonder at the sheer impossibility of the world changing so much in such a short space of time. All her Jane Austens are, of course, pre-Kindle paperbacks with faded receipts.

She doesn't envy these Regency ladies. Not even the rich ones who have a bit more control over their lives. And, despite the happy endings, she doesn't envy Austen's heroines either, battling through what she sees as a thicket of restrictions on their freedom. She wouldn't go as far as to call it a Regency Taliban – but some of the parallels are spookily close. It's amazing, she often thinks, that these books are so popular with women. Maybe it's relief that the bullets have finally been dodged, to an extent. It's *Pride and Prejudice* if you want to celebrate progress made, she thinks, or *The Handmaid's Tale* if you need a reminder of the restrictions and, more latterly, the threats that still exist.

Her mind drifts further. Why can't she be more like Elizabeth Bennet? Why can't she accept Freddie's offer of a life upgrade as Lizzy had Darcy's, albeit eventually. Darcy had offered Lizzy a similar escape to riches, and she'd (finally) swooned at the offer. For the flat in Spain, read Pemberley. For the Porsche: a phaeton with ponies, maybe? She muses, can see herself tootling about in a phaeton with ponies, until an image of Freddie dive-bombing into the UEA Broad washes the scene away in an enormous cold and muddy splash, ducks fleeing noisily in all directions.

Today, she's in the middle of a modern book, a family drama. Her go-to genre when she isn't in the mood to look back or forward, an *as-it-is* book. The world as it is. Twenty-first century turmoil. It's good so far: wife is unhappy, on the edge of an affair, telling ever more complicated half-truths as she edges closer to the edge. It's called *Edging to the Edge*. Ludicrous title. It nearly put her off. But she's read the author before so trusted her form. Even though the blurb has *edge* in it six times.

The doorbell rings. She thinks she knows who it might be, so she isn't too disappointed at being disturbed...

'I'm sorry about last night. I–'

'It's not a problem. I can guess what happened. Come in.' Alice hits the kettle. Wonders if her Japanese tea ceremony silence might help. But Emma's in no mood for silence.

'We had a huge bust up, about the money. It wasn't so much the private health thing, although he's always been dead set against that. As am I. In principle. It was the charity thing. The wound to his bloody macho pride. That weighed more than Mag's health and welfare. You were right when you said we should do our own little private deal. What did you call it? Two no-nonsense women tearing up the rules of etiquette? I shouldn't have told him. I can see that now. I should have booked Mags in and pretended a cancellation came up at short notice. I had to rush her in and out. I should have bluffed it. Blagged it. I wish I had. At least Mags would have had the operation. I could have handled Keith.'

'I'll write you another one.'

Emma smiles, shakes her head sadly. 'I think it would cost me my marriage. Cost Mags her dad. I couldn't do that to her.'

They sit in silence for a moment. Two teas between them, untouched. Emma looks up. 'But thank you.'

Alice nods weakly, desperately tries to stop her tears from rolling. Fails miserably... 'It's so unfair,' she whispers, her voice trembling. 'I simply wanted–'

'I know,' Emma cuts in. 'As I said, if I'd taken your advice, kept it a secret, not blabbed to him about it. I should never have told him.'

Alice knows this isn't the moment to load Emma with her problems, about Freddie and the true story of the money, and what it's doing to their marriage, how she's having to weave ever more complicated dance steps to stop him from whipping her life, and the children's lives, out from under them, like a magician ripping a tablecloth from a fully-laid dinner table. But it is ironic, she muses, Emma thinking it best to keep secrets from her husband, just like she's keeping secrets from Freddie. Is it really the best way? Is it really the only way?

41
____

THE LION KING

Another surprise 'treat' from Freddie. Even Alice doesn't know where they're going. But they're going. In his car. *His* car. The mustard pot, she's dubbed it, silently. Down the A11, almost grazing the speed limit. So, she's guessing London. She had wondered if he'd got tickets for a Norwich away match, but the Canaries (Alice is picking up the lingo) are away at Blackpool, and they're heading south. But the kids are happy enough, the roof's down, the wind is blowing Poppy's hair all over the show and she and Ryan are either shouting excitedly at each other, trying to guess where they're going and what the treat might be, or they're raising their arms in the I'm-not-holding-on pose so popular on the big rides at the theme parks. Freddie does voice a little 'Now, now, settle down' warning, as if he's afraid one, or both, of them might be sucked out by a freak vortex. But what with the tornado of air circling the car, they clearly can't hear him.

Alice feels happy. Ish. Freddie is happy, the children are happy, Alice is happy. Ish. This is what you should do with two point three million pounds, she thinks. A little treat for the whole family. She's tried to wheedle details about what they're doing out of Freddie, but he's steadfastly refused to divulge a word, obviously enjoying his power of patronage greatly.

They pass Thetford, Alice always feeling smugly confident that they would pass Thetford, what with Freddie having a couple of million quid to spend. She does suffer a slight scare – *Please don't let him be heading for Devon* – but her fears are rendered unfounded when he crosses the M25. Destination London now increases to ninety-nine per cent. She notices Freddie checking his (new) watch occasionally, but he doesn't seem bothered, he doesn't speed up noticeably, so she guesses they're doing something in London and have time to spare. The satnav eventually announces their arrival at Redbridge Tube station, causing huge excitement for Ryan and Poppy who love riding the Underground.

Freddie shushes them away as he buys the tickets, not wanting to reveal their destination, and they pile onto a train that's heading for Ealing Broadway. This causes Alice to wonder. She's sure Ealing's in west London. She's no expert on the city, so she's no idea what delights Ealing – or its *Broadway* – might hold for them. But they change at Mile End and take a District line train heading for Wimbledon, which immediately serves up tennis in Alice's mind. But it's October, and as the train pulls into Westminster, Freddie stands up with a huge smile on his face and leads them towards the exit. Alice knows enough about London to realise what's coming. And when Freddie delays them for a few minutes, pretending to consult the train timetable, and his watch, she notices they're minutes from midday.

The children gasp at Big Ben as they reach the street, and it starts to bong like *News at Ten* has turned up the volume. Alice has worked out enough to have her phone ready to snatch a video of their gobsmacked faces, and Freddie's proud one. They stroll along the embankment licking overpriced ice creams and

Alice's suspicions are raised again as Freddie causes them to loiter within spitting distance of the London Eye, constantly glancing at his watch – as if...

The view of Big Ben from the top of the London Eye is even better than the view from the street. Ryan and Poppy gawp and point, and Alice feeds her arm through Freddie's.

'Thank you,' she whispers.

'Oh, this is the warm-up,' he replies with a twinkle. 'You wait for later on...'

Later on turns out to be hosted by the Lyceum Theatre, just off the Strand, where Freddie has tickets to see *The Lion King*, eliciting screams from Poppy to match those that greeted Norwich's first home goal of the season. Alice wonders if she needs to have a quiet word with her – about the etiquette of screaming in public. It's fine at Carrow Road, scream all you like. But in a packed, but relatively quiet, café off Oxford Street, not really the done thing.

They snatch selfies in the foyer in front of the publicity banners, a habit usually dismissed with eye-rolling by Freddie, but somehow, he's morphed into an average thirteen-year-old as he asks perfect strangers to record the moment for the four of them. Alice even wonders if he might have signed up for Instagram or TikTok. She wonders who'll be reeling more, her or him...?

Afterwards, they stroll through the West End, Alice hugging Freddie close as they watch the children chattering and pointing at sights they usually only see on the telly. A *ristorante italiano*, it is agreed by all, will be the perfect place to eat, even though *The Lion King* was set in Africa. And almost immediately they find Uno, with an outside terrace in Covent

Garden. They order, and the pizzas are the best they've ever tasted, and the most expensive Freddie has ever paid for. But, as with his ability to pay outrageous prices for watches and cars, he barely trembles as the credit card machine demands three figures for a couple of pizzas, a few drinks, and some house-brick-sized portions of tiramisu.

They toilet in sequence, with Freddie being the last. Alice notices a slight kerfuffle as he exits the restaurant, a tight squeeze as a number of young men rush out through the door, pushing past him, all noisy chatter and sharp elbows. Freddie is jostled and looks annoyed.

'Blooming oiks,' he grumbles as he returns to their table, sitting down and rubbing his foot. 'One of those idiots stood on my foot.'

He lifts his jacket off the back of his chair, stands, preparing to put it on when Poppy squeaks, 'Daddy, where's your fancy watch...?'

PART 5

ROOSTING CHICKENS

42

THE MUG

Freddie looks at his wrist like it belongs to a yeti. He rubs the bit where his watch should be.

'Wait a minute...' he blurts, turning and scanning the street. 'One of those oiks has taken it. I could feel someone grabbing me, just as one of them stamped on my foot.' He drops his jacket back onto the chair. 'Oi! You lot...!'

Poppy's eyes widen; Ryan's mouth drops open; Alice's brain engages. She grabs Freddie's arm.

'No, Freddie,' she says, standing and taking a firm hold of him. She's shocked at how strong he feels as he struggles to free himself. She's not going to be able to hold him.

'But they've taken my watch. I *know* they have.'

'Leave it,' Alice says, not wanting the children to witness too much more. 'It's gone, Freddie. They're a gang. Look at them. Professionals, probably. They're not going to say "Oh, sorry, mate, yeah, here's your watch". There's four of them, Freddie.' Then she lowers her voice to a hiss and presses her mouth to his ear. 'They probably have knives...'

The pressure on Alice's grip lessens. Freddie's *Daily Telegraph* is often full of knives, especially in London. His face turns from anger to a mixture of confusion, disappointment and fear.

'Let it go,' Alice whispers again. 'Don't make it worse. *The children...*'

Freddie sits down.

'Have they stolen your watch?' Ryan gasps, sitting up straight, like he might be preparing to join Freddie in a sprint down the street to tackle a gang of vicious, knife-wielding muggers who've made off with his dad's watch.

Freddie sucks in a deep breath. 'I'm not sure. Maybe I left it in the car.'

'No, you didn't. You were looking at it all the time on the train, and on the Eye. I saw you.' Poppy, ever the detective, has got Freddie bang to rights.

'Yes. I did have it. So, let me see. I think I took it off when I washed my hands in the toilet, in the theatre. Maybe I left it there.'

'Let's go back,' Ryan says, standing up. 'Somebody might have handed it in.'

Freddie shakes his head dubiously. 'They'll be shut now. I'll call them in the morning. Anyway, let's not let it spoil our weekend. We're not finished yet. The hotel's around the corner.'

'The hotel?' Three voices: indistinguishable incredulity.

'Yes. Tomorrow we've got a boat ride on the river and a picnic in one of the parks. Although if anybody has anything special they're dying to do or see in London, we might be able to squeeze it in...'

Alice grabs his arm as his proud smile returns.

'Thank you,' Alice says, kissing Freddie's cheek as they get ready for bed. 'That was such a lovely day. The children are absolutely thrilled. And so am I.'

Freddie shrugs. 'Yes, if only I hadn't been mugged in a restaurant. I feel such a fool. I'm sure, now I think about it, I saw one of those guys more than once, walking past our table. I'm quite certain now that they targeted me.'

'What did the police say?' Alice asks, Freddie having slipped out while she took care of the children.

'Well, you were right. First thing they asked me was had they been violent; did I see any weapons? Knives? Guns, even. They told me that stealing luxury watches is quite a thing nowadays.'

'Really?'

'Yes. It's very common. Have you heard of the boxer, Amir Khan?'

Alice shakes her head. A *Strictly* dancer, perhaps. One of the Norwich City players, for sure, especially the blond one on the wing. But a boxer? No chance.

'Well, anyway, he had a seventy-thousand-pound watch taken off his wrist in the street, *at gunpoint*. There are gangs of thugs doing it. It's really dangerous.'

Alice looks shocked. She hadn't really thought they'd have knives; she only said it to stop Freddie from chasing after a gang of four young hooligans and getting himself beaten up, especially with the children having free ringside seats for the night's main event.

'It could only have got worse, Freddie. Even if they weren't armed, there were four of them. They could have given you a right beating. The watch isn't worth it for the children to possibly see that, don't you think?'

'I do. But I wasn't thinking that then. I was angry. And I felt a mug. Stupid. I took my jacket off because I wanted people to see my watch. How stupid; how vain is that, Alice?'

She hugs him. 'Let it go, Freddie. It wasn't your fault. Let it go.'

'I felt something happening with my arm, but when one of them stamped on my foot I was distracted.'

'Let's not let it spoil the weekend, for the children. They're having such a nice time.'

Freddie nods. 'I'll get on to the insurance company on Monday. It's lucky, I had a look at our household policy when I bought the watch and bumped up the amount insured for a single item. So, it'll be covered.'

Alice smiles. 'You see? Not such a fool, after all. It's insured, and nobody's hurt. We can enjoy the rest of your weekend treat.'

***

The next morning, after breakfast, they ride the river bus up and down the Thames until Poppy begins to find her sea legs going a bit wobbly. Then, having stocked up on some picnic items, Alice hails a taxi to take them to Regent's Park. The taxi ride perks Poppy back up again: taking a black cab appearing to be one of the most decadent things it's possible to do in London, on a par with riding in a yellow taxi in NYC.

There's a band playing in the bandstand; and ducks desperate to be fed in the pond; and the ice-cream prices are astronomical; and Freddie has more tickets, for Roald Dahl's *Enormous Crocodile*, which is playing at the Open Air Theatre.

'You've surpassed yourself,' Alice says, squeezing Freddie's arm as the curtain goes down to yet more screams from Poppy. They have plenty of time to catch the Tube back to Redbridge...

THE SECOND LIGHTNING STRIKE

'No. I remember that sign, there. I could see it as I parked. And this white Fiat was next to us. I remember it. I saw the National Trust sticker.' Freddie is getting impatient with all the suggestions that he might have parked it *over there*, or *over there, by that tree*, when he knows exactly where he parked. And it's gone.

'So? What? Has it been towed away? But you bought a ticket, didn't you?' Alice enquires, rather desperately.

'Yes, I bought a ticket. All the way through to midnight tonight. There's only one explanation.'

'You think it's been stolen?'

Freddie nods, almost casually: the mugging and car-theft victim getting used to his role: desperately trying not to look too desperate.

'So, what shall we tell the children?' Alice looks over to where the children are scouring the four corners of the car park in case, well, in case Freddie parked it somewhere *over there* and then completely forgot where. 'This will spoil everything for them. And what are we going to do? We're too late for a train, even if we could get back into London to catch one. Oh, Freddie. This is so unfair.'

Freddie sighs. 'Look, let's make this as simple as possible. Especially for the children. I think I need to call the police, to report it, for the insurance. And then, unless they suggest otherwise, I'm going to give Poppy the thrill of her life and call another taxi. Let's go home, love. We have the money. And let's sort the rest of it out later.'

Alice hugs him. 'It was a lovely weekend, Freddie. Wonderful. You're right. Let's make as little of it as we can, for the children. Then sort all the paperwork out tomorrow.'

In the taxi (*late booking, close to midnight on a Sunday evening, one-way drop-off to Norwich, four passengers, that will be £250 please, sir. Card payment only*) Alice's heart breaks for Freddie. He's done everything right, ticked every family treat box, organised tickets for trains, theatres, boat rides. How could life treat him so cruelly? She squeezes his hand and smiles at him numerous times on the way home – Poppy asleep between them, Ryan enjoying the ride in the front seat – in an attempt to put the proud smile back on his face. But within seconds of every squeeze and smile from her, his mouth droops into a miserable pout, his mind obviously turning over and over the events that have spoiled the weekend – at least for him.

They've tried hard to shield the children from the worst of the injury, and the news from the police that their car, a mustard-coloured Porsche, registration FRE66IE, has been spotted on camera, speeding north on the M1, probably driven by joyriders, had been painted as good news. Had the car been stolen for export, the police have advised, it would be in a container at Felixstowe by now and not speeding up the M1.

The police are confident they could have it back within the week. As long as the joyriders don't decide to torch it. Then it'll be the paper storm of insurance. But it was speeding, so the police are after it and, with luck, the joyriders might simply ditch it and do a runner when they get near to home. Especially with the blues'n'twos on their tail.

44

THE PINK DILDO

THE EXCITEMENT HAS BEEN NUCLEAR, and it's been building for weeks. With Alice and Poppy having taken to walking to school with Emma and Mags, the girls have spotted a couple of friends being allowed, occasionally, to walk to school minus parents. So, they've begged, and they've pleaded, and Emma and Alice have wallowed in the joy of so much childish delirium being produced by the promise of so little. Neither Emma nor Alice have wanted to relinquish the pleasure of accompanying their children to school, so the fact the dangled bait of the *last Friday of every month* has been seized as a sort of jackpot win by the girls, has comforted Emma and Alice that the small sacrifice (on their own part) is worth the huge prize (for the children).

So, it's the first last Friday, and Emma is taking her turn being the invisible escort, not that the girls know they're having one. Emma and Alice have promised that Mags can use her scooter (when she's had her operations) and Poppy can go on her (lottery funded) bike, whenever the weather is good enough. Alice wonders if she'll have to learn how to rollerblade in order to keep up when it's her turn following at a discreet distance as the invisible escort.

Ryan's new school is too far for walking; she calls for him to hurry up. She remembers he had swimming the day before and, as usual, he never takes his towel and trunks out of his bag. She locates the bag and unzips. Instead of the expected damp towel and trunks aroma she's hit by the unmistakeable smell of bubble gum. She's caught a whiff of it before over the last week or so, never been able to identify the source. Ah well, at least she's solved that little puzzle; Ryan is the secret *Bazooka Joe* aficionado.

At first, she thinks it's a dildo, all bright pink and smooth. *What the...?* Then she sees the brand and it dawns, like a slap. It's a vape. The gasp from behind removes her options in the should she/shouldn't she dilemma.

'What are you doing?' he gasps, a sort of last-chance saloon indignation, not much belief behind it.

'Yesterday's swimming stuff,' she replies, holding the sodden bundle in one hand, like an unwanted FA Cup runners-up medal.

His eyes meet hers, flash to the vape in her other hand, then return to her eyes. Does he think that she doesn't know what it is? Then he looks at the floor, defeated. Alice knows, well, she hopes, he's not yet streetwise enough to think she might have thought it was a dildo.

'Come and talk to me,' she says, when the standoff shows no sign of an end. She tells herself all the worse things she might have discovered in his bag: cigarettes, drugs, porn – *a dildo!* And her heart is tugged by his look of desolation.

He sits next to her, picks a fingernail, swats at his cheek. It takes him a while to begin in barely a whisper.

'All the other boys were doing it. Teddy's dad imports them. Teddy sort of nicks them from his dad. He's super disorganised, Teddy's dad. Teddy tears the packaging, by accident, then Teddy's dad can't sell them. So, Teddy takes them and sells them to us, cheap. They were laughing at me, daring me, said I probably couldn't afford it. I just wanted to fit in,' he says.

She could cry for him. He brushes his cheek with the ball of his hand.

'They haven't been nice. They saw our car...'

Alice adds two and two. She's seen the other cars at the school gates. She's not a big car person, but she knows a big car when she sees one. Rusty would have made quite an impression, she can see now. Why hadn't she thought and taken the mustard pot, saved his blushes? She realises, once again, how far out of the loop she is when it comes to moving in the millionaire circles Freddie is placing them in.

'They take the pi– the mickey. Call me the poor boy, or Oliver, or UC.'

'UC?'

'Universal credit.'

Alice winces at the casual but sophisticated cruelty of children.

'One of them got hold of the register the other week, saw our address. They thought that was hilarious. They all live outside the city in mansions; at worst they're in the Golden Triangle. Not where we live...' The Golden Triangle is Norwich's to die for zone as far as estate agents, and anybody who lives in Norwich, are concerned.

She could hug him. Isn't sure whether it would make it better or worse. He's at that age where he sometimes shrugs her off when she ruffles his hair.

'Say something, Mum,' he says, not looking up, when another silence closes in around them.

That's another thing she's noticed. It's been recent, she can't remember when she first heard it: *Mum*. She's not Mummy anymore, not with Ryan. She's somehow morphed into Mum.

So, when did that happen? And how? And why? Is it a hormone thing? Can't be. Yet there it is: Mummy leaves stage left, enter Mum stage right. A rite of passage in the parental journey that she never saw coming – doesn't welcome at all. She doesn't hate it; she simply prefers Mummy. She knows it had to change. He couldn't still call her Mummy when he was an adult – only Prince Charles had done that: called the queen Mummy, that is, not Alice. So, is Freddie now Dad instead of Daddy? She'll have to look out for that, but it's almost a given. At least Poppy is still Mummy and Daddy's little girl. Long may that last.

She leans over and pulls him close, he doesn't resist, and his tears soak into her blouse and melt her heart.

'Are you angry?' he says after a few moments of muffled sobbing.

'No,' she says, 'I'm more worried about your health.'

He sits up, case for the defence. 'I try not to inhale it. I just puff it and blow it out real quick. I don't really like it. But they were all doing it, and...' And he trails off, his breathing shallow, until he sucks in a huge juddering breath. 'I hate it,' he says, quietly, as if it's no big thing: *I hate cabbage; I hate Ipswich Town.*

'Then don't do it.'

'No, not that, although I do hate that.'

'What then?'

He sucks in another breath. 'School.'

'School? But you love school.'

He shrugs. It's a *not anymore* shrug.

'What about history? You love history.'

'That's one of the worst lessons. The books smell; they're all musty and yellowy. They were written in the 1970s; I checked the date at the front. And the teacher's useless. Mr Dankworth. He has a clock on his table, like one of those chess timers. "One minute to read page twenty-six," he announces, and we read in silence. You can't turn the page if you've finished, not until he makes the next announcement: "Two minutes to read pages twenty-seven and twenty-eight." If you haven't finished, you have to turn the page anyway. The boys call him The Conductor, because he does nothing except boss you around. We do that for half the lesson. Then he collects the textbooks, and we have to write notes on what we've read. You can't make notes as you go along. You have to do it all at the end. He corrects it before the next lesson and you lose marks if the dates are wrong or missing, if you misspell any of the names. It's so boring. The test at the end of the year is all on what's in the book. We don't discuss anything; we don't make anything – except copies of the smelly old textbook.'

Alice is shocked. She knew after all the primary school projects and dressing up as Egyptians that secondary would be a bit more 'academic'. But this seems a bit more... *Dickensian.*

'Why haven't you said?' She knows the answer.

'I didn't want to let you and Dad down. Dad, especially,' he mumbles. 'I know how good he thinks the school is. How much I'll get out of it. But it's horrible, Mum. I hate it. I was good at maths in primary, but here, they don't really teach, they don't help you. They simply hand out the textbooks, tell you the page, and you have to work out what to do and then do pages of sums. That's it. They don't explain anything, we don't do investigations, you can't really ask questions.'

'Why not?'

He looks embarrassed. Alice can guess the reason.

'The other boys take the– the mickey...'

He gives her a weak little smile. Possibly pleased she understands, she thinks.

'Most of the other boys help each other in their dorms at night. But I'm not a boarder. Now I hate maths as well. I ask

Dad, but I'm starting to worry he'll think I'm thick if I ask him too much, or he thinks it's easy.'

'Don't say that. You're not thick. And you are good at maths; this simply isn't good teaching. And Dad will always help you. And he won't think you're thick. Neither will I. It's always harder to learn if you're not being taught well. This isn't your fault, Ryan. You need to understand that.'

They sit in silence, Alice cursing herself. She should have seen this coming. This is her job. This is what she does. She looks after them, helps them with all their little problems. Except, this time, she hasn't. And with a problem that isn't so little: making new friends in a different school full of children who aren't like Ryan. She's taken her eye off the ball, got distracted by the money issues. She saved Poppy, but let Ryan go. She should have taken Freddie on, as she had over Poppy.

'Where's your watch?' She says it absent-mindedly, can't be sure why she's noticed. Has somebody, a bigger boy, taken it off him? Her alarm bells are ringing now. Albeit late.

His hand whips up to his wrist, rubs where his watch should be. He takes a breath, shrugs it out.

'They wear Tags to school.'

'Tags?'

'Tag Heuer. It's another status watch, but sportier than Rolex, unless it's the Daytona. Tags are linked to Formula One, all sporty, they have stopwatches and lap-timers and that kind of stuff. They wear their Rolexes at home, going out for dinner. Not to school.'

Alice hasn't understood half of what Ryan's just said. But she's got enough.

'Would it help if we bought you a Tag?'

He shrugs again, sighs again. 'I think I'm too far gone and, to be honest, I don't like them, the other boys. They're not like me, and I don't really think I want to be like them.'

She squeezes him as the pride swells inside her. 'That's a lovely answer,' she says, ruffling his hair, meeting no resistance. 'I wouldn't like you to turn out like them.'

'Will you tell Dad?' he asks suddenly; she feels he's been building up to it.

'About the vape?'

'Yes.'

'Well, if we're going to have a serious conversation about moving you to a different school, I think it would be an important reason. That, and how unkind the other boys have been, and the crap history lessons...'

He pulls away, his eyes wide with hope, shocked by her choice of language, and reddened with tears.

'Really? Are you serious? Would you...?'

'I'm serious, yes. Because it is serious, isn't it? I don't want you unhappy at school. Neither does Dad. And we certainly don't want you vaping simply to try to fit in. You will stop that, won't you?'

He nods, then his brow furrows again. 'Will Dad be angry?'

She shakes her head. 'I don't think so. I think he'll understand, as I do. He might be angry with himself, as I am, for not seeing this coming. Perhaps we've made a mistake, by moving you to this school. Let me talk to him.'

He nods, looks at the clock. 'I'll be late.'

She loves him for noticing, for still caring.

'What have you got this morning?' she says.

His eyes flick up, consulting his mental timetable, she thinks. 'Double history...'

She tries not to, but can't resist: she smiles. He smiles too, another little sheepish one.

'Look, I'm not teaching till after lunch, how do you fancy going out for the morning, get a coffee and a cake, have a chat about anything and everything? I know we often don't have time. Then I'll take you in after lunch?'

He looks torn. 'But what about...?'

She laughs. 'What? Double history? With The Conductor? I think you can safely miss one crap double history lesson without your whole future being blighted, don't you?'

45

———————

THE SMALL BOAT

THERE'S a message on Alice's phone that afternoon as she's leaving work. Can she come in and talk to Mrs West, Poppy's headteacher? ASAP. It's important. 'I'll tell you what it's about when you arrive.' Like she means now. Not tomorrow. Not next Tuesday at half past ten. Now. This is a shock. Poppy the subject of a talk – not even a chat – a *talk* with the headteacher? Ryan? There've been a couple. Little tussles in the playground; arguments over swapped football cards. But Poppy? In trouble? Falling behind? Bad behaviour? Friendship issues? As likely that Poppy has punched the caretaker or laundered her dinner money. Alice diverts towards Poppy's school, her mind ablaze.

Ryan vaping? Now Poppy in some sort of trouble? How has this happened? Under her nose? Without her getting a sniff that anything was brewing? She prides herself on knowing her children. Prides herself that they bring their little problems to her – because they know she solves them. They trust her. They talk to her. This is her job. This is her most important job. So why haven't they come before things have got to this stage? The vape in Ryan's bag and him being unhappy at school stage? The phone call from Poppy's headteacher stage?

270

The answer is screaming at her again. She's been so tied up with Freddie and the money and trying to protect the life they have that she's taken her eye off the children. They've let them have their dinner in front of the TV instead of all together too often. Why? So she and Freddie could whisper, and she could scheme. She's lost touch with them. She hasn't been there to ask them how they are, listen to their little tales, notice the small changes and hesitations that would have led her to a bit of gentle probing; it never took much to get them to confide. She'd noticed that Kelly hadn't been around to play for a while, decided to ask Poppy if things were all right between them. But had she? No. She'd been too busy, tripping Freddie up as he planned to move them to Beverly Hills.

She wants to scream. She's angry with Freddie. But most of all, she's angry with herself. This is her job. This is who she is. She wants to slap herself. How could she have let this happen? Rusty cleans the muck out of her exhaust pipes and Alice is in the headteacher's office in eight minutes.

'This is a bit delicate, Mrs Cash,' Mrs West begins, looking unusually defensive, embarrassed even. Mrs West is a scientist by training: chemistry, Alice thinks. She could never see her as a natural fit with primary school children, unlike Ms Gibson, Poppy's latest squeeze, who is also in the room. 'Ms Gibson has some information to share.'

Ms Gibson looks horrified at being drawn into the conversation so soon – at all. She takes a shuddering breath and unclasps her hands, like she's afraid Alice might be about to hit her. If a seven-year-old were to draw a primary school teacher, they'd draw Ms Gibson: flat shoes; denim dungarees; mid-length hair that was probably quite tidy a couple of hours previously;

dangly kangaroo earrings; no make-up; a kind mouth; a harassed look haunting her eyes.

'Yes, well, at the moment it's still only a bit of hearsay, but we thought it best to ask you to investigate before we said anything to Poppy. We'll deal with the boy involved.'

'A boy? Which boy? What's happened?' Alice's world suddenly feels decidedly unstable. Ryan vaping? Poppy 'in trouble with a boy' – two oxymorons in one day? She dreads hearing what Freddie might have to say that evening... What would Ryan call that? A hat-trick?

'It's an older boy, only a year older, but he's in Poppy's year because– well, you see...'

Alice looks at Mrs West, pleads with her eyes that she spits it out if Ms Gibson can't. Mrs West takes the bait.

'We're pretty sure the boy has been bullying Poppy. Specifically, taking money from her. I'm talking to his mother after school. It's a delicate situation, we don't believe Poppy has done anything wrong here, we think she's a victim but, well, she's never been in any trouble before and we don't want to frighten her with a visit to the headteacher's office, but she won't tell Ms Gibson exactly what's been happening, so we thought it best if we asked you to probe a little. Find out exactly what's been going on?'

***

Alice collects Poppy at the usual time. She skips across the playground like you'd wish any seven-year-old to do and starts babbling about the art they've done that afternoon; the kangaroo earrings Ms Gibson was wearing; can she put her painting of them on the fridge for all to see? When it's dry? Does Mummy like it? Of course she does, it might look like two elephants in need of reconstructive surgery but no matter, it can go on the fridge.

Alice had been planning to drive to Earlham Park, there's a café, talk to Poppy somewhere nice, somewhere quiet. But the traffic is snarled up and her heart is playing a Van Halen drum solo. She turns around and cuts into Poppy's Antipodean monologue.

'Is somebody taking money from you, Poppy? Somebody at school?'

The silence in the back tells Alice everything she needs to know. She wishes now she'd waited until they'd got to the park, so that she could hug Poppy.

'Who is it, Poppy?'

'Ahmed.'

Poppy's head is down; her hands are open on her knees. Her voice is nearly a whisper. Why are her children always whispering to her? A tear plips into Poppy's small, pink clean palm. She always washes them after art. Always needs to. She leans further forward, like she's not sure where the tear has come from. She touches it with the index finger of her other hand, rubs it around in a small circle.

Alice is doing a very easy jigsaw puzzle, creating a picture of Mrs West's defensiveness, her embarrassment, at bullying in her school. Worse, at bullying by one of the refugee children she's had to work so hard to integrate in the face of some of the parents who have complained, loudly, at how much of the teachers' time they take up with their poor English and the lack of support from a county education authority that barely exists anymore. The car behind honks her; the traffic's moving again.

'How much money has Ahmed been taking, Poppy?'

Alice watches in the rear-view mirror as Poppy wipes a tear away. Why won't this fucking traffic go any faster?

'Five pounds.'

'Five pounds?' Alice feels a dam on the verge of breaking, all ready to flood her. 'How often?'

'Every week.'

The dam suddenly looks more unstable, pink vapes and five-pound notes already lapping over the top and seeping through growing cracks in the decidedly unstable-looking concrete.

'Every *week?*' Alice tries to keep her voice even. 'Your pocket money? Since when?'

'Since nearly the start. After the holidays.'

The traffic slows then stops in front of them. Alice wants to get out of the car, wrap Poppy in her arms. Months? Fucking months of suffering and Poppy's said nothing? How has she missed this?

'Is Ahmed in trouble?' Poppy asks, now looking out of the window. Her cheeks are red and damp.

'Well, a little bit. For taking your money. He probably doesn't understand the rules. Once he learns the rules, he'll be fine.'

Poppy continues to stare at the shops and houses, but her concentration is clearly elsewhere.

'Am I in trouble?' she says after quite a long hiatus.

Alice twists in her seat. 'Of course not, Poppy. Why would you be in trouble?'

'Because I helped him to break the rules. I gave him the money.'

'Oh, Poppy, he *made* you give him money. That's the rule he broke. It's like stealing.'

Poppy suddenly looks up at Alice, like she's just worked out something really complicated, like six times seven.

'But Ahmed didn't make me give him money.' Poppy is looking distinctly bemused.

'What do you mean?'

Poppy shrugs. 'He didn't *make* me give him money.'

More honking from the cars behind.

'Christ!' Alice pulls off, glances at Poppy in the rear-view.

'So, why did you give it to him?'

Poppy shrugs again. 'Because he didn't have any. He didn't have any birthday presents. He didn't have any proper shoes either, they had holes in them, his socks got wet whenever it rained.'

'Hold on,' Alice interjects, before Poppy can get any further with Ahmed's wardrobe contents. 'Go back to the beginning. You first gave him money after the holidays. Why?'

'Because it was his birthday; he didn't get any presents; his family is poor.'

The traffic crawls again, why didn't she wait until they'd got to the bloody park?

'Okay, so what happened? Did he just come up to you and tell you he got no presents?'

'No. I asked him what he got.'

'And he said nothing because he's poor? So, what happened next?'

'I brought my five pounds in the next day and gave it to him.'

'You– You just *gave* him five pounds? He didn't *ask* for it?'

'No. And he wouldn't take it. I said I wanted to give him a birthday present. But he said no.'

'So, what happened next?'

'I bought him a present. From the corner shop.'

'With your pocket money?'

'Yes. I tried again the next day, and he said his mum said he could take it.'

'What did you buy him?'

'A chocolate orange. He shared it with me.'

'Right. And then what? You said you'd given him five pounds every week.'

'That's right. When you gave me my pocket money, on Friday, I gave it to Ahmed on Monday.'

'Why?'

'I told you. Because he's poor. His family are poor. He needed it more than me.'

Alice considers her seven-year-old daughter negotiating this strange set of circumstances on her own. An odd, somewhat frightening, set of circumstances that Alice, until now, has known absolutely nothing about.

'So, let me get this straight. Ahmed never *asked* you for money, he never said he'd do anything bad to you if you didn't *give* him money. It was one hundred per cent *your* idea, *your* decision?'

'What's a hundred basen?'

Alice checks a trembling smile. 'It means completely, absolutely, yes with bells on. This was absolutely, completely *your* idea?'

'Of course.'

In the face of some furious honking on the Unthank Road, Alice turns the car.

———

'I need to see Mrs West right now, it's very important.'

'She's with a parent at the moment, but she'll be free after that if you'd like to wait.'

'Is it Ahmed's mum?'

'Well, yes, it is, but—'

'Then it's even more important that I see her now. Please tell her that I have new information about Ahmed and the money, and she must hear it now, before Ahmed and his mum leave.'

Mrs Buston is of the formidable school of secretaries. First-class honours. Maybe also a PhD. There aren't many who get one over her. But she rises slowly from behind her desk, looking a little stunned, and knocks gently on Mrs West's door before slipping inside. She's out of view for all of twenty seconds before reappearing, looking surprised, and ushering Alice and Poppy inside.

Mrs West is behind her table. Ahmed is sitting on an adult's chair facing her, crying. Knowing that Ahmed is a year older than Poppy, but held back a year because of his English, Alice has pictured a much bigger boy. But he's small, smaller than Poppy, frail-looking. His mum is next to him, she's also small and frail; she's holding his hand and looking very confused. Poppy goes straight over to Ahmed's chair, bunches up next to him and takes hold of his other hand. He smiles timidly.

'Thank you so much for coming back, Mrs Cash. Ahmed is telling me quite a strange story here. And I'm very pleased to see you here, Poppy. I'd like you to tell me what you think of Ahmed's story. Is that all right?'

Poppy nods, smiles at Ahmed.

'Ahmed says he never asked you for money.'

'That's right.'

'Oh.' Mrs West looks completely flummoxed, like Poppy has recited the periodic table, backwards, in Spanish. 'Okay, and he also said he never *made* you give him money?'

'That's right.'

'He said that giving him money was your idea...?'

'That's right.'

'Are you sure?'

'A hundred basen.'

'What?'

'Absolutely. Completely. Yes, with bells on.'

Alice catches Mrs West's eye, unable to conceal a smile amid her tears. Mrs West presses on.

'So, this was *your* idea?'

Poppy nods.

Mrs West looks like she can't remember the first element on the periodic table. 'So, why did you give him money?' she asks, tentatively, as if the answer might involve the rewriting of some of the fundamental laws of the universe.

'Because he didn't have any. And he didn't have any birthday presents. And his shoes let water in, and his coat did too. And because he's my friend.'

Poppy says this in the most matter-of-fact way possible. *Why did you have breakfast this morning, Poppy? Because I always have breakfast in the morning, and because I was hungry. What did you expect me to do?*

Alice feels she will never be prouder of Poppy. Poppy might – quite possibly will – go on to win the Nobel Peace Prize, but Alice knows she will never feel prouder of Poppy than she does now. If only the world was full of Poppies, it would be a much better place.

Ahmed's mum breaks nervously into the shocked silence.

'Ahmed is bad boy?' she says, in hugely accented and hesitant English.

'No!' Alice says.

'No!' Mrs West says.

'No!' Poppy says.

Ahmed's mum smiles. Ahmed smiles.

Mrs West is shaking her head.

'Mrs Khalil, can I ask you? Does Ahmed bring money home from school?'

Mrs Khalil looks confused. Mrs West reaches for her bag, pulls out a five-pound note. 'Does Ahmed bring these home every week?'

Mrs Khalil's face breaks into a huge smile. 'Thanks you very much,' she says to Mrs West. Then Mrs Khalil stands up, goes around Mrs West's table, and kisses her on the cheek. 'Thanks you very much,' she says again, looking like she's won the lottery. 'Ahmed give pounds for me every week. He say pounds is from school.'

Mrs West shakes her head, points at Poppy. Mrs Khalil looks confused again. Mrs West points at the five-pound note, then nods and points at Poppy again.

Mrs Khalil returns to her side of the table, wraps Poppy and Ahmed in her arms and sobs quietly.

On the way home, the second attempt, Alice catches Poppy's eyes in the rear-view again.

'You said Ahmed didn't have very good shoes; they leaked water. But he seemed to be wearing some very nice new trainers today.'

Poppy looks out of the window, then brings her gaze back to the mirror.

'I bought them for him. For his birthday. Although they were a bit late.'

'You bought Ahmed *trainers* for his birthday? As well as the chocolate orange?'

'Yes. Are you angry?' she asks.

'Why would I be angry?' Alice replies, while wondering if Poppy is capable of the biggest wind-up of all time. Decides she isn't.

'Explain to me how you bought Ahmed trainers for his birthday. Where did you get them?'

'In M&S.'

'You bought Ahmed a pair of trainers, in M&S?'

'Yes.'

'On your own?'

'Yes.'

'When?' Alice asks, not really knowing whether she wants to hear the answer.

'We went for coffee with Mags and Emma, one evening after school. I said I was going to the toilet.'

'The M&S café?' Alice remembers it's next to the children's shoe department. 'You went out into the shoe department and bought trainers for Ahmed while I was having coffee with Emma and Mags?'

Poppy nods, like it's the simplest ruse in the MI5 instruction manual.

'How much did they cost?'

'Nineteen ninety-nine. They were late because we didn't go for a coffee in M&S for a while.'

'How come I didn't see them?'

'I said I didn't want the box, and I put them in my schoolbag. The box would've been nice, for the present, but the shoes were more important, so I said I didn't want it.' *Smiley showed me how.*

'How did you know his size?'

'I looked at his shoes when we changed for PE.' *Smiley again, an old trick. Norwich Rules.*

'And how did you pay for them?'

Poppy shrugs, an easy one, evidently. 'I had four five-pound notes in my piggy bank. Four times five pounds is twenty pounds. Daddy taught me that. I got a penny change. We learned how to work out change with Ms Gibson in maths. But twenty pounds take away nineteen ninety-nine is an easy one. You just add a penny to nineteen ninety-nine.' She looks back at her mother's eyes in the rear-view mirror again. 'But now I don't think you're angry.'

'Good. I'm surprised that you didn't know how I'd feel about this,' Alice says, deciding, for the moment, not to congratulate Poppy on her change-giving prowess. Instead, she tries to put herself in Poppy's shoes over the last couple of months, planning the great shopping trip to M&S to secretly buy Ahmed some trainers for his birthday? She can't think of anything so complicated and daring that she might have attempted herself, aged seven. 'So why did you think, before, that I might be angry?'

Poppy surveys the shops outside the car window.

'Because of the boats.'

'The–' Alice wonders if she's in a film. One of David Lynch's earlier ones? The one with the guy with all the hair? *Rubberhead?* Something like that. The one where reality seems to bend like rubber. Is that what it was all about?

'Which boats?' Alice says, with as steady and normal a voice as she can manage.

'The small ones.'

'Explain that to me.'

'Daddy says the people in the small boats are taking all the jobs. That's why he doesn't like them. But Ahmed isn't going to take anybody's job, he's only eight. He wants to be a doctor when he grows up, like his mum and dad, and go back to Syria, so he won't take anybody's job. And you never said anything to Daddy, so I thought, maybe–'

'Maybe that I agreed with him? No, Poppy, I don't, and he knows that. And by not saying anything, I was trying to tell him that it was no use starting that conversation. But if I'd thought for one minute that you were listening in, and thinking that I did agree with him, then I'd have said something.'

Wait till your father gets home, Alice thinks as she fights back a smile, and more tears, resolving to give Freddie a bit of a talking to re the compassion shown by their seven-year-old daughter. On a whim, she swings the car into The Forum car park, then sets the pair of them up with the full afternoon-tea experience under the glittering chandeliers of the Assembly House tea room. Poppy's eyes look ready to pop, the full afternoon-tea experience under the glittering chandeliers of the Assembly House tea room is a treat usually reserved for birthdays, anniversaries, and any other 'special occasions' that Alice can concoct.

'This is a reward,' Alice says, as Poppy takes her first sip of a banana milkshake. 'For being brave, and for being kind. To Ahmed.'

Poppy smiles, wipes a dribble of banana milkshake from her upper lip. 'Daddy was right; it was too small.'

Alice wonders what's coming next. Has Poppy negotiated extra universal credit payments for Ahmed's family by sneaking down for a chat with the ministers at the Department of Work and Pensions while Alice was hoovering the living room? Having tea with George Smiley while she was there? 'What was?' Alice asks, with more than a hint of trepidation, and huge interest.

'The boat. It was very small. Much too small.'

'The boat that Ahmed came on?'

'Yes. After I gave him the shoes, he told me. He said it was one of those rubber boats, but it wasn't big enough for all the people. He said he counted the people in it; there were more than twenty-nine.'

'More than twenty-nine? What do you mean?'

'He said he was practising his English, and he didn't know thirty then, so when he got to twenty-nine, he had to stop, but there were more.'

Alice stares at Poppy, at the tear rolling down her cheek.

'He said it was night-time, and there was a big moon. He liked the moon. But it was windy, and cold, and raining. And his shoes and trousers got wet because his mum had to carry his little brother out to the boat, and he had to walk in the water.

And it took a long time. And the engine was loud and smelly. But it broke, the engine, and some of the men had to row. And the water started splashing over the side, into the boat. And he felt sick. He *was* sick. And it took a really long time...'

Alice wonders if she knows who it is sitting opposite her, wonders how Poppy has discovered these facts in the life of an eight-year-old Syrian refugee, and decided, entirely off her own bat, that she was going to do something about it.

Later, at home in the garden, Alice collars Poppy with something that has been playing on her mind since their chat in the Assembly Rooms.

'Tell me, Poppy, your sudden dislike of bacon and ham in your sandwiches, your wish for two satsumas and two Club biscuits in your lunchbox, and your unusually large appetite at breakfast and teatime. Is that because you're giving some of your lunch to Ahmed, and he's a Muslim, and he doesn't eat pork?'

Poppy's eyes widen with what Alice is sure is astonishment.

'I share it with him,' Poppy says, hesitantly, after staring at Alice for a few moments, like she believes Alice might have superpowers. 'He has free dinners, but they're rubbish, he eats it all but he's still hungry afterwards. How did you know?'

'I'm getting to know you, Poppy,' Alice says, proudly. 'Now tell me why Kelly doesn't come round to play anymore. I think I might be able to guess the reason...'

Poppy takes a breath. 'She said I shouldn't be friends with Ahmed. She said he smells. She said her dad said they were taking all the jobs.'

'And what did you say?'

Poppy straightens up, like she wants to get this next bit right.

'I said, a good friend doesn't tell anybody else who they should be friends with. And that's when she said we weren't friends anymore.'

Alice marvels at how Poppy has taken on board advice she'd given to Ryan, it must be nearly a year ago, when there'd been some playtime bust up between him and his friends. She'd had to go in to see Mrs West to sort it out.

'So, what do you think of that?'

Poppy shakes her head. 'Ahmed's a better friend. Can he come round to play?'

'Of course he can,' Alice says, smiling.

'Daddy won't mind...? About...?'

'About the fact that he's Syrian? And he arrived on a small boat? No, Daddy won't mind. Tell Ahmed to bring his mum as well; we can have a chat and a cup of tea while you're playing. I imagine she might not have that many friends to chat to.'

Poppy looks doubtful. 'She can't speak very much English.'

'I know, but I'm an English teacher, I could give her lessons.'

Poppy seems to consider this, then shakes her head. 'She won't have any money to pay for English lessons.' Alice charges scandalous amounts of money giving private English lessons, twenty, sometimes even *twenty-five* pounds, for an *hour*. Alice stares at her. Poppy cocks her head to one side.

'You won't charge her any money, will you?'

Alice smiles. 'What makes you think that?'

'I'm getting to know you, Mummy,' Poppy shoots back with a grin.

So now, Alice realises she's really boxed herself into a corner. She has to inform Freddie that Ryan is leaving his private school, and that Poppy is buying presents for a Muslim asylum seeker who arrived on an extremely small boat. But it's more than that, she knows. This has gone on long enough – too long. She's let the children down by not being honest with

Freddie. By not telling him how she really feels about their life together, including the children. She knows the time has come. She can't put it off any longer. She's going to have to confront him; tell him the truth, finally. Better cook his favourite for tea tonight, she thinks. Or maybe Red Dragon Pie would be more appropriate...?

Her phone rings. Unknown number.

'Hello. Alice Cash.'

'Hello? Are you a relative of Frederick Cash?'

'I'm his wife. Who are you?'

'I'm calling from Accident and Emergency, Norfolk and Norwich Hospital...'

46

THE MERCY DASH

ALICE IS DOING 123mph on the A47, heading for Colney, when her brain finally informs her that it decided to take the mustard pot (returned undamaged by the police) while she was evidently incapable of considering her options. She's never driven it before and isn't sure how she's managed it this time without sight of the three-hundred-page manual – or at least a quick-start supplement. She's driving in a daze, one of those out of body experiences she's read about; overtaking like Lewis Hamilton; *this little thing sure can move when you put your boot down.* She takes her foot off the accelerator and checks for blue lights, but what's the point? She's nearly there anyway and she really doesn't give a fuck. She'd tell them what's happened, and they'd probably give her a 130mph blues'n'twos escort.

Emma has taken charge of the children in a flurry of nurse-like efficient kindness. They can stay as long as Alice needs. They can sleep over. She'll feed them, wash their clothes. No problem. As long as Alice needs. 'Just go. Go to Freddie...'

She'll never find the car again in the car park, so probably won't have to pay any fines, cos she's not wasting time hunting for the machine or the app or whatever the latest time-wasting and money-making wheeze is. She's a double millionaire, so she can park anywhere she fucking well likes. Amazing what your mind does when you're incapable of thinking straight.

Nurses in blue, some in pastel green, talking to her, she can't take in a word of what they're saying, but she follows them. Corridors, trolleys, the smell of cleaning stuff, beds, Freddie, wires, cables, bleeping machines. She starts to cry, takes his hand. His eyes are closed, no response, but his hand's warm and the bleeping and flashing lights confirm that he's alive. There's a woman in a white coat; she must be a doctor; she's talking. She says the words Alice has pushed from her mind all the way here: she says 'heart attack' and the room spins like the washing machine is revving up for the final rinse and spin...

'Mrs Cash? Mrs Cash? Here, drink this. It'll make you feel better.'

Alice takes the paper cup: it could be water; it could be a sedative; it could be gin; it could be anything. She drinks it in one.

'Are you feeling a little better? It's quite a shock, I know.'

She's ridiculously young, looks like she should still be in school, sixth form at a push. Looks almost as scared as Alice feels. Her name tag says *Nurse Ali Baker*. She wonders if she's another Alice. Nobody has ever called her Ali. What is her mind doing? Nurse Ali Baker has her hand on Alice's arm. They're trained to do this, Alice thinks. But it feels nice, comforting, like she really cares.

'I'm fine. I'm okay. As you said, a shock. The doctor said Freddie has had a heart attack?'

'That's right, that's the prelim diagnosis, although we're still doing tests. It doesn't look like it was a major one. He's stable.

I'll ask the doctor to fill in the details. When you're ready I'll take you back in to see him. He's still under sedation. The ambulance was called immediately, and luckily it got to him really quickly. That's such an important thing.'

'I'd like to see him now.'

Nurse Ali Baker leads Alice back to Freddie's bed. Alice is grateful for the light touch on her elbow all the way. She might be young, but she's either paid attention during her training, or she's got her head screwed on. Probably both. Freddie looks as he had fifteen minutes earlier.

The doctor returns, repeats what the nurse has obviously repeated already. Not been in long, they're still doing tests, he's had an X-ray, ECG, he'll have an echo, blood thinners, blood tests, probably a mild heart attack, they're hopeful, sedation, lucky they got him in so quickly. Alice asks questions, doesn't hear, doesn't understand, doesn't remember many of the answers. She latches on to certain words: hopeful, mild, lucky... Remembers them. Clings to them like small boats in a storm.

When she's run out of questions they leave her with him. She sits by the bed and holds his hand, talks to him. That's what people always do to unconscious patients, on the TV, in films, in the family drama books she devours. Some ridiculous notion tells her that he might be able to hear her. She read somewhere, doesn't make it true, especially if it was on the internet, but she read that hearing is the last sense to go when people are unconscious or in a coma. So, there's a chance. Not that he's in a coma. Well, they didn't say. And she didn't think to ask. They can induce them. He's just unconscious. Or sedated. Not that she knows the difference. So, she talks to him. Tells him she loves him.

'I might not say it as often as I used to, but I do. I love you, and I love our children, and I love the life we've given them, and how they've turned out. I never thought I'd say it, but I love going to the football, with Ryan looking so happy sitting next to you in his scarf and bobble hat, and Poppy screaming her head off. I love doing all that as a family, and the lunch before. It's my favourite day of the week because of that.

'And you'd be so proud of Poppy. You won't believe what's been happening in school. They called me in today. They thought she was being bullied, some older boy taking money off her. But he wasn't. She's been *giving* money to a little Syrian boy who didn't get any birthday presents because his family is so poor. Her own idea. He'd refused to take it when she first tried. She forced him to. She bought him shoes because his own were leaking. I'm so proud of her. She said she didn't tell us because she thought you... well, me too, she thought we wouldn't like it, because his family arrived on a small boat, and she's heard you kicking off about small boats. And she thought I agreed with you because I never said anything. And I told her that I didn't agree with you. And I told her, I said you'd be proud of how kind she'd been. That it doesn't matter about small boats. What matters is that we're kind. And she's been kind. And brave, too, to do what she thought we wouldn't like, because she thought it was the right thing to do. I feel terrible that she didn't think she could tell me. I'll never forgive myself for that. She's struggled with this on her own.'

She wipes her eyes, rubs his hand, tries to compose herself. The volume of tears pouring down her face doesn't seem natural. She's never cried this amount. Her hands are soaked, like she's had them under a tap. The front of her skirt is sopping. It's like all the tears she's stored up, with all the words she hasn't said, have poured out together. She looks for any change in Freddie's heart rate, or any of the other numbers and squiggly lines that she doesn't understand. They don't seem to have changed; she really has no idea. But she does have more words, and almost certainly, more tears.

'I think we did right to keep her at her school. I know you think it's a bit rock and roll, but she's learning to be kind. She's learning about the world we live in. About different people. You should be really proud of her...'

She wonders if she should go on, go further. What if he can't hear her? What would be the point? But what if he can? And she wants to. She wants to tell him everything she's never been brave enough to tell him. Just in case. So, she fights back the tears and ploughs on, vomiting the words like she's lost control of them...

'Ryan's doing well. He's trying to be brave. For you. But it's not been easy for him. The teaching's not great there, Freddie. At his new school. He hates history now. He used to love it, but not anymore. And they don't explain the maths. He's embarrassed that he has to ask you more and more questions. He wants to be taught well, he's desperate to show you how clever he is, not demonstrate how far he's falling behind.

'And another thing, the other boys haven't made him welcome. They found out where he lives, so they know... they know he's not really their type, whatever type that is. So, there's been a bit of mickey-taking. A bit of piss-taking. And apparently, Rolex isn't the current watch to have; they wear a different one, can't remember what it's called. Tap, or something. It doesn't matter. But he hasn't said anything because he... he doesn't want to let you down. But he's not happy, Freddie. It all came out this morning. He was crying.

'You see, I found a vape in his bag. He's doing it to try to fit in. All the other boys do it, so he's been joining in. He's so unhappy, I think we need to move him to where he should have gone, with his friends. He'll learn more if he's happy, and if he's not mixing with kids who are vaping, and he's vaping too, just to fit in.'

She wipes her eyes again, blows her nose, notices that

Freddie's pulse is up a little. She wonders if she should stop, takes a deep breath instead.

'I probably should have said something sooner, Freddie. Probably before you even won. I'm sorry I didn't. I should have. Maybe it's too late. But... You see, I'm not sure I want all the things you want. Now that we've won. I really don't think I want to give up work. I like my job. I like the children at school, my colleagues. I like my days there, all of us working together for something we believe in, to help the children. I enjoy it. I like doing it. I'm good at it. I should've said it before. In fact, they've offered me head of department. Daniella is desperate for me to take it, and I think I want to. It would mean going nearly full-time. She said I could do eighty per cent. And with the kids older now, I think I'd like to.'

She notices Freddie's pulse has risen, wonders again if she should stop talking, or call the nurse, but she feels it's kind of therapeutic, for her, whether he can hear her or not, she feels the need to say it out loud. All of it.

'And I like where we live, Freddie. I have friends here. Emma has the children now. She said as long as I want, as long as I need. She's ready for them to sleep there, no questions asked. She'll feed them and look after them as if they're her own. She just told me to go. Go to you. Practically pushed me out the door. They're nice people. Not like the crew we met at that hotel, looking down on us. I don't want to move house, and live next door to people like that. And neither do the children. Ryan's unhappy that he doesn't see his friends much anymore, and I know Poppy will be happier where she is. She's known there, the headteacher was almost crying when we worked out what Poppy had been doing. They think she's wonderful. They know her.'

A light begins to flash on the monitor beside the bed. Freddie's pulse is up some more, the figures have turned red, an electronic bleeping noise starts wailing for attention. Suddenly, a pastel rainbow of medics appears. The young nurse is there as well, Nurse Ali Baker, smiling at Alice, her hand on Alice's shoulder, ushering her out as the curtains are whisked around the bed. Alice feels her legs giving way, doesn't want to leave Freddie's side but doesn't have the strength to resist. The young nurse reassures Alice, but her words don't register; they're just noises as behind the curtain the hushed voices sound ever more frantic.

For half an hour, forty minutes maybe, Nurse Ali Baker sits with Alice, holding her hand, telling her to stay calm, Freddie's getting the best possible care. It's a specialist ward, cardiac experts, all of them. The nurses included. And Alice tries to remember the last things she said to him.

Did she kiss him goodbye this morning? She thinks so. Did she tell him she loved him? She can't remember. She wants to ask questions, but she's afraid. In case the nurse can't give her the answers she wants to hear, which would make her think the worst. So, she doesn't ask. Is he going to be alright? Or is he going to...? No, best not ask. The nurse wouldn't be able to say, of course she wouldn't, and that would sound like bad news.

They say your life flashes before your eyes when you're about to die. Alice wonders if she's experiencing something similar. Does it happen when somebody you love is about to die? And is it their life you see? Or do you see your own? Or perhaps your life together? And Alice tries to banish the thought because it's morbid, and Freddie's not going to die. They said he was lucky. It was mild. Everything was so fucking hopeful... And now? And now yet more tears come. A torrent of them. And Nurse Ali Baker hugs her and soothes her. And now all

Alice can see is a cascade of images like a Facebook page scrolling on fast-forward. Their first meetings; walking home from school together; his old-fashioned leather satchel, his dad's, he'd said; Freddie on one knee, proposing; buying their house; their first holiday; Ryan being born; Poppy; Freddie buying that ridiculous sports car. She wants to stop the flow of images, but they keep coming, and she's afraid they'll reach the final one, and it'll be Freddie... It'll be Freddie, in that bed, where she left him, but he won't be...

She sobs quietly, squeezing Nurse Ali Baker's ridiculously small hand. He can't die on her. Christ, he's only forty...

Alice pulls her phone out, it's almost an instinct; she needs to know the kids are okay. Nurse Ali Baker ignores the *No Mobile Phones* stickers plastering the walls.

Emma answers on the third ring and Alice drinks in her calm reassurances that the children are fine, they're playing, about to have dinner. She decides not to tell Emma what's going on, not wanting to put her in the position of having to say that everything is going to be okay, when... There's an odd moment when Alice thinks she hears Poppy, sounding distraught, shouting 'Before he dies...' But Emma bats it away calmly, they're playing.

And then the door opens, slowly, and Alice kills the call quickly. There's a white coat, but Alice can't look up at the face because her insides are shrinking, and all the air is leaving her lungs, because she knows what happens next. It always happens like this in the books she reads, in the films she watches, the doctor stands there and says nothing, but you can tell. You can tell from the look on their face...

47

THE VITAL STATISTICS

KEITH IS MAKING DINNER. Veggie-*con-carne-sin-carne*, as he called it, until Poppy told him what that meant, and he nearly dropped his knife in surprise. Having completed her chopping duties, Poppy is now playing with Mags and Emma on the floor. They're playing doctors and nurses. Emma hadn't been keen, had suggested teachers or builders (the Lego usually being a favourite) but Poppy and Mags had insisted.

Poppy has Barbie; she's the doctor. Mags has her favourite Teddy; he's the nurse. Emma has Ken, the patient. Ken isn't feeling well at all, so Barbie and Teddy are fussing around the bed, plying him with litres of sugar-free lemonade and a constant stream of injections.

'I think he's looking a bit better,' says Barbie after the fourth injection. She nods to herself. 'How do you feel, Ken? Better?'

Ken lifts his head and looks around. 'I think I feel better,' he says. 'Thank you. You've been very kind.' Emma sneaks a look towards the kitchen where Keith signals five minutes with his fingers. 'In fact,' says Ken, sitting up straighter, 'I think I feel a bit hungry. Will dinner be ready soon?'

'Wait a minute,' Teddy says suddenly, worry in his voice. 'You don't look well anymore. I'm going to call an ambulance.'

'No,' says Ken, sounding put out that his dinner might be postponed. 'I'm sure I'm feeling better.'

'Call an ambulance,' Barb says. 'Hurry. This is an emergency.'

Before Ken can protest again, Teddy drags a boat out of the toy box and starts nee-nawing loudly.

Emma's phone begins to warble on the sofa. She snatches it up, ready to pass it to Keith, but it's Alice.

'Hello,' Emma says, standing up and moving towards the door. Ken is now face down on the boat, and Teddy and Barbie are hauling him around the room, nee-nawing furiously.

'Emma? Hi. Just thought I'd check in. See how you all— What's that noise?'

'It's nothing. It's the children. They're playing. We're just about to have dinner.'

'Go faster!' Barbie demands. 'Before he dies.'

'What? Did someone say...?' Alice's voice is filled with panic.

'No!' Emma snaps. 'They're playing. Some shopping game, I think. Pies. They're buying pies. Look, how's Freddie? Any news?'

'Oh, no, not really. They're still monitoring him. You know...?'

Emma nods silently, eyes all the while on Ken's rather rickety journey over the sofa and under the table. 'That's good.'

'The children okay? They're not brooding? Worrying?'

'No, they're fine. They've asked a few questions, as you'd expect, but they're fine. Really.'

'Good. I was just worried. You know?' There's an uneasy little silence, like Alice might be about to say something more. 'Oh. Hang on. I think the doctor's here. I have to go...'

'Okay. I'll…' But the line is already dead.

Keith gives Emma a thumbs up from the kitchen. Emma slides back into the game, taking control of Ken on the boat.

'Are we going home now? I'm feeling much better,' he announces, jumping off the boat and standing up on the sofa.

'We thought you were going to die,' Barbie says. 'Are you sure you're better?'

'Yes, I'm much better now. I feel ready for dinner. You've done a great job. I'm going to be fine.'

Poppy looks directly at Emma, her thoughts completely hidden behind her eyes…

Alice looks up slowly, dreading what she's going to see, the next few seconds of her life stretching to infinity. The doctor smiles, and Nurse Ali Baker lifts Alice to her feet like she weighs nothing at all.

Alice stares at Freddie. Stares at all the wires and the oxygen mask, and the thousands of pounds' worth of machinery that's keeping him alive. They've given him a little more sedative but there's nothing to worry about. False alarm. All a precaution. They're still saying things are positive; he's been lucky. She grabs his hand again.

'Come back to me, Freddie. Come back and talk to me about what *we* want. Together. Let's see if we can compromise somewhere, meet in the middle. I'm afraid, Freddie. Am I losing you somehow? Because we don't seem to want the same things anymore. I'm frightened.'

The hours stretch in both directions. Alice calls Emma again. Everything's fine at home. The children are playing. How is Freddie? It's all positive. He's been lucky. They're very hopeful. Alice almost feels the more she says these words, like some magic incantation, the truer they will be. They *have* to be...

She's surprised to find a chart at the bottom of Freddie's bed; she'd have thought all his data would be on computers. And the chart, to be honest, is pretty sparse: name, time of admission, general stuff. But the time of admission causes her to think. It says he arrived at four forty. So, he must have come from work, he always finishes at five. Why hadn't work called her? It's strange. It's not even six yet; there could be somebody still at their desk, tidying up the end-of-week stuff on a Friday evening. She calls the bank; a female voice answers almost immediately.

'Hello? Is that Tasha? It's Alice Cash here. Freddie's wife.'

'Oh hello, Alice. How are you? If you're looking for Freddie, he's long gone I'm afraid.'

'No. It's... I'm at the hospital; I'm with Freddie. He's had... well, they think he's had a bit of a heart attack. A mild one. They're still doing tests. And I–'

'Oh my goodness. I'm so sorry. That's terrible news. Is he going to be okay?'

'Well, they're saying lots of positive things, but they're still doing tests.'

'If there's anything we can do, Alice, call me. That's horrible; he seemed so well today, in a really good mood. Tell him not to worry about the bank, we'll cover him until he's well. I won't expect him all of next week, at least. Let me know whatever we can do.'

'Well, that's sort of why I'm ringing. I'm a bit confused. You see, he was admitted at twenty to five, so I assumed you'd called the ambulance to the branch...?'

'No, it's Friday. Freddie has his early finish on a Friday.'

'His *early finish?*'

'Well, sorry, it's a study hour. He gets it because he's a deputy. Every Friday, he finishes at four.'

'Right... And he leaves the bank?'

'Yes, you can study at home if you like, the bank doesn't keep tabs. He doesn't have to study at all if he doesn't want to, it's kind of a perk for the deputies, but you know what Freddie's like. He probably goes to the library.'

'Right, of course. Thank you, Tasha. It was nice to talk to you.'

Alice kills the call as Tasha's saying something else about not worrying... Freddie leaves work at four o'clock every Friday. She sits next to the bed and looks at him. He looks peaceful. Peaceful – ish. Being hooked up to a load of medical machinery isn't a traditional peaceful look. But he looks calm. Unworried. Whereas Alice is starting to worry. She can't help herself. She's starting to worry big time. Her brain is galloping in all directions and frightening her. Freddie always leaves the bank at four o'clock on a Friday...

So, two questions, she thinks as she tries to hold the panic in check: *Where do you go? Every Friday? When you leave the bank at four? Not five? For your study hour? And second question, maybe more important than the first: who called the fucking ambulance?*

Alice goes to the nurse's station. Nurse Ali Baker isn't there. Another nurse looks up from a computer terminal, smiles.

'Hello. I'm with Freddie Cash. Can you tell me, was anybody with him when he came in?'

'Yes, it was his wife, I think.'

Alice's left knee buckles under her. The room starts to sway. She fights it, places her hand on the countertop and grips it hard. She fears she's going down. Going out. 'No,' she says, as steadily as she can manage, almost as much to herself as to the nurse. '*I'm* his wife.'

'Oh, I'm so sorry, I assumed she–'

The young nurse she knows, Nurse Ali Baker, comes out of a room; the nurse on the desk signals frantically to her to come over.

'Ali, who was the woman who came in with Mr Cash? I assumed it was his wife. I'm so sorry.'

Alice waves the apology away with the hand that isn't welded to the countertop. She has to keep a grip on her emotions, but they're starting to build up, like those NASA rockets do just before they launch.

'I heard him calling her Mandy, I remember cos I love Barry Manilow. You know the song?'

Alice hates Barry Manilow. 'What was she like?'

Nurse Ali Baker thinks for a moment. 'Very glamorous, well dressed, quite a bit of make-up. But she was a bit strange and, if I'm honest, I assumed she was his wife as well, but she didn't exactly behave like a wife. She wasn't crying or anything; she almost behaved like she thought it all a bit of an inconvenience. It was like she couldn't wait to get away. Like she had something better to be doing.'

'She didn't leave a name? A full name?'

'No. She simply disappeared as soon as we started treating Mr Cash. It was quite odd. But she might have saved his life, whoever she is. One of the paramedics told me they were around the corner from the flat when the call came in, they were with him in minutes because of her. It's quite possible she saved his life.'

'The flat? What flat?' Alice's fingers are turning white on the countertop.

Nurse Ali Baker shrugs. 'I don't know. Where he had the heart attack I suppose...'

48

THE SLEEPLESS NIGHT

Alice sleeps in the chair by Freddie's bed. Or, rather, she doesn't. She's nipped home for a shower and a change of clothes, reassured the kids who are worried, but they swallow her optimism. 'He isn't feeling well, but he's getting better; the doctors are simply keeping an eye on him; he'll be home soon.' *Lucky, positive...* Poppy's having a lovely time with Emma and Mags; Ryan is happy on his PlayStation.

So, she sits (as opposed to sleeps) in the chair next to Freddie's bed. His pulse is steady; the machine is bleeping quietly. And she wonders.

Who is Mandy? It sends a chill through her every time she thinks the name. She doesn't say it out loud, doesn't want to hear it coming out of her lips, knows that will start a whole new thing when she has to say it aloud, as she fears she will, in the not distant future. There's no Mandy working at the bank, she's sure. He's never mentioned a Mandy. She's not going to get anywhere chasing Mandy.

So, she tries to go through all the places Freddie might go during his study hour. Study hour? Why has she never heard of such a thing? Early finish, every Friday? Why has he never told her? Why hasn't he come home? Or suggested collecting Ryan or Poppy from school? Spent a little extra time with them? Took them to the park? A coffee shop? McDonald's? Why hasn't he? Instead, he was with Mandy.

The chill seeps through her body again. It's an actual physical thing, she always thought it was something writers just wrote. But *the chill*, it's physical. A doctor could measure it, she's sure, with some fancy gizmo. Something happens to her body, the muscles; they tremble, physically, like a wave of cold electricity ripples through her body every time she thinks the name.

Mandy.

Where was he? And a worse thought: what was he *doing?* With Mandy? In her flat? What were they doing *together* in her flat? Every Friday?

Then she remembers. The nurse told her Freddie's belongings are in the drawer next to the bed. She fishes out a plastic bag: car keys, wallet, coins, phone... They know each other's password, so she's in it within seconds, feeling like her marriage might be crumbling before her eyes as she does what they do in those novels she devours about... about marriages crumbling. Why does she read them? Why couldn't she be like normal people, and read normal books? Like the ones where people chop each other up with knives or saws? Or the ones with goblins or aliens? No, she reads the ones about marriages falling apart.

Straight to his WhatsApps, praying there won't be a Mandy, because this has to be all a big mistake. Mandy must be someone who picked him up off the street, or wherever he was, and called the ambulance. This thing about a flat must be an error, a confusion. Mandy has to be a terribly busy woman who needed to be somewhere else after she'd saved Freddie's life. Well dressed? Make-up? A cosmetics rep for House of Fraser? He could have collapsed in the street. Near the flats, outside the flats. That has to be it. She can't think of another plausible explanation that isn't...

There's no Mandy in his WhatsApps. No Mandy in his contacts. There's no Mandy in his notepad. No photos of women she doesn't recognise, just a few of herself and the kids – and about thirty million of the yellow car. But there's no Mandy. She can't make up her mind whether this makes it better – or a whole lot worse. If Mandy is– If Mandy is Freddie's– If Freddie didn't want Alice to find out about Mandy, then he wouldn't have her phone number, or photos of her on his phone. Of course he wouldn't. They know each other's password. They don't hide secrets on their phones. Which makes it worse. Much, much worse. Mandy is a secret. Mandy is *his* secret. So, Mandy wouldn't be on his phone.

And there's that chill again, every time she thinks the name.

She finally sleeps. Fitfully...

Freddie's awake, the monitors are bleeping sedately. Alice rubs her eyes. There's daylight. A different day beginning. A very different day, she fears.

'How are you feeling?' It seems ridiculous to be asking it, the name *Mandy* screaming in her ears, demanding attention. Is she imagining it, or does he look different? Changed? By the heart attack? The drugs? Or by something else? Has he heard what she said the day before? She pushes her fingers through her hair.

'I don't know,' he says. 'Tired. Like I haven't slept. Is it Saturday?'

'Yes. They sedated you. Have you seen the doctor or a nurse this morning?'

He shakes his head. 'Not today. I was waiting for you to wake up.'

There's something between them. She can feel it. Something unspoken. Something broken. Is it her? Because she's heard the name Mandy? Or is it him? Because he's afraid she's heard it? Or because he heard everything she'd said? Why didn't he wake her?

'They're positive,' she says, blithering, not knowing what she can say that's true, or still true, if more test results have come back overnight. She needs the doctor. She needs to sort out all the medical stuff before... before she sorts out everything else. Before she sorts out his study hour, his early finish – and Mandy.

'What have they said to you?' he asks.

'Yesterday?'

'Yes.'

'They thought it was a heart attack. They said a mild one. They were hopeful, positive. They said you were lucky; they got to you really quickly.' She remembers all the important words. 'There are still test results to come in.'

He takes a deep breath. She takes his hand, grips it. Wonders if she should. If she can...

'How are the children?' he asks, suddenly looking worried, more worried. Like he wants to steer the conversation before she...

'They're fine. Send their love. I told them you're okay; you're getting better. They wanted to come, but I don't want them to see you, not like this, all the wires, the machines, it'll frighten them more. They slept at Emma's. I must ring her again. She's been wonderful. Carte blanche for them to stay as long as we need. They miss you. Want you home.'

He smiles weakly at her.

A doctor comes in. A different one. Asian. Male. Alice prays Freddie doesn't say something, anything. Hopes he's on his best behaviour. The doctor's very positive. They have more test results. Everything is mild, hopeful, positive, he's been lucky.

The word *lucky* translates into *Mandy* in Alice's head and she feels sick. Mandy, the woman who probably saved his life. They're going to keep him for another night, more tests, observation, then if all the tests are good, home tomorrow to rest, tablets to take, blood thinners, follow-up next week, more tests, but it's all very *hopeful*, they're feeling *positive*. He's been *lucky*.

Alice wonders if her luck has finally run out...

She drives home to wash, to change, to check on the kids, on Emma. Nothing feels real. She drove to the hospital yesterday fearing she was losing Freddie. Now she drives home, sure she'll lose him, but for a different reason. Where was he? What was he doing? Who is Mandy? When is she going to confront him? Because she knows she has to. She *has* to. Doesn't she?

The children are excited, but with a wariness that tugs at Alice's heart. They want to see him. She tells them tomorrow. He needs to rest. A little problem with his heart, but it's all positive; it was very mild; the doctors are very hopeful; he was very lucky.

'I don't know how to thank you,' Alice says to Emma, over tea and biscuits, after she's told her all there is to tell about Freddie. Well, about his health.

'Your children are lovely,' Emma says. 'It's a real pleasure to have them. Mags has had such fun; Ryan is so kind to her, like a real big brother. As long as you need, Alice. We'll call to return the favour someday, you know that.'

Alice laughs, then she starts to cry. Can she tell Emma? Should she? She thinks Freddie's having an affair. She thinks their marriage might be falling apart.

49

THE ENGLISH INQUISITION

FREDDIE'S SITTING UP. The machines are still bleeping, almost merrily. The oxygen mask has gone. He's got a bit more colour, doesn't look so close to... he's looking a bit better.

They chat. Nonsenses. Although they're not. The doctors have been asking him about his diet: does he exercise? Does he smoke, drink...? But Alice can't concentrate on Freddie rabbiting on about how he can start walking, they've suggested that, maybe jogging later. Perhaps they can play badminton together?

'Where were you when this happened?'

He looks shocked. She feels shocked. It just came out on its own. Like she has no control over her mouth. Like she's watching a film, and the actor says something you don't want them to say, as they always do, and you think, *No, don't say that...* She doesn't feel she's asked it. She shouldn't.

'I can't remember.' But he looks shifty. Like he's lying. And that only makes it worse. Makes her press on.

'So, did you call an ambulance for yourself?'

'I– I– I think so.'

'From work?'

'Can I have some water?'

She passes him the cup. Her hand is shaking; some water spills onto the sheets.

'Because it says you were admitted at twenty to five. So, you must have come from work... Did work call the ambulance? Did Tasha call it?'

He sips the water. She feels cruel. Like she's hounding him, hunting him, backing him into a corner. She knows she shouldn't – he's in hospital. But it's *her* who's backed into the fucking corner. He's lucky, it's all positive, mild, hopeful. Is she hopeful? Is she positive? Who the *fuck* is Mandy? She sits on her hands to stop them from shaking, to stop him from seeing them shaking. Or is she afraid she might hit him?

'Who's Mandy?' She gulps at the sound of the name out in public. Sharing the room with them: Alice, Freddie and Mandy, all together in a hospital room at the N&N. It suddenly makes it real. Makes her real. Mandy. Like she's walked into the room, all fancy clothes and make-up. Somebody they know. Somebody *he* knows. The woman who probably saved his life. Is she his lover? Is she a prostitute? Is *she* what provoked his heart attack? Afternoon sex after his early *fucking* finish when he should have been studying and could have been picking up the kids or with her...?

'What?'

'What do you mean, *what*? It's a two-word question. The woman who called the ambulance? The woman who quite possibly saved your life?'

He looks trapped. Like a small animal. Rabbit in the headlights. Rat in a trap.

'She's not who you think she is,' he says, it's almost a gulp, involuntary, like one of his Smiley spies weighing every word so they don't give themselves away.

'So, who do I think she is?'

Now he's been rumbled. What's the word his spies use? Blown? He's blown. *Norwich is blown.* She waits for an answer; he's weighing more words. It's clearly an intricate calculation.

'How can you be sure she's not who I think she is, if you don't seem to know who I think she is? Shall I tell you who I think she is? Would that help?'

Freddie looks wretchedly unhappy. She almost feels sorry for him, but now she's getting angry, based mainly on how sorry she feels for herself, how badly let down she feels, how foolish she might have been, how easily she might have been duped, betrayed, conned – all the words have spy connotations. But also, it's odd, how her women's fiction family dramas now seem to be blending with Freddie's espionage fiction. Women in her books are also duped, betrayed, conned. She used to think their reading habits had nothing in common; now, she's not so sure.

But it's not just the 'affair', if that's what it is, that she feels she's been conned by, hoodwinked over. It's everything else. What also gives her a huge source of pain and anguish, is that she's somehow been duped into believing she lives a small life. That there's a better life out there if she'd only wear the right watch, drive the right car, send the children to the right schools, drive up the right drive to the right house in the right area...

She studies Freddie. He reminds her suddenly of a frog, splayed and pinned on a dissecting table.

'Are you having an affair?' Words she'd never expected to utter in her life. Words from one of her women's novels. Not real words, real-life words, but words that characters say, not real people. Not her.

She loves him, she really does. He's kind and can be funny and he's good with the kids and he's never even really got angry with her. He doesn't get drunk. He's a good man.

His mouth moves, but there are no words coming out. Just a sort of twitching movement, like his brain has malfunctioned, alongside his heart. He shakes his head, but she's no idea if that's a no, or another twitch, or a denial of the legitimacy of the question. She hopes it isn't another heart attack.

'Is Mandy a prostitute?'

'No, no, no!' He gasps. His eyes fill with layers of what? Shame? Fear? Again, she can't be sure. Is his *No, no, no* a denial, *Mandy isn't a prostitute*. Or is it a rejection of the question? *Please, don't ask me that... she can't be asking me that...*

'So, who is she? How long have you been seeing her? They said at the bank you always leave early on a Friday.'

He swallows. She notices on the monitor his BP and pulse numbers are spinning like a fruit machine, she knows she really shouldn't be doing this now. He shakes his head. Again, she doesn't know why. Is it denial? Is he berating himself? Realising what he's done, whatever *it* is?

'Freddie, I'm scared. What's going on? Are you leaving me?'

She almost gasps aloud as she says it. She had no idea she was going to say it. It's like she's listening to a play on the radio. Where did those words come from? Who wrote this script? This is not part of her life.

'No,' he says, eventually, after too many moments when he looked like he wasn't going to say anything. And was it a *no* meaning *I'm not leaving you?* Or did it mean, *Don't ask me that?*

'Tell me, Freddie.'

'I can't.'

'You...' She feels her life, her marriage, her family, everything that was pretty rock solid only a few days ago, is now starting to shift, to slide, to crumble. Earthquakes must be like this, she thinks, when everything starts to move and topple around you. You quite literally watch every part of your life collapse, fall apart, get crushed, killed. She wants this conversation to stop, to go back to wherever it came from, because she can't believe it's come from her. But she can't stop, not now, not now he's said–

'You have to tell me, Freddie. I'm your wife. Who is she?'

The silence stretches beyond breaking point. What is he thinking? That she'll say *Okay, never mind, are you hungry?* She stares at him and can't recognise the feelings she's having. She now doesn't recognise this man in the bed. Does she know who he is? This man she thought she knew, sitting in this hospital bed, wired to machines that are helping to keep him alive, but, apart from that, who is he? Does she really know him?

'Last chance...' she says. Why does she say that? What does she mean? Her heart is hammering so hard she's going to be in a bed soon, attached to the sort of wires and monitors that are keeping him alive. 'Tell me, or...'

Or what?

He shakes his head again. He looks like a child. She got a more adult reaction out of Ryan when she found the vape. Poppy told the truth about the money immediately. How can Freddie behave so differently? Why can't– Why *won't* he tell her?

'Listen, Freddie. You tell me, or... or it's over between us. This isn't what I signed up for when we married. We don't have secrets from each other. Secret women. I don't have a secret man. We tell each other the truth. We always have...'

Except, she hasn't. And she knows it, can see it now, how she's always kept her secrets, not told him, not explained how she feels. She takes a deep breath, stands up, turns for the door, puts her fingers on the handle, waits for him to say something, anything...

50

____

THE IPPON

ALICE STARES AT HER PIZZA, her oven chips, her baked beans. Such an ordinary dinner on such an ordinary day. Except it's not. Has she left him? Is that it? Is that all it takes? Has she done it? Has she done what the women do in some of the books she reads? The ones where they're not killing or being killed by someone? Although, in some of them, they leave *and* kill. Or get killed after having left.

The kids are in front of the TV again, another 'treat' because she needs to think. Yes, yes, she knows she shouldn't. But she needs to work out what's going on. What has she done? Are Ryan and Poppy now part of a broken family? Not that they're aware of it. Not yet. Is she a single mother? She almost laughs aloud at the idea. Almost.

The children are still their happy, normal selves, a little down because Freddie's not there, but they're enjoying the treat of having their dinner in front of the TV, again, and she'd told them Daddy's getting better; he'll be home soon. They're so good about it, they never argue about what they're going to watch. They take turns, Poppy's idea, Ryan agreed. Are they now from a split family? Is Freddie an estranged father, with a younger-model new girlfriend? Soon to be new wife? Has she *done* that? Has *she* done that? Or has Freddie?

She swats tears away; the children mustn't see her cry. She shovels a forkful of chips into her mouth and chews angrily. What does she do? What does she do now? Now that she's left him. Has she? She feels like a writer in the middle of a novel, who doesn't know what to write next. Writer's block, they call it. So, what's she got? Wife's block? Jilted wife's block? What does she do? What's the next word on the next line on the next page...? She honestly has no idea.

She suddenly remembers she has the extra point three in the bank. Three hundred thousand pounds. She barely thinks about it. But she knows, if they divorce, she's due half the money. Another million pounds. Give or take. Will she fight him for it? She thinks she will. Thinks she will in the way she thinks DCI Banks will catch the criminal on the TV. Not in a real-life way. She can't think like that. Not yet. But will she have to think like that? Does she need a solicitor, for example? Her mind swirls through what feels like a draft script for a detective show. Could she? Would she? Can she?

Two smiling faces stare at her from their wedding photo. It seems such a long time ago, the time when that photo made her smile – yesterday morning, it was. Now, she stares, wonders where the happiness she'd felt on the day, used to feel whenever she looked at it, has gone.

There's a little cough behind her left shoulder. The children, dressed for judo, with delighted little smiles on their faces at having got themselves ready, without her having to remind them, again. She feels like telling them it's off for some reason, burst water main, some nonsense. But she knows they'll be disappointed. She can't do that to them. Not now. Not now that they're...

Out on the mat, Poppy has been matched with a lad called Josh, who's a sliver taller than her but much stockier, has a crew cut, a missing front tooth and a colourful transfer on his left forearm. Makes him look like a right nasty (little) piece of work. A bruiser. To be fair, Poppy looks a bit of a bruiser herself with her own missing incisor. They're doing *randori*. Alice knows that one; it's a sort of gentle sparring where they can practise what they've been taught. They've got a grip on each other's jacket at the collar and are circling, like extremely small sumo wrestlers. Every now and again, Josh tugs roughly at Poppy's collar and she responds by stepping quickly aside so he can't sneak in and trip or throw her. Her neck is reddening from the coarse material and the constant tugging. Alice wishes he wouldn't be so rough with her. Their faces are set in intense concentration as they circle and circle...

How can she do this? Pretend everything is normal for Ryan and Poppy when in her mind her own world is imploding? Their world is imploding. Is she in denial? Should she go back to the hospital tomorrow and behave as if nothing has happened, nothing has changed, accept it all like, well, like the royals do? Always have. They've always had mistresses and lovers. Is that what Freddie's doing? Taking a lover because he's now rich? It's bonkers, but it's as sensible an explanation as she's managed to come up with. Should she simply accept it? As long as it's only that, and not the break-up of the family? Could she?

But then another plotline opens up in her mind. She got the impression from Tasha that this study hour has been going on for a while. A long while. Before the win. So, has this... *thing*, this *Mandy* thing, been going on since before the win? Because that would make it different. Not some madcap fling because he was rich, but something that was going on from when he was normal Freddie, Dad Freddie, husband Freddie. That would be a whole lot worse.

Suddenly, there's a kerfuffle on the mat, and Alice turns her head just in time to see something quite extraordinary. It's so incredible, it makes her gasp out loud. In one fluid movement, almost dance-like, it looks like a blur, Poppy spins so her back is to Josh, and ducks forward with her left leg lifting behind her like a figure skater on one skate. In a flash, no more than an instant, and with apparently little effort on her behalf, Josh flies high over Poppy's shoulder, his feet arcing through the air like shooting stars, and lands slap bang flat on his back with an enormous *BLAM!* It's like a gunshot.

Alice knows this is *ippon*: the perfect, clean, unanswerable, total victory; the ten-point, holy grail of all judokas. The children's attempts at throwing each other usually end in little tumbles as a pair will topple into a small heap of limbs. They only ever see a proper *ippon* when the instructors demonstrate on each other, effortlessly whipping their opponent over their shoulder and smashing them onto the mat – the *tatami* – with a force and brutality that provokes little gasps from the children, and from Alice. This is an equally awe-inspiring sight.

Josh stares up from the mat looking stunned, his head twisting left and right like he's never seen the building before, certainly not from this angle, and clearly never having been thrown for such a clean ippon before, especially not by a blonde-haired girl who's a bit shorter and slighter than he is. Poppy is now standing above Josh, still holding one of his arms in her hand, looking like she's in complete control of him.

On the other mats, all movement and noise stop. Heads turn, including the instructor's, mouths open in shocked expressions – like Alice's. The look on Ryan's face is slightly different to everyone else. There's shock, yes. Everybody's looking shocked. But Ryan's shock is of a different order.

There's a hint of admiration. Pride. But a smear of something else as well. Fear maybe? Like that girl in the film; Alice can't remember what it was called, set in a hotel, when Jack Nicholson comes through the bathroom door with an axe. Ryan looks a bit like that girl did. A bit.

Poppy stands above Josh with a strange look on her face, like she's discovered a power she hadn't known about before and is now calculating how useful it could be to her. She catches Alice's eye, nods a little conspiratorial nod, smiles, then stretches out her other hand and hauls a bemused-looking Josh to his feet.

Girl Power, Alice thinks, wondering if it might run in families...

51

THE DEALER

Freddie's sitting up in bed with a breakfast tray on his lap. There's toast, juice, tea. He looks up as Alice enters the room, but then immediately looks down again. She closes the door and sits on the chair next to his bed, puts her bag on the floor.

'How are you?' she says. She's considered not asking. Considered starting with, *We have to talk.* But she couldn't. She couldn't be that heartless. He's still her husband – for now. He's still the father of her children. He's still in hospital. But...

'They're letting me out,' he says to his half-eaten toast. 'Maybe tomorrow, they say, but you know what it can be like.'

'I've brought you some clean clothes,' she says.

He nods. Unable to speak? Whatever. There's a silence. She's decided to give him a chance to come clean. To explain. To confess. To beg forgiveness. Whatever it is he needs to do. If he does – come clean, explain, confess, beg forgiveness – she's decided she'll give him a chance. One. For the children.

Eight hours previously, at a sleepless 2am, she was leaving him, taking half the money. But by three thirty, she was giving him a chance. And by five, she was leaving him again, no matter what he said. Now, she's prepared to give him a chance. One.

For the children. God knows what she'll be doing by lunchtime…

But it must be over. Now. No more contact. No more 'study hours'. No more Mandy. He comes home when he's finished work; he plays with the children; they do something together. Plus, he has to tell her. All of it. How long? When did it start? Everything. Those are her conditions. The silence stretches beyond polite.

'We have to talk,' she finally says, staring at him, but he's more interested in studying his half-eaten toast. 'Freddie, I need to know what I'm dealing with here.'

Nothing. Has he nodded off? Had another heart attack? Is he simply blanking her? He has to say something.

'Talk to me, Freddie. I need to know what's going on. Is our marriage over?' The words almost stick in her throat, choke her. She can't believe it's come to this so quickly. Why won't he say anything? Why is he pushing her away? The silence makes her angry. She's promised herself she wouldn't get angry, but this silence, this pushing her away, ignoring her, she can't stand it. It's so unlike him. Is it– The thought hits her like thunder. Is this what he wants…?

The door opens, a nurse comes in, all crispy pastel polo shirt and bonhomie. 'So, how are we feeling, Mr Cash? Hmm, I see your blood pressure is a little up.'

Alice looks out of the window as the nurse fusses with a drip. She assures him it's nothing to worry about, it'll fluctuate over the next few days, she'll make sure to let the doctor know but he's not to worry.

'I've never slept with her,' he says, a whisper, after the nurse has closed the door and the silence has become oppressive.

'So, what is it?'

He shakes his head.

'If you're not sleeping with her, what are you doing?'

Another shake of his head.

'How long have you been seeing her?'

Yet another shake, barely noticeable this time.

'Months? Years? Since before the lottery?'

A nod, more of a tremble. 'Before.' Hardly a word, more of a gasp.

'Jesus Christ, Freddie.' This makes it worse. She's been through this scenario, at 2am, and at five. Before the lottery means it's not some madcap, too much money in his pocket, too much temptation, nonsense. This is *before*. When they were fine. When they were him, her, Ryan and Poppy. No millions, no delusions of grandeur, an ordinary happy family. Like the fucking cards: Mr Cash, the banker; Mrs Cash, the banker's wife, but also a teacher; and the children, Master Cash, the banker's son; and Miss Cash, probably Ms Cash, knowing Poppy, the banker's daughter. A happy family. She wipes away a lone tear. Then she stands up.

'I can't stay with you on this basis, Freddie. Not if you've got some secret lady friend, Mandy, and you won't tell me what you do with her. I can't do that. It's treating me like an idiot. If you're having an affair, I'm leaving you, unless it stops now. This minute. If she's a prostitute, I'm leaving you, unless it stops now. This minute. If it's some fetish you've got, I don't know, something from your schooldays, whips and leather, or whatever, then as long as it stops, Freddie. You look for advice; we look for advice; you show me that you want the life we have, we *had*, with me, with the children. But, if you won't tell me what you're doing with her, if you expect me to trust you with a mystery, secret woman then I'm leaving you. It's not a marriage anymore. We can't keep secrets from each other. Can't you see that?'

Silence.

She turns for the door. Stops. Turns back.

'Actually, Freddie. That's not true. I haven't always been honest with you. For the best of reasons, but I haven't. I have some secrets. I should have told you long ago. But I didn't. So, I'll tell you now.' She takes a shuddering breath. 'When you've moaned and groaned about our life, how much better it would be if we, if *you*, won the lottery. Well, I never really agreed. I never shared that dream. And shall I tell you why? I should have told you long ago. I was happy. I was happy with you, happy with the children, happy with our home, their school, our car, our holidays. Christ, there are millions of people in the world, in this country, who don't have what we have, what we *had*. A home, food on the table, nice children, love. God, Freddie, what more did we need? So, why didn't I tell you? Why wasn't I honest? Because I didn't want to spoil your dream, and I never thought it would come true. I just wanted to make you happy with what we had. But it looks like that wasn't enough.'

His heart rate is up; she can see it on the monitor. So is hers, she can feel it in her chest.

'Have you really nothing to say to me, Freddie?'

The moments pass like aeons; she can almost feel the planet turning beneath her feet. 'Right, listen, this is what I'm going to do. I'm taking our house, our family home, off the market. I'm cancelling Ryan's place at that school. He's not happy, he's vaping to try to fit in. The teaching is Dickensian. He's got no friends. Then I'm going to look after our children. I'll bring them to see you when you're fit to see. But when you're ready for discharge, I don't want you back at the house. Come and get some more clothes but find yourself a place. Stay with Mandy if you like. Although that might not be a good idea, with your heart, you know? Probably not a good idea to go through with the mansion either, because when we're divorced, half the money will be mine. That's the law. I'm your wife. Half the money is legally mine. I'll need it for the children. Now, I'm making the first phone call to the estate agent. I'm taking our family home off the market.'

She pulls out her phone, hunts for the number with trembling fingers, listens to it ringing, knows this call will start a process that is going to change the whole direction of her life, and of the children's lives. She's amazed at how calm she feels. It's like she's reading one of the family drama novels she loves so much. Nice family, trundling along together, nice house, nice car, nice holidays, nice life – and then *boom*, husband has an affair, marriage disintegrates, wife leaves with the children, husband shacks up with his (usually much younger) lover. She has never, *ever* thought she would be that wife. Freddie? Take a lover? Who would take him?

She loves him, of course she does. He's the father of her children, the only man she's ever slept with. One of only two men she's ever kissed. Properly. But what would any other (younger) woman see in him, with his rapidly balding head, his pot belly, his waddle of a walk, his Man at C&A wardrobe (before it went bust), his conversation limited to test cricket and televised snooker and his dicky bow and, now, dicky heart? She can't imagine anyone else ever 'falling' for him, or even simply 'fancying' him, even while drunk. Them that is; he never gets drunk. The call connects. She's amazed by the feeling of control it gives her.

'Hello, it's Alice Cash here, Mulberry Lane. I'm sorry but we've decided to take the house off the market.' Why does she apologise? It's her house, she can sell it or not sell it. She's no need to apologise. 'No, we've simply decided to stay put. Thank you for your help. I'll come in and sign anything I need to over the next couple of days. Okay? Fine. Thanks. Goodbye.'

She disconnects, takes a breath. It wasn't so difficult after all. She thinks she knows how Poppy felt, last night, on the mat: *Ippon!*

Freddie is looking at her like he doesn't recognise her. Like she's a different person. For some odd, inexplicable reason, she quite likes that look. He looks shocked. She wants to shock him. Like he's shocked her.

'About Ryan, Freddie. I know we have spaces in year seven, so I'll talk to Daniella in the morning and get him transferred asap. And I'll come and see you, and bring the children, if you let me know where you are, but our marriage is over.'

It's at this point that she starts to cry. She's been amazed at her businesslike composure up until now but telling him their marriage is over is the final straw. Simply saying the words does the damage, makes it real, convinces her that she really does mean it. He starts to cry too. He's a pathetic sight with all the wires and his roly-poly little tum.

She picks up her bag, turns and opens the door. She thinks he mumbles something. Sounds like, 'She's my dealer.'

'Your what?' She stops in the doorway, like there's the smallest chance he's said what she thinks she heard him say.

His head is down, staring at his belly. 'She's my dealer. Mandy is.' She hears it clearer this time. Still can't believe it.

'Your *dealer*?'

He looks up at her, shrugs, nods.

Alice's mind starts to close down. She sees him snorting cocaine off a toilet cistern. She sees him injecting something into his arm in a filthy public toilet. It makes no sense. She steps out of the room, closes the door quietly behind her, and runs down the corridor.

52

THE CAR PARK

ALICE RUNS to the car but once inside doesn't trust herself to start it. Instead, she sits at the wheel gasping for breath, staring at a blurry world through yet more tears. How has she produced so many? Her mind is blank for a moment.

Drug dealer? It makes no sense. Freddie? *Drugs*? Another woman, she could have sort of understood. A prostitute, even. Sex. But drugs? Which drugs? He barely drinks: it takes him a week to finish a three hundred quid bottle of wine; he doesn't smoke. Alice has never taught any of the PSHE at school, so she doesn't really know much about drugs. Less than the average year six child, she imagines. Ryan probably knows more than she does.

Then her heart thumps like a hammer has hit it – can drugs provoke a heart attack? There's cocaine. Could that do it? You sniff that. Off toilet cisterns with rolled-up fifty-pound notes. She's seen that on the telly, DCI Banks, probably. Not him – the criminals. And LSD. Is that still a thing? That's a tablet. You go on trips. Freddie, on a trip? She almost laughs. Mallorca's his idea of a trip. And crack. But isn't that just more cocaine? Yes, crack cocaine. One of the American shows, probably, CSI somewhere. And what else? Speed? No, wasn't that the mods and the rockers? *Quadrophenia?* What else is there? What could he be on? What's that stuff they inject? Heroin. That's the one. That's the one that seems to hold the most danger: addiction, withdrawal, cold turkey – and heart attacks... Please let it not be heroin. But that is simply ridiculous.

She plays with the jigsaw. Another piece slots into place. *Before the lottery.* This has been going on since before the lottery win. And just as that made the sex scenario worse, so it makes the drugs scenario a lot, lot worse. Is it work? Is he *so* unhappy at work that he's started doing drugs to get through the day? People do that. She's read about it. In *The Guardian.* She can't see Freddie doing that. He'd talk to her. They'd talk... And then she wonders. Would they? Would they really? Has she talked to him, before today when their marriage exploded? Has she told him what had been worrying her? And has she listened to him, *really* listened, about what worried him? Did he hate work so much that he's resorted to drugs because he didn't feel he could talk to her? But it still doesn't make sense. Freddie? Drugs? Christ, she almost wishes it had been a prostitute.

The world outside the windscreen seems to be continuing without any care for what's going on in her life. Why shouldn't it? This is her little drama. Nobody else cares, mainly because nobody else knows, and they probably wouldn't care if they knew. Not even the children know. Yet.

So, how does she tell the children? What does she tell the children? Does she blame Freddie? It is his fault. Does she do what all the jilted women seem to do in her books? Does she load all the blame on to him? Does she make the children hate him? Because this isn't her fault.

But she knows she can't. Freddie's 'crime' is against her, not against the children. And she wants them to grow up knowing him and loving him. So, she can't even tell them the truth. That it's all his fault. But what can she tell them? How can she explain that Mummy and Daddy don't love each other anymore? That Daddy won't be living at home anymore? At least he won't be living with Mandy, she suddenly realises in an explosion of relief that it wasn't another woman, it wasn't sex, it wasn't any of the usual things that split families up after twenty years of marriage and two children. Two beautiful, lovely children who deserve so much more than this.

And suddenly the relief is gone, as quickly as it came.

The days stretch. Like the summer holidays. Just without the fun. Without the relaxation, the colourful blouses, the sandals, the deckchairs in the garden, the ice-cream van tinkling around the corner, long sultry evenings, the laughter. Alice considers them a happy family. There's a lot of laughter in their house. Usually. Not so much now. There's an atmosphere. She doesn't like it. It's eggshells. Everybody walking on eggshells, afraid to say something in case... In case it leads to something else. Something worse. And nobody wants to find out what could be worse.

The children are quieter than usual. As if... as if they think they might have done something wrong – but don't know what. They're never naughty, so Alice hates this feeling that they might think they could have done something wrong, when they haven't. It's Freddie who's done something wrong. And maybe they might think Alice too, because she's thrown him out. But she doesn't feel she can tell them. So, there's just this atmosphere. Like waiting for something bad to happen. Like animals are meant to be able to sense storms and earthquakes before they hit. Can the children sense that a storm, or an earthquake, is about to hit...?

53

THE OTHER DEALER

FREDDIE HAS a room at the Holiday Inn at Tuckswood, the nearest (and cheapest) hotel to the hospital. It's the standard sort of room he, Alice and the children have stayed in so many times before, on little away day, out-of-season trips they've taken to the coast, up to the Broads, the kids having the treat of their own room with a connecting door: how easy it had been to create some excitement for them. It has a bed, chair, TV, fridge, coffee. Bright colours, a bit scuffed here and there. You could film a scene for DCI Banks in here.

Alice is delivering another bag of socks and pants. They've danced around the issues. *How is he feeling? Fine, a lot better. When is he back at the hospital?* And she is interested. As he is interested... in the children. *How are they? Fine. Missing you.*

'Have you told them yet? About us? About...?' he says, not looking her in the eye.

'No, Freddie. We said you should do that.'

'Right, yes. We did.' He looks dejected. Broken.

She feels mean. Thinks she might do a better job of it, when the children start crying, as they will. She wonders if she can trust him to do it right. If there is a right way of telling your children, your seven- and eleven-year-old children, that you're not going to be living with them anymore? That they can come and visit, and he can take them to McDonald's, and see them at the match every fortnight, but the rest of the time? Is there a good way of telling them that? Because they've still told them very little so far. Nothing about what really matters. Daddy is still recovering. *It's taking a little more time than expected...* Alice waiting for Freddie to tell them. Freddie, apparently, just waiting...

'Which drugs?' she says, in a flat tone, the tone she'd use were she asking him which biscuits he'd like her to pick up from the supermarket.

'What?'

'Cocaine? Heroin?'

'*What?*'

'Which drugs is she dealing you? What are you on? Are you an addict?'

Freddie's mouth falls open. It could easily be another heart attack.

'Drugs?' he whispers.

'Dealer?' she replies.

'No!' He gasps, penny dropping, fifty-pound notes dropping, two point three million quid dropping. '*Investments.* Mandy's a *trader*. Stocks, shares. She deals in derivatives, financial instruments.'

Alice wonders for a moment if he's lying. He's regretted telling her, so now he's backtracking. But his face shows her he's not. So, she wonders instead if this is somehow not as bad as sex, or drugs. At least it isn't rock'n'roll; he hasn't run away with a band of twenty-year-old girls as their lead singer. Investments?

So, that means he's been gambling again. Back to his icy thingies, that he'd promised, so long ago, he'd stopped. She made him promise, wouldn't marry him until he did. Her mind is spinning wildly. So, he hasn't been sleeping with a lover, or a prostitute. And he hasn't been sniffing or snorting or injecting whichever drugs you sniff, snort or inject. He's been gambling. Is this better? Does she feel relief? Is there a lifeline here? How would she know? She only reads these family drama books; she doesn't write them.

'For you.' He nods to himself. She does feel relief, she realises, a little, that it wasn't a prostitute or drugs, but it's ebbing fast.

'You stopped that. We talked about this. *Years* ago, Freddie. That time you lost money on the ice things. You said you'd stop. You said you'd *stopped*. So, you're gambling again? You've been gambling?'

'It's not gambling, it's investing.' His tone is weaselly, like he knows his argument is piss weak.

'So why wouldn't you tell me? Why did I have to threaten you with divorce before you'd tell me?'

'I knew you wouldn't be pleased.'

'Oh, no? And why wouldn't I be pleased if you were investing and not gambling?'

His piss-weak argument has been flushed.

'I think I have a problem.'

She stiffens. 'You think... No, Freddie. Don't do that. Don't you *dare* try to do that. I have a problem, Freddie. The children have a problem, and the problem is *you*.'

'I did it for you. I did it for the children. I simply wanted to do something to make us a little extra nest egg, so we could have nicer holidays, the kids could have some extra treats, we could give up work, for good. We couldn't do that with what we won. It wasn't enough.'

'Not enough? Jesus, Freddie, we won two point three million pounds. Don't you think that's a big enough nest egg?

It's a bloody mansion nest, filled with golden ostrich eggs. Why would you think we needed more?'

Freddie mumbles. 'It's not that much really, not when you think about it. House, holidays, car. The children will probably go to university, inflation could soar, interest rates could plummet, we have the mortgage. We couldn't retire on it. It's not enough.'

'So, you were gambling?'

'Investing. Over the years, I've probably made close to thirty thousand.'

'Over the...? Over the *years*? What years? Jesus, Freddie. What the fuck are we talking about here?'

She doesn't swear often. Freddie doesn't like it. But it does act as a warning, to him, that she's angry, or hurt. And he doesn't like that either. He dislikes that more than he dislikes the swearing. So, he lets it pass. As usual.

'Before the lottery, I only ever used my bonuses. I got a thousand pound bonus a few years ago, for example, a year later it was worth two and a half grand, remember we went to Casa Lola at Easter? I said I'd got a bonus, well the bonus was a year earlier, and I more than doubled it. And you remember when we went to Crete? Five stars? That was a small lottery win that I more than doubled by investing it, as a surprise for you. I said it was a bonus. I did it all for you and the children.'

'So, you lied to me?'

'It was a secret. I wanted to surprise you. I didn't win enough to do something really nice, so I invested it and then told you.'

'But you won the lottery and didn't tell me?'

'It was only a thousand or so, the holiday was nearly four grand. I did it all for you. I've always made a profit over the years.'

'The years?'

He looks down.

'How many years, Freddie?'

'Since, well, the ISAs...'

'The ISAs? So, you never stopped?'

He looks up, pain on his face. Alice's brain somersaults. *Hold on. Wait a minute. Wait a fucking–*

The heart attack? Freddie's heart attack? It was caused by the sex. That's what she'd thought when she'd first heard Mandy's name. The sex with his lover, or with the prostitute, the fetishy stuff, in the flat. Whatever. That brought on the heart attack. And then? And then, it was brought on by the drugs. The cocaine, the heroin. So? So now, so now it's the gambling... It hits her like a train. Or like a 70mph juggernaut. Or what being thrown for *ippon* by a seven-year-old girl must feel like.

'Jesus, Freddie. How much have you lost?'

He swallows; she notices the sweat beading on his head, she knows she really shouldn't be doing this now, but when your husband suddenly confesses that he's gambled away enough money to give him a heart attack, she feels entitled to turn the screws a bit.

'How much have you lost?'

'Most of it.'

'Most of what? Most of the *lottery win?*'

He nods.

She takes a breath. So, 'most' of the money is gone. She rolls the thought around her swirling mind. There are certain planets where that might not have been the worst option she could have imagined. There are certain universes, not long in her past, where she's prayed that the money would be gone. She hadn't cared where; she simply wished for it to be gone. She wonders if she seriously meant it. He's lost somewhere in the region of two point three million pounds, and she really isn't that bothered? *Really?*

'What's left?' she asks, flat again. *Do you fancy KFC or Macky D's?*

He shrugs. She feels like slapping him. She never has before, so it's an odd feeling. She clenches her fists in an attempt to get control of her emotions – but then fears she might punch him. 'The car. Some wine. The watches…'

She waits for more. Then concludes that there isn't any more.

'Right. So, I see what you mean by "most of it". What were you gambling on?'

He takes a breath. Doesn't contradict her use of the word.

'Cryptocurrencies.'

'Cryptocurrencies? Are they a real thing?'

He nods.

'And this Mandy? She advised you to put everything, except your car and the watches and a couple of bottles of wine, into cryptocurrencies?'

He nods again.

'Can we sue her? Negligence? Incompetence?'

He sighs, like it's a non-starter. 'Mandy gamb– invested everything she had. Everything. It was a too-good-to-be-true opportunity…'

'That turned out to be too good to be true?' Alice remembers the nurse saying how Mandy had left in a hurry when she'd come in with Freddie. Like she had something better to be doing. Well, now Alice knows what she had to do. She had to deal with her own bankruptcy.

'I'm sorry.' He looks at the floor.

'I can work that out on my own.' She wonders whether she can say the next thought that enters her mind. She doesn't wonder for long. 'You remember you put three hundred thousand pounds into my account when you won? Don't you dare even dream of asking for half of that when our divorce is going through. Don't dream of asking for one penny – or I will sell my story to *The Sun* or *The Star*. I will. I'll do anything to protect my children from your madness. Don't for one second think I'm bluffing. Now, I want you to sell your car and the watches and put the money in the bank. I'll deal with any wine that's left. We will need to talk.' She turns to the door, for the second time in what feels like a lifetime.

'Please don't go,' he croaks.

But she's too far down the corridor to hear him.

54

THE VISIT

'*When can we see Daddy...?*'

The days bleed into each other. An open wound that festers and weeps, blood and pus, an ugly orangey-yellowy colour. The children mope. It's not something they usually do. But now they do. They mope. Poppy's even lost interest in reading. There's a *Duckling in a Dungeon*, or in Danger, or in something else beginning with a D and she hasn't touched it in days. She's busy, or she can't find it, or – the killer – she wants Daddy to read it when they see him next. And they've started to bicker. Poppy and Ryan. A little. And Alice hates it. She hates the destruction. The destruction of what they had. And she can't really understand it. Because he never told her. But she can only conclude it was his work. That he hated it so much that he resorted to this...

'*Can we see Daddy soon...?*'

But she finds it difficult to understand. He showed no signs. Not that she'd know what the signs might be. His grumpiness, obviously. But he'd never turned to drink nor, mercifully, to drugs, or a lover, or a prostitute. As they often do – in the novels she reads.

'Is Daddy coming home soon...?'

And she wonders if it's fixable. Can they put it all back together again? What would it take? He'd need treatment, surely? Is he a gambling addict? She's heard of Gamblers Anonymous. They'd have to talk about it. And that seems to be the hardest thing.

She'd have to hear how unhappy he was. How unhappy he really was. And for how long? And she'd have to confront the sad fact that he'd never told her, and she'd never noticed, never guessed, never asked. That's almost the saddest thing...

———

Alice takes the children to see him. It's been six days of lying to them and she hates herself. She hates Freddie too. He's promised he'd tell them. When they were all together. About what was going to happen. How things would be arranged. Nothing about the money, just the domestic arrangements as he called them. The break-up of our family had been Alice's choice of words. But he doesn't.

The worst thing? He changes the venue of the visit, as he calls it. *Thank you for coming to visit me.* Not at the hotel. He's back in the hospital. Well, in the cafeteria. So the children will think he's still there, she guesses. Being treated. Or waiting for an appointment. Or some such nonsense. And like children, they're too excited to think anything else.

He tells them about statins. He talks about badminton. Walking. Jogging. Everything except the domestic arrangements. And Alice feels betrayed. Like he's waiting for her to have to do it as the children ask again and again, as they will, as the days turn into weeks into months.

'When can we see Daddy again...?'

55

THE BUTTERFLY

IT'S BEEN two weeks since the heart attack. The children know something is up. Alice can feel it. They're close. They talk. They'll suspect. Worst-case scenario – they might work it out. Or simply guess. Alice dreads the moment. Ryan, maybe even Poppy, coming to her with the question. *The* question. Or one of the possible questions.

'Is Daddy not coming home?'

'Has Daddy moved out?'

'Are you and Daddy not friends anymore...?'

'What does divorce mean...?'

Her heart breaks every time one of them approaches her, looking inquisitive. Looking like they have a little problem that they know she can solve for them. Because that's what she does. That's what she's always done. But she knows – *this* time, she knows she can't.

Freddie visits, collecting some more clothes (on the Q.T.) while he's about it. The children are all over him, telling him how much they're missing him. Ryan talks about his new school, and Freddie says nothing about the change. They tell him about how they had a sleepover with Mags, in a tent in her garden; about the next Norwich match, at home to Bristol City, is he coming? *Pleeeze! But only if you're well enough...* And Poppy finds a book about an animal in peril somewhere on the planet and she reads it to him, breaking Alice's heart.

He tells them about statins, again, and how they will help him get better; about the long walks, perhaps jogging, that he'll be doing. *Yes, of course you can come with me.* He says he's staying at a 'clinic'; he still needs to rest. And they swallow it all like, well, like children.

And with the children reassured, and satisfied because he's staying for tea, Alice and Freddie sit on the sofa, on their own, no DCI Banks, no chocolate Hobnobs, and discover that they don't know what to say to each other anymore.

'I'm sorry,' Freddie finally whispers, looking at his shoes. 'If I could turn back the clock, I would.'

Alice sighs. *I'm sorry too*, sounds too harsh, too cutting, too final, too, *It's all your fault.* Even though it is. But she does want him to recognise how he's betrayed her, without rubbing his nose in it.

'Is there any way I can put it right?' he says. 'For the children? I don't want them to get hurt.'

Alice feels like screaming. Yes, for the children, of course for the children. *But what about* me? *Am I not getting hurt?*

But she doesn't scream. And she decides not to say anything either. Because this might be the olive branch she's been secretly hoping for. An opportunity, an excuse even, to attempt to maybe start, to see, if it might be possible... Can she forgive him? She guesses she'll soon find out. It could be now or never.

There are a few moments in your life, she's often thought, when you know you're making a big decision. A huge one. A life-changing one. A decision that will have implications for years into the future. Going to university. Or not going, in Freddie's case. Choosing a career path. Marrying somebody. Having children with them. Huge decisions that you don't take lightly because you know at the time that they matter, will matter, for years to come. Decades to come. They'll open some doors, and close others. She's always had a 'no regrets' mindset when faced with one of these moments. Think about it, carefully, then make the decision knowing that, even with hindsight, it was the right decision, given what you knew at the time.

She didn't think she'd be facing another one of these moments. Certainly not so soon. Going, or sending, either her or Freddie into a care home had seemed the most likely next big fork in her road. But suddenly, at the age of forty, here's another. This decision, these next few moments, will shape her life, Freddie's life, her children's lives, for decades into the future.

The older you get, it seems to Alice, the more you notice these moments. Recognise them as they're happening. Going to university had been on automatic pilot. Her parents assumed she'd go; all her friends were going; it hardly seemed like she was making a decision at all, but she still knew it was an important moment. Having finished her degree, she thought long and hard before deciding to be a teacher. Marrying Freddie had been a big one, especially as her mum had been so against it. She'd had to make a stand there, knowing that marrying Freddie might fracture her relationship with her mother. Having children had been an easy choice as they'd both wanted them. And then, she'd left him. That had been a blur. She'd been angry, frightened. That one hadn't really registered; it had happened so quickly; she hadn't really taken the time to think. It had been more like a dream – or a nightmare.

And now, another. Maybe the most important one of all, and she's completely on her own.

She's had little time to think about this. So, Freddie's lost all the money? Great. Problems solved? No private school for Ryan; no move to a gated community near Hampstead Heath or Monte Carlo; no more sports cars. Fine. She could live with it; only a few days ago she was praying for it. But. The big but. She would have preferred to have the discussion. The chance for them to sit down and think about what they really wanted. To do with the money. Both of them. Together. She knows she's partly to blame for not being honest with him.

And so, although there is a part of her that is happy all her most recent problems have gone away, there is another part that would have preferred to have had some control over the money – that is, some control over Freddie. But he's banjaxed that possibility, and she's angry about it. She's angry that he hasn't been honest with her – for years. He's been gambling his little bonuses, yes, for the best of reasons, but the fact is, he's kept her in the dark. Treated her like a child. Somebody who couldn't be trusted with big decisions. And that hurts. She's hurt. He's hurt her. Is there any way he can put it right? She takes a breath...

'I want what we had, Freddie. Well, what I thought we had.' She says it quietly, looking at his bald spot because his head is down. 'I want what we planned when we got married. That we'd be honest with each other. That we'd grow old together, see the children off into the world. Not much more, certainly no less. I was never unhappy with those plans. Were you unhappy with them? *Really* unhappy? I know you didn't like your work, but our life, before this? Were you really unhappy with that?'

He looks up, seeming confused, like he's never really thought about it before. 'I felt as if I'd let you down.'

'How?'

'I said I'd be a manager. We'd have a bigger house, a nicer car, nicer holidays...'

'We had enough, Freddie. More than enough.'

'I felt you expected more.'

'Who? Me? Or your dad?'

His eyes glass over; she feels like she's pressed on a fresh bruise, but she knows the bruise is almost a lifetime old.

'I wish now,' he says, almost to himself, like it's something he wouldn't really want to confess, but he's sort of forgotten she's there, 'I wish I'd ploughed my own furrow, thought more about what *I* really wanted to do: taken the loan, gone to university, not joined the bank, not simply tried to please my dad.'

This is the equivalent of a religious conversion. Freddie? Not working at the bank? Like his father had? Like his grandfather had? This is Freddie shedding his skin in front of her; telling her he's gay; speaking fluent Russian and confessing to being a sleeper agent.

She wonders if she dares. It's suddenly obvious to her, but to him? Is it too big a risk? Would it only make it worse? Her mouth makes the decision while her brain ponders in neutral.

'You're still young, Freddie. You've got plenty of working years left. Twenty or so...'

He seems shocked, she's not sure what by: the twenty years still to come, or the possibilities...

'Do you really think so?'

She smiles, marvels how, despite his balding pate, his pot tum, and his two-days' worth of stubble finally making an impression on his chin, he can suddenly remind her of Ryan: open, innocent, infinitely trusting.

'Of course. What would you have done if you hadn't joined the bank?'

'Maths,' he says, quick as a flash, *The Flash*, the DC Comics

Flash, squeezed into a red latex suit with a few more wobbly bits on show.

'Well...?'

'Well, what?'

'Do it.'

'What? A maths degree? I'd still end up in an accountant's office for another twenty years. Bossed about by teenagers with degrees in media studies because of my age. I've missed the boat, Alice. Nobody would want me now. Nobody would take me seriously.'

'I meant teach it,' she says, before she has time to think.

His reaction would've been no different had she said 'astronaut'. His eyes threaten to pop. He smiles just like Ryan, shyly. What was that old word that nobody uses anymore? *Bashfully*? That's the one.

'I'm serious,' she continues, wondering if she is.

'Don't be silly.' He flaps the idea away with his hand, an irritating wasp at a family picnic on Mousehold Heath. But, to her amazement, Alice has spotted a butterfly flitting out of the long grass, heading their way.

She's never entertained the idea before; Freddie's always been a banker, but the thought flutters randomly around her mind, all bright colours and tiny wafts of air: too delicate to fly far?

'Why not?' she blurts, desperately trying to turn the delicate flicks and flashes of colour into a picture that he might see for himself. 'That's why most teachers teach, the love of a subject. And you love maths.'

He shrugs, like a butterfly resting on a flower, without the puff for now to fly anymore.

'The best teachers transmit the love, and the students follow the scent.' She likes this butterfly analogy; it's poetic. Although Freddie the butterfly? Is it quite simply ridiculous? Not the analogy – although that's a bit of a stretch – but him, teaching? She ploughs – well, flaps – on, furiously.

'I can see you teaching, Freddie. You always look so happy whenever you're helping Poppy and Ryan with their maths. But you never see how they look at you, you're always concentrating on the numbers. Poppy especially, she sees you as some kind of mathematical wizard, making the numbers work for you, so easily. There's hero worship there when you're helping her.'

'Is there?' He looks shocked. Genuinely shocked, like he'd only ever seen the numbers, and never noticed Poppy, and the way she looked at him.

At that moment, Poppy scuttles in, holding the class bear in one hand and a toilet roll in the other. It's Poppy's turn to bring Barney home. Alice remembers a garbled conversation with Poppy about Mzzz Gibson announcing an Ancient Egyptian project. Poppy has to do something Egyptian with him. Alice takes a leap of faith and tries to remember one of the prayers she must have known as a child.

'Poppy! What do you think about Daddy becoming a teacher? A maths teacher, in a secondary school?'

Poppy has her hand in the kitchen drawer, pulling out the Sellotape, scattering paper napkins as it snags. She stops, considering the idea, like it's a choice between pizza or a Big Mac for tea. Alice prays to any god, even the Ancient Egyptian ones, who might be in the area.

'Yeah,' Poppy says at last, still chewing the idea, but she's nodding now, it's obviously making sense in her mind. 'He'd be very good. Better than Mrs Cooper in year two. I saw her using her fingers once, for eight times seven. Daddy *never* does that. Daddy *always* knows *all* the answers. *And* he never shouts.'

Alice looks at Freddie, like the chief inspector of Ofsted has just pronounced him *Outstanding*.

Poppy joins them on the sofa, the toilet roll behind her like an advert with puppies.

'If Daddy was a maths teacher, in secondary, then you could both teach me when I go! You should do it, Daddy. You'd take to it like a duck to lemonade.'

There is a silence as Freddie and Alice stare at Poppy. Her face is deadpan – almost. Her eyes are flicking from Freddie to Alice and back again, there is mischief in them.

Alice hugs her, makes a mental note for the Assembly House in the very near future. That tall thing they do with every flavour of ice cream on the planet in it, a double portion of *ron y pasas*. Plus syrups and sprinkles. The knicker thingy. Poppy skips back outside, toilet roll now playing out like a firehose: career-change for Daddy sorted.

'You see?' Alice says, wondering if both she and Poppy are seriously deluded.

'I couldn't teach,' Freddie sighs, huge disdain: *I can't bloody fly!* 'And, you know what they say: "those who can, do: those who can't, teach".'

Alice laughs. She's not sure she's done that for weeks. It's an unusual feeling. But that old chestnut? *Those who can't, teach...?* She's heard it before, demolished it a thousand times. 'Did you know that Einstein was a teacher? Stephen Hawking? Marie Curie? They all taught *and* did. Only a fool can't see it's possible to do both.'

'Really?'

'Yeah. And you know what Aristotle said?' It's obvious he doesn't. 'Those who know, do. Those who *understand*, teach. And, of course, we'd have the holidays together. All of us.'

There's suddenly a new look in his eye; she wonders for a moment if he's trying to work out whether Aristotle said the stuff about the holidays as well. But it's not that. He's wondering; she can see Ryan in him again, without the pot tum or the balding pate, choosing GCSEs, not too far into the future.

'You could retrain. We spend a lot of our lives working – the least you should do is try something you think you might enjoy. They're scouring the world for maths teachers, Freddie. Especially since Brexit. They're getting them in from India. It's costing them a fortune, and here you are, sitting on the doorstep.'

'But I don't have a maths degree, remember? My dad saw to that.'

'You don't necessarily need a degree to teach anymore, Freddie. They've changed the rules for some of the new training schemes.'

'I don't think I'd be confident enough without a degree, and some teacher training, *proper* teacher training, not simply throwing you in the deep end to cover the shortages, like you said they're doing.'

'Then, do a degree. And then do a PGCE.'

'*Me?*'

'You've got better A level results than I have. You got a good grade in maths.'

'I got an A.'

'There you go,' she says, smiling at his pride starting to re-emerge, and because she knew he got an A, of course she did. Poppy might not know what it is but even she knows Daddy's got an A in maths. 'They'd hoover you up in an instant. You'd probably end up with a first.'

'You think?'

'Yes. I do.'

'But they don't give degrees away at Tesco, do they? There are tuition fees, and I'd have to take three or four years off work.'

Alice suddenly feels the world turning on its axis again, it's happening a lot lately, a slow, grinding rotation of billions of tonnes of earth and water and magma revolving in space – all caused by a butterfly's lazy flapping...

'I'll support you,' she says, as easy as that. But she feels the power in her hands, under her feet, in her words.

'How could you support me? It would take years, Alice. Three or four years. We only just manage to afford a holiday with the two of us working.'

'I have the money.'

'What money?' he says, confusion furrowing his brow.

'I've got three hundred thousand pounds in my bank account. You gave it to me, don't you remember?'

Freddie looks as if he's been thrown for *ippon*; his mouth drops open.

'But I gave that to you,' he says. 'To buy things, for *you*.'

'This *is* for me.'

'But, Alice, this could use up over half of that. What with fees, and me not working. Possibly more. How is that for you?'

'Because I'd get a new Freddie. Well, actually, no. I wouldn't get a new Freddie. I'd get the *old* Freddie back. The one I married. A Freddie who's excited about a new career, like you were when you first started at the bank. I can see it in your eyes. You heard what Poppy said. You'd be good at it. You'd enjoy it. I can't think of anything I'd rather spend the money on. I love my work, you know that. Think what we'd be like if we both loved our work...'

'You mean, you'd take me back...?'

He looks pathetic, desperate. A broken man. Actually, he looks like a boy, pleading for a second chance, promising he won't do whatever he's done again.

She cocks her head to one side, Poppy-style, appraising him, possible new boyfriend material? 'I might,' she says, feigning indecision, almost savouring the moment. She has his future, her future, all their futures, in her gift. 'One condition.'

'No more gambling?'

'*Two* conditions.' She smiles. He almost does.

'What's the second?'

'You do your degree. Or whatever you need to do. You train to be a teacher. If you think it will make you happy. And if you don't, then you choose something else. You use what's left of the money to find something that will make you happy. Because that's what will make me happy, and the children.'

'Are you serious? I mean, not just about me doing a degree, but about the money. That's yours, Alice. You owe me nothing. In fact, if I'm honest, and we are being honest here, I owe you. I shouldn't have given you three hundred thousand pounds. I should have given you half. Or, maybe, better still, I should have asked you more, made decisions together. About what to spend it on. I messed that up, didn't I? I've messed everything up. I've lost the money, half of it was *your* money, I can see that now, and I could still lose you. I'm so sorry, I know I've hurt you. Could you really forgive me?'

Alice picks up his hand. 'You can fix it, Freddie. *We* can fix it. If we want to. We can put our life back together and fix the bits that needed fixing. That means we talk. And you do something else, like teaching. If you really want to do it. If you think it will make you happy. And if we're both working full-time, if I take the head of department job, then maybe we also share the housework and the shopping duties a bit more evenly. Maybe even some of the cooking? And no more secrets between us...?'

Freddie nods, looking her in the eye. He takes a breath... 'Do the children know?'

'Know what?'

'You know. About what's happened. The money. That I moved out...?'

'I don't think so. I was afraid they were going to guess. I wonder if they might have, but are too scared to ask.'

'You never told them?'

'No.'

'And they never asked?'

'No.'

'What would you have said if they had?'

Alice shakes her head. 'I honestly don't know.'

Ryan trots in, ball in hand, sweat in rivers.

'Poppy says Dad's going to be a teacher!' The look on his face tells Alice volumes of stories with floaty music and happy endings.

'I'm thinking about it,' Freddie says, guarded, hopeful maybe.

'Oh, go on! Please. You'd be *brilliant.*'

Freddie blushes, looks away, paws his eyes. 'You think so?'

'*Think* so? Dad, you're miles better than most of the teachers I've ever had.'

Alice sends Ryan one of her 'meaningful' looks, loaded with enough data to widen his eyes.

'Well, actually, thinking about it, you're miles better than any of the teachers I've ever had. You explain things clearly, and you never get impatient. You'd be brill. You know your shit.'

Ryan's so excited, he doesn't seem to have noticed what he's said. Freddie is clearly too flattered and confused to take it in. Alice decides that shit happens – and trusts Ryan to know the difference between *you know your shit* and *you know you're shit...*

Freddie stares at Ryan, glances at Alice.

'Can I have a phone?' Ryan asks suddenly, like a volcano erupting without warning.

Alice almost laughs, pictures Ryan at the wheel of a car in a few years, *Lord save us!*

'We said when you were fourteen,' Alice says, but she says it kindly, like it might be negotiable, under the right circumstances... She thinks she might know what has provoked this particular eruption.

There has been a constant stream of blue envelopes, postmarked Mallorca, with beautiful precise, careful copperplate writing, landing on the breakfast table. She's sure he's writing back. She's spotted a little writing pad and a pack of envelopes in his bedside drawer – not that she was snooping. She wanted to tell him that airmail paper and envelopes would be cheaper – and maybe more romantic – but she hadn't wanted to embarrass him.

'Is it because lots of kids in secondary have them?' She knows they have them at home, even though they're not allowed them in school, but what she really wants is to stoke this conversation – smoke him out.

'No, it's not that...' he says, trailing off, like there's a second part to the sentence that starts, *It's...*

'It's... well, it's just that I've been helping Rosalita with some English. We've been writing each other letters.'

'Yes, I've seen them! Is she any good?' Alice asks mischievously. Freddie's eyebrows lift; Alice gives him a smile.

'Yes, she is. She's really good. And she's been helping me with my Spanish.' He looks at Freddie, who gives him an impressed little nod. Alice thinks Ryan is getting ready to strike.

'So, what's all this got to do with a phone?' she asks, like a line in a Ayckbourn play.

'Well, she's just had her thirteenth birthday–'

'I hope you sent her a card.'

'Wha–? Yes. Of course I did.'

'Good.'

'And she got a phone, for her birthday, from her parents, and she wants us to use WhatsApp, for the English... and the

Spanish! So it doesn't take so long. Like it does with the letters.'

Alice nods knowingly, like this isn't the worst reason for wanting a phone years earlier than they'd agreed. She looks at Freddie, who gives a little shrug like he's way out of the loop on this one, but he can't see the harm if it's going to help Ryan with his studies.

'There'd be conditions,' Alice starts, looking gravely at Ryan who nods like a death-row inmate seeking a last-minute pardon. 'We'd put parental controls on it.'

Ryan nods some more; *As many as you like.*

'And no video calls...'

His face drops. Pardon rejected.

'...unless you were on wifi. We wouldn't want you using up a ton of data.'

His eyes brighten, his face lifts, like he's won the lottery. More manic nodding.

'Video calls? *Really*?' It's clearly a jackpot win.

'Of course. You're going to have to speak to her face to face. It's the best way of communicating, so you really understand what the other person's saying. Isn't that so, Freddie?'

'Yes. Yes, it is,' Freddie stutters, looking as pleased as if he's been allowed to have a phone too.

'And you could help him choose a good one, couldn't you? You know a lot more about phones than I do.' They share a smile, Freddie having confessed his use of a secret burner phone for his illicit negotiations with Mandy – his dealer.

Ryan jumps out of his chair, kisses them both. Alice thinks the PlayStation present of a couple of years previously has been trumped – and might now see significantly less use...

Poppy stumbles in with a huge wad of toilet roll wrapped in Sellotape, and probably containing a bear.

'Dad's going to teach maths!' Ryan blurts, shock in his voice, like he doesn't really believe it. The whole Norwich City squad are popping in for tea.

'I know. Cool,' says Poppy, handing the mummified bear to Freddie. 'Now, do you think Barney can breathe in there...?'

The doorbell rings.

Alice goes to answer it. Strange, she can't see anybody's shadow through the frosted glass. She opens the door, looks down. It's Mags, holding an untidy bundle of toilet roll in one hand and an envelope in the other.

'Mummy said I have to show you this,' Mags says, holding up the envelope, before brushing past her and heading inside in search of Poppy. Alice pulls a letter out of the already-opened envelope. It's from the hospital, a date for Mag's first operation. Alice gasps, looks over the road. Emma is running across. Alice decides to meet her halfway...

56

ONE YEAR LATER…

ALICE DASHES ALONG THE CORRIDOR, books under her arm, bag swinging off her shoulder, almost late for year seven, *Taming of the Shrew*.

'Mrs Cash! Mrs Cash!' The voice arrests her; it's Reda. 'Mrs Cash. My mother, she say yes. She say I can do the sleepover…'

'That's wonderful,' Alice replies. 'I told you she would.' What she doesn't tell Reda, is that in her weekly English lessons with Reda's mother, Alice has managed to persuade her that a sleepover wouldn't harm Reda's spiritual well-being in any way. There's another shout in the corridor.

'Mr Cash! I done the homework!' It's a voice full of pride, desperate to show what he's achieved. Alice knows Tommy, he should be lining up outside the *Taming of the Shrew* class by now, but he's not; he's chasing Freddie along the corridor, book in his hand. Alice earwigs the exchange.

'Look, Mr Cash. I got it. On my own. I didn't ask my sister. It's eight, isn't it? Eight!'

Freddie takes the book, eyes it carefully, then nods. 'Well done, Tommy. Brilliant.'

'Thanks, Mr Cash. Gotta dash, got Shakespeare now: *Taking all the shoes*, it's really good.'

'Don't be late,' Freddie warns.

'Hi, Mrs Cash,' Tommy yells as he passes her. 'Got Shakespeare now. *Taking all the shoes...*'

'*Taming of the Shrew*, Tommy. *Shrew*.' She needs a word with Freddie.

'You've got Tommy all fired up,' she says as Freddie reaches her. 'That takes some doing. I'd heard he hated maths.'

Freddie shrugs. 'He's very keen. Loves puzzles.'

Alice nods. 'Eight's the answer? So, not too difficult a puzzle that one?'

Freddie smiles. 'It was quite tricky. But the answer's thirty.'

'But...'

Freddie's smile widens. 'What was it you said the other week? The right answer isn't always the most important thing. Enthusiasm can be more valuable in the long run?'

Alice nods. 'You're getting it, Freddie. Look, I wanted to ask you. How did the observation go this morning, with Daniella?'

'Oh, great,' he says, beaming. 'In fact, she said the maths department would need a new teacher in September. She said she wanted me to apply. They could appoint me on a temporary contract, as long as I was still doing my training. Then she'd give me a permanent one once I'd finished.'

'Oh, that's wonderful. You'd like that, wouldn't you?'

'The chance to teach Ryan, and Poppy in a couple of years? I'd love it.'

'Oh, well done. You deserve it. All the work you're putting in.' She kisses him on the cheek.

From behind them, at the other end of the corridor, comes a huge cheer.

'Put him down, Mrs Cash! You don't know where he's been.'

It's a gang of girls from Alice's tutor group, blushing and laughing. Freddie looks horrified.

'Off to classes, you lot. I'll kiss my husband whenever I like. In fact, I might just give him another...'

There are screams and shrieks from the girls, who scuttle away at speed.

Alice straightens Freddie's dicky bow, a fashion tic he's adopted to give himself a bit of personality around the school.

'You've nicked yourself shaving; there's a spot of blood on your collar,' she says.

'Bugger. I'll pop it in the washing machine tonight. We've got one of those Stain Devil thingies, haven't we? I'll splosh on a bit of that as well.'

'Apart from that,' she says, quietly, 'you look like a million dollars.'

He blushes, smiles, then turns and walks towards his class. He makes it halfway down the corridor before slowing, stopping, turning, and heading back. Alice watches him as he returns. In his dark suit; red, satin dicky bow; and shiny brogues, he really looks the part. He reaches Alice and stops, quickly checks up and down the corridor, before kissing her on the cheek.

'You too,' he says, blushing again. 'In fact, you look like two point three million pounds...'

ACKNOWLEDGEMENTS

My thanks, again, to all at Bloodhound Books for your continuing support and hard work. Special thanks to Betsy, for giving this one a second look. I'm also grateful, once again, to Better Book Design for another wonderful cover.

Thanks to my editor, Abbie Rutherford (abbie-editorial.com). Her forensic eye, sound advice, and 'dogged' pursuit of perfection have (once again) improved my scribblings immensely.

Finally, thanks to my wife, Jill, most memorably for the evening we spent at Giuliani's Beach Pizzeria in Benicassim, using the back of the menu to invent potential areas of conflict between a husband and wife over how to spend a lottery jackpot. Of course, it was all in the pursuit of fiction. But we keep buying the Cuponazo tickets...

A NOTE FROM THE PUBLISHER

Thank you for reading this book. If you enjoyed it please do consider leaving a review on Amazon to help others find it too.

We hate typos. All of our books have been rigorously edited and proofread, but sometimes mistakes do slip through. If you have spotted a typo, please do let us know and we can get it amended within hours.

info@bloodhoundbooks.com

www.ingramcontent.com/pod-product-compliance
Lightning Source LLC
Chambersburg PA
CBHW030524190726
48283CB00006B/1755